Sarah Harrison has written many bestselling novels – *Life After Lunch*, *Flowers Won't Fax*, *That Was Then*, *Heaven's on Hold*, *The Grass Memorial*, *The Dreaming Stones* and *Swan Music* are all available from Hodder & Stoughton – as well as children's books, short stories, articles and scripts. She lives in Hertfordshire. To find out more information about her novels, visit Sarah's website at www.sarah-harrison.net.

Praise for Sarah Harrison:

'Rich and engrossing' *Yorkshire Post*

'Crisply drawn . . . convincing . . . accomplished.'
Christina Koning, *The Times*

'Harrison's perceptiveness, reliably elegant style and compassionate awareness of the subtle vagaries of the human heart make hers a book you're neither likely nor willing to forget.' *Harpers & Queen*

'A consummate storyteller, Harrison weaves their tales into an absorbing page-turner.' *Woman & Home*

SARAH HARRISON

The Nightingale's Nest

HODDER

First published in Great Britain in 2006 by Hodder & Stoughton
A division of Hodder Headline

First published in paperback in 2006 by Hodder & Stoughton
A Hodder paperback

3

A CIP catalogue record for this title is
available from the British Library

ISBN 978 0 340 82858 7 (B format)
978 0 340 82857 9 (A format)

ISBN 0 340 82858 7 (B format)
0 340 82857 9 (A format)

Typeset in Plantin Light by Palimpsest Book Production Limited,
Polmont, Stirlingshire

Printed and bound by
Mackays of Chatham Ltd, Chatham, Kent

Hodder Headline's policy is to use papers that are natural,
renewable and recyclable products and made from wood grown in
sustainable forests. The logging and manufacturing processes are expected to
conform to the environmental regulations of the country of origin.

Hodder & Stoughton Ltd
A division of Hodder Headline
338 Euston Road
London NW1 3BH

For Ollie and Finty

Chapter One

One evening in the late summer of 1965 I turned a corner in north London and fell headlong into the past.

It was like falling in love – swift and overwhelming, a tumultuous mixture of shock and recognition. And I was swept, too, by a piercing realisation of what it had meant to be young, and how long ago that was.

I hadn't realised how close I was because I'd approached the area by car from a different direction, without the signs and landmarks I might otherwise have taken into account. Plus, it was the end of a long day, (I'd been to see my mother, now in an old folks' home), and I was driving on autopilot, anxious to get back. Then suddenly I saw the corner of the road with its elegant red-brick houses, the old-fashioned street lamps, and the trees with the protective iron cutlet-frills around their trunks, the raised pavement curving invitingly away down the hill. I was swamped by a wave of conflicting emotions, and had to pull over.

The furious gesture of the driver behind was wasted because, unusually for me, my eyes were full of tears. When I'd finally got a grip on myself I parked the car in a side street, got out and began walking. There was no conscious decision; I was simply being drawn, magnetised, back to that place and the time it represented.

Not so long, perhaps ten years, had passed since I'd last been here, but it was the more distant past that rushed back to claim me. And even after ten years there were differences.

It was like meeting other people's children, whom one hasn't seen for a while: their parents seem the same – as one does oneself – but the children are proof if proof were needed that any amount of water has flowed under the bridge. Here, the trees which had been scarcely more than saplings had grown tall and leafy, their branches linking hands. Many of the houses had been subjected to tasteful modernisation. There were residents' parking arrangements in place along one side. Where one road began and the next – what I thought of as 'my' road – began, a paved promontory had been put in place, so that they now in effect formed two cul-de-sacs, end to end. The consequent lack of through traffic added to the feeling I remembered so well, that the moment I turned off the main road I entered another world. An invisible curtain seemed to close behind me. I hadn't just imagined it all those years ago: the air, the light, the atmosphere were different here, sequestered and just a little eerie. These were family houses; there must have been plenty going on this summer's evening – children playing, teenagers listening to radios, dogs larking about, people eating supper, changing to go out, cutting grass in their back gardens – but for now they were becalmed in the sinking sunshine. I found myself walking softly, conscious of my footsteps.

Just before I reached Number Seven I crossed to the opposite side of the road, the better to take it all in. Whoever lived there now had not apparently felt pressured by surrounding 'improvements' to make many changes. The house was a good deal less spruce than its intensively maintained neighbours, but the impression it gave was not of neglect but of an amiable confidence, as though the occupants, like those before them, felt no need to compete. The small front garden still boasted elder and crab-apple trees, masses of periwinkles (at this time of year no more than a tangle of unchecked greenery), the same untidy beech hedge and two mossy, cracked stone urns on either side of the door, in which had been planted trailing fuchsias, red, white and purple. There were the same iron bell-pull and dolphin door knocker, and the boot-scraper on the front step. There were curtains, but no nets, at all the windows except, I noticed, the one on the top floor. I wondered who slept in that attic room now, under the eyes of all those people; if, indeed, the people were still there.

I was unsure whether to go and knock on the door – would that be considered rude? And more importantly, if admitted, would I be setting myself up for the sort of anticlimax that all too often accompanies an attempt to revisit the past?

As I stood there gazing, a car, one of those Mini Mokes that the girls liked so much, drew up at the pavement a few yards beyond me, and a young woman got out, smartly dressed in a short-skirted pink suit and white polo-neck jumper. She glanced at me before locking the car door, and then again as she turned to go in. The glance radiated a cool, public-spirited suspicion and sure enough she asked: 'Can I help you?'

Maybe she thought I was a nuisance caller of some sort: a Jehovah's Witness or a sales rep. I smiled apologetically.

'No – I worked for the people who lived at Number Seven over thirty years ago, and I couldn't resist taking a look.'

By any standards, I appeared what I was – a respectable elderly party. This, along with my manner and voice, must have reassured her, for her own manner became less guarded.

'I'm sorry, we've only been here a few months.'

'It doesn't matter, how would you know, anyway?'

'I do know the Parkers are away on holiday.'

I didn't straight away make the connection. Still, I chanced my arm. 'Do you think they'd mind if I took a quick look in the garden?'

'Well . . .' She hesitated, quite properly, for I was a total stranger asking her to take responsibility for my nosiness. 'I tell you what, why don't I come over with you, then if one of the neighbours spots us they'll realise you're not casing the joint. We all know each other.'

It was a nuisance, but she was being more than fair. 'Thank you. I'll only be a minute.'

I came down the steps from the raised pavement and together we crossed the road.

'This is very good of you,' I said. 'My name's Pamela Griffe, by the way.'

'Lilian Owen. Not at all.'

As she opened the gate I had a bright idea and took a card from my handbag.

'There. That's me.'

'Oh, for heaven's sake, there's no need . . .' She waved it away, blushing slightly, embarrassed to have elicited this proof of identity.

'Please – it will make me feel better about imposing on you.'

'Oh, all right then.' She took it from me without looking at it, and slipped it in her jacket pocket. We were in the front garden now. 'Anyway, here we are . . . Is it as you remember?'

'This part is. Surprisingly so.'

'The Parkers are awfully nice. They invited Tom and me over for drinks when we first arrived. Giles was with Wiggins Teape, the paper people, but he's retired now, they have a grown-up family and a tribe of grandchildren . . . I *think* they said they inherited the place from a friend, or a relative. Anyway, they liked the place as it was. And once you've got used to it it's rather nice to go into a house that isn't all stripped pine and Habitat.'

Now, the penny dropped.

'Giles?' I said. 'Giles and Georgina?'

'That's right!' She relaxed visibly. 'Do you know them?'

'I used to know Georgina quite well. A long time ago, as

I say, but still . . .'

'What a coincidence – what a shame they're not here.'

'Never mind,' I said. 'I wonder, could we go round to the back garden?'

'I don't see why not, now we're here. Especially as you're an old friend.'

She motioned me to lead the way; trusting or, perhaps, testing me. A black and white cat miaowed, tail waving, by the flap in the back door.

'Annie,' said Lilian. 'Trying it on. Take no notice, next door are feeding her.'

There was one change, I noticed. The kitchen had been extended in some way, and the door on to the back garden no longer opened from the end of the hall, but from the dining room.

A moment later, and for the second time that evening I was stopped in my tracks by the powerful force field of the past.

Lilian must have noticed, for she hung back tactfully. 'Take your time. I'll be quite happy perched here. It's a nice excuse to do nothing for a few minutes.'

Her earlier suspicion seemed now to have been completely dispelled by my connection with the house's owners, and the emotional reaction which I could do nothing to disguise. She sat down on the low patio wall and took out her diary, which she began scanning assiduously.

I murmured my thanks and wandered away from her, conscious of each step, each breath, each headlong heartbeat. Almost nothing had changed. Some of the shrubs had been replaced, but others had grown and spread, and the trees were taller so that the garden was if anything even more secretive than I remembered. I found myself blessing Georgina. We had been as different as two young women could be, but this much we had shared: the magic of the garden.

Behind me I heard a man's voice – a neighbour perhaps,

briskly enquiring, and Lilian's soothing reply – but I didn't even turn round. The garden wasn't large, but this end of it, now as then, was overgrown and secluded, so I had already become invisible. I followed the winding path I knew was there, barely visible stepping stones set into the rough grass. I had to push aside branches, fronds and twigs, which softly swung closed again behind me, cutting me off. Here a huge spider's web, a perfect cartwheel of silvery filaments with the speckled owner suspended at its centre, blocked my way. I stepped aside respectfully and negotiated the undergrowth beside the path rather than disturb his filigree flytrap. Now I could see the high wall, covered by a thick shroud of ivy. Breaking against the foot of the wall was a surf of vegetation allowed to grow, and die back, and grow again, to find its own level in the twilight of the tall trees. In early summer, I remembered, bluebells had flourished here.

And – yes. This was where it had been. I could still pinpoint the very location of the nest, in the far right-hand corner beneath the elm tree. Those of us who'd known about it never had to say that it would be our secret, but it had become so; as if, in protecting the nightingale, we were protecting ourselves.

There was no sign of it now, but I stood and gazed down at the place, hidden close among the greenery between the grey, muscled roots of the giant tree. So perfect and particular. So safe.

As I walked back, once more careful not to break the spider's web, my legs were trembling. Lilian was examining a rose bush as if it were a scientific specimen.

'They've got some mildew here . . .' she murmured. 'I might pop over with my lethal spray.' When I made no comment she straightened up and smiled. 'So – interesting?'

'Yes,' I said. 'Thank you.'

'My pleasure.'

We walked round to the front of the house and out into the street. I felt as though I'd been holding my breath, or under water. As I burst back into the present, everything seemed very clear, and bright.

'Would you like to come in for a moment?' asked Lilian. 'Have a quick coffee – or something stronger?'

I realised I probably looked rather pale. 'That's very kind, but I won't. It's been a long day and I was on my way home.'

'If you're sure.' She glanced around. 'Were you in a car?'

'I'm parked up near the main road.'

'OK. Goodbye, then.'

'Goodbye.' I turned to leave, but she had a sudden thought.

'Oh, I wonder – would you like me to tell the Parkers you were here?'

I hesitated. Would I like that?

'No,' I said, 'don't bother. We've been out of touch for so long, you know how it is.'

Dazzled by tears, I walked away.

Chapter Two

Whenever I arrived back at Woodlands, it was with a mixture of satisfaction, astonishment, and anxiety: satisfaction on account of my modest achievement; astonishment that it was still there; and anxiety about what I might find. Today, these sensations were overridden by another more powerful one: the siren song of the past, which haunted and debilitated me so that I could not bring myself to get out of the car but sat and stared, trying to recalibrate myself.

The name 'Woodlands' was picked out in rustic pokerwork lettering on a slice of varnished oak on the gatepost – not that there was any gate. The front door stood open in a risky, symbolic gesture of welcome.

Perhaps there had been woods in this part of west London a hundred years ago, but not now, or for some time. The house, a three-storey, double-fronted Victorian villa, belonged to a row that stood stranded like out-at-trouser gentry on what had become a brutal dual carriageway, surrounded by utilitarian pre- and post-war development, low-rise offices and filling stations. A couple of hundred yards away stood the grubby red-brick church of St Cuthbert's, whose doors opened twice a week, on Wednesdays and Sundays, to admit a dwindling number of faithful, mostly black. The incumbent, Peter Archard, had been *in situ* for over ten years. He was a clever, exhausted-looking bachelor in his late fifties with the pouchy face and bad colour of a drinker, which may have explained his continued presence in this spiritual wasteland.

On arrival he'd called round and expressed the not wholly serious hope that we – 'the Woodlanders' as he sardonically called us – might swell the congregation. I told him I considered it unlikely and so it had proved. But there was no doubt he liked and was amused by us. He continued to call round once a fortnight or so, for a late-night glass of whisky and a chat rather than for any charitable or evangelical purpose.

There had originally been a double garage at Woodlands, testament to the bourgeois heyday of the house, but I'd long since had it converted into a games room. We still had a substantial pull-in off the high road, and this was where I sat for a moment in the hot, toxic London evening with the rush of traffic noise in my ears, trying to find a place in my head to imprison the clamorous ghosts of Crompton Terrace.

I didn't get long. Two minutes after I switched the engine off Hannah came out at the trot, looking harassed, arms folded as though it were cold, or more likely as if stopping herself from knocking someone's teeth in. She opened the passenger door and got in, slamming the door after her and leaning back panting, like a fugitive seeking sanctuary.

'Thank God you're back!' she said. 'There's been hell to pay here.'

It wasn't that bad; all fairly routine stuff for the current residents of Woodlands. We were a volatile household at the best of times. This afternoon, while I'd been revisiting the past in the form of first my mother, then Crompton Terrace, Doreen had pinched some cigarettes allegedly belonging to Maeve and there had been a spat resulting in Maeve's being taken – in her glory, I had no doubt – to Outpatients for a stitch in her eyebrow. The wholly unrepentant Doreen had retreated with her contraband to her room and propped a chair under the door handle. Moreover she had done so without baby Kyle, and was refusing to have anything to do with him, responding to all entreaties with a certain brutal logic relayed wincingly to me by Hannah: 'You cunts take care of him, you're the fucking do-gooders.'

It was Dorothy's day off, and since Josie had accompanied Maeve to Outpatients that had left Hannah singlehandedly looking after four infants – Kyle, Maeve's baby Jackson, and six-month-old twins Anthony and Arlette, whose mother, Alex, had overdone things on a visit to her own mother the previous evening and was laid low with alcohol poisoning. It was a source of astonishment to Hannah how Alex had managed to get back from Plaistow at all, the state she was in but, like all good shepherds, we did our best to rejoice in the lamb that was missing and was found.

The other girls, as was often the case when mayhem not of their doing broke out, had kept a low profile, Hannah said. This was not necessarily a good sign. A good fracas provided ideal cover for illicit pot-smoking, drinking and light thieving of the kind which had sparked the trouble in the first place. But at least they had kept their babies with them so that Hannah could give her full attention to the impromptu crèche.

'Are Maeve and Josie back now?' I asked.

'Oh yes,' said Hannah grimly.

I got the picture. Wronged on two counts, Maeve would be incorrigible.

We went in, and Hannah immediately ran upstairs on some unspecified errand, passing both baton and buck to me. The other Woodlanders were assembled in the kitchen for their tea. This was generally served at six, but the afternoon's ructions meant that it was now well after seven and the natives were restless. The usual industrial quantity of fiery red Bolognese had been disinterred from the freezer and Josie, a formidable Barbadian of immense stature, was stirring a cauldron of the stuff, and another of spaghetti. The older babies, Kyle, Tina and Aaron, were glaring at each other in the playpen preparatory to being put in their high chairs. The little ones were in bouncers, on their mothers' knees, or, in one case, being bottle-fed.

The newly returned Maeve was sitting in the best chair, wearing her suture with queenly hauteur. Doreen was grating Cheddar into a bowl. A packet of Marlboros lay open and unattended on the worktop nearby – an olive branch of sorts, I surmised, unless Doreen planned to lure her adversary into making a move so as to trap her hand in the grater. Alex's twins, thank God, were sleeping peacefully in their baskets, allowing their whey-faced parent to sit, whimpering, at the table with her head in her hands, her fingers thrust into her shock of piebald-bleached hair. The others – Janice, Roz and Ilyena (a waif-like Russian girl whose ballerina-like beauty disguised a violent temper and a practised way with a penknife) – had the slightly smug air of women who had not been involved in the afternoon's shenanigans and who therefore deserved their tea and looked forward to it with relish.

Roz was bottle-feeding Sean. If any of the Woodlanders knew that Breast was Best, they weren't letting on. To a woman, they considered it 'yukky' and wanted to 'keep their figures'. By which I suppose they meant their bustlines, since I'd always understood that breastfeeding encouraged the dilated uterus to contract more effectively . . . but what did I know? I'd never had children. I was humbled, almost awed by these fierce, fecund young women who'd deigned to accept my help.

Janice was reading a hospital romance entitled *No Cure for Love*. Little Natalie lay on a changing mat on the floor next to her. Ilyena held a fork before her face, poised between opposite forefingers; every few seconds she would release the fork and catch it again between her fingers with the effect, and doubtless the intention, of gratuitously adding tension to an atmosphere already seething with the stuff. In his bouncer her baby, Dasha, in an unconscious parody of his mother, squinted furiously at his balled fists. At ten weeks the squint showed no signs of improvement and I had made an appointment for them at the hospital orthoptic clinic.

The kitchen swirled with cross-currents. An uneasy peace had been restored, but it was incumbent on me, as do-gooder-in-chief, to reinforce that peace by stroking each ruffled ego, spreading praise and encouragement and demonstrating by my every word and gesture that everything had been entirely, incontrovertibly, my fault for not being present when I was most needed.

This I could do: diplomacy, the restoration of the status quo by means of a little well-judged self-abasement, was my special talent. The local social services were probably correct in regarding Woodlands as at best the quixotic venture of a slightly dippy old bat, and at worst an extreme and dangerous example of loony liberalism, but what I lacked in managerial skills I made up for in crisis management. After decades of experience I could not always avert trouble, but I was jolly good at defusing it when it came.

I greeted everyone, and apologised profusely for not having been around. The greeting met with silence, the apology elicited a grumpy murmur of agreement. Only Josie was genuinely pleased to see me though not wholly, I suspected, for reasons of friendship.

'Nearly ready, Pam!'

'Wonderful. I do hope you haven't been waiting for me.'

'No darlin', it was that wretched hospital!'

Thus prompted, I sucked my teeth sympathetically over Maeve's stitches, and then picked up the Marlboros off the side and dropped them in her lap. She pocketed them without comment. In the complex dynamic of the house it was Doreen, the undisputed malefactor, who would require the most attention. Accordingly I stood leaning on the worktop, watching admiringly while she finished grating the cheese. Her domestic skills were sketchy, but it wasn't hard to admire her: though unkempt, she was wonderfully handsome, with the strong, androgynous features of a Cherokee squaw.

'Thanks, Doreen,' I said. 'That looks nice.'

She pushed the board to one side and wiped her hands on her jeans. 'Where were you earlier?'

'Visiting my mother. She's in a home in Winchmore Hill.'

'It's all homes with you, isn't it?' said Doreen. 'All homes and no home.'

Doreen had an unerring instinct when it came to inflicting pain. She could identify and exploit vulnerabilities in others the way some people could remember names, or eye colour. But stifling pain was another of my specialities.

'This is my home,' I said, and continued immediately, before she could place another shaft: 'I gather Kyle's been as good as gold all afternoon. He's an absolute credit to you, Doreen.'

She muttered something about that being nothing to do with her, and Maeve sniffed. Kyle pronounced a plague on all our houses by hurling a small metal spinning top which struck Janice's Natalie a glancing blow on the head. Fortunately Janice had been too engrossed in the goings-on in *No Cure for Love* to see what happened and – perhaps because Josie had begun dishing out the spag bol – no one rocked the boat by shopping the culprit. Maeve picked up Natalie and passed her to Janice, and then collected Jackson and put him in the sought-after freestanding high chair. Again, though it was not her turn, no one challenged Maeve's right to this privilege: her injury was qualification enough. The three small bowls of those babies who were on solids were apportioned and left to cool. Doreen took the first adult plateful and sat down next to Alex, who turned away, blenching.

'You want some, darlin'?' enquired Josie. Alex shook her head. Josie tilted the ladle invitingly. 'Come on, honey, a little bit will do you good.'

'Take it away, for Christ's sake!'

'There's no need to bring the Good Lord into this.'

'He'd never touch it, it looks like shit,' moaned Alex.

'It good food, young lady!'

'If you say so . . .'

'I do. Here.' Josie put a small helping down on the table in front of Alex, nudging her elbows with the edge of the plate to make her sit up. 'Let me see you do your very best now. You want those twins to be motherless?' Alex rolled her eyes in a 'spare-me' look. 'Course you don't,' continued Josie undeterred. 'They depend on you, Lord bless them.'

The other mothers paid no attention to the substance of this exchange, but they had some respect for Josie, a mother herself and one who had proved that in spite of the age difference she could overcome any one of them in a straight fight. They allowed her to deliver herself of her homily and waited patiently for their spaghetti.

Hannah returned after her well-earned breather and took her place at the table next to Ilyena, who finally put down the fork.

'OK,' said Hannah, 'own up. Who's been putting what they shouldn't down the upstairs toilet?'

After supper, no one having confessed and the air growing ever more sulphurous with accusation and suspicion, I went to work with the plunger. In theory this type of making-good was the responsibility of whoever had caused the problem, but in practice I was a noted soft touch. Josie sometimes accused me of being afraid of the girls, but she was wrong. I wasn't in the least afraid of them: I loved them. I experienced a kind of ecstasy of humility – something I'm sure

Josie's Good Lord never intended – in looking after them. If I was ever hard on one of them it was not because I wanted to be but because I felt I should.

To my considerable relief the loo did not offer up its secrets, but after a minute or two the water level dropped sharply, with a rich gurgle, and then slowly stabilised. I knew that the drain's revenge was merely postponed and that in a week or two we would have to call out Dyno-Rod whose representatives would remove the cover from the manhole in the back garden and with a sort of sardonic relish haul out the evidence for all to see. The mothers would watch with interest, unembarrassed, screaming with laughter and pointing, but I, the one to whom no taint of guilt adhered, would cringe, and remain well out of the way until it was time to write the extortionate cheque.

I put some bleach down the bowl, scrubbed and flushed. As I stood there with the brush in my hand Roz appeared in the doorway, carrying Sean.

'Is it OK now?' she asked.

This enquiry, I knew, constituted a confession. 'Oh yes,' I said heartily. 'All back to normal.'

'Since I had him I come on so heavy I have to use a sanny as well,' she confided.

'Not to worry.' I replaced the brush and washed my hands. 'Soon dealt with. But try and remember not to put it down the loo.'

'Yeah . . .' She was already wandering off, with an air that said that was quite enough honesty for one day.

Between then and ten-thirty lights-out the house gradually quietened. I'd always had the feeling that an evening routine was best for the babies and happily Josie agreed with me, so we tried to see to it that they had bottles, baths and ordered bedtimes, even those too young to sleep through the night.

Dorothy and I lived at Woodlands. I considered myself to

be on duty at all times; the other three were on a rota. Two people couldn't really cope if anything seriously unpleasant blew up, but we always made sure that one of the others was on the end of the phone if we needed reinforcements. Given that there'd been an incident during the afternoon the law of averages suggested that there would be no more major disturbances that day. This wasn't always true. Sometimes 'a ruck' as the girls called it would raise everyone's temperature and the place would be like a hot spring, bubbling, smoking and periodically boiling over for hours to come. But based on experience I was reasonably optimistic for tonight.

Josie and Hannah cleared the supper things, and Hannah laid the table for breakfast and put out the mugs for hot drinks before leaving. Josie and I had a general tidy-up and made ourselves available for help with the babies' bedtimes.

After that, most of the mums whose babies had settled went down to the games room. On a shelf below the window were piles of board games but they were used even less than the ping-pong table. I had recently invested, with rather greater success, in table-top football and a miniature pool table, but there was no escaping the fact that television was king. TV was the girls' god, their relief, their relaxation, their escape. They didn't just sink down in front of it, they sank *into* it. They were allowed to smoke in here, too, and babies weren't allowed after eight o'clock; if they needed attention from their mothers it had to be upstairs. So I always felt I was seeing them as they really were, or as they had been before the fall, so to speak, just a bunch of young women lolling around, chatting, laughing, smoking, drinking tea, indulging in horseplay, leafing through magazines, but always with the magic blue-grey light flickering in the background.

After looking in, I usually left them to it. They didn't want me around, and there was always paperwork to do at this time of day. Blasted paperwork, the bane of my life! Finances provided a constant source of worry. I'd been, briefly, a rich woman when I sank my fortune into Woodlands' predecessor all those years ago. No more. I'd made some wise investments which yielded an income and which impressed my bank manager sufficiently to allow me a huge overdraft, and as well as Woodlands I still owned my mother's house, which I let to carefully vetted and approved students from a local technical college. But there was little doubt that when they eventually carried me out of this place it would be to a pauper's grave, unless the girls in a late fit of sentimentality forked out for my send-off. We had a clutch of small grants and endowments from various charitable trusts and every autumn I put on my Jaeger suit and did the rounds, ensuring that old friends stayed faithful and new ones were encouraged. Unfortunately we weren't the sort of good cause to attract the Lady Bountifuls. There would be no Woodlands Ball at the Dorchester, or Christmas Fair at the Connaught Rooms for us. We relied on the odd maverick benefactor and whatever goodwill we could drum up and we managed, just. Paying the staff constituted the biggest outlay and I was fortunate they were so tolerant. Delays always affected the youngest ones most keenly, and among them there was the quickest turnover: Hannah had done well to last six months but I wasn't betting on another six.

The mothers contributed a fiver a week, and over and above that it was what they could, if they could. We operated on an honour principle. Madness, really, but it did mean that something came in from them, and however little it was given freely. A very few of them had parents who helped, others were on benefits, one or two – usually those who would be moving on soon – had part-time jobs. We shopped for dry goods once a month at the Houndsditch Warehouse and for meat and veg at the scruffy local market off the high road. The mums bought their own toiletries and cigarettes and paid their way if they went out, though if they needed to do something important such as go to court, or the doctor, or visit a relation for some pressing reason, Woodlands pitched in. Correction, *I* pitched in. I was Woodlands. My fortunes rose and fell with those of this place. If I had started it as a business it would long since have gone to the wall. I was blessed with better health and strength than anyone had a right to expect at my age, and if ever there was an incentive to maintain both, this provided it: when I went, Woodlands would too.

Labour of love or no, that didn't prevent the paperwork being a headache. Wolves still had to be kept from the door, records kept up to date, organisational problems solved, begging letters written, and complaints dealt with by letter or phone according to urgency. All that on top of unheralded visits from disaffected fathers, parents, employers and sadly, from time to time, teachers. I wanted to create a place of sanctuary for the mothers, but all too often I was caught in the crossfire between my charges – determined at all costs not to be grateful – and their families, friends and associates, equally determined to be under no obligation to some mad old biddy with more money than sense. Even the staff went about their business with a wary air, alert to the first signs of the ship going down. I walked a tightrope.

I had a large room, a sort of bedsit, on the first floor. My one indulgence was an en suite shower and loo. This facility was in theory sacrosanct, but the rest of my room was not. I never locked the door. The mothers couldn't lock theirs and I thought it right to be subject to the same regulations. Hannah had introduced a system of 'red engaged' signs which meant 'do not disturb', and they were free to use this if they wanted. The chair beneath the door handle employed by Doreen this afternoon was strictly discouraged.

I generally left my door wide open during the after-supper period, for two reasons. One was in order to be visible, and accessible. So far in their lives these girls had been excluded, or had excluded themselves, from a great deal that most took for granted: family, education, sympathy, a moral code, the giving and receiving of affection. The very least that Woodlands could do was to include them; to embrace them and their babies no matter what. I told myself that it was not the least but the most important thing we could do – to provide an exemplar of grown-up reliability and dependable care.

The second reason for my open door was self-interest. I hated the admin., and welcomed interruption. This evening it came at just after nine o'clock in the form of Doreen and Roz. Roz was the prettiest of the mothers in a conventional sense – fresh-faced, silky-haired, generally well presented, and baby Sean was plump, smiley and sweet-smelling. She and Doreen had struck up a close, odd-couple friendship. Josie sucked her teeth knowingly over this liaison, but I chose to take it at its face value. If it made them happy and hurt no one else, it could only be a good thing.

I knew why they were there, but there was a little ritual to be gone through just the same.

'All right if we come in?' enquired Doreen, doing so.

I was working out rotas for both staff and tenants (as we called them) for the following month. 'Of course,' I said, 'nice to see you. Mind if I just finish this?'

'Carry on.'

Roz sat on the white wicker chair and Doreen lounged on the bed. 'Sean and Kyle all tucked up?' I asked, not looking up. It was like dealing with shy and potentially snappish wild animals – too much eye contact would be perceived as threatening.

'Yeah. Little devils.'

'End of a long day,' I observed ambiguously, summing things up to everyone's advantage. I filled in the last box in the week and pushed the pages aside, turning my chair to face them.

Roz picked at her fingernails. 'Sean's got a rash.'

'Oh, I'm sorry – did you show Josie?'

'Yeah, she gave me some cream. He never had a rash before.'

'It's been so hot,' I offered. She was a picture of anxiety, poor child, furrowed brow, pursed mouth, pick-picking away. 'Would you like me to take a look?'

Doreen gave a minute twitch of scorn which I pretended not to see. Roz said: 'He's asleep now.'

'Well, he can't be too uncomfortable. Would anyone like a biscuit?'

'Biscuits in the room!' Doreen rolled her eyes but they both had a plain chocolate Club anyway. With the biscuit half-wrapped like an ice cream in one hand, Doreen reached out to the bedside table and picked up a book.

'What's this then?'

'*A Town Like Alice.* By Nevil Shute.'

'Blimey – man or a woman?'

'Man.'

'Daft name.' She riffled the pages disparagingly as if seeking, and failing, to find anything of the remotest interest. Which since she could barely read was certainly true. 'What's it about?'

I had learned to ignore her studied lack of interest. She glared witheringly at the book's cover. Roz glanced at me from beneath lowered lids. I told them about Jean, and Joe, about the women prisoners' forced march at the hands of the Japanese, about Joe's theft of the chicken for 'Mrs Boong', their post-war reunion in Australia, and the ice-cream parlour in the 'bonzer town' of Alice Springs. Neither of them gave the impression that they were paying much attention, but when I'd finished giving them this summary, Doreen tossed the book towards the end of the bed, and said laconically: 'Go on then, read us a bit.'

Her tone implied that she was doing me a favour. She didn't know it, but this was true. As I began to read – the part where the women first meet their unlikely Australian saviour – my heart was full to breaking. I was no great reader-aloud; my rendition was straightforward rather than expressive. I trusted in the quality of the writing to do its own work. Every time I read to them, two or three times a week, I was almost unbearably moved to be doing so. But I was very careful not to let this show.

Among those who came to be read to, Doreen was the constant, sometimes on her own, sometimes accompanied by one or two others. She always behaved as if it were the first time, the result of the merest idle curiosity on her part. I colluded in this, making sure that there was a fresh book on the bedside table each week whether or not I'd finished the last one. I laboured long and hard over the selection of these books. In the past couple of months we had read among others from *Jane Eyre*, *Bonjour Tristesse*, *The Hound of the Baskervilles* and (a particular favourite of mine and a triumph), *The Secret Garden*. I carried out a sort of ad-hoc abridgement of each text, careful to select passages which, when heard in sequence and linked by my explanations, would give the shape of the whole story.

Occasionally, one of the others would get bored and leave. Never Doreen. She'd lie there until I'd finished, or had to stop. Only then would she get up, rub her face, mutter ''Night then,' and go. In the whole time I'd been reading to her she had only offered one comment, which was that Edward

Rochester was asking for a knee in the nuts. Naturally I colluded with her in the pretence that each occasion was random, an aberration. Any admission of mutual indulgence would mean the end of the readings.

Tonight, both Doreen and Roz stayed until I closed the book at ten to ten.

'Better end there,' I said. 'I ought to try and get a bit more work done.' I didn't mention the ten o'clock curfew – these rules existed but I tried not to be heavy-handed about them.

Roz got up at the same moment as Josie appeared in the doorway, her coat already on.

'Sean's crying, darlin'. Don't worry, he only just started!' she added as Roz rushed past. 'I'm off, goodnight.'

' 'Night, Josie.'

When they'd gone Doreen swung her legs off the bed. 'I dunno,' she said. 'I've heard of being hung for a sheep, but crucified for a fucking chicken . . .'

Nevil had made a hit.

I made my rounds, saying goodnight to everyone, offering my opinion on Sean's rash, fetching glasses of water, admiring photos and recommending transistors be turned off. I wasn't as green as they thought me, I knew the radios and the lights would go back on once I'd left, but it didn't matter. I wasn't ever going to be a martinet. We all had to get along.

When everything was reasonably quiet I went down-stairs and switched on the intercom. In spite of what I'd said to the girls I wasn't planing to do any more work. I was elated by the success of the reading and tired, too: a lot had happened since I'd set out that morning to visit my mother.

One of the reasons Doreen's earlier remark had hurt was that I myself recognised the irony of my mother being in one 'home' while I operated one for other mothers in a different

part of town. It was undeniably true that in her nineties she
needed professional care of a sort I wasn't equipped to
provide; however it was also true that I would have found
looking after her full time almost intolerable. I could put up
with any amount of the girls' rudeness, roughness and even
occasional violence – I'd been to A and E half a dozen times
on my own account – but my mother's mental and physical
deterioration tried me beyond endurance. Our relationship
had been at best guarded and at worst vexed, but she'd always
been tough. It was her decline I found hard to forgive.

I felt terribly guilty about it. Guilty at not being a more
loving daughter (though I tried my best not to let her see it);
guilty that I was looking after others and not her; most of
all, guilty that I was happy doing it.

At least the onset of senility had made her more tolerant
about the Woodlanders.

'How are things with those women?' she used to ask
when she had all her marbles, usually as I was just about
to leave. She didn't just disapprove of the mothers, she
despised them. And it was no good my telling myself that
she hadn't even met them, because I knew if that were ever
to happen she would dislike them even more. In her eyes
single mothers were no more than tarts, and their children
bastards.

'Doing fine, thank you,' I'd reply, reminding myself that
she was old, lonely, probably jealous.

'It's more than they deserve,' she said. 'You're wasting your
life.'

'That's not how I see it.'

'People like that are no good. Scum, your father would
have said.' She often put this word in his mouth, though I
could never remember, nor even imagine, him using it. 'They
take advantage of you and then they're off.'

'But Mum,' I said, 'that's the whole idea.'

That usually shut her up. One thing she couldn't deal with was sarcasm, however mild. But I'd got no pleasure from having had the last word. There were often tears in my eyes as I drove away. I had no other relatives: when my mother went, I would be the sole remaining Streeter. We should have provided a source of comfort and companionship to one another. If she were to die tomorrow I knew that I would suffer excruciating pangs of remorse. But as time went by we had increasingly brought out the worst in each other.

I saw now that there had been something symbolic in my return to Crompton Terrace. Not only had it broken the long return journey between my mother and Woodlands; it had also brought back to life that strange, wonderful, frightening and formative time. The time that more than my parents, my upbringing, even more than Matthew, had influenced the subsequent course of my life. The memories bloomed once more in my head.

I walked out into the small back garden and lowered myself gingerly on to the rickety lounger that stood on the grass. It was a warm night. One or two of the girls' bedroom windows still glowed orange behind their cheap curtains. A baby was snickering, in the early stages of waking to demand a feed. It was never completely quiet here.

I slipped off my shoes to feel the grass under my feet, and tipped my head back. I would have lain down but I was not confident of the lounger, or my own ability to get back to the vertical without disaster. Out of reach of the city's sulphurous orange glow there were still plenty of stars; the tail lights of an aeroplane, winking rhythmically; a calm, freckled moon.

I resolved to write to my mother the next day – or soon, anyway. A pleasant, newsy, filial letter which it would be no shame for one of the carers to read aloud to her.

I wondered idly what my original benefactor – the one who had made me rich beyond my wildest imaginings – would have made of the use to which I had put my tainted inheritance.

Chapter Three

When I was eighteen, the same age as the century, I went from sweetheart to widow in the space of a few days. I was a wife for just three heady, sleepless nights in the Esplanade boarding house in Pevensey.

It was more romantic than it sounds (not that we needed romantic surroundings to do what we so much wanted to do) – a small whitewashed villa at the apex of the long curve of the bay, its windows gazing out to sea. In spite of its name there was no esplanade; the villa's tussocky garden was separated from the shingle by no more than a bleached wooden fence, and a gate with a giant hook-and-eye latch to secure it against the offshore wind. A little further along the beach to the west was the area where the fishermen kept their boats. Inland to the east stood the castle fortress of King Henry VIII. Behind us lay the small town, itself peaceful but alive with honest war effort and scarred, like every town, by terrible loss. I think that was when I saw for the first time how closely freedom and safety are linked, that one is not possible without the other.

We were both virgins, of course, Matthew and I. Our marriage certificate was our licence to make love. We might not have been so self-controlled but for the war which had fanned our passion by denying us the opportunity to indulge it. We had met six months earlier, at a chapel hall dance, a week before Matthew left for France. I hadn't been interested in anyone till then. I was a bright girl who'd got into the grammar school and was trying to decide what to do next. Marriage was the last thing on my mind.

My parents were older than other girls' parents, late marriers themselves, and my mother hadn't had me till she'd turned thirty. They were solid, lower middle class and proud to have got there. My genial father, Gerald Streeter, had risen to be works manager at the Speedwell bicycle factory; my mother, Phyllis was a housewife of iron routines and terrifyingly high domestic standards. Their house in Catford, south London, gleamed. The only task she delegated – grudgingly, and only as a gesture to her husband's managerial status – was the weekly wash, which a Mrs Budd carried out under her gimlet-eyed supervision. Though she never said as much, she certainly considered herself a lady in all but birth, but would have conceded that those born to it were more entitled to the term. That was in the nature of things. As a girl she'd had a pretty voice and taken part in amateur theatricals, which was how they'd met. She would never for a single second have considered the stage as a career. If Dad wanted to embarrass her, he used to say aside to me, but loud enough for her to hear: 'I was a stage-door johnnie, you know.'

Mum liked to make him out to be a 'typical' man, part wide-eyed innocent, part satyr, part domestic tyrant, but none of these was remotely accurate. He was just easygoing and let her think, or say, or pretend, whatever she liked.

He was quite unconcerned, too, about my lack of interest in the opposite sex. 'Don't you be in any rush, Pammie,' he'd say, 'you've got your whole life ahead of you.' Mum, while pleased I'd got myself a decent education, definitely wanted me to have an admirer – some nice lad with good intentions that she could have kept an eye on and spoilt with homemade cake.

As it was, my parents didn't even know of Matthew's existence till he came back on leave. He asked for my father's permission to marry me on their second meeting. In truth we'd probably have gone ahead anyway, but we weren't two of nature's rebels. We wanted everyone to be happy. I thanked my lucky stars that Matthew was the sort of man everyone instinctively liked and respected. Dad granted his permission at once, all gruff and pink-cheeked with emotion. Mum was thoroughly put about by the speed of it all, as though that in itself were somehow indecent. She had been deprived of the cake-consuming period of supervised courtship, but she could see we were dead set on it, and gave us her blessing.

If I say Matthew was a 'good' person it might give the wrong impression – that he was dull and virtuous. I suspect that interpretation stems from childhood when the command to 'be good' means to be seen and not heard. I'm talking about something quite different. If I say that he charmed people that's not quite right either, because charm is seen as something suspect or bogus, a facility employed to bamboozle the unwary. He hadn't a mean bone in his body; his instinct was to like his fellow man, to get the best out of life and put the best in, to say yes if he possibly could, to give and not to count the cost. He wasn't handsome, but he shone out. If he smiled at you, you were the better for it. If he shook your hand you were instantly warmed.

When he kissed me I knew what bliss was.

So it wasn't so hard for my parents to let me go. We had a little ceremony at the Wesleyan chapel, alongside the hall where we'd first met, and a tea afterwards for which my mother at last got to make that cake – and what a cake! It was a triumph, so the occasion became almost as much hers as ours. In the afternoon we caught the train to Eastbourne, and from there to Pevensey, and walked hand in hand with our small suitcases to the Esplanade. A wintry sun shone on fine, sleety rain and made a rainbow over the marshes, so although we were starved with cold, we felt blessed.

The landlady was called Mrs Doyle. If there was, or ever had been, a Mr Doyle, he was not in evidence. She was a handsome, kindly woman in late middle-age, heavily skirted and tightly corseted in the pre-war way, but also glossily made up and the very soul of discretion. She presided over our little honeymoon like a benign deity, there if we needed her, invisible if we didn't. Her sole other guest was a commercial traveller whom we only saw at breakfast, but it was the measure of her quality that she treated him like a king as well.

It was late March, by turns spring-like and freezing. We took long walks on the beach, and to the castle, but there was no question of us being turned out between breakfast and tea. She made us sandwiches for the middle of the day, to eat out or by the fire in the parlour which she lit in the morning and kept burning all day for our benefit. She was a wonderful plain cook whose food had the flavour and warmth that can only come from a person who loves cooking, and eating. There was nothing to do in the evenings in Pevensey, but that didn't matter, because we went to bed early.

Many times since then I've read a lot about how in our day ignorance and lack of experience made for sad, bad experiences of sex, to the extent that sometimes whole marriages were blighted. Well, we were both utterly inexperienced, but I can't imagine that we could have had more mutual pleasure and excitement. Except, of course, that it would have got better with time, and time was what we were about to be denied.

When, on our last morning, we said goodbye to Mrs Doyle, she was warm and friendly as ever, but betrayed no special extra emotion. We had been paying guests and she had treated us according to our youth and our newly-wed status. Doubtless, times being what they were, there would be plenty more couples like us and she would be just as good to them. I was glad she'd kept it businesslike. My own feelings were quite enough to deal with, without having to take account of someone else's as well.

As we walked to the station Matthew carried his own case and mine too, tucked under his arm, his other hand holding mine. I remember thinking that this was how it would be from now on: someone to share difficulties as well as pleasures. The Great War – how can a war be great, I ask you? – was about to reclaim my husband, and yet I refused to consider the possibility that 'from now on' might mean something entirely different.

On the mainline train back to London engine smoke scudded between us and the cold, gleaming countryside outside. We both felt the shadow of imminent separation creeping across us, and we went quiet. I linked my arm through Matthew's and laid my head on his shoulder, closing my eyes to keep the tears in.

We went back to my parents' house in Catford. In my bedroom, now legitimately ours, I sat on the bed and watched my new husband change back into a soldier. He had lovely skin, smooth and pale as marble, and reddish-brown hair that was a lighter colour, almost gold, under his arms and at the top of his legs. Till then, the war had not left a single mark on him. He was whole and perfect.

When he was done he sat down next to me in his stiff, rough uniform and put his arm round my shoulders. He took my left hand in his, rubbing the thin gold ring with his thumb as if it were Aladdin's wonderful lamp and could grant us our wish.

'Well, Mrs Griffe . . . I do love you so.'

I couldn't speak. He kissed my hand, and then my mouth. Licked a tear off my cheek. 'Don't cry, sweetheart. Everyone says it won't be long now. Then we'll have plenty of time.'

He was right. One week later he was dead, and I had all the time in the world.

We only had those few days, but they changed my life for ever. It wasn't only grief that separated me from other single girls of my age: it was that I had joined the ranks of the widows. We had no rarity value; there were tens of thousands of us, each dragging her individual tragedy like an untidily packed suitcase, a disobliging *memento mori* for the as-yet unbereaved. Even my parents managed to give the impression that for me to miss Matthew too much, or to show that I did, would be something like bad form, when so many others out there were in the same position. And many of them, their tone gently implied, almost as if I should be comforted by the fact, *had been married for years, and had children*. It was as if my fledgling marriage to Matthew simply did not, could not, count for so much as all those longstanding ones, exemplary or otherwise.

They didn't mean to hurt me, but their thoughtless attempts to cheer me up made me bleed inwardly. In telling me that I was in some way fortunate to have lost Matthew before things went any further, before we had built a life together or got to know each other better, or had a family, or even had time to quarrel, they were driving home the very aspects of my loss which I found most agonising.

When I was ten a woman from up the road, Mrs Coleman, had a stillbirth. I knew because my mother told me, in the slightly disapproving tone she reserved for matters of a highly personal nature. She must have thought it best for me to know because of the Colemans' other children with whom I played from time to time. I remember coming in from school one afternoon and hearing voices in the front room. I recognised Mrs Coleman's. As I crossed the hall she burst into tears. It was the first time I had ever heard an adult cry, and it stopped me in my tracks. Appalled but paralysed, I stood there listening.

'John Anthony!' she sobbed. 'We christened him, he had a name, two names! He was our lovely boy, but no one talks about him, they all want me to forget, so they can forget, but I can't, I *can't!*'

Some programmed reflex caused my mother, doubtless rather alarmed by this outburst, to get up and push the door to. I wasn't quick enough and she saw me. She made a fierce 'run along' gesture and I needed no second bidding. I fled.

Now, though, I knew exactly how that poor woman had felt – that because her son's life had been scarcely more than an eye-blink the world wanted her to discount him. But John Anthony had been a part of her family, and of her, a real person, her 'lovely boy' who only a few days before his birth had had his whole life before him.

Matthew and I were like that. We too had had the best part of our lives before us. Our whole life together, light on plans but heavy on dreams, had been there for the living. I mourned not only what I had lost, but what never happened: the love-making and the fallings-out, the scrimping and the strokes of luck, the treats, the trials . . . The babies.

I articulated none of this. I was very young, and in those days quite conventional. I accepted my parents' well-meaning view of the situation and to all intents and purposes fell in with it. The end of the war came, and there was a party at that blasted chapel hall. This time, at my mother's instigation, I made a cake, too, though not as good as hers. I remember feeling like a ghost: present but unconnected, barely visible. No one made a fuss, of me, or any of the other hardworking, quiet-mouthed war widows. Talking about it, people doubtless reasoned, would only have made it worse. Perhaps they were right. And after all, with so many of us, where would it have ended? There would scarcely have been a cheerful face at the party! I didn't care. I was glad of the privacy. And besides, it was my husband's uniqueness for which I craved recognition, the singularity of our love, not its commonplaceness.

Without the warm, healing poultice of sympathy, I carried my brief memory of Matthew around with me like a speck of glass that gradually worked its way into my system and became buried – a minute, needle-sharp, stifled pain, too deep to dislodge. Maybe that was what the expression 'the iron entering one's soul' means.

After a year of living at home, helping my mother and being, I sensed, a slight worry and embarrassment to her and my father, I did the sensible thing (I say that without resentment, it *was* sensible) and took a secretarial course. I went daily by bus to the Eileen Nair College in Rathbone Road, Dulwich, and over nine months learned shorthand, typing, filing and bookkeeping. The twenty or so girls on the course were no older than me but none of them was in my position. One or two of them claimed to be nursing broken hearts over young men killed in the war. Many had lost fathers, or brothers. But none was like me, a widow. I hugged my widowhood to me, saying nothing: feeling, if I'm honest, a mite superior.

I owe much more than my livelihood to that year at the Eileen Nair. It was my salvation, preventing me from becoming the sort of joyless, sour-faced prig whom Matthew could never have loved. I had something useful to do, and I made a friend for life.

I befriended Barbara Chisholm believing I was doing her a good turn, long before I realised it was the other way round. She was a thin, plain, solitary girl who smoked at every opportunity and was a fearsomely quick study. No one was unpleasant to her, she wasn't ostracised, but they tended not to include her. In spite of my secret suffering I was nice-looking and conventional, as I've said, and easily assimilated. Smugly, I thought Barbara was left out, when she was leaving herself out.

We ate our lunch in the college canteen – either what the canteen itself provided, or the sandwiches we had brought with us. The food wasn't nice, so most of us brought our own and sat at a long table specially set aside for the purpose, as they do in schools today. Barbara always had a small flask of tea and a bun. She'd sit quietly at one remove from the rest of us, watching, and no doubt listening, in her detached way. I recalled how I'd felt at the street party, and wondered if that's how I'd looked to other people. She was lonely, I decided, and forbidding in her loneliness.

She'd always eat her picnic quickly, and then put away the thermos and go outside for a cigarette. Smoking was forbidden inside the college, and frowned upon outside the front of the building because of the bad impression it conveyed, but Barbara wasn't easily deterred. I'd watched her – she smoked, urgently, absent-mindedly, without affectation, like someone who *needed* to smoke. Though she was plain she was saved from mousiness by a long nose and heavy eyebrows which gave her face a certain distinction. Her clothes, though, were hopeless even then, not even eccentric, but frumpy.

To be fair to myself, I may have been in danger of getting priggish, but I hadn't yet done so. My desire to befriend Barbara was genuine – I felt sorry for her and I detected a possible kindred spirit. Also (and this *was* self-serving) I didn't want anyone else, no matter what their status, to suppose I was the same as all the others. One afternoon in November, when we'd been on the course a couple of months, I got up from the table when she did and followed her outside.

It was a damp, raw day and there was the usual one-legged man stumping up and down the pavement opposite accompanied by his lugubrious greyhound, with a collecting box strapped to its back. The man had a placard round his neck proclaiming LIFE RUINED AT WIPERS, PLEASE HELP. I experienced my customary twinge of disapproval. It hadn't yet occurred to me that this prim response to the man's desperation was pretty close to the way others had reacted to me after Matthew's death. They acknowledged I'd been through something terrible but it was not deemed suitable to make too much of it. There was a delivery van parked outside the Criterion Café, and a lad shovelling horse droppings into a bucket. Two women with prams stood on the corner, jiggling the prams as they gossiped.

Barbara Chisholm was sitting with her back to the building, on the low wall that separated the front garden from the road. Her feet were on the pavement. She had positioned herself near the College's imposing name-board so that she could not be seen from the windows but (this may or may not have been intentional) her proscribed activity, viewed from the other side, was taking place directly beneath the words EILEEN NAIR.

'Hello,' I said, 'may I join you?'

She was in the middle of taking a drag, and didn't answer but made a little tucking-in gesture with her skirt, to show there was plenty of room. I sat down. The wall felt cold and clammy under my thighs. My feeble altruism wilted a little, but I could hardly go straight back in.

'Nasty day—' I began.

'I'd offer you one,' she said, as though I hadn't spoken. 'But I'm on a ration.'

'That's all right, I don't. Or not often,' I added.

She nodded, as if this was what she'd expected to hear. Already I had the oddest feeling that everything was the wrong way round – the opposite of what I'd expected.

'What do you think of it so far?' I asked. 'The course?'

'The course is fine.' She placed a slight emphasis on the first two words that implied an unfavourable comparison with something left unmentioned. But I was unwilling to pick her up on this, and said instead:

'I find the shorthand hard. But I suppose it will come.'

She nodded. 'Yup.'

'You're so quick. You must be miles ahead of the rest of us.'

She shrugged, not denying it. Her cigarette was almost gone, but she continued to smoke the stub to the bitter end, holding it between finger and thumb like a working man.

'And you're married,' she said.

The unrelated nature of this remark and its suddenness, the fact that she wasn't even looking at me, took me by surprise.

'Yes – no.'

Now she looked at me, raising one eyebrow. 'Which?'

'I was. I'm a widow.'

She betrayed no particular reaction, but dropped the last fragment of her cigarette to the ground and placed a sturdy black shoe on it.

'Really?' she murmured.

I could scarcely believe I'd heard her. I was incensed. I hardly knew her and wasn't yet familiar with her vague, detached way of speaking.

'Of course, *really*.'

'Do you have children?'

'No. There wasn't time.'

She gave a sardonic little sniff. 'There's always time.'

'I beg your pardon?'

'I said,' she repeated slowly, tucking her big bony hands into her armpits for warmth, 'there's always time for that. It only takes a couple of minutes, you know.'

That was enough for me. I'd offered the hand of friendship and had met with nothing but rudeness. Fortunately for both of us the exchange was cut short by the appearance of one of the teachers.

'Mrs Griffe, Miss Chisholm . . . Will you come in now please.'

It was not a propitious first exchange, and I wasn't anxious to repeat it. But I can only suppose that her curiosity was aroused by it as much as mine, because about a week later she came up to me as we trooped out of bookkeeping, our last class of the afternoon. More accurately, she drifted alongside; it was impossible to tell whether her presence at my side was accident or design.

'I was thinking of going over to the Criterion for a cup of tea,' she said offhandedly.

'Really?'

If she noticed the sarcasm she didn't show it. 'Mm . . .'

'Good idea,' I replied.

'What about you?' The question was open-ended, more enquiry than invitation.

'I hadn't thought about it.'

I saw her head turn away, but not enough to conceal the ironic tweak of her mouth, the lifting of an eyebrow.

'Maybe I will,' I said. Even to my own ears I sounded a bit defiant, as though she'd thrown down the gauntlet for a duel instead of a cup of tea over the road.

We walked across, she with her rangy, loping stride, coat flapping, I marching smartly slightly ahead of her to demonstrate my independence.

The Criterion was poor-respectable. Like it or not, I was my mother's daughter, acutely sensitive to such nuances. Not poor-rough, nor smart-respectable, and certainly not posh. That is to say it was clean but sparse, it served beans on toast as well as Battenberg cake, and the tea came in mugs from an urn on the counter, not in pots, cups and saucers at the table. The other customers were a scattering of elderly ladies, two men in clean but shabby suits, with briefcases, and a smartly dressed woman who was making a great show of waiting for someone – looking at her watch, peering out of the window and so forth.

I hadn't been to the café before but from her manner Barbara obviously had. Away from the curious eyes of the Eileen Nair I felt less prickly, and relaxed somewhat. We ordered two teas and a buttered teacake to share, and sat at a table in the corner. Barbara immediately got out her Park Drives and this time offered them to me as well. I took one. It was true I didn't smoke often – with me it was a social affectation – but I didn't want to seem standoffish. There was nicotine on her fingers and they shook slightly. Rather surprisingly she produced a nice little black leather-covered lighter.

'That's smart,' I said.

She looked at it as if baffled. 'I suppose so. Someone gave it to me.'

This too was a surprise. She didn't look like the sort of girl to whom people gave lighters.

'I'm sorry,' she said, 'about your husband.'

That was the first step towards our friendship – that she hadn't apologised to *me*, but expressed sorrow, in however formulaic a manner, over Matthew. I nodded dumbly.

We neither of us spoke for a moment. Barbara smoked unconcernedly for a while and then asked: 'What was he like?'

That was step two.

I was still struggling. She waited, not exactly patiently, it was more neutral than that; she didn't press me, or ask a second time. She simply sat there and got on with things till I was ready. She stubbed out her half-smoked cigarette, cut the teacake in two, and started to eat her half steadily, unselfconsciously, as though she were on her own. Sipped her tea. Lit another cigarette.

Eventually I managed: 'What do you want to know?'

'Well . . .' she puffed vaguely. 'What did he look like? Colour of eyes? Hair, straight or curly? If any?' she added – not smiling, but it broke the ice.

I told her. She listened. Again, there was something comforting in her almost businesslike reaction. She did not assume an expression of sympathy, but paid attention, occasionally saying 'Mm' or 'Yes' as if I were giving her my views on moral rearmament or birth control. I had thought I craved sympathy, but this matter-of-factness was tremendously comforting. It was as if Matthew were at last getting the attention and respect he deserved, even if it was from a stranger.

When I eventually ran out of steam it was quite dark and we had drunk a second mug of tea. Around us, the clientele had changed. The old ladies and the threadbare businessmen were gone, and the smart woman had finally given up on whoever she'd been waiting, or pretending to wait, for. Now there was a gaggle of factory girls in the far corner and another table full of lads, eyeing them up.

'He sounds nice,' said Barbara. 'You were lucky.'

That was step three.

On the way home on the bus I became tearful and had to pretend I had a cold, but it wasn't all sadness from talking about Matthew. There was relief, too. And for the first time I was able to see that I had indeed been lucky. In a strange way Barbara's words, spoken in her casual, almost offhand way, had restored Matthew to me – the real, passionate Matthew whom it had been my good fortune to love and to marry.

There was one more stage to the development of our friendship, and it was even more unexpected.

It took a while to develop, because we didn't spend that
much time together. Barbara remained on the fringes of life
at Eileen Nair, and I continued to be one of the herd. Neither
of us envied the other but we each respected the other's position. I think we both liked the oddness of our association, its
unexpectedness, and didn't want to jeopardise that by
becoming too familiar. The others looked at her a little differently because we were friends, but any attempts to include
her were repelled by her poker-faced air of self-sufficiency.

One of the girls asked me about her. 'What's she like?'

I didn't have an answer. I said she was nice – what on earth
did that mean? – and the girl gave me a look that said she'd
take my word for it. I realised I knew next to nothing about
Barbara except what I could see. Her identity, as far as I was
concerned, rested solely in her interest in me. Rebuking myself
for my selfishness, I took the next opportunity to restore the
balance. It was late December, the last day of term, and the
Criterion had a small Christmas tree in the window and a
holly-wrapped collecting tin on the counter, coyly labelled:
'Compliments of the season from our staff'.

'My treat,' I said grandly as we sat down.

'Why?'

'No reason. Because.' She made her wry face. 'Because I
feel like it.'

'That'll do.'

They were serving 'chef's' fruit cake and we had a slice
each with our tea. I asked Barbara what she would be doing
on Christmas Day.

'Getting through it,' she said grimly.

'Oh dear,' I said. 'You don't like it much.'

'Correct.'

'Who will you be with?'

'Nobody.'

'Barbara . . .' I was dismayed. 'From choice, or necessity?'

'Both.'

'Would you like to join us?' I asked. It was on the face of it a reckless invitation – I could just imagine my mother's reaction on hearing that a perfect stranger was coming to Christmas dinner. On the other hand I was pretty sure what the answer would be and to my considerable relief I was right.

She gave a faint smile that told me not to be silly. 'No thank you.'

In anyone else I might have thought this bluntness quite rude, but I was used to her manner by now. I also knew that I could, without giving the least offence, be as direct with her as she was with me.

'Why do you hate it so?'

'For a start –' she began the process of lighting a cigarette – 'I've never liked it. Even when I was a child. All that forced merriment . . . Games, forsooth!' She shuddered. 'I was never any good at it, and then one was made to feel one was letting the side down.'

She drew on the cigarette. That first drag was like much-needed fuel to her. Sensing there was more to come I played things her way and didn't press her. She exhaled slowly. Smoke drifted up past her face, her narrowed eyes. In retrospect, I realise that she was deliberating, weighing up the advisability of her next remark, its effects and consequences.

'Also,' she went on, gazing out of the window, turning the cigarette packet on the table with her long, stained, ringless fingers. 'I miss my son.'

It was never her intention to shock. I had asked her a straight question and she was returning a straight answer. I should have been flattered, but at that moment I was too flabbergasted to do anything but blurt out:

'Barbara! You've got a *son*?'

'Had.' To allay my worst fears she added: 'I had him

adopted. Or other people did it for me. He went when he was one week old.'

'How *awful*,' I breathed, though part of me was shamefully thrilled by the awfulness of it.

She shrugged. 'It's what girls like me do. At least I had time to get to know him. Some of them went at birth.'

'But didn't that make it harder – to give him up?'

'No.' She gave me a level look. 'He was mine for that week. And he still is, wherever he is.'

'Do you know the people?'

'I didn't want to. If I'd liked them I'd have been jealous, and if I hadn't – it doesn't bear thinking about.' She stubbed out her cigarette, with hard, grinding movements. 'He had to go, and that was it. I'm sure he's well looked after. And whoever they are he'll be used to them by now. They'll be his parents and he'll think all parents are like them.'

I could tell from the way she said all this that it was an acquired philosophy, one she'd rehearsed many times in her head. After my initial shock I instinctively knew how to proceed. Barbara above all people did not want sympathy. When I had needed comfort she'd provided it with her straightforward curiosity, her interest and attention.

'Did he have a name?' I asked.

'Freddy. To me. I don't know what he's called now.'

'Freddy's nice. Dashing.'

She gave her almost-smile. 'I thought so.'

'Who was the father?'

'A man called Reg Parsons that I worked with at the factory. He was the foreman. I don't know what possessed me . . .' She shook her head in bafflement as she took out another cigarette. 'He gave me the lighter, actually. He was stupid and ugly. But then so was I.'

'Barbara—'

'No, I was. Stupid to let him do what he did, and too plain

to feel I could say no. Pretty girls have a lot of power. You must know that.'

It was a compliment of sorts, but it wasn't something I'd thought about.

'He wasn't wicked,' she went on. 'He didn't *force* me to do anything. That's what makes it even sadder.'

'Does he know – about Freddy?'

'No. I just left and got on with it.'

I couldn't begin to imagine it: the fear, and the loneliness. 'What did your parents say?'

'I didn't tell them, either. We'd already fallen out, it would only have confirmed them in their opinion of me.'

I was awed. 'So what did you do?'

'I cast myself on the mercy of the Emmanuel Home for the dirty and disgusting.'

The colourful language, so unlike her, offered a measure of her strength of feeling. I scarcely needed to ask my next question.

'What was that like?'

'Horrible. They looked after us but they made sure we knew that no one else would. We were untouchables. There was a war on, our boys were dying, and yet girls like us were doing this sort of thing.'

I remembered Matthew, and our honeymoon in Pevensey. 'But you'd done nothing wrong!' I protested.

'Oh yes I had,' she said curtly. 'Not just in their eyes, in mine, too. I deserved my punishment. I shan't do that again.'

I wanted to tell her how wrong she was, how much she would be denying herself, but this was not the moment.

'Still,' she said, 'I got a reward as well as retribution. I got Freddy. And to the great annoyance of all concerned I had an easy birth. I'm surprised they didn't push him back in and make me do it all over again.'

This time, I could think of nothing to say. We both stared

out into the dark, lamplit street. It had begun to rain. The one-legged Ypres veteran lurched past, his greyhound padding next to him.

'So that,' said Barbara, 'is why I don't like Christmas.'

Chapter Four

I went to work at Seven Crompton Terrace in my late twenties. I confess I've never been sure exactly how I got the position. I had considerable experience by then, and the assurance of good references, and I suppose I was quite nice-looking and smart, but my qualifications were no better than those of hundreds of other young women of my age in London at the time. Perhaps the Jarvises didn't have many applicants, but that would have been surprising considering it was a peach of a job. Or perhaps – though they never afterwards struck me as in the least fussy – there were certain things they didn't care for, such as curly hair, or big feet, or a particular verbal tic, and I just happened not to score black marks on the day.

Since leaving college, I'd been in the typing pool at a tea-importers, then secretary to the classified ads manager of a north London newspaper. For the last two years I'd been working at Osborne's, a small publisher of children's books in Maiden Lane. I was secretary to the commissioning editor, Max Darblay, a florid man with a stomach ulcer. He was alternately lecherous and bullying – in fact it was possible to predict the degree of his nastiness on any given day from that of his hot-handedness the day before. I could deal with him, he was harmless enough. What astonished me was how he had achieved such a position of power at Osborne's when he detested children and despised authors. The former he referred to as 'little darlings' in a tone that would have curdled milk, the latter as 'whimsy-merchants'. Those who did not by any stretch of the imagination qualify as whimsy-merchants (some of our authors wrote fast and furious adventure stories) were dismissed as 'clerks' on the assumption, I could only suppose, that people who produced this stirring escapism did so because they themselves led such unconscionably dull lives. That would certainly have accounted for his embarrassment when one of the new 'clerks', D.L. McAlpine, came into the office prior to lunching with Roddy Osborne, the managing director, and turned out to be a giant of a man: a Cambridge rowing blue and much-decorated veteran of both South Africa and the Dardanelles, who wrote his tales of heroism, danger and endeavour in between exploratory trips to uncharted regions of the globe. I remember noticing that he had two fingers missing on his right hand. Once he'd got over his embarrassment, Max Darblay dismissed McAlpine as the exception that proved the rule.

When I took the job at Osborne's I'd been under the illusion that publishing was a glamorous business. Elsewhere it may well have been, but our branch of it (McAlpine apart) was not. My day consisted of long periods of routine correspondence, filing, tea-making and diary-adjustment, enlivened by Darblay's rather pathetic advances and subsequent fits of pique. Still, it was a reasonably prestigious job that paid enough for me to leave home and rent a small top-floor bedsit off the Tottenham Court Road, and my time there resulted in one real and lasting benefit: a realistic, even a mildly sceptical, appreciation of human nature.

Darblay's importunings and uncertain temper taught me the value of holding steady and maintaining one's self-possession. I won't say that he didn't reduce me to tears on a couple of early occasions, but I only allowed the tears to fall in the cloakroom, or in the bus on the way home. In the

office, I was a model of unflappable efficiency. My aloofness infuriated him, but he must have been grateful that I
made no recriminations or complaints, that my own behaviour was as unvaryingly calm and reliable as my work, no
matter what he threw at me. He never uttered a thank-you,
nor an apology, but on both the Christmases that I was there
I received a generous bonus, which was far more useful.

Those authors that I met I liked, in the main, but what
intrigued me was the gulf between the writer and what he
or she wrote – the gulf occupied by that wonderful thing
which I lacked, the creative imagination. McAlpine was
certainly an exception, being every bit as fearsomely intrepid
as his heroes, but those whom Darblay dismissed as 'whimsy-
merchants' were, I had to admit, a surprising lot. The author
of a series of enchanting fairy books was a big woman in
brogues and a tie; the stories about Piers and Posy, orphaned
twins at large in a mysterious other-world on a quest for
their missing brother, were written by an elderly solicitor
from Eastbourne; the chronicles of a magic bicycle were the
work of a war widow with four children; Armand the Alligator
was the creation of two gentlemen friends from Leeds, and
so on. We may not have been the biggest or most renowned
publisher of children's books, but I was nonetheless vouchsafed this glimmer of insight into literary inspiration: like
lightning, you never knew where, or in what form, it would
strike.

Also, who knows? Perhaps the fact that I had experience
in a broadly 'artistic' milieu was a contributory factor, along
with my unexceptionable ordinariness, in my being offered
the job with the Jarvises.

The advertisement in *The Times* was brief and a little coy.
Amanuensis required, shorthand and typing, general duties.
Successful candidate will be able, amiable, adaptable. There
followed a Post Office box number.

Within a week of sending off my application I received a letter from a Mr Christopher Jarvis, the Sumpter Gallery, Bowne Street, W1, inviting me for an interview not at the gallery but at a private address in Highgate. My heart sank. I wondered if this meant that Jarvis was looking for someone to help more in the domestic arena; the words *general duties* and *adaptable* took on a new significance. If that were so, I was not the woman he was after; my domestic capabilities were strictly limited to what was required by my simple, single life. But I could hear Matthew's voice in my ear saying: 'Best foot forward, Mrs Griffe,' and after all, I reasoned, I could always say no.

It was a beautiful day in early May when I presented myself at Seven Crompton Terrace for the interview. There was pink and white blossom on the trees in the road, and more in the gardens beyond. It made a delightful change after my poky flat and dark office in town and my heart lifted in spite of my nervousness.

Crompton Terrace was more modest than the road by which I approached it, Hardwick Row. Number Seven, though three storeys high, wasn't grand, but it was pretty, and there was a quirky charm about the front garden with its knobbly red-brick path and crab-apple tree. A glamorous little red roadster (a Riley, I found out) was parked at the kerb outside. I approached the door and stood in the open-sided porch. Tendrils of early honeysuckle waved from the wooden uprights, and cobwebs clung in the far corners. On the tiles to the right of the front door was a large riding boot, its leather cross-hatched with age, in which stood an umbrella, a walking stick and a butterfly net. None of them looked as if they got much use; I suspected that they were there for show.

The dolphin door knocker was polished to a high shine. Assuming I was expected, and not wanting to sound peremptory, I knocked quite lightly. In less than a minute, the door was opened by a tall, elegant, middle-aged man in shirtsleeves. The moment he saw me he put a finger to his lips and pointed with his other hand to something above my head. Obediently, I looked up. Beneath the eaves of the porch was the rough brown cup of a swallow's nest, the head of the occupant just visible above the lip.

I smiled appreciatively. The man smiled back and beckoned me in. When he'd closed the door he said:

'Mrs Griffe?'

'Yes.'

'How do you do. Christopher Jarvis. I'm sorry to shush you like that, but we feel rather honoured by our residents and don't want to disturb them.'

'Of course.'

'May I take your coat?'

'Oh . . . thank you.'

We were in a hall, with a flight of stairs, that narrowed into a corridor towards the back of the house. A second door, half-glazed, seemed to give on to the back garden. Mr Jarvis hung up my coat.

'Come through.'

He led the way into a room on the right of the hall. It was set out like a small library, with books lining every wall and a leather-topped table in the bay window, covered with more books, papers and catalogues. On another smaller table just inside the door stood a telephone and a typewriter. There was a fireplace opposite the window, and someone had placed a shock of bluebells in a pottery jug on the hearth, which still held the rubble of yesterday evening's fire. On the floor was a Turkish carpet in rich reds and blues that matched the curtains, and the lamps, too, had an oriental look, coloured enamelwork on great bulbs of brass.

'This would be you,' said Jarvis, pointing to the smaller

table. He nodded at the larger one. 'That's me, when I'm here.'

'I see,' I said. I wasn't at all sure what it would be like working in the same room as my employer, and may have sounded rather doubtful. To appear keener, I added: 'What a lovely room.'

'It is pretty, isn't it?' he agreed, rubbing his hands together. He was extremely handsome, with a smooth olive skin, auburn hair, and a little moustache. His pale blue shirt was soft and loose. He may have been a gallery owner but he looked more like an artist himself.

'My wife and I love this house,' he went on. 'The street is so secluded, somehow, and although the rooms aren't large everything's perfectly proportioned. It's a good example of the very best in English domestic architecture.' He smiled again. 'I'll show you around afterwards.'

His easy charm was disconcerting. He had a way of making everything sound as though I had already got the job. I warned myself not to get complacent, and to prepare myself for polite rejection.

'Do sit down,' he said. There were two strappy leather chairs – I later learned they were called 'safari chairs' – on either side of the hearth, and a chesterfield with some rather battered tapestry cushions. I took one of the chairs and he sat on the end of the chesterfield furthest from me, his arm along the back, his legs crossed, still smiling.

'Oh –' I said, remembering something. 'I brought my references.' I took them out of my bag and handed them over. He didn't so much as glance at them, let alone open the envelopes, but put them on the side table next to him, on top of an uneven pile of magazines.

'Thank you. I'm sure they're impeccable. Now!' he went on, in a tone that was almost gossipy. 'Tell me why you're here.'

This complete reversal of roles might have thrown me, but I'd had a useful training in unpredictability from Max Darblay.

'Your advertisement was unusual,' I told him, 'and I believe I have the necessary qualifications.'

'Ah, but to do what?' he asked teasingly.

I had the cutting in my bag, and took it out. 'To be an "amanuensis",' I read, 'with additional "general duties".'

'What about "able, amiable and adaptable"?'

'I haven't had any complaints,' I said.

He laughed. 'Well done! All right, that was unfair of me. Let me explain . . .'

It turned out that what he wanted was, as he put it, 'a paragon that may very well not exist' – a general factotum combining the qualities of 'accountant, diplomat, and favourite aunt'. Basic secretarial skills were a prerequisite but by no means the most important part of the job.

'You see,' he said, 'we're both pretty helpless. We need help!'

He struck me as anything but helpless. Lazy, perhaps; disinclined to do anything that didn't appeal to him. I suspected him of being indulged as delightful and attractive people often are.

'Would I be working for more than one person, then?' I asked.

'Yes. My wife and me. Though perhaps as we are one flesh that doesn't count.'

'That depends,' I said, 'on what sort of work she wanted me to do.'

He seemed to think this was hilariously funny, throwing his head back and roaring with laughter. 'A very good point!'

I waited patiently. When he'd stopped laughing, he said: 'She wants keeping in order, like me. Amanda's hospitable to a fault – we have a very full life with lots of visitors and house guests and so on and she needs a major domo – a coordinator. A clear head and steady hands. Which,' he added, 'from my first impression, you have.'

'Thank you. I hope so.'

He chuckled a bit more and then seemed suddenly to realise that he should be conducting things in a rather more businesslike way. He asked me earnestly about my typing and shorthand speed, and then cut across my answer with:

'No, dammit, just tell me everything about yourself.'

I told him a lot, but nothing about myself. I told him about the jobs I'd done, including the current one and why I wished to leave (being sure to cite his advertisement as the main reason); I told him about my education, and where I was brought up, and where I lived now. I explained that I was a widow. I fancied that I'd given him a great many facts while revealing nothing personal. But he was no fool; I can see now that he must have intuited a great deal from my appearance, the way I spoke, everything about me. He sat with his hands linked behind his head, listening with rapt attention. When I'd finished, he brought his hands down to his knees with a slap, and said:

'Excellent! Tell me, would you like a look round?'

I'd decided early on, when he'd first mentioned it, what my answer would be to this invitation.

'That's kind of you, but I won't, thank you. I have to be back at my desk by lunchtime.'

'Of course, I forgot, you're a working woman.' He got to his feet, and I did the same.

In the hall, the generally informal tenor of the interview emboldened me to ask: 'Have you had many applicants for the job?'

'Dozens!' he said. 'Dozens and dozens. It's been positively humbling.'

I wondered, if this was so, what the un-humbled

Christopher Jarvis must be like. I half hoped to meet Amanda before I left, but there seemed to be no one else about. At that moment I thought I did glimpse someone, a slight figure, appear at the end of the corridor, and then almost as quickly disappear, but the house was so quiet I thought I must have imagined it.

'I'll be in touch soon,' he said. As he opened the front door, he held up his finger to remind me about the swallows, and I nodded to show the message had been received. And so we parted in silence, the door closing with scarcely a click behind me. It was only on the way back to Maiden Lane that I realised we had not exchanged one word about money.

One week later I received a letter saying that the job was mine if I wanted it, at a salary of £250 per annum – considerably more than I was earning at Osborne's – and that the Jarvises would like me to begin as soon as possible, subject to the terms of my present employment.

I still saw Barbara, every so often. She was never one to take the initiative in these matters; with hindsight I realised how privileged I had been when she suggested that first cup of tea. She must have seen something sympathetic in me despite our inauspicious start. Anyway, our mutual exchange of confidences had sealed a lasting friendship which thence (it was tacitly understood) it was my duty to foster. Were it not for me, heaven knows whether we should ever have seen each other after we left the Eileen Nair. On the other hand something told me that had she really needed me, or known that I needed her, she would have been in touch. We had established a closeness which didn't require proximity. We understood one another.

I wanted to tell her about my new job, and chose the rather sticky day on which I handed in my notice to meet her at the Lyons Corner House in the Strand. Ever since college Barbara had worked for Rice and Claydon, a firm of bespoke tailors in Jermyn Street. At first I'd been rather uncharitably surprised that a business so dependent on appearances should have employed Barbara, a woman who cared so little about hers. But she had obviously made herself indispensable, and it dawned on me that perhaps drabness and reserve were important in a place habitually visited by gentlemen without their wives. Her thin figure suited the current fashions, and these days she was always, if not exactly chic, at least quite smart, in a neat costume, with her straggly hair bobbed to shoulder-length.

The weather had changed abruptly in the ten days since my interview, and I scurried down the Strand under an umbrella, thinking how grubby my stockings were getting and that I would have to wash them tonight because I had no others ready to wear. In the lobby of the Corner House I shook the worst of the wet off my umbrella and stood it with more than a dozen others just inside the door. Barbara was already there, at a table in the far corner, smoking a cigarette and gazing into space. She always had that ability to cut herself off from her surroundings so as to appear perfectly at ease in them. If I had been waiting for someone on my own I should have needed a newspaper or a book to occupy me, so as not to seem restless or forlorn, whereas Barbara gave the impression that she could have sat there all day, idle and detached, at one with herself.

I went over and we greeted each other casually, as if it had not been several months since our last meeting. A pot of tea and two cups were already on the table.

'I took the liberty,' said Barbara. 'It only just came, and I knew you wouldn't be late.'

'Shall we order teacakes?' I suggested. It was a sign of our improved circumstances that we now had one each.

'They're on their way. I asked them to begin toasting when you arrived.'

'You're so organised!' I exclaimed.

She pulled her face. 'It's a case of having to be, these days.'

This was my cue to ask how her work was going. She always said laconically that it was just the same but then went on to mention various small things that had happened, mostly concerning the amusing goings-on of clients. In her dry way she was a good raconteur. I was prepared to bet that the gents-about-town who brought their custom to Rice and Claydon would never in a hundred years guess the conversational capital that was being made of them by Mr Rice's thin, pale, spinsterish secretary.

When we'd polished off the teacakes, she lit another cigarette and said, glancing away from me as she did so: 'So what was it you wanted to tell me?'

'I've got a new job!'

I described to her the idiosyncratic advertisement and even more idiosyncratic interview. She listened attentively, where appropriate giving her small, sniffing approximation of a laugh.

When I'd finished, she asked: 'So what exactly is it they want you to do?'

I shrugged, my eyes wide and excited. 'I've still no idea, really – I'm jumping into the unknown!'

'Watch out,' she said. 'Be careful. I've heard about these artistic types and what they expect from their employees. You'll wind up as someone's muse.'

I could think of worse fates, but didn't like to say so. 'He's not an artist,' I said, 'he runs a gallery.'

'Same difference. Artistic circles. What about her, what's she like?'

'I didn't meet her, she wasn't there.'

'Perhaps there was a reason for that. Perhaps she was prowling the attic, scowling and slavering like Bertha Mason.'

I laughed. 'I don't think so! The impression I got was of a rather disorganised society hostess.'

'They're the worst,' said Barbara. This time we both laughed.

By the time I left Osborne's three weeks later, I would have been happy to clean public lavatories if it meant I could escape Max Darblay. If ever I needed proof that he relied on me, his fury at my departure provided it. He seemed to take it personally, not expressing the least interest in where I was going, and setting out to avenge himself on me for my impertinence. The importunings stopped, but the capricious bullying got worse. And without the need to hang on to my job, I found I was more susceptible to it. Only the knowledge that I would soon be away from this horrible man once and for all kept me going.

On my last day, Roddy Osborne, who was at least a gentleman, came into our office to wish me well. Darblay's smile was a frozen snarl.

'We shall miss you,' said Roddy, 'shan't we, Max?'

'Indeed we shall,' said Darblay through gritted teeth.

'That's the trouble with really good staff,' went on Roddy, 'you can't keep them. They seek fresh fields, and it's right and proper that they should. Still, we've been lucky to have you these past two years, and I'm sure you'll enjoy working at the Sumpter.' I had mentioned Christopher Jarvis in the context of the gallery for simplicity's sake.

Darblay's face lit up with interest. His whole manner changed. 'Oh, you're going to work for Jarvis, are you?'

As soon as Roddy had gone, Darblay said: 'Now then, Mrs Griffe, why don't you let me take you to lunch as a mark of appreciation?'

I demurred, wary of this sudden change of heart, but he was insistent. He took me to a restaurant in Floral Street where I had often made bookings on his behalf for lunches with our more profitable authors, or those we were trying to woo away from bigger companies. It thought itself grand, and was certainly expensive. I disliked walking in there with Darblay, and disliked even more the possibility that I might be taken for one of his despised protégées (I knew from the way he spoke to them on the phone that he made no attempt to conceal this attitude from others). But it was worse than that. It became apparent from the moment we arrived that not only was I to be subjected to a farewell burst of lecherousness but that he was trying by implication to pass me off as a close woman friend, using phrases like 'the lovely lady', and 'my charming companion' when relaying my order to the waiter, and waving away the wine list with: 'It must be champagne!'

The restaurant staff politely fell in with this pretence, but I was sure they had the measure of him, and would be discussing us unfavourably behind the scenes. I squirmed at the thought of what they must be saying about him, that boorish fellow from Osborne's, and worse, about me, the opportunistic young woman happy to accept his heavy-handed attentions. Still, I told myself, after today I would be free of Darblay. I could put up with his nonsense just once more. It was even possible, I reminded myself, that he meant well and was attempting in his inept way to give me a treat.

I had cold consommé to begin with, he had asparagus, which he consumed with exaggerated relish, and much slurping and smacking of lips. At least the disgusting performance prevented him from talking too much. But when our main courses arrived – salmon for me and steak in pepper sauce for him – he finally revealed the reason for this whole charade.

'So how did you find Mr Jarvis?' he asked.

'He seemed very pleasant,' I replied. It didn't seem appropriate to be discussing my future employer with my present one in quite these terms, but the finer points of etiquette had never bothered Darblay.

'Pleasant, eh?' He chuckled.

Sensing trouble, I remained silent, determined not to give him any more to chew on.

'You don't know much about him, do you?' he asked.

'I know enough,' I said.

'I doubt it!' He charged his own glass, but I put my hand over mine. 'I very much doubt it!'

It was obvious he was going to fill in the gaps in my knowledge whether I liked it or not. I concentrated on my salmon, which now seemed about as appetising as cardboard.

'Jarvis is not pleasant,' he announced. 'Far from it. He's queer as they come.'

I had never heard the expression but from the context and Darblay's manner I inferred that it was insulting.

'I'm really not interested,' I said primly.

'There are a lot of nancy boys in the art world,' he went on, through a glutinous mouthful of pepper sauce and potato. 'If you want my opinion—'

'I don't, Mr Darblay.'

'Listen.' He became hectoring, leaning forward and wagging his fork at me. 'This is good advice I'm giving you, young lady. Jarvis is a mucky piece of work, up to all sorts. Men and women. I'm sorry if that shocks you, but you ought to know.'

I was, in fact, a little shocked. I'd led a relatively sheltered life and although I knew that 'all sorts' went on in the wider and more sophisticated world (I had met the creators of Armand the Alligator) I never expected to come into contact with it myself.

I remembered something with which to refute Darblay's unwelcome 'information'.

'Mr Jarvis is married,' I said. 'I shall be working for both him and Mrs Jarvis.'

Darblay laughed heartily at this. 'I bet you will! Most of

these queers are married, and the wives fall into two cate-
gories. Those who put up and shut up, and those who are,
if you take my meaning, in on it.'

This was too much. If he had intended to upset me he'd
succeeded, but I gathered all the resources accumulated over
the past two years, got to my feet, and spoke not loudly, but
firmly and clearly so that those at nearby tables could hear.

'I refuse to put up with any more of this. You are a rude,
revolting bully and I find your advances repulsive. And by
the way,' I took my purse out of my bag, removed a handful
of notes – I have no idea how many – and slapped them
down on the cloth, 'your table manners are a disgrace.'

I closed my bag and walked from the room. There was a
hush. Everyone watched me. I was not an exhibitionist, used
to attracting the attention of others, so it was quite an ordeal.
One of the waiters opened the door for me with a flourish,
colluding in my grand exit.

Out on the pavement I was quite giddy with shock and
relief. I managed to go fifty yards or so, far enough to be
sure Darblay wasn't coming after me, before stepping
unsteadily into the doorway of a ladies' clothes shop and
leaning against the wall. Almost at once a middle-aged woman
in a black dress emerged from the shop and said in a thoroughly unfriendly tone: 'Are you all right, miss?'

I gasped that I was, but that I had felt rather strange on
coming out of the restaurant up the road. She must have
noted my flushed face and the champagne on my breath,
because the eyes in her over-made-up face became hard as
jet.

'I'm afraid,' she said, 'that you can't hang about here.'

I suddenly realised what she was thinking. I was being
moved on! I started to laugh and couldn't stop. I tottered
back on to the pavement, the tears running down my cheeks.
The woman stared with a furious mixture of disapproval and

anxiety, her worst suspicions confirmed. I had never in my life excited so many contrasting and extreme reactions as I had in the past hour. I was still laughing as I went down the road, and people gave me a wide berth.

When I got back to the office I went to see Roddy Osborne and told him that I'd felt unwell during lunch, and would have to go home. He was kind and concerned and asked in his courteous way where Darblay was. I told him, in a small, suffering voice that as far as I knew my host was still in the restaurant. Osborne looked politely surprised. The notion that I had queered Darblay's pitch with his superior put wings on my heels as I left Osborne's for ever.

My elation was shortlived. Alone in my room that evening Darblay's salacious warning came back to haunt me. What exactly had he meant by a 'mucky piece of work, up to all sorts'? About the wife probably being 'in on it'? In on what? It was infuriating that notwithstanding my brave and spirited behaviour earlier, the horrible man had succeeded in unsettling me. I was reminded that Barbara, too, had cast not entirely serious aspersions on 'artistic circles', amusing at the time but which now began to trouble me. The golden prospect of my new job in the sunlit uplands of Highgate was tarnished. But I had burned my boats, and could only go forward.

That was the Friday, and I was due to start work at Seven Crompton Terrace on the Monday. With my natural nervousness exacerbated by Darblay and, retrospectively, Barbara, it was hardly surprising that I found something to worry about that was within my control.

What on earth would I wear?

After my early tomboyishness, the appreciation of my femininity brought about by Matthew, and the grey indifference of widowhood, I had settled into a style that suited the life I led: one dominated by work, evenings in or at most out with a girlfriend, weekends spent catching up on chores, visiting museums and galleries, or at home with my parents. My small wardrobe comprised a sort of uniform, not quite drab but not stylish either, calculated to cut down the need for decisions. Each item would go with almost any of its companions, a policy designed for convenience rather than excitement. Subject to the requirements of laundry, dry-cleaners and mending-basket I could step into almost anything and be ready for the day.

Now, I was thrown into an agony of uncertainty. In spite of all Darblay had said I did not wish to appear prim, or schoolmarmish. I did not want Christopher Jarvis and his wife to be laughing at me behind my back. The awful thought occurred to me that perhaps I had been selected *because* I was dull. Then I remembered how certain remarks of mine at the interview had seemed to impress and amuse Jarvis – my feeling was that he had liked me, we had liked each other, my fears were groundless. On the other hand if he had perceived me as being in the least attractive, was that a good thing in all the circumstances Darblay had hinted at? And even if none of it were true, the practicalities of the job were still a mystery: I had no idea what would constitute my daily routine, or if there would be any routine at all. And then there was Seven Crompton Terrace itself, not an office but the Jarvises' home. If Christopher Jarvis's own sartorial style was anything to go by, little Pamela Griffe in her business suit might become an almost offensively provincial presence around the place.

This uncharacteristic panic destroyed all sense of proportion. The issue overshadowed everything else. It was a measure of my ridiculous fears that in the end I was driven to go downstairs and knock on the door of Louise Baron, in the room immediately below mine. She was a cheerful, glamorous girl but our lives – and hours – were very different and we had never progressed beyond friendly acquaintanceship. Now she was so long opening the door that I concluded she wasn't in and was about to trudge back up the stairs in despair, when she appeared, wrapped in a red silk kimono, her blonde hair in disarray and her eyes smudged with make-up.

'Hello!' she mumbled drowsily.

'I'm so sorry, I woke you up, it doesn't matter,' I gabbled, but she beckoned me over conspiratorially, and whispered through a haze of last night's scent and smoke:

'No, Pamela, it's nice to see you, but can you give me five minutes?'

'Of course! I didn't mean to disturb you, it's not important.'

'But a cup of coffee is,' she whispered. 'And I'd much rather have it with you than him. You're just the excuse I need to chuck him out. I'll knock on the ceiling, is that all right?'

I agreed, and went back upstairs, telling myself I didn't *have* to take Louise's advice. I couldn't help but admire her casual breaching of the no-men-in-the-rooms rule, but for a male companion still to be around at ten thirty in the morning posed problems which I didn't envy. Our landlady didn't live on the premises but the caretaker and his wife had a room by the main entrance and acted as her deputies and informants. They were merciless, and for Louise to be caught smuggling a man from the building would mean expulsion with immediate effect.

Just the same, there was a thud on my floor a few minutes later and I went back down. She was waiting for me in the doorway, still in her kimono, but with her eyes wiped and hair brushed, her face wreathed in smiles.

'Come in,' she said, 'sorry about just now.'

'That's all right, I shouldn't have called so early.'

Her room, the same size as mine, had a higher ceiling which made it seem bigger. It was full of colour, and she'd thrown the window open. Admittedly there was no view except of the blank wall of the department store warehouse next door, but it was pleasant to have the early summer sunshine pouring in. An orchid corsage, of the sort to be purchased at vast expense from Moyses Stephens, stood in a jar of water on the bedside table. To my relief the bed itself was tidy, the counterpane pulled smoothly over the pillows and a thread-bare stuffed badger slumped against the bedhead.

'Brock,' she explained. 'The only faithful man in my life.'

She lit the gas ring and put on a kettle. 'You will have some coffee, won't you? I'm absolutely dying for one.'

'Thanks, that'd be lovely.'

'No milk and sugar I'm afraid.' She assembled two cups, a china jug, a wooden spoon and a brown paper packet of coffee grounds. Then she took a packet of cigarettes from the drawer in the bedside table and offered me one. When I declined, she said:

'Don't worry, why d'you think I opened the window?'

'It's not that,' I explained. 'I don't often smoke.'

She returned to the kettle and poured its contents into the jug, giving the mixture a stir with the spoon. As she waited for the grounds to settle, she said: 'I hope you weren't shocked, Pamela – about Miguel.'

'Not at all,' I replied, not quite honestly. 'But I was a bit worried. How on earth did you get him out?'

'I keep a selection of larger clothes. Not to mention a hat.'

'What?' I laughed incredulously. 'He walked out of here dressed as a woman?'

'Mm . . . Miguel became Maria.' She handed me my coffee with a sly smile, but then burst out laughing herself. 'He looked a picture!'

'But what about when he's outside?' I said. 'In the street?'

She shrugged. 'That's his problem. They're only my responsibility this side of the front door. He'll just have to find somewhere to put his own clothes back on, or behave in a very ladylike manner till he gets home.'

I shook my head in astonishment. 'I can't believe he agreed to it!'

'Beggars can't be choosers. Besides, it's in the contract.'

'The contract?'

'The agreement. If they want to come back here, they have to do as I say. And any man who really, truly wants to come back will agree to anything, believe me. As I'm sure you know,' she said kindly.

'What about getting in?'

'Once the guard-dogs are asleep, nothing wakes them. But you do have to be patient. Now Pamela, what can I do for you?'

After all that, my nervous taking about clothes seemed very small beer, but I was here now.

'I wanted to ask your advice.'

'Ask away.'

I explained my predicament, being sure to include Darblay's comments to spice things up a little.

'Jiminy,' said Louise. 'I see the problem.'

This at least was a relief. 'I'm so glad you do. I don't usually worry about this sort of thing.'

'Don't you? God, I do, all the time. But then it's my business.' I knew she worked at Maison Ricard, a fashion house in Chelsea, both as an assistant and a mannequin, modelling clothes for the rich clients.

'That's why I thought you'd be the person to ask,' I said humbly.

'Right.' She adopted a businesslike tone. 'Here's my opinion, for what it's worth. You went to the interview dressed as you normally would be for work.'

'Yes.'

'And this man hired you on the spot.'

'Well, not on the spot exactly—'

'All right, but from what you say he must have made up his mind almost at once, or he'd never have contacted you so soon afterwards.'

'I suppose so.'

'So why change?' Louise raised her shoulders, and hands, palms uppermost. 'You were obviously exactly what he was looking for.'

'Perhaps, but now I'm actually due to start work there I'm worried that I won't fit in.'

'Just a moment ago,' she reminded me, 'you were worried about fitting in too well. And *besides*,' she overruled my rising objection, 'you have no idea whether anything that poisonous man said was true. I mean, who would you rather work for, that pig or Christopher Jarvis?' She read the answer in my face at once. 'There you are then.'

'So,' I said, 'you think I should wear the same suit?'

'Not necessarily *exactly* the same suit.' Louise couldn't conceal a note of mild exasperation. 'But you don't have to pretend to be something you're not. You could always add a little something, a gesture towards your changed circumstances.'

'Such as what?'

'I don't know . . .' She dropped her cigarette end in her coffee cup and went over to a lopsided wardrobe in the corner of the room. When she opened the door, colourful clothes burst from it like some sort of conjuring trick. 'Sorry, not very tidy – let's see . . . I know . . .'

After a moment's rummaging she brought forth a silk scarf printed in a geometric pattern of fuchsia pink and blue. She motioned me to stand in front of the mirror on the mantelpiece, twirled and furled the scarf with a practised hand and held it beside my face.

'It suits you. It's Fortuny, it was a present, but it does nothing for me.' She laid the scarf over my shoulder and went to close the wardrobe, saying over her shoulder: 'Have it.'

'Are you sure? Thank you.' She had been so friendly and generous with her time that I could hardly turn her down, though I was by no means sure whether I wanted the scarf.

'I tell you what,' she said, 'I'm quite jealous of you going to work for those people.'

'Why would you be jealous?'

'Not of the work itself,' she explained hastily. 'I couldn't type or manage anyone's life to save my own – but seeing the artistic crowd at close quarters. Be honest, Pamela, you'd be disappointed if they weren't just a *little* bit louche.'

I considered this as I sat on the bus en route to my parents' house next day. I supposed Louise was right to the extent that I had been seduced by the disordered elegance of Seven Crompton Terrace, and the slightly eccentric charm of its owner. She was also right that I should not allow spiteful innuendo to affect my attitude before I had even begun. The proof of the pudding was in the eating. As to the scarf, it was a well-meant present but I doubted I would wear it.

Sunday dinner with my parents (it was always 'dinner' – 'lunch' wasn't in their lexicon) had an unvarying pattern. I would arrive at midday, and my father, newspaper in hand, would open the door, with a 'Hello Pammie!' and a warm kiss. My mother would emerge from the kitchen, removing her apron, and we'd exchange a more restrained greeting before all going into the front room. It often took us a while to shake down together, and we had developed a routine for dispelling the slight initial awkwardness. When we'd exchanged kisses and ascertained that I was fine and they as well as could be expected, my father would clasp his hands together and announce that he was ready for a bottle of ale, and ask whether I'd 'be wanting anything'. I would, naturally, decline. My mother, familiar with this exchange and its outcome, would already have bustled off to the kitchen, and would return with the beer, and a glass, on a tray which she'd place on the side table. Then all three of us would sit down in the front room and make what could only be described as small talk for about ten minutes. During this period it was understood that while we might very well cover matters of life and death – the birth of a neighbour's grandson, or the demise of the old man from next to the shop – we would touch on nothing personal. There was a time and a place for everything.

When my mother rose, saying she must go and get on if we were any of us to have any dinner, it was my cue to offer to help. She would say no, but suggest that I might like to come and keep her company, since my father was probably going to 'have his nose in the paper' anyway.

My father would give his blessing to our departure by saying, with a wink that he knew when he wasn't wanted and he'd expect his dinner piping hot in front of him at one. My mother and I would raise our eyes at one another and retreat. It was during this next half-hour in the kitchen that my mother and I would exchange whatever confidences we chose to. Then, over the dinner table, my mother would relay what I had told her to my father, being sure to sift out anything she deemed contentious or unsuitable.

'Pam's starting a new job tomorrow,' she announced over the mutton and caper sauce.

'Is that right?' said my father admiringly. 'Congratulations. I can't keep track of you, girl.'

'I've been at Osborne's for over two years,' I reminded him. 'I needed a change.'

'What's the money like?'

'That's not the point, Gerald,' reproved my mother.

'Pardon me, but it is – they're paying you more, I hope?'

'They are, actually.'

'Jolly good show!' said my father, picking up on my 'actually' to parody my new posh way of speaking. 'How much?'

'Gerald!'

I told him. He whistled. 'By the centre! Well done, Pammie.'

'The man runs a picture gallery,' said my mother, as if my princely salary required some explanation, 'and his wife's a very busy woman, so Pam will be working for both of them.'

'Sounds like you'll be run off your feet.'

'I hope so.'

'Just make sure they don't take advantage,' he said.

'Don't worry, Dad, I will,' I assured him. He can have had no idea how fervently I meant it.

I presented myself at Crompton Terrace, scarf and all, on the dot of nine o'clock, having arrived early at the bus stop and dawdled for some minutes to achieve this perfect punctuality. A bottle of milk stood in the porch. As I waited, I felt a swift rush of air above my head and remembered the swallows' nest. One of the adults had just returned; its sleek forked tail protruded from beneath the eaves. I reminded myself that to get off on the right foot I must keep my voice down.

The door was opened by a pretty, distracted-looking woman with round blue eyes that drooped at the outer corners.

'Hello? Yes, hello?' she asked, as if talking on the telephone.

'I'm Pamela Griffe,' I explained, very quietly. 'I start work here today?'

'Oh my goodness, yes of course . . . Come in.'

I had the distinct impression she'd forgotten all about my arrival, if she'd ever known at all, an impression reinforced by her saying as she closed the door after me: 'I'm afraid my husband's not here. Maybe,' she added vaguely, 'he'll have left some instructions for you.'

So this was Amanda Jarvis. After two minutes I could already see what Christopher Jarvis had meant by her needing assistance. I had rarely met anyone who gave off such an air of helplessness. It was oddly comforting to realise that I could be genuinely needed.

'Don't worry, Mrs Jarvis,' I said firmly. 'Even if he hasn't, I can be busy familiarising myself with things – or perhaps there's a job you'd like me to do?'

'Heavens!' She gave a nervous little laugh. 'I shall have to think. May I say, that is a terribly pretty scarf you're wearing.'

I wished Louise had been there to hear it. 'Thank you.'

She touched the corner gently with her fingertips. 'Silk . . . it's absolutely sweet. Where did you get it?'

'I'm afraid I can't remember,' I said. 'But I do love it.'

God forgive me, what a good liar I was. Still, I fancied I'd given the desired impression – of a woman who bought enough elegant scarves for it to be hard to recall the provenance of any one.

'Let's just peep in here,' she said, opening the door of the room in which I'd had the interview. She stepped inside cautiously, as though wary of what she might find. It looked much the same as on my last visit. Jarvis's desk was in turmoil, the one assigned to me was empty.

'I don't know . . .' murmured Mrs Jarvis. 'I wonder what's best.'

I decided to take the initiative. 'When will your husband be back?'

'I don't know,' she said again. If the Jarvises were ever to have a coat of arms this phrase should clearly be on it. 'He was at an opening in Hampstead last night.'

From this I inferred he'd spent the night elsewhere. I felt a flutter of anxiety in my stomach, but squashed it.

'I'm here to make myself useful in any way I can,' I said. This may have been rash, but she seemed so loath to give instructions of any sort I was pretty sure I was safe from heaving coal or washing the windows. 'Perhaps there are some calls I could make for you?'

'I suppose there might be.'

'I'll tidy up in here,' I said. 'And if there's anything at all you'd like me to do, you can let me know.'

'Thank you . . .'

I put my handbag down beside the desk, and draped Louise's scarf over the back of the chair. Mrs Jarvis hovered. But when I advanced purposefully on my employer's desk she darted forward as if electrocuted.

'Oh, Mrs Griffe! No, I'm sorry, he doesn't like anyone fiddling with his papers.'

'I just thought I might straighten things out for him. I assure you I'd be wholly discreet, and I wouldn't throw anything away.'

'No, I know, it's not that – but I still think it would be best if you didn't. Until he gets back.'

'Very well,' I smiled cheerfully. It had now become a point of honour with me to be of some assistance to this fluttery, jittery butterfly of a woman. 'May I make you a cup of tea, or coffee? If you show me where everything is that could be one of my tasks.'

'Yes, what a good idea!' Her relief at this suggestion was painfully obvious, but it wasn't an offer without self-interest: a hot drink would be welcome, I needed something to do, and I was curious to see more of the house. I was also interested to know whether there were any domestic staff at Seven Crompton Terrace. I had yet to see any, but it seemed unlikely that a reasonably well-to-do couple like the Jarvises, whatever their bohemian pretensions, would employ no help at all. If that turned out to be the case, it didn't bode well for me.

I followed her down the hall, and the passage, to the back of the house. There was a second small staircase here, presumably service stairs, or leading to a servant's room of some sort. Beyond this to the left I glimpsed a dining room, the predominant colours yellow and black, with elegant modern furniture, the walls covered with bold, startling abstract paintings. At the end of the passage the door stood open on to an untidy garden; a cluster of basket chairs crowded on the small terrace, and a couple of sparrows, pecking the ground around the legs of the chairs, flew off at our approach.

Amanda Jarvis waved a hand towards the garden and pulled an apologetic face.

'Not our strongest point, I'm afraid, but so pretty. And the other night we heard a nightingale – would we have a nightingale if everything was tidy?'

I agreed that they probably wouldn't.

She led the way through a door on the right, entering, as before, with an air of extreme caution, like a lion-tamer approaching his charge with a whip and a chair. I saw that her lack of confidence made her almost a stranger in her own home.

'Here we are,' she murmured. 'The kitchen.'

I glanced around. Each room in the house appeared to have a distinct character – the rich, souk-like clutter of Jarvis's office, the killingly chic dining room, and now this: a scarcely touched Victorian kitchen with a flagged floor, a stone sink, a black iron stove and a lazy-susan draped with damp cloths. A big deal table was littered with crockery and cutlery, both clean and used, a breadboard with a cut loaf, a pat of butter with a collage of crumbs, and a covered cheese dish.

'Oh dear,' said Mrs Jarvis. 'Dorothy's late.'

Judging by the kitchen I was pleased to hear of Dorothy's existence, but doubtful as to her competence. 'Never mind,'

I said, 'tell me where things are, it'll be good practice.'

'Let's see . . .'

It was plain within seconds that my employer had no more idea than me where things were kept, but between us we assembled a tea-caddy, teapot, cups, spoon and sugar. There was half a bottle of milk in the larder, but it had turned sour. I remembered the bottle in the porch and went back to fetch it. The mere act of doing so made me feel more at home.

'Christopher prefers coffee,' volunteered his wife, sitting down at the table. 'But I'm not sure where it is.'

'Tea will be perfect,' I said. While we waited for the kettle to boil I busied myself clearing the table, stacking the dirty things in the sink, putting the loaf in what I hoped was the bread bin, and the butter and cheese in the larder. Mrs Jarvis watched me with her hands to her cheeks like an astonished child – it was gratifying in a way. I opened cupboards until I found one containing crockery, and put the clean things away, all the time wondering if I was making a rod for my own back, and resolving to keep an eye on Dorothy when she condescended to put in an appearance.

'. . . decided against having a live-in help,' Mrs Jarvis was saying, as if reading my thoughts, 'because we like to have house guests, and it means we can use the top-floor bedroom.'

I remembered the dim, swift-moving figure I'd spotted as I left the house on my first visit.

'Is there anyone staying here at the moment?' I asked.

'Yes, there is,' she replied. 'Suzannah. We almost always have one or two orphans in residence. There are so many talented young men and women who can't afford anywhere to live. It's our pleasure to help them.'

During this little speech she was the most animated I'd seen her. I remembered what Christopher Jarvis had said about his wife being very hospitable, and found myself warming to her; the combination of a generous, giving nature and a complete lack of domestic or organisational ability can't have been easy.

While we drank our tea, she began to remember odd calls that needed making – a grocery order, her dressmaker, her husband's god-daughter – and correspondence to be attended to, including bills, at the mention of which actual tears welled in her eyes.

'Naturally,' she said, 'I can't possibly ask you to help me with that sort of thing . . .'

'Why not?' I replied. 'It's what I'm here for. I'd be glad to.'

'Really?' She appeared incredulous. 'I am *such* a stupid woman.'

'Not having an aptitude for that sort of thing doesn't make anyone stupid,' I said. 'And two heads are better than one. We could sit down together and be through it all in no time.'

'Oh!' She gave something between a little gasp and a sigh. 'I should be so, so grateful!'

When we'd finished, she went off to make a list and look out the bills and I 'got in the sink' as my mother would have said. I'd washed up our cups and was well into the rest of the dirty crocks when the back door burst open and a girl burst in, pulling off her hat and coat in a great flurry.

'Forgot my purse, then the bleeding bus was late, so crowded I nearly couldn't get on, strap-hanging all the way, overshot the stop—' She stopped abruptly. 'Who are you?'

'*You* must be Dorothy,' I said, taking a slightly mean pleasure in having the advantage over her.

'That's right.' Keeping her eyes on me like a rabbit with a snake, she reached for a far from clean pinny that hung on the back of the door, and put it on. 'Dorothy Viney.'

'I'm Mrs Griffe. I started work here today.'

'In the kitchen?' she asked warily.

'No. In Mr Jarvis's office. But he's not here at the moment so I'm going to be helping Mrs Jarvis out with a few jobs.'

I detected a fleeting, sceptical look. I was too much of an unknown quantity for her to weigh in with her opinion, but I could guess what it was.

'I've done most of the washing-up,' I said pointedly. 'But now you're here I'll leave you to it.'

'Righty-o.' She glanced towards the stove. 'You boil the kettle?'

'Mrs Jarvis and I had some tea.'

'Good, I've got a mouth like a— I'm gasping.'

I turned away quickly so she wouldn't see my smile. Even without the prior evidence, it was clear Dorothy would not have passed muster in my mother's house, but I couldn't help liking her.

Mrs Jarvis wasn't in the dining room, or her husband's office. I found her in the drawing room at the front of the house. This room managed to be both glamorous and comfortable-looking in cream and pale pink. There were art books on a glass coffee table, a mantel-mirror with a frame of carved roses and songbirds, fat-cushioned sofas, an oriental lacquered screen and a gramophone on a purpose-built stand with dozens of records on the shelf beneath. Mrs Jarvis sat at a bureau in the bay window. Pieces of paper lay on the floor around her feet. It was obvious the bureau had been so full that, when opened, the papers had simply burst out. She turned doleful eyes towards me as I came in.

'Oh, Mrs Griffe—'

'Pamela,' I said. It seemed natural with her.

'Pamela . . . I can't find a thing.'

'Don't worry.' There was an upright chair next to the door and I moved it so that I could sit beside her. 'One step at a time.'

I spent almost all day in the drawing room with Mrs Jarvis, and by the end of it we had filled two waste-paper baskets, paid the bills, made an appointment with the dressmaker and placed the grocery order (after a systematic audit of the kitchen cupboards and further throwing away which had Dorothy gawping in astonishment). I also reminded her about calling her husband's god-daughter, which she did at lunchtime while I went for a walk. She had asked me if I wanted to have lunch at the house, but I preferred to go out. Apart from the cheery Dorothy the Jarvises employed one other person, a peripatetic cook – or 'Chef' as they called him – who (it was explained to me) prepared either lunch or dinner according to circumstances, or when they were entertaining. Mrs Jarvis was very worried about having placed the order without consulting Chef, but I pointed out that we'd confined ourselves to staples and necessities, those things any household would want in the store-cupboard, and that she could confer with him about specific menus in due course.

Since Chef was obviously a person of some influence, I put my head into the kitchen before I took my midday break, to introduce myself. Dorothy was applying a carpet-sweeper to the floor of the corridor and made a face as I approached.

'Going to say hello?' she asked, and when I nodded: 'Good luck, he's a proper little ray of sunshine, I don't think.'

Chef, whose name I came to learn was Cecil Organ, was thin, pale and glum. His salad days had been spent as a sous-chef at one of the big hotels on the south coast, but the stress and strain of the job had made him ill. Surely nothing could have been less stressful than preparing meals for the distraite and undemanding Mrs Jarvis, but to look at him you wouldn't have thought it.

'Will you be in for lunch, then?' he asked, giving the distinct impression that an affirmative answer would probably sound his death knell. But when I told him I was going out he looked even more downcast, as though I had just swelled the growing band of ingrates who spurned his cooking.

'Very well,' he said. The unspoken 'suit yourself' hung in the air.

'Told you,' hissed Dorothy as I came out.

I glanced out through the glass-panelled rear door into the garden, and saw that someone had moved one of the chairs on to the grass, and left a gauzy shawl, or scarf, hanging over the back, which was towards the house. A small movement made me glance again; a pale hand appeared and flicked at something, an insect perhaps, or a leaf, on the 'shawl', which I now saw was the long hair of a woman reclining in the chair.

When I came back after an hour, refreshed by my walk in the sunshine, and a sandwich eaten on a bench at the top of the hill, the woman was no longer there. It occurred to me as Mrs Jarvis and I ploughed through the contents of the bureau that afternoon that, whatever her husband's proclivities, he had gathered about him a household consisting almost entirely of women.

At five o'clock, as I was leaving, he returned home, and expressed his desolation at not having been present on my first day.

'Mrs Griffe! I was delayed last night and it was simpler to stay with my friend in Hampstead. How have you been?'

'Very well,' I said. 'Mrs Jarvis and I have been busy.'

'Good, excellent!'

His wife came out of the drawing room and he kissed her warmly. 'Amanda, darling heart . . . I understand you've had a good day.'

'We have.' She gave me a wan, doting smile. 'Pamela is an absolute treasure, Chris. We must be sure to hang on to her.'

'We will!' he cried. 'I knew the moment I met her that she was one of us!'

They saw me off from their doorstep, beaming, arm in arm beneath the swallows' nest.

As I walked up the hill to the bus stop, I felt my first day had gone well. But whether or not I was 'one of them' was something on which I reserved judgement.

Chapter Five

I came to learn that while Amanda Jarvis's helplessness was real, her husband's was a charming affectation. In reality he was a shrewd, confident man. The Sumpter Gallery was successful in both artistic and commercial terms: it prospered, and the Jarvises were well off. Mrs Jarvis's anxiety about bills was based not on an inability to pay, but on her own pathological fear of figures. In my mind, though never to her face, she soon became 'Amanda'.

There was a sort of game being played, of which I soon learned the rules. With Amanda it was not just acceptable but positively desirable to be firm and decisive. I was never less than respectful, but I took charge. In Mr Jarvis's case, no matter what his apparent disorganisation, *he* was the one in charge. I was immensely grateful to his wife for not allowing me to meddle with his desk on that first morning. It amused him to characterise me as being fierce, and fearsomely efficient, and himself as slightly afraid of me, but nothing could have been further from the truth. I quickly realised that beneath the boyish charm lay a far tougher and more complicated proposition. In other words, my Osborne's training stood me in good stead.

Only once did it let me down, and that was enough. I happened to walk into the office when, unknown to me, his wife was with him and they were having what appeared to be an intense, personal conversation. I realised my mistake straightaway, but I hadn't even had time to say 'sorry' and withdraw before he snapped:

'Get out, will you, for God's sake, are we to have no privacy at all?'

For that instant his eyes were cold and his mouth mean. It was a shocking transformation. Amanda Jarvis didn't so much as turn her head. A few minutes later she bustled out, still without looking at me. He summoned me back, all smiles and sweetness, but I never forgot that look.

My work for him consisted mostly of routine tasks – correspondence, making calls, keeping everything in order and Jarvis himself running to time, of which the last was by far the most difficult. Often, artists would come to the house to see him, and I'd be introduced, and then left to my own devices while they talked in the drawing room or the garden. The artists, like the Osborne's authors, were a surprising bunch. One of the most radically innovative and sought-after among them was Paul Marriott, a neat little man in a collar and tie who looked far less like the popular idea of a painter than Jarvis himself. Others (usually the less successful) played up to their role, affecting eccentric clothes, hats and, in the case of one woman, a clay pipe which stunk the place out. One or two were authentically strange and I couldn't help but feel respect for these people who perceived a world so different from that which the rest of us inhabited. I sensed that the mysterious house guest, the woman whom I had glimpsed in the passage and in the garden, was one of these. Why else would she be so reclusive, so fearful of human contact?

But artists apart, what made my job pleasurable, and interesting was Seven Crompton Terrace itself. Because I was working in the Jarvises' home I became part of the ramshackle extended family of employees, friends and deserving cases they had gathered about them. And as I found my feet I acquired a sense of where and how I fitted into the social hierarchy of the household. Mine was in many ways a privileged position. I was an employee, but several rungs above Dorothy, and even the lugubrious Chef. My relationship to Amanda was almost that of paid companion, and I spent long hours closeted with Mr Jarvis in the office, from which Dorothy inferred I must be privy to all kinds of inside information.

One day when I'd been there for a couple of weeks, as I was going out at midday I almost tripped over Dorothy on her hands and knees in the porch.

'Steady on!' she yelped. 'Mind me!'

She was scraping bird droppings off the tiles with a bone-handled table knife.

'Wretched birds,' she grumbled, chipping away. 'Can't see why they don't get rid of them, horrible messy things.'

'I think it's nice having them there,' I said. 'Should you be using that knife to do that, Dorothy?'

She looked at me as if I were mad. 'I'll wash it.'

'I should hope so!'

She got to her feet and peeked through the side window of the porch from which there was a view of Jarvis's desk, to check that the coast was clear before asking:

'So how are you getting on then?'

'Fine, thank you.' I prepared to be on my dignity, but Dorothy was a girl whose indifference to rank made that almost impossible.

'What do you think of them?'

'They're charming.'

'Isn't he just?' She grinned collusively. 'I wouldn't say no.'

'Dorothy!'

'He's too many for her, don't you reckon? She's such a ninny she can hardly blow her own nose.'

'That's not true, and anyway you shouldn't speak about them like that.' I looked over my shoulder and spoke in a reproving stage whisper, but Dorothy was unabashed.

'Don't worry, they're out the back by now. Have you met the other one?'

'What other one?' I asked, though I was pretty sure I knew who she meant.

She rolled her eyes upward. 'Her upstairs. The lodger.'

'Suzannah – no, I've seen her about,' I said. 'But we've not been introduced.'

'Course you haven't. You want to go up the top and take a look some time.'

'No I don't,' I said, though of course I was now madly curious. 'I don't have any reason to go upstairs at all—'

'You use the lavvy, don't you?'

'Dorothy, for heaven's sake,' I began, but I couldn't stop myself from smiling and she pressed her advantage. 'Course you do. Next time you go, if you get the chance, you nip up and see.'

'But how would I know if she was in there?' I protested, giving myself away completely.

Dorothy winked. 'Because I'll tell you.'

I collected myself. 'Excuse me, I won't have any lunch hour left at this rate.'

'She's a tramp, I reckon,' said Dorothy. 'Both kinds.'

The day after that was a Saturday so I had to contain my curiosity, and hope it would die a decent death over the weekend. I decided to go and look at the gallery. It was remiss of me not to have done so before, but I had been so preoccupied with other aspects of the job that I'd entirely failed to focus on this, its *raison d'être*.

Bowne Street, W1, was a narrow road off Hanover Square. It had the discreet and muted air of a place that did not need to advertise itself because those who mattered – the wealthy and discerning – would know how to find it anyway. The Sumpter Gallery was two-thirds of the way along, the name on a brass plate by the door. A single picture stood on an easel in the window, which was itself no more than a high, white box. The picture was of wavering concentric black circles disappearing into infinity. As I stared at it the circles seemed to move, like water going down a plughole, sucking me in, which was doubtless the artist's intention.

I confess I felt rather nervous. The outside of the gallery spoke of utter exclusivity. Would I be treated contemptuously, or even shown the door? I stood there dithering for a moment, but just then a couple came along and walked straight in, talking animatedly. They appeared smart and well-to-do, but not in the millionaire bracket. If they were nobility, it didn't show. I could hear Matthew saying: 'Come on, Mrs Griffe, you're as good as anyone!' I pulled myself together and went in.

There was a small foyer, where a young man sat at a table, legs crossed, a book in his hand. He smiled pleasantly, said 'Good morning' and offered me a catalogue, which I took. 'The gallery is that way,' he said, pointing to double doors on my left.

I went through. It was like the Elysian Fields! The gallery was a great white atrium. Light streamed through glass panels in the roof. Tall rectangular columns divided up the area, and around the walls the pictures were hung far apart, not competing with one another, but each the master and focus of its own space. Apart from the other couple I was the only person there. No disdainful curator was patrolling the room. I began to relax. I should have known that Christopher Jarvis would not have presided over a snobbish operation; he had his faults, but airs and graces were not among them.

Having taken the catalogue, I didn't look at it, but put it in my bag. I didn't want to be tied by the printed page. I was not naturally adventurous in my tastes; till now I had only been to the National Gallery and the occasional exhibition at the Royal Academy. But the spacious, uncompromising beauty of this place took my breath away.

About half the pictures were of the kind the Jarvises had in their dining room at Crompton Terrace – striking, abstract juxtapositions of shapes and colours, some of them sharp and angular, others sinuous like the painting in the window. The other half were more conventional – 'representational' was the word I'd heard used – and it was one of these which made me pause and stare.

It depicted a female figure looking out of a window, a subject which might have been sentimental in other hands, but not here. The window itself occupied two-thirds of the canvas; the view beyond it was of grey streets and buildings, blurred as if by rain. The figure to the right of the window was tall and thin, her arms folded, her shoulders slightly hunched, a picture of tense unhappiness. I could not decide if she was waiting for someone, or watching someone depart. Or whether she was simply locked up in her own despair. The artist had used a limited palette of greys, blues and black to give his picture a wintry light, but the woman was in a flimsy, sleeveless dress. I longed to wrap a shawl around those hunched shoulders. But her expression and attitude, as well as being desolate, repelled sympathy: if she was lonely, I thought, it was because she was a recluse. She had brought it on herself.

I gazed at this picture for some minutes before moving on. There was no other quite like it in the gallery, so in my naïve way I assumed it was the only one by that particular artist. There were some fine, uncompromising portraits, half a dozen landscapes of open countryside that reminded me of Pevensey, and a great many atmospheric interiors and finely executed still lifes.

I remained at the gallery for over an hour, and before I left I returned to the woman by the window. The dramatic impact of the picture was intensified by my having looked at so many others. The woman's isolation appeared even more deliberate; her figure seemed to vibrate with an angry hopelessness.

As I was going I encountered my fellow visitors. The woman smiled at me.

'Interesting, isn't it?'

I agreed that it was.

'What do you think of the famous Stannisford?'

I must have looked blank, for she pointed at the largest of the abstract paintings, which hung immediately opposite the entrance.

I expressed myself lost for words. Her husband leaned towards me. '*Me too,*' he said in a stage whisper.

His wife nudged him. 'He doesn't care for it.'

'Neither does this young lady!' he chuckled. 'Can't you tell?' I took the line of least resistance and agreed, and he was still chuckling as I went out.

In truth I'd never heard of Stannisford, and had scarcely noticed the painting. I walked for about ten minutes till I came to a respectable small hotel, went into the non-residents' lounge and ordered coffee. I took out the Sumpter catalogue from my bag and leafed through it till I found what I was after. 'Nobody' by S.R. Murchie, 1928; painted in oils, priced at £50. My instincts had been correct – there were no other pictures by Murchie in the exhibition. I made a mental note to ask Christopher Jarvis about the artist when I got the opportunity.

After some shopping and a light lunch I went home. Louise must have heard my footsteps on the stairs, for she popped her head out.

'Hey – how are you getting on?' She held the door open. 'Come on, I want to know everything!'

She'd been delighted when I got the job, but with our very different hours I'd scarcely seen her in the intervening weeks. Now that I was used to Seven Crompton Terrace, her cluttered, colourful room struck me as less *outré*. We took up our positions, I on the chair and she on the bed, ankles crossed, head against the wall, cigarette in hand. She wore a long, loose mandarin tunic and trousers in olive green.

'It's going fine,' I told her. 'I'm enjoying it.'

'The scarf worked, did it?'

'Mrs Jarvis complimented me on it on my first morning. She actually asked me where I got it.'

'What did you say?'

'I said I couldn't remember.'

'Pamela! You should have said you had this terrifically stylish friend who knew it would suit you down to the ground and lent it to you specially because she knew the elegant effect it would create.'

'The point was to make them think *I* was stylish,' I reminded her.

'True. But anyway,' she said, 'who cares about you? I want to know about *them*, the decadent artistic crowd – are they as bad as you feared?'

'No,' I replied cautiously. 'Not yet.'

Louise hooted with laughter. 'There's no pleasing you, is there? You were scared to death they were going to be dope-fiends or white-slavers or whatever, and now they turn out to be model citizens—'

'I never said that.'

'Tell me then.'

I did my best to describe the atmosphere at Crompton Terrace, and the character of its occupants, but it was hard to convey the exact tenor of the place. The amusingly chaotic aspects of the household were easy enough, but I was unable – and perhaps unwilling – to express my sense of an undertow, the presence of something darker beneath the surface. Or maybe I was unwilling to try, because already I felt that whatever the secret was, I was now part of it. One of them, as Christopher had said.

'I should so *love*,' said Louise, 'to be a fly on the wall.'

'Oh,' I said, 'it's all quite ordinary, really.'

When I arrived for work on Monday it was to find that a second house guest had arrived. There was no question of missing this one: as I came through the front door he was emerging from the kitchen, in pyjamas and unlaced brogues, with a slice of toast in his hand.

'Morning!' he said gruffly. 'Sorry to affront public decency like this, two seconds later and I'd have been out of the way.'

'That's quite all right,' I said.

Hearing our voices, Christopher Jarvis came out of the office, pretending to be outraged.

'For God's sake, Rintoul, cover youself up, there are ladies present!'

'I've already apologised.'

'He has,' I said.

'Yes, but just the same it's disgraceful . . . Rintoul, this is my *sine qua non* Mrs Pamela Griffe. Mrs Griffe, may I present Edward Rintoul.'

We said 'how do you do' and Rintoul added: 'I shan't shake you by the hand – marmalade.' He was a bear of a man, barrel-chested and, as his imperfectly fastened pyjamas revealed, impressively hirsute.

'Right,' he said, 'I'll stop embarrassing everyone and run along.'

'Please do,' said Jarvis, rolling his eyes at me in a 'did you ever?' expression as Rintoul went up the stairs. When we were in the office, he said: 'Hard though it may be to believe, he's one of the most gifted miniaturists working today.'

I wasn't completely comfortable with him talking like this about his friends. He wasn't to know that when it came to creative people I could believe anything. I took the opportunity to mention my visit to the Sumpter Gallery.

'You did? Excellent! What did you think of us?'

I realised that since my opinion counted for less than nothing, I might as well be truthful.

'I thought it was quite wonderful. I was bowled over.'

'No! You were?' He beamed with delight. I might have been the art critic of the London *Times*. 'Have you seen much contemporary art?'

'Almost none,' I said. 'Only here, really.'

'You see?' He seemed to be addressing the world at large, through me. 'People aren't stupid, nor necessarily conservative by nature. We have an inbuilt artistic sensibility, Mrs Griffe – you have it, I have it. Experience and training add knowledge, which is an aid to appreciation, but not its basis. So tell me, what did you make of our Stannisford?'

I said a private thank-you to my fellow visitor for having pointed this out to me. At least I could now say, honestly: 'Not much.' Jarvis looked rather crestfallen, and I reminded myself that I was referring to the most valuable painting at the gallery. 'I mean, it wasn't my favourite. There were others that I preferred.'

'And which were those?'

I mentioned one or two of the abstract works that had impressed me, and then added: 'I particularly liked the Murchie,' congratulating myself on this casual use of the artist's surname.

'Ah,' he said. '"Nobody".'

'Yes.'

Jarvis's tone and expression became more searching. 'Could you say why?'

'Yes – it was dramatic. It seemed to be part of a story, but it was impossible to say what the story might be – or at least I could guess at lots of things, it could have been any of them. And it was very bleak and sad.'

'But you liked it for that?'

'Yes.' I considered how to explain why. 'I sort of – respected it. The picture was its own world, not concerned with mine. Or anyone else's. It turned its back on me but drew me in at the same time.'

There was a short pause. 'My goodness, Mrs Griffe,' said Jarvis very quietly. 'You're quite a critic. That was an impeccably articulated response.'

I was not aware of ever having blushed before, but I believe I did then. 'It was how I felt.'

'I can tell.' His eyes continued to rest on me, admiringly, so that I wanted to turn his attention to something else.

'Do his pictures sell?' I asked.

He smiled, probably at my naïvety. 'The artist's very young, there isn't a big enough body of work yet for a market value to have been established. Anyway,' he went on, sitting down at his desk. 'Had we better make a start?'

It was still only early summer, but the day was hot. Although we had the windows open the atmosphere in the office was stifling. The task he allotted me was to check on transport arrangements for the exhibition due to begin in August, for which many canvases were coming a considerable distance. These arrangements were made no easier by the uncertain temperaments of those I was dealing with. I had to place several telephone calls to iron out details. Mr Jarvis retreated to the drawing room, with the intention of writing catalogue copy for the same exhibition, but his concentration must have been affected by the heat because he kept coming in and out to 'see how I was getting on'. At eleven thirty, when he was on the third such visit, there was a tap on the door and Dorothy appeared with a jug of lemon squash.

'Mrs Jarvis thought you might appreciate this, sir.'

'What an extremely happy thought. Pour us both a glass, would you, Dorothy?'

Dorothy put the tray down on a side table. As she poured she sent me an elaborately meaningful glance whose message was completely lost on me. I frowned, both to discourage her and to signal my incomprehension. But on the way out she gave me another look, accompanied this time by a minute twitch of the head, and a roll of the eyes upwards. What was the girl on about?

At the door she seemed to have a brainwave, and turned to ask: 'Sir, Chef asked me to check how many for lunch?'

'Oh, heavens, don't ask me . . . Just Mrs Jarvis, myself and Mr Rintoul I believe – but you'd better ask my wife.'

'I will, sir.'

Before she closed the door I was aware of her grimacing once more in my direction.

At midday I was quite sticky with the heat, and left the office to go upstairs to the bathroom on the first floor. I couldn't help but glimpse Christopher Jarvis's feet on the arm of the sofa in the drawing room, and hear his deep, slow breathing, the only sound in the house. There was no sign of his wife anywhere, and I couldn't see anyone in the garden. I imagined that Dorothy and Chef would be having a cigarette outside the back door as they often did late morning, she sitting on the step, he leaning up against the wall.

I went quietly up the stairs. After I'd used the lavatory I went into the bathroom, washed my hands and splashed my face with cold water. The house was well equipped with bathrooms. Apparently Amanda had spent some time in America as a young girl, and learned to appreciate the benefits of transatlantic plumbing and the superior facilities it provided. Apart from this, the guest bathroom, there was an outside lavatory beyond the kitchen, and Mr and Mrs Jarvis had their own bathroom, connected to their bedroom. A pity, I often thought, that all this convenient modernity didn't extend to the kitchen.

I came out on to the landing. The silence up here had something secretive about it. Suddenly, I understood Dorothy's speaking looks. Those present for lunch had not included Suzannah, the girl from the top floor. She must have gone out. Now was my opportunity to take a peek.

The struggle with my conscience was shamefully brief. After all, I only intended to pop my head round the door for a second. There was a door in the corner of the landing that gave on to the back, the servants', stairs, but I went boldly up the main ones so as not to appear furtive, so that I could say to anyone who asked: 'I was just looking for Suzannah.'

There were three bedrooms on the first floor: the Jarvises' and two others, of which one was occupied by Rintoul, the other empty. Hers, the only bedroom at the top of the house, was, as Amanda had indicated, the maid's room. The door was closed. Sticking to my resolution, I walked briskly over and tapped on it. No reply came, and I pushed it open.

Whatever the room had looked like before, it was now nothing more nor less than an artist's studio, containing a bed with a dust sheet thrown over it. A carpet had been rolled up against the wall beneath the window, the small wardrobe and washstand had been pushed together in the far corner, and a large, battered suitcase spewed clothes and shoes. The centre of the room was taken up with a trestle, on which clustered tubes and saucers of paint, a bottle of turpentine, brushes in jars, stained rags and one or two used mugs. There was also an easel bearing a canvas with a few preliminary charcoal lines. Sheets from a sketchpad littered the floorboards. Opposite the easel a full-length mirror with freckled glass stood propped against the redundant wardrobe, along-side a couple of large folders tied with tape.

But it was the wall beyond the easel, facing the door, that caught my attention. To my astonishment, the artist had begun painting *on the wall*. No wonder Dorothy had been by the ears!

I hadn't intended to go further than the door, but now I went in, treading softly this time in case the floorboards creaked. There could be no doubt now that I was snooping.

The painting was on the left-hand side of the wall, nearest the window. But I noticed she had removed a framed picture from the centre, signalling her intention to do more. So far she had completed two portraits, of Amanda Jarvis and Dorothy. To my untutored eye the style was free – 'loose' was the term I'd heard used – but it was most effective: both women were instantly recognisable. She had brought out a certain likeness between them, a surprising similarity between Mrs Jarvis's vague, distracted prettiness and Dorothy's slightly blowsy charm, but I couldn't have said whether or not this was deliberately subversive.

I gazed at the painting for a minute or so and then hurried out. I was shocked at myself, but quite thrilled, too. On the first-floor landing I encountered Rintoul, coming out of his room, fully dressed this time in a flannel shirt, balding corduroy trousers and the same brogues, now with socks.

'Hello there!'

'Hello,' I said, reddening. 'I was just checking that the lady upstairs – um, Suzannah? – wasn't in for lunch.' I had no need to make an excuse to him of all people, but I was flustered.

'She's gone off somewhere,' he said. 'What about you, will you be joining us?'

I shook my head rather too vigorously. 'No, I prefer to go out and get some fresh air.'

'Call this fresh?' He wiped his brow. 'Chance'd be a fine thing.'

'Well, to get some sunshine, anyway.'

I heard the phone ring, and began to go down the stairs. Rintoul fell in behind me. 'Don't care for it myself,' he said. 'My mother always said if it was sunny I should go out and enjoy it instead of sitting around indoors doing the things I preferred doing. It's only weather for God's sake. It's what goes on in the great outdoors.'

We reached the hall and I headed for the office. Rintoul followed.

'Lord and master in there?'

I hesitated, not sure how Jarvis would feel about being literally caught napping. 'He was in the drawing room . . .'

Rintoul glanced in. 'Nope.' He entered the office ahead of me. Jarvis was on the telephone. When he saw Rintoul he made a welcoming face and gestured to him to sit down. Since they were obviously to have a private conversation, and it was almost lunchtime anyway, I picked up my bag, and the lemonade tray, and excused myself.

The tray was my pretext for leaving via the kitchen. When I went in there, Chef was arranging slices of cold pie on a platter. The back door was open and I could see Dorothy perched on the step in the sun, a tendril of smoke hovering above her head.

'Going out then?' asked Chef. He was the first to complain of the heat, but he still managed to sound resentful.

'For a while, anyway – until it gets too much for me.'

At the sound of my voice Dorothy had twisted round, and now she stubbed out her cigarette, scrambled to her feet and hurried in, her face split by a gleeful grin.

'Well?'

I couldn't resist teasing her. 'What?'

'Did you go and look?'

I wasn't sure if Chef was in on the secret, but she noticed my expression and linked her arm flirtatiously through his. 'Don't mind him, I tell him everything, don't I?'

'Maybe you do,' he said. 'And maybe you don't.'

'He knows all about it,' she insisted. 'So what do you reckon?'

I decided against expressing any shock. 'It's very good of you.'

She shrieked with laughter, and then clapped her hand over her mouth. 'D'you think so?'

I nodded, and she nudged Chef, who dropped a tomato and sighed heavily. 'Hear that? I've had my portrait done and it's a good likeness! Pity it's on a ruddy wall, eh, or it might be worth something!'

'Dorothy,' I said more seriously. 'Do you think Mr and Mrs Jarvis know about it?'

She shrugged. 'I dunno. Who cares? I'm not telling on her, anyway.' She glanced at me suspiciously. 'You're not going to, are you?'

'No,' I said. 'Of course not.'

'You won't, will you, Chef?' She tilted her head to look into his face.

'Do what?'

She grinned again. 'He won't.'

Chef returned to his slicing. As I left the kitchen Dorothy followed me into the hall and pulled the door to behind her.

'Oy . . . !'

'What is it, Dorothy?'

'Did you get a chance to look in theirs?'

'I beg your pardon?'

'Their bedroom.'

'Of course not!' I pretended to be outraged at the suggestion – I could scarcely admit to my undignified curiosity, but Dorothy took that as read.

'I suppose she was in there, was she – taking a nap?'

'I have no idea.'

'There's two beds for show, but he sleeps in the dressing room.'

'I don't know why you're telling me this, Dorothy. The Jarvises' sleeping arrangements are of no interest to me whatsoever.'

'Really?' She gave me her infernally knowing grin. 'You're the only one, then.'

I suppose I was being hypocritical, but not entirely so. Any suspicions I'd harboured about the Jarvises' marriage had their origins in Max Darblay's vicious gossip, and not in my own observations. What I had seen since coming to Crompton Terrace was a wholly benign partnership based on mutual understanding and affection. Whether or not there was also a spark of passion I couldn't tell, and had no real wish to know. Even if everything Darblay had said was true, the Jarvises' was a relationship far closer and more harmonious than many more conventional marriages, and what didn't hurt either of them was not for me to judge.

I determined to be led into no more gossip with Dorothy.

It was almost unprecedented for Barbara and me to meet more than once a month these days, but her calm, laconic company offered a welcome change from the rather too colourful circumstances of Seven Crompton Terrace.

The warm weather continued, and the evenings were long and light. We met up at the Albert Memorial and set off around the perimeter of the park in the direction of Kensington Palace.

Almost at once she said: 'You look different.'

'Do I? In what way?'

She pulled her head back the better to assess me. 'Happier.'

'Well I am, much.'

'And something else . . .'

'Oh dear.'

'No,' she said, 'it's good. More alive.'

I knew she was right; that my few weeks with the Jarvises had changed me. I could feel it. The very air I breathed, which had been stale and unrefreshing, now hummed with possibilities and mysteries and unknown quantities.

'I'm glad it's suiting you so well,' she went on. 'Especially after all the grim forebodings.'

'Oh,' I said, 'I didn't take him too seriously.'

'Maybe not, but I was a bit doubtful myself.'

'Me too. To be honest I was frightened to death.'

'I bet,' she said, 'that it's the things you're a little afraid of which are making it exciting.'

'That's true,' I agreed.

That night in bed I thought of Matthew, and realised how long it was since I'd done so. I said 'sorry' to him, but he seemed to be smiling even as he drifted away.

Chapter Six

'They've got people coming for a lunch party on Thursday,' Dorothy told me. 'Chef's in a terrible two and eight 'cause they haven't said how many.'

'Perhaps they don't know yet,' I said. 'It's only Monday. I'm sure they'll tell him by then.'

She pulled a face. 'You're an optimist, intcha?'

'Yes,' I said. 'I suppose I am.'

It was true I was in high spirits. My meeting with Barbara had proved to me what in a way I had known but been too cautious to admit – that I was enjoying myself. That each day I woke up with a sense of pleasurable anticipation and excitement about whatever lay ahead. I seemed to be witnessing the emergence of a different me, one submerged for a long, long time. No wonder that in my half-waking dream Matthew had smiled at me: he must have been pleased at the return of the bright, curious, slightly mischievous girl he'd once known.

At the Jarvises I remained the efficient, unflappable, soberly dressed young woman they'd employed, I made sure of that. I flatter myself they'd never have guessed how altered I was on the inside.

It transpired that Suzannah, when she left the house that day last week when I'd been into her room, had gone to stay with other people. Dorothy, of course, was the source of this information, which related to Chef's annoyance about numbers.

'Don't ask me where,' she said. 'She's a proper fly-by-night. One day she's here, the next – whoosh. But her stuff's still here, so she's coming back.'

I couldn't resist asking: 'Do you clean in there?'

She rolled her eyes. 'Pull the other one! I changed the sheets, that's all. Not that they needed it. It's stifling up there this weather, I reckon she's been sleeping on top. In the buff probably.'

I made no comment. I knew Dorothy was dying to know more about me and what I got up to when not at Crompton Terrace, and these little sallies were intended to test the water, to get a rise out of me which I wasn't going to provide.

'That Mr Rintoul's a messy bugger,' she offered, by way of a second go. 'But he's not working, so I do clean in there. D'you think they teach them at art school – oil-painting, watercolours and how to live in a pigsty?'

'I wouldn't know,' I said.

'Bet your place isn't like that.'

'Put the kettle on would you please, Dorothy?'

Christopher Jarvis and Rintoul had gone out together somewhere, so I was entirely at his wife's disposal. I didn't have to ask about Thursday's arrangements; it wasn't long before the issue of the menu came up.

'I wonder if the weather's going to hold?' Amanda murmured. 'It makes such a difference if it's hot – no one wants a big cooked meal. That would make it easier for Chef, too. He's always so put out when we can't give an exact number.'

I could see both sides of this, but it seemed to me that some factors at least could be established which would help the poor man.

'Let's see,' I said. 'You won't be fewer than, say, four, will you?'

'Good gracious, no.'

'And not more than . . .' I plucked a figure from the air. 'Twelve?'

She thought about this. 'Not as many as that . . . Eight, I should say, unless – no, no, not more than eight.'

'Then perhaps you could tell Chef there will be eight? If it turns out not to be so many that won't matter.'

Her face puckered with worry. 'He does so hate waste when he's been to a lot of trouble.'

I noticed that it was not the Jarvises but their cook who hated the waste, but he couldn't have it both ways. For all his glumness I rather liked Chef, but the tyranny of his disapproval had to be overthrown, for everyone's sake.

'There won't be that much left over, I'm sure,' I said. 'And why don't you order a salmon? Then you could have it hot or cold, depending on the weather.'

'That's a very good idea, Pamela.' She brightened up, and I was really pleased to have been the cause of it. She might be ineffectual (Dorothy's 'ninny' was too harsh) but hers was a genuinely sweet, generous nature.

I fetched a pad and pencil to write down her grocery orders, asking casually as I did so: 'Has one of your guests left? There seem to be fewer people in the house.'

'Suzannah, no, she hasn't left. She's gone to stay in Eastbourne for a few days. I believe she comes back tomorrow.'

I made a mental note to tell Chef. 'Perfect weather for a trip to the seaside,' I said blandly. She agreed, fanning her hand in front of her face.

'A sea breeze would be so welcome . . . I find the heat quite trying. We go to Italy in July, it's Christopher's favourite place in the world although I'm afraid it's out of the frying pan into the fire as far as I'm concerned. But the house is beautifully cool so I loiter in there through the middle of the day.'

It was the first I'd heard about them going away, and I

wondered how that would affect me. July was only a few weeks away; it was so like them not to mention anything about their plans. Would they want me to take my holiday at the same time? Or would they leave me with enough work to keep me occupied? Or – and this was the most attractive option – would I be left with no specific tasks, but simply required to keep an eye on things in their absence? I was a little ashamed of myself for thinking it, but the prospect of being free to observe, and perhaps to explore, was irresistible.

We made the list, and I placed the orders, including a five-pound salmon from the fishmonger's. These days I always scouted round the kitchen before Chef arrived to ensure we missed nothing, and didn't buy things she already had. We wrote out the menu for Chef, 'for eight': artichoke soup (hot or cold); salmon (hot or cold) with peas, new potatoes and hollandaise sauce; strawberries and cream. I brought the household bookkeeping up to date while she wrote some letters, and then I offered to walk up to the village and post them. She asked, apologetically, if I'd collect some shoes of her husband's from the mender's while I was there. I was only too happy – it was another beautiful morning, and she always worried that I didn't have enough to do when her husband wasn't there, so this suited both of us.

Before I left I reminded her to give the menu to Chef as soon as he arrived. We smiled at one another, like children discussing a grumpy adult: co-conspirators, becoming friends.

I noticed as I left that the swallow-babies' heads were visible. It would soon be time for them to learn how to fly. This would present quite a problem for the parents, because of the nest being on the inside of the porch. The entrance to the porch was wide and open, with wooden arches on either side, but the little ones would need to begin their maiden flight with a swift, difficult swoop if they weren't to collide with a wall.

And then there was a tiled floor . . . I did hope that nature and instinct would protect them. Like the Jarvises, I'd begun to feel proprietary about the swallows. Perhaps later today, with the lunch party in mind, I would suggest to Amanda that I make a discreet sign warning visitors about the nest.

It was mid-morning and the sun was hot, but not yet oppressive. I took my time. Now that I was working at Crompton Terrace, Highgate village appeared different. When I had first come here for my interview I had thought it terribly smart and exclusive, perched on its hill far above town. Now I saw it with different eyes. This place couldn't fool me: it had a double life.

The cobbler was a chatty soul. 'Top-notch shoes, these,' he remarked as he wrapped them up. 'Lovely leather, made in Italy. I shouldn't say it, but the Italians know what they're doing.'

I acknowledged the compliment on Mr Jarvis's behalf. It flashed across my mind that this sort of detail would have delighted my father, but unaccountably incensed my mother, who would have filed Italian shoes under 'unnecessary', the male equivalent of 'showy'.

The cobbler glanced at me with a twinkle of curiosity. 'Staying with them, are you?' I told him I worked there. 'They're an interesting couple,' he said. 'Always have a houseful.'

It occurred to me that as a local tradesman of long standing he'd probably picked up a good deal about the Jarvises, and it certainly wasn't my place to gossip about them. I paid for the shoes and left, buying a sandwich at the baker's before returning down the hill.

When I got back I put my swallow-notice idea to Mrs Jarvis, who was delighted.

'I think you should *definitely* do that, Pamela. It would be too awful if anything happened.'

'Mr Jarvis won't mind?' I asked.

'Quite the opposite, he's dotty about our swallows. He always says it's an honour to have them here.'

She supplied me with a wide-nibbed pen and some black ink, and I spent the next hour writing out the notice in my best calligraphy, taking a childish pleasure in each smooth 'O', downward sweep and upward flourish. I was almost done when she popped her head into the office.

'Pamela – oh, doesn't that look nice, you are clever . . . Listen, I don't feel like eating any lunch today so I've let Chef and Dorothy go, and I want to lie down in my room for a while. Will you be all right?'

I assured her that I would. It occurred to me, perhaps unworthily, that her decision to give Chef the day off was not unconnected to her having handed over the luncheon menu for eight. Still, what did it matter? It was rather nice to know the house was empty but for the two of us.

'Have you had something to eat?' she asked anxiously.

'I bought a sandwich in the village.'

'Do please use the garden if you'd like to,' she said. 'It's a little untidy, but there are plenty of chairs, and cushions and what-have-you.'

'Thank you,' I said. 'I might well, if you're sure you don't mind.'

'No, no, you must, you do so much for us . . .' Her gratitude was touching when in fact I felt that where she was concerned I did very little, and none of it at all demanding. She made to leave, then added: 'There's a parasol out there if you want to use it. It's a bit of an awkward thing, but I'm sure it won't give you any trouble . . .'

I finished the notice, and put it on top of the bureau in the drawing room for her final approval. Then I collected my sandwich, and a glass of lemon squash from the tidy and deserted kitchen, and went out to the garden. I was very conscious that this was another turning point, a very definite step forward in my relations with the Jarvises. Or at least with Mrs Jarvis, but I couldn't believe that he would object to or countermand the granting of this small privilege.

Her description of the garden as 'a little untidy' was an understatement. Seen from the house it was a sunlit area of brick terrace and daisy-spattered grass, with a thick shrubbery beyond. Once I was out there I realised that the shaggy grass was at this time of year scarcely more than a clearing on which the romping vegetation threatened to encroach unless cut back – something which had been attempted with more energy than expertise.

I tested one of the chairs and sat down. As I found a spot on the ground where my glass would stay upright I noticed one or two cigarette stubs and a wine cork among the daisies. Bees hummed, and a cloud of small yellow butterflies hovered over a sweet-smelling bush covered in white flowers. Admittedly I was no gardener, but I rather liked it – I could have been out in the countryside. About to bite into my sandwich I glanced self-consciously up at the Jarvises' bedroom window, but the curtains were drawn.

When I'd finished, I decided to have a look round. It wasn't a large garden, perhaps eighty foot long I judged from its neighbours, but the end seemed mysterious and far away, cloaked by trees and shrubs. An inviting little stepping-stone path led into the jungle and I followed it. It wound away so that almost at once I felt cut off from the house and the open garden behind me. The air was deliciously cool and the glossy dark leaves of rhododendrons seemed to breathe moisture. There were several quite tall trees, and when I reached the wall at the end I found a couple of giants growing in either corner, like the pillars of a four-poster. Ivy crawled over the ground and up the wall which was damp and green, as if covered in verdigris. It was another world.

I stood there for a moment, savouring the cool, shaded seclusion. I wondered if anyone ever came here, and why. Just then my question was answered by the gleam of a small object among the moss and ivy at my feet. I bent down to pick it up. It was a hairslide in the shape of a cluster of strawberries and white strawberry-flowers, the fruit and petals prettily enamelled. I was about to put it in the pocket of my skirt when I saw something else in among the leaves, near where the slide had lain. It was, to my astonishment, a bird – a tiny, brown bird, sitting on its nest, frozen with fear, trying to be invisible. I too kept still as a statue, full of a sense of wonder, and privilege, desperate not to alarm her. I knew that skylarks nested on the ground, but suddenly I remembered something Amanda Jarvis had said and it gave me a childish thrill.

I was looking at the nightingale!

With exquisite care I took a step backwards . . . And another . . . Another still . . . until I could turn without frightening the bird and make my way back between the sheltering branches, leaving her safe.

When I emerged on to the grass my heart was pattering as if I'd run a mile and I felt ridiculously pleased with myself. I had absolutely nothing left to do indoors, so I remained in the garden. I collected up the cigarette ends and corks (there turned out to be more than one) from the grass, and did some simple weeding around the edges, only pulling up those plants of whose identity I was certain, like thistles, plantains and dandelions, and putting them in the dustbin. Rather pleased with the effect I'd achieved, I went to the lean-to at the side of the house, next to the outdoor lav. There didn't seem to be a lawnmower, but I found a stiff broom and swept the terrace, collecting the rubbish up with a dustpan and brush and emptying that into the dustbin too.

With the bit now well and truly between my teeth I went round to the front of the house and started on some weeding there. This, being a smaller area, responded even better to my efforts. Setting aside my complete ignorance of all things horticultural, I began to wonder if care of the garden might not become another of my responsibilities, but the look on the face of a passing neighbour, and her faint, baffled, 'Good afternoon' told me that I didn't yet look the part.

I was clipping the top of the hedge with some rather blunt shears when I heard Amanda calling my name. I'd been in a world of my own and felt suddenly quite guilty as I rushed round to the back, pink, perspiring, grubby-handed and wild-haired. But she displayed only relief, putting her hand to her breast and closing her eyes with a smile.

'Pamela – thank heavens! I thought you'd disappeared!'

'I hope you don't mind, Mrs Jarvis. I had nothing else to do so I was amusing myself with a little tidying up in the garden.'

'Tidying? Oh!' She looked about her, noticing for the first time the results of my amateurish labours. 'Oh!' she cried again, putting her hands together, her eyes and mouth round with astonishment. You'd have thought I was Capability Brown and had created nothing less than a sweeping prospect with a neo-classical gazebo and artificial lake. 'Pamela! Is there no end to your talents?'

I beamed. Her reaction was more than I could have hoped for, as well as far more than I deserved. 'I was really just fiddling about – and I was very careful not to pull up anything I didn't recognise.'

'Of course you were . . .' she breathed. 'It's marvellous the difference you've made.'

'I did a bit at the front, too,' I said. She at once flew round there, with me in her wake, and again declared herself completely overwhelmed.

'The thing is,' she said, 'we could do with help, but Christopher objects to the idea of some stranger wandering about in the garden. He likes to feel that any of us can come out here at any time and have peace and quiet. He sees it as a sort of sanctuary, but the trouble is that at this time of year it runs wild.'

The word 'sanctuary' reminded me of something and I took the hairslide out of my pocket.

'I found this,' I told her, but not where, or what else I had found.

She took it from me and examined it, rubbing her thumbs over the bright enamelled surface. 'What a pretty little thing . . . I think it might be Suzannah's. Could you bear to go up and pop it in her room?'

'Of course.'

I was only too glad to. For one thing I needed to wash my face and hands and comb my hair, and for another this meant that I had not just been allowed, but sent, into the attic room, and could feel less guilty about my previous visit. I believe Amanda had an almost superstitious aversion to going into her guests' rooms for fear, perhaps, of what she would find. She could have had no idea how justified those fears were in this case!

Cooler and cleaner, but already beginning to feel quite stiff from the unaccustomed exercise, I went up to the top floor and into Suzannah's room. She couldn't have taken much with her to Brighton; it looked exactly the same as before. But for one thing – the sketchy lines on the easel were now taking shape, and it was possible to make out the beginnings of a portrait. Or at least a picture containing a seated figure. I put the hairslide on the washstand, and stood back to get a better look. The shock of dark hair, the heavy drooping shoulders, the big hands clasped between the knees – there was no mistaking Edward Rintoul.

I found this both surprising and pleasing. Surprising that one artist should come here for the express purpose, as far as I could see, of sitting for another; and pleasing because I had recognised it. What with Christopher Jarvis's comments on my art appreciation, and his wife's on my gardening, I was in danger of becoming quite big-headed. Except that the nagging sense of things I didn't know, or understand, kept me in my place.

I went back to my desk, and having nothing to do took a book on the Dutch Masters from the bookcase and sat reading, and staring open-mouthed at the pictures. When five o'clock came Mr Jarvis and Rintoul had not reappeared, and I went to find Amanda to say that I was going.

She was in the drawing room, also deep in a book, a novel. She had changed into a pale blue bias-cut dress with a soft frill around the scoop neck and looked pretty and, for once, relaxed.

'Are you off, Pamela? You've done so much today. I can't thank you enough.'

'It's been a pleasure, really.' I didn't say, 'It's what you pay me for,' because I fancy it rather pleased her to think of me as an exemplary, competent soul who did things out of the kindness of my heart. In spite of the comings and goings at Crompton Terrace I was sure she was lonely.

'Before you go,' she said, closing the book, 'I wanted to ask if you'd join us for lunch on Thursday?'

I was taken aback. 'That's very kind of you. I don't know – I mean, are you sure?' What I meant was that *I* wasn't sure. I'd become used to being an observer. My pretensions to being one of them had never extended to sitting round the table with them and their artistic friends.

'Perfectly,' she said. 'I know Christopher would like it, and I certainly would.' Seeing my disconcerted expression she added with an uncharacteristic hint of mischief: 'Don't worry, I'm sure you'll be able to make yourself useful, even if that means mopping up the bores for us.'

This, as intended, made me laugh. 'If you put it like that, what can I say? Thank you, I'd love to.'

I couldn't imagine that there would be any bores at the party, or even that the Jarvises numbered any among their acquaintance. But on the bus home I experienced a thrill of nervous excitement. Whoever was going to be there, I would meet them! My life had changed out of all recognition.

The following day it was equally hot and, even though Mr Jarvis was back, nobody felt inclined to work. Once we'd done the correspondence and I'd brought him up to date on the previous day's developments, he retreated to the garden, and I occupied myself with leafing through a pile of Sumpter's back catalogues. I told myself that this was to better acquaint myself with the gallery, and the taste of its owner, but all the time I was looking for more pictures by S.R. Murchie.

There were only two, in an exhibition held exactly a year ago, and they didn't disappoint. One was called 'The Garden'. It showed a small, walled garden viewed from above, as if (I found myself thinking) from an attic room. The garden itself was one of many, a whole terrace of such gardens, with more beyond, none of them elegant or well kept, or even romantically neglected like the one here. These were not the gardens of the self-indulgent well-to-do, but the backyards of people with little time for flowers or sitting in the sun. Most had some sort of vegetable patch – rows of cabbages, bean-sticks, carrots and potatoes – with the rest of the space, whether grass or concrete, given over to bicycle-maintenance, washing lines, prams, dogs, cats and dustbins.

What marked out the nearest garden from its neighbours was its emptiness, as though this was a house where no one lived. The whole area consisted of nothing more than long, scorched-looking grass, as I imagined the African veldt to be, with here and there great stooks of fierce-looking weeds that had pushed their way through. Its air of desolation was unutterably sad.

No figures featured in the painting: despite all the evidence of teeming occupancy, not a single person could be seen. The only sign of human life was a hand, or part of a hand, in the bottom right-hand corner of the canvas. The effect of this, even on the printed page, was to make me feel that I was actually there, that it was my own hand, resting on the sill as I peered down into that empty garden. I shivered.

The second picture, 'Summer, 1927', was gentler than the other Murchies I'd seen. It showed the interior of a large, sparsely furnished room. The time I guessed to be a summer's afternoon, something like this one. A half-curtained French window admitted a soft panel of light, but the rest of the room was not dark. A girl and a dog lay together on a sofa. She was furthest away, and with her back to the artist, not posed but curled in childish sleep, with rounded shoulders and legs bent up. Her shoes, pink, with a small heel, lay on the floor. The dog, a greyhound, had somehow managed to gather its lanky limbs into the remaining space, but its whip-like tail and pointed head hung over the edge of the sofa, and its eyes gazed soulfully out at me. The effect was of two companions, overcome by the lassitude of a hot day, who neither knew nor cared how they looked.

I wondered how this effect was achieved. Had Murchie taken a photograph of such a scene, and worked from that? Had he worked from memory? Or had he been there? I liked to think it was the last, because there was something trusting in the girl's carelessly hunched figure and rumpled hair. Neither she nor her dog minded being watched by the artist as they dozed off.

At four o'clock Jarvis came in, and suggested that I go home.

'Nothing doing here,' he said. 'You might as well. Good work in the garden, by the way.'

'I enjoyed it,' I said.

He nodded at my desk. 'I see you've been doing some homework.'

'I hope you don't mind, I saw them on the shelf—'

'Of course I don't mind; on the contrary, I'm delighted you're interested. Did you find the Murchies?'

'Yes.'

'The girl with the dog is my god-daughter. You'll meet her on Thursday.'

From this I inferred that his wife had told him she'd invited me. 'I'll look forward to that. It's a lovely picture – happier than the others.'

'I think so,' he agreed, adding: 'You might meet the artist, too.'

'That would be wonderful!' I was genuinely thrilled. 'There's so much I'd like to ask him.'

'We'll have to see what we can do,' said Jarvis with a smile. 'Now you cut along home. I'll see you in the morning.'

He withdrew into the garden again. As I came out of the office I saw Dorothy in the drawing room, topping up the flower water with a long-spouted can. There was no chance of slipping away unnoticed; she spotted me at once and came over with that gleeful expression so typical of her.

'What's all this?' she asked *sotto voce*.

'All what?' She was cheeky and we both knew it. I always resolved to be more aloof with her, but could never keep it up.

'Out in the *garden*,' she said, raising her eyebrows and pouting. 'Invited to the *luncheon* party? What you been up to?'

'I haven't been up to anything, as you put it. But Mr and Mrs Jarvis have been very kind, it's true.'

'Kind?' She put her head on one side. 'I doubt it.'

'I think it was kind. Perhaps they wanted their guests to meet the person who answers the telephone.'

I could hear my note of self-justification, and knew it was quite unnecessary. Why should I have to justify anything to the Jarvises' parlourmaid? But I could never escape the feeling that Dorothy's experience here was longer than mine, and she was possessed of a sound intuition.

Now she said, a touch self-importantly: 'There'll be more to it than that, take it from me.'

'For goodness' sake, Dorothy . . . Such as what?'

'I don't know, do I? But he always has his reasons.'

'Well,' I said, 'let's see, shall we?'

Dorothy made a face that said indeed we would, and returned to her watering. She really was incorrigible. I dared not give up my feeble attempt at dignity, for fear of being taken over altogether by this likeable, manipulative madam.

In the porch, I noticed that one of the baby swallows was perched on the edge of the nest. There was no sign of its parents, but it was clear that flying lessons were about to start. Several droppings spattered the tiles. Dorothy would have to clear them up before Thursday. I hoped that she would neither use the bread-and-butter knife nor disturb the birds: she had a robust working-class attitude towards God's creatures – broadly speaking it was that they were all right in their place but in the case of the swallows, this wasn't it.

There was a woman walking down the hill towards me. She wore a long cotton skirt, a loose black shirt, sandals and a frayed, broad-brimmed straw hat. Over one shoulder hung a long-handled raffia basket. She'd bundled most of her long hair up into the hat, but several strands had escaped and trailed over her shoulders. She looked like a gypsy except that as she got closer I could see how pale she was.

I was almost sure this was Suzannah, the guest from the

top floor. But I wasn't sufficiently confident to say anything to her as she went past. For her part, she didn't seem to notice me at all. She appeared entirely preoccupied, in a world of her own.

To satisfy my curiosity, I glanced over my shoulder when she'd gone by, and saw her open the gate of Number Seven, and go through. Some instinct must have told her she was being watched, for quite suddenly she turned her head and looked directly at me. It was no casual glance; I could feel the intentness of that look. For a second – less than a second, before I hurried on my way – I had the uncomfortable sensation of being the whole focus of a stranger's attention.

When I got home, Louise was on her way out, done up to the nines, and disposed to stop and chat. I'm afraid I wasn't concentrating overmuch on what she had to say, but apparently she had a new job.

'I'm not going to give up the other one,' she told me, 'because this one will be nights, and not even every night to begin with, so I'll see how I get on, but it'll mean twice the pay and huge tips . . .'

I was pleased for her of course, but I couldn't really take it in. Increasingly, even when I wasn't there, I inhabited Seven Crompton Terrace. The house in Highgate had become my reality, and everything outside it muffled, distant, indistinct.

The next day couldn't come soon enough for me.

Chapter Seven

All that week it was hot. Too hot. As the days went by, the blue sky faded to the colour of pewter, and beneath it London seethed and simmered. Sunshine smiles gave way to a trudging, sweaty stoicism.

At Seven Crompton Terrace only Dorothy, never the most punctilious worker, maintained her usual pace, though complaining loudly of the heat. Everyone else in the house was lethargic. We kept the curtains at the front drawn from midday onwards. Amanda stayed indoors, and her husband was uncharacteristically tetchy, not with me, but with the world in general – short with people on the phone and inveighing against recalcitrant transporters, temperamental clients, and politicians who had failed to foresee the problems of peace.

Jarvis had never spoken of his wartime experiences, and I'd never asked, both because it was not my place and because such conversations made me too sad. Now, in passing, I learned that he had served in the desert in Mesopotamia.

'You know, I thought I could tolerate heat till I went over there,' he told me. 'I'd always flourished in high temperatures, hot sunshine made me cheerful and energetic. I flattered myself I should have been born an Italian. But there . . .' He closed his eyes and shook his head at the memory. 'It was like nothing I'd ever come across before. Solid, ceaseless, like a blast-furnace. I'd say intolerable, except that there was no choice but to tolerate it.'

'So this,' I suggested with caution, 'must be nothing to you.'

'It's certainly nothing to *that*,' he said. 'But I don't care for these protracted spells of hot weather any more. Unless I'm on holiday with nothing to do but sit under an olive tree with a jug of wine. They remind me too much of the damn desert. And everything that went with it.'

His face had grown quite bleak and pinched. To take his mind off the war, and those aspects of it which I didn't want to discuss any more than him, I asked: 'What did you do before you joined up?'

'I practised,' he said, and seeing my baffled expression added: 'I was already a professional soldier.'

If he had wanted to astonish me, he succeeded. I mumbled something gauche about having had no idea.

'Well of course you didn't. And it's of no great interest now, anyway.'

In spite or perhaps because of his uncertain mood I sensed that he was disposed to talk. There was no escaping the area I'd wished to avoid. I remarked, respectfully, on the great difference between soldiering as a career, and the art world in which he operated now.

'Not so great,' he said. 'Look at all those remarkable poets who found their voice in the trenches. Soldiers are individuals like anybody else.'

'Not quite like, surely,' I suggested. 'You could say that of any group of people. We all make our choices.'

'Or war makes them for us,' he said curtly.

'Was it not your own decision, then – to join the army?'

'Hardly.' He shook his head. 'I was carried along on a tide of family tradition, expectation, and misplaced patriotism.'

'Misplaced?' I asked, and realised as I said it how impertinent that sounded. But he seemed the opposite of put out – in fact for the first time in the conversation he smiled wryly.

'I might have known I wouldn't be allowed to get away with that! Perhaps true patriotism is never misplaced, but the notion that therc is anything in the least sweet or right about naïve young men gargling their last on foreign soil to satisfy the grandiose whims of a bunch of hidebound halfwits is nothing short of preposterous. It would be ludicrous if it wasn't so damned tragic— I'm sorry.'

I couldn't speak. The memories which I'd thought were receding rushed back and snatched my voice away. My eyes stung; I covered my mouth with my hand. After a long moment of reflective silence, it was Jarvis who recovered first.

'I apologise,' he said again, and then caught sight of my face. 'Mrs Griffe – Pamela – are you all right?' I nodded dumbly. He was all concern. 'What a rude devil I was to go ranting on like that. I dare say you have your own painful memories. Who doesn't? Please don't think for a moment that I was belittling what men did out there, I saw it with my own eyes – the selfless courage, the devotion, the grace. It was astonishing. It still astonishes me. It's the arrogance and wastefulness of the old men that I can't forgive.'

I pushed my chair back. 'I think if I may – I need some fresh air.'

'Of course, of course.' He hurried over, opened the door, took my arm. 'May I get you something? Would you like a glass of water?'

'No. Thank you . . .' I didn't want his sympathy, his solicitous hand or his offers of assistance however kindly meant. I wanted only to be alone. To his credit he realised this and stepped back.

'Please don't think of returning till you're ready,' he said. 'I'm here if you need anything.' Quietly he pushed the door to, but not shut, after me.

I would have gone into the back garden, where it was cooler, but I could see Rintoul lying flat on his back on the grass with his hat over his eyes. From the kitchen came the sound of Dorothy and Chef talking desultorily as they went about their business. A cold drink would have been welcome, but I couldn't face Dorothy's bright, perceptive questioning. Instead I crept unsteadily up the stairs and swallowed a few mouthfuls from the tap in the bathroom, using my cupped hands. Then I came down and went out into the porch. Even the swallows were stunned by the heat, so no flying lessons were in progress, and there was a little shade here. I leaned against one of the wooden uprights, breathing deeply.

I was overcome with shame. Until now I flattered myself that I had kept my composure, and remained self-possessed. Any anxiety I'd had about my new job had stayed well hidden. And I had managed to learn quite a lot about the people round me while not giving anything away about myself. But this moment's weakness would have undone all that. My reputation for iron unflappability was a goner.

I mustn't leave it too long before returning to my desk – getting back in the saddle, my father (who had no knowledge whatever of horses or riding), would have said. My legs still felt rather shaky, so I embarked on a few turns to the gate and back. On my second return journey something at the top of the house caught my eye and I looked up to see Suzannah at the top-floor window. She gave no sign of recognition, and disappeared almost at once as though embarrassed at being seen.

Seconds later the front door opened and she came out, closing it behind her. She was wearing the same long skirt I'd seen her in the other day, with her stained painter's overall over the top. Her silvery-brown hair was in two thick plaits, but since it wasn't completely straight many hairs had escaped and stuck out like fine wires. Her face and collarbones, though pale as ever, gleamed with sweat.

'Hello,' she said. 'I wanted to say thank you.'

Her voice was light and soft, her tone inconsequential. It was like a young boy's voice.

'What for?' I asked.

'My hairslide, that I dropped in the garden.'

'I didn't know whose it was,' I said. 'But Mrs Jarvis thought it must be yours. I'm glad you've got it back.'

That was clearly that so far as the hairslide went, but she didn't go right away, and perched on the low wall between the porch and the office window. I took advantage of the pause to come back into the shade.

'We haven't been introduced,' I said, rather stiffly. 'I'm Pamela Griffe. I started work for Mr and Mrs Jarvis a few weeks ago.'

'Yes, I know.' She seemed to assume, correctly, that I already knew her name. 'How are you?'

I answered what I took to be a formulaic question in a formulaic way. 'Very well thank you.'

'I mean are you feeling better?'

Now I remembered that she had seen me tottering back and forth to the gate.

'Oh, I'm sorry – yes, thank you. It must have been the heat.'

'Ghastly, isn't it? I work in my room up at the top and it's complete hell in this weather. Edward – my sitter – bought us an electric fan, but he's on strike today until it gets cooler.'

'I saw him out on the grass.'

'I'm having to get on with other things.' She stopped and gave me a searching look. Her eyes were very light, almost transparent; looking at them was like looking into water, or clear glass. 'I suppose,' she said, 'you will have seen what I'm doing up there?'

Of course, she knew I'd been into the room to return the hairslide, but I still answered cautiously: 'I could tell it was Mr Rintoul on the easel.'

'Not that,' she said dismissively. 'The mural.'

'Yes,' I said, 'I did notice.'

'Good, because that's much more important.' She gave me another quick, sharp, glance. 'You do realise it's a secret – a surprise?'

'I didn't, actually, but I haven't told anyone.'

'I made Chris and Amanda promise they wouldn't go in, and as far as I know they've kept their word.'

For someone so fey and reclusive she was amazingly confident of the mural's effect. I hoped for her sake that the 'surprise' would be a pleasant one for the Jarvises – but then she knew them much better than me.

'It's Dorothy you want to be careful of,' I said.

'Yes, I saw she'd been in and changed the bed. You're right, she has a mouth like a torn pocket. But I suspect she likes a secret, too.'

This remark displayed a pretty shrewd understanding of our resident gossip. But now the subject changed again.

'Talking of secrets, where did you find it – the hairslide?'

'At the end of the garden.'

'I hope you walked carefully.'

She was sounding me out. She wasn't going to mention this second secret to someone who didn't already know.

'Don't worry,' I said, 'I was so close I almost trod on her, but I saw her in time.'

'Good.' Something in those pale eyes told me that she was pleased we had established a small bond. 'Have you heard her sing?'

'No. But then I'm not here at night.'

'You should stay one evening. It's worth it.'

I was trying, and failing, to imagine how this private concert might be arranged, when she said: 'I believe I'll see you on Thursday.'

'That's right.'

''Bye for now, then.'

She made to go in, but just before closing the door she paused and pointed up at the swallows' nest. 'Nothing shy about them, is there? But then they don't sing.'

I waited a moment or two before following. Jarvis was no longer in the office; the room was tranquil. There were two tumblers on the desk, one containing water, and the other a sprig of the fragrant white shrub in the back garden, the one the butterflies liked so much.

I sipped the cool water and breathed in the flowery scent. My bad moment about Matthew had passed, and was never to be mentioned again.

'You met her then,' said Dorothy the next morning.

Chef had not yet arrived when I went into the kitchen to make coffee. I wondered what it would take to keep something private in this house.

'M-hm . . .' I murmured as absently as I could, as I filled the kettle and busied myself assembling cups and saucers. 'I found something of hers and returned it.'

'She's a funny one, isn't she?'

'She seemed very nice,' I said, 'but she was only thanking me, we didn't speak for long.'

'Did she mention about painting all over the walls?'

Just for once, I was not going to give in. 'No.'

Dorothy gave me a sceptical look. 'And you wouldn't tell me anyway.'

'No, Dorothy, as a matter of fact I wouldn't.'

'Suit yourself.' She opened the broom cupboard with a clatter and took out the basket caddy containing polish and dusters. 'Better get going, I suppose, people coming tomorrow. Know who they are yet?'

'No, I don't.'

'You're a proper old Chinaman this morning, you are,' she

said, cheekily but without the least rancour. I couldn't be bothered to remonstrate. I'd made my point, and wanted to remain friends.

On the day of the lunch party it was hotter still. And the sky was low and leaden, stifling the least breath of air. The caretaker, the newsvendor, the bus conductor and assorted passengers all volunteered the opinion that the sooner it thundered the better. One man put our minds at rest by claiming to have suffered all night from the particular headache that presaged storms.

Mr Jarvis's car wasn't outside when I arrived, and I thought he must be out, until I saw it parked for some reason a little further down the street. In the porch I stood on tiptoe to peep at the swallows' nest, and could make out nothing at first; then I caught sight of a fluffy head and realised there must be one non-flier, a late developer, still in residence.

As I closed the front door Mr Jarvis came out of the drawing room.

'Morning – any more of this and the nation will grind to a halt. I've ordered ice.'

'What a good idea.'

'May I say how pretty you're looking today?'

'Oh—' I glanced down at myself as though I hadn't got up early and spent an hour deciding what to wear. 'Thank you, I wasn't sure . . .'

'You'll be the smartest person at the table,' he assured me. 'With the possible exception of my wife, of course, who always looks charming. And by the way,' he added, 'I've left a short list on your desk – after that, I think your assistance on the domestic front would be appreciated.'

Dorothy was in the office, flicking the bookshelves with a feather duster.

'Don't worry,' she said, 'I'm off now. Just taking the

opportunity.' The way she said this implied that she was constantly on the lookout for extra work.

'How's Chef?' I enquired. 'All quiet out there?'

She shook the duster out of the window. 'More or less. He's a lot better now he knows it's for eight, and all cold.'

I did a quick mental calculation: apart from those of us already here, and assuming Edward Rintoul was included, there would be three guests. It crossed my mind that Dorothy might well know their identity, but I buttoned my lip. I'd know soon enough, and what's more by this time tomorrow I would actually be in possession of information *not* available to her.

'That's a nice dress,' she commented disarmingly as she went out. 'Don't worry, you'll be able to hold your head up.'

By eleven I'd completed Mr Jarvis's list, and spent the next hour helping his wife to lay the table, arrange flowers (something I'd never done, and for which I had no real aptitude), and liaise with Chef. Mr Jarvis kept his head down in the office; Dorothy was set to putting a high shine on the drawing room. At midday Amanda went upstairs to change, and I found myself at a loose end. I wasn't quite sure where I ought best to be when the others arrived. To wait in the drawing room would look presumptuous. Should I open the door to them? Remain in the office until summoned? Loiter self-effacingly in the background? I opted for the latter and went into the garden, where I could give the appearance of usefulness while being available for introduction when required.

My labours of a week ago might never have taken place. The weeds were back, the terrace was dusty and littered with petals, and there was a fresh crop of cigarette ends on the grass. I was too smartly dressed for weeding, but I picked up the cigarette butts, and then fetched the broom to sweep the bricks. Within seconds I was pink and perspiring.

Edward Rintoul came out just as I'd swept the rubbish into a corner. He was wearing the same loose, shabby clothes he'd had on when I met him on the stairs, but with sandals. His feet were not a pretty sight.

'You're so *busy*,' he exclaimed plaintively. 'Why must you be so *busy*? It's not the weather for so much activity.'

'I've finished now,' I said.

'Thank God for that.' He seemed to take my activity as a personal affront. But he was right, it was too hot. I put the broom back in the shed while he kept up his litany of complaints.

'It's hotter than hell up there in Suzannah's attic – I'm sitting for her, you understand.' I nodded non-committally. 'She doesn't seem to feel it, the girl's in a world of her own, but I'm melting. I've suggested I take my clothes off and make it a life study, but for some reason she didn't go for the idea, why would that be?'

'I can't imagine.'

He guffawed. 'Nor me.'

I thought to myself that I must seek out and study some of Rintoul's miniatures, and they had better be good, because he was an awful man. Thank heavens at that moment Mr Jarvis came down, and he went in to talk to him. In spite of the heat I preferred to remain in the garden for the time being, and occupied myself in arranging the chairs, and dusting them off with a shammy leather I found in the shed. I saw the parasol Amanda had mentioned, leaning up in the corner between the house and the garden wall, and considered trying to put it up, but then I remembered she had described it as 'tricky', and since no one else had attempted it I left well alone.

By the time Dorothy answered the door to the first guest I was little more than a grease-spot, and felt relieved when Amanda called me in, and it became obvious the party would convene in the drawing room.

I passed Dorothy in the hall and she gave me a look as

much as to say 'How about them?' I couldn't pretend I wasn't a little nervous, and her cheerful assumption that we were co-conspirators made me smile.

The Jarvises and Rintoul were present – but not, I noticed, Suzannah – and two of the guests had arrived together, but coincidentally, I gathered, from light-hearted remarks being bandied about. The moment I walked in Amanda greeted me warmly and introduced me to them.

'This is Pamela Griffe, our wonderful Pamela. In a few short weeks she's made herself completely indispensable, hasn't she, Chris?'

'Certainly has,' agreed Jarvis. He offered me a champagne cocktail, which I declined, but fortunately there was lemonade as well which I accepted gratefully. I almost never drank alcohol, from lack of opportunity more than anything else, and wanted to stay clearheaded.

The two guests were Christopher's god-daughter Georgina Fullerton, a very pretty, nice, unaffected girl of about eighteen; and Paul Marriott, the neat, drab little man who painted the Sumpter's most eye-catching abstracts. I'd seen him before once or twice about the place, but we'd never been introduced. He shook my hand briefly and at once continued talking to Rintoul. He seemed gauche rather than rude, and I didn't take offence, especially as Georgina went out of her way to be pleasant.

'I've heard about you,' she said. 'Amanda thinks you're the best thing ever.'

'It's very kind of her to say so. I just do whatever I can.' I thought this might sound rather Uriah Heep-like, and added: 'This is a lovely place to work.'

'Oh, it must be!' she exclaimed enthusiastically. 'I love it here so much, it's one of my favourite places in the world.' I wondered how much of the world she had seen – more than me, I was sure, but that wasn't saying a great deal. As if reading my mind, she said: 'I've just got back from Switzerland – l'Auberge des Colombes, have you heard of it?'

I admitted that I hadn't. 'It's a finishing school,' she explained. 'So now I'm finished, can't you tell? I can speak French, I know which cutlery to use and how to address bishops and members of the aristocracy, how to write and answer invitations and how to get in and out of a sports car without showing my knickers. I'm ready for anything!'

I laughed. 'It sounds like it.'

'Honestly, a terrible waste of Daddy's money, but it made him happy and I had lots of fun. The other girls were a very jolly crowd, and all different nationalities, we were an absolute Tower of Babel at mealtimes – I mean obviously we were supposed to speak French but we were always breaking down. It was quite strict, mind you, no boys or anything like that, so I've got some ground to make up.'

Christopher Jarvis had joined us during this last effusion and gazed affectionately at his god-daughter. He must have been listening to the conversation, for he said:

'You know you can come here whenever you like, Georgie. You won't meet many aristocrats or bishops but you can be free as a bird.'

'Oh Uncle Chris!' She linked her arm through his and squeezed it. 'You're so sweet. I shall definitely take you up on that.'

'And what about the Season?' he asked in a mock-serious tone.

She grimaced extravagantly. 'Don't *say* that word! I won't have anything to do with that ghastly business.'

'I think it's a frightfully good idea,' he teased her. 'I've told your parents I'll chip in so you can do it in style.'

'Aaah!' She buried her face in his sleeve. 'Please, no! I couldn't stand it!'

Jarvis sent me a look that was near enough a wink. It was

obvious they understood one another and that the Season was as much anathema to him as to her.

Just then Suzannah came into the room, and the group opened out again to welcome her. She had put on a dress for the occasion, ankle-length, long-sleeved and rather shapeless but in a vibrant deep violet, and her hair was loose, held back with the strawberry hairslide. On her feet were flat, moss-green grosgrain pumps, like ballet slippers. She was nobody's idea of a beauty, and certainly not interested in fashion, but today her pale, fairy strangeness was spellbinding.

This time it was Christopher who performed the introductions, and while he fetched her a cocktail Suzannah fell into quiet conversation with Marriott. Georgina began talking to Edward Rintoul. Amanda murmured something about Chef and slipped out of the room. I was left momentarily on the sidelines, and just as well, because three words were ringing in my head:

Suzannah Rose Murchie.

S.R. Murchie! The strange, reclusive young woman from the top floor was none other than the artist behind 'Nobody', and 'The Garden' and 'Summer 1927', those pictures which had so attracted and disturbed me when I first saw them, and which still haunted me.

My astonishment must have been plain to see, because Christopher Jarvis came over and said: 'Surprised?'

'Yes, I am.' I was a little put out at having been strung along, and couldn't help sounding it. 'You said the artist would be here. But I had no idea it would be her.'

'I admit it was rather naughty of me not to tell you before,' he said, 'but you were so passionately articulate in your praise of her work that I couldn't resist the treat of seeing your face when you found out.'

I was mollified, as he knew I would be. Although I did my best to hide it I was quite shamefully susceptible to his flattery. To disguise it, because I was still a little on my dignity, I muttered something about going to help Mrs Jarvis, and excused myself. His light hand on my arm told me the excuse was accepted, if not believed. As I left the room I told myself that I must make an effort to rebuild and maintain my outer shell of composure, which had already cracked more than once and was in danger of disintegrating altogether. No matter what my employers' kindness, I still felt that this was a household in which it was unwise to drop one's guard altogether.

I was in the hall when the doorbell rang. A second later Dorothy emerged from the kitchen looking distinctly warm, poor girl.

'Don't worry,' I said, 'I'll answer it.'

The new arrival was standing in the porch with his back to the door, gazing up at the swallows' nest. He must have heard the door open, but he didn't immediately turn round. Instead, he reached up a hand as if to touch it.

'Don't!' I cried, before I could stop myself. The hand paused, and was withdrawn. He turned slowly to face me. Already embarrassed by my outburst, I had to bite down hard on another exclamation, this time of horror.

'I'm so sorry,' I said. 'But there's still a young one in there. You couldn't have known.'

'No,' he agreed. He didn't, thank heavens, seem in the least put out. 'Am I allowed to come in?'

'Yes of course – please, do.'

Thank goodness my miserable discomfiture was ended by Amanda, who came flying along the corridor, exclaiming in delight.

'Ashe, how lovely! Thank you, Pamela. Ashe, let me introduce Pamela Griffe. Pamela, this is one of our oldest and dearest friends, John Ashe. Come through and have a drink, we're not in the garden because of the heat . . .'

She led him into the drawing room, and I heard

Christopher Jarvis's welcoming cry of 'Ashe!' I went in the
direction of the kitchen, my heart pounding. Before going in
I paused to get a grip on myself, but the door opened and
Dorothy appeared, saying over her shoulder: 'So I'll tell her
we're ready, shall I?' She turned and almost bumped into me.
'Oops! What are you doing there? You know what they say,
you won't hear any good of yourself.'

'I was coming to see if there was anything I could do.'

'Too late, I'm afraid. Who was that at the door?'

When I hesitated, she gave me one of her keenest and most
knowing looks.

'Met him then, did you? Our Mr Ashe?'

I could only thank God I wasn't sitting next to him at lunch.
Not even the Jarvises, with their rather playful attitude to my
sensibilities, would have subjected me to that on a first
meeting. I was placed between Suzannah and Paul Marriott,
on the side of the table by the garden windows. Directly
opposite me was Edward Rintoul – I never imagined I could
be so pleased to see him – with Ashe and Georgina on either
side of him. Amanda Jarvis sat at the head of the table nearest
the kitchen door, flanked by Ashe and Marriott, and her
husband had his god-daughter on his right, and Suzannah
on his left.

I could only think that the others must either have met
John Ashe before, or be remarkably unshockable. I had never
seen such a terribly disfigured face. Or, at least, half-face, for
the right-hand side was perfectly unmarked. It was a real
effort not to stare; my eyes kept involuntarily returning, in
horrified fascination, to what they least wanted to see.

He seemed to have been slashed by giant claws. The left-
hand corner of his mouth was dragged upwards towards the
corner of his eye, which was similarly pulled down. The web
of skin which was left, or had been constructed, so as partly

to conceal the skull-like gape of his mouth, served to make it even more grotesque. What was visible of his damaged eye was milky and vacant like that of a dead animal. The skin around this devastation was pitted and scaly, the grain not uniform, as though pieces had been randomly stitched together.

Amanda Jarvis served the chilled, snow-white artichoke soup from a tureen on the sideboard. But bile sat at the back of my throat and when my bowl was put in front of me I could scarcely bear to look at it, let alone take a mouthful. For the second time that day I found myself thinking: Why did nobody warn me? Why wasn't I prepared? What possible pleasure or advantage could there be for them, or me, or this unfortunate man, in giving me such a shock?

Except, I supposed, that in the case of Ashe himself, he must have become used to it. Every day of his life he must suffer the horrified stares, the shaken whispers, the pointing and unguarded remarks of children. What, in God's name, must that be like? How could he bear it? And yet he was so calm. More than calm: still. His presence at the table would have been formidable without the scars; with them it was remarkable. He was doing more listening than talking and when he turned towards Rintoul on his left, and consequently towards me, displaying the clean half of his face, his dark eye was unblinking, his expression quietly attentive. He must once have been a handsome man, black-haired, olive-skinned with high, wide cheekbones like a Tartar. He wasn't tall – scarcely more than my height – but he was powerfully built, his broad shoulders slightly incongruous, like a prizefighter's, in an expensive dark suit.

At one point in those first few minutes after we sat down he glanced directly across at me. I experienced a sharp jolt of embarrassment. He seemed to know that I'd been watching him, and even what I'd been thinking. Not, with his experience, that it would have been hard to do so. My face burned, and I fiddled with the napkin in my lap. I didn't want to be of the smallest interest to John Ashe; I should have preferred complete invisibility to a single moment of that hard, inscrutable attention.

Thank goodness Paul Marriott was saying something to me. In my confusion, I didn't catch all of his question and had to ask him to repeat it.

'I wondered what you were doing, Mrs Griffe, before you came here?'

'I was working for Osborne's – the children's publisher.'

'I know them,' he said. 'How was business when you were there?'

'Pretty good, I think. As far as I could tell. I was secretary to the commissioning editor and they seemed to be taking on plenty of new authors.'

'Years ago,' he said, 'before the war in fact, I did some illustrations for one of their books.' Because of the nature of his current work he must have considered this needed some explanation, because he added: 'I needed the money, and was very glad of the job. And it stood me in good stead in all sorts of ways.'

'What was the book?' I asked. 'Can you remember?'

'As if it were yesterday. It was called *Jumping Jonah*, written by a rather fierce lady who was the scion of a noble house. I suspect her forebears of having been slave traders because it was frightful twaddle about a little negro boy who could jump over anything. I had a good deal of fun depicting him leaping over elephants, banyan trees, that sort of thing. It was in rhyme, too . . .' He frowned for a moment as if he all at once, and for the first time, found the whole enterprise rather puzzling.

It was long before my time, but I did remember seeing the book displayed on the shelf behind Roddy Osborne's desk.

'What happened?' I asked.

'The book did very well – the author went on to write a

whole series, I believe – but a couple of my paintings found a buyer and I decided to concentrate on that.'

'I meant in the book – to Jonah.'

'Oh, I see!' He gave a sharp little laugh. 'Let's think – I believe I last showed him jumping over a river, carrying a long rope, so that a whole string of other children could swing across, to escape from an army of man-eating rhinoceroses. Or do we think "rhinoceri" . . .'

'I shall have to look out for it,' I said. 'Is it still in print?'

'Somewhat surprisingly, it is. I know that because I receive microscopic royalties twice a year.'

We were invited to pass up our empty soup plates, but because mine was still virtually full I got up and volunteered to do the clearing. As I removed John Ashe's plate I noticed his smell, dry and fresh as clean linen. When he glanced up and said, 'Thank you,' I shivered.

I returned to my place. Amanda rang the bell and Dorothy came to take away the plates, and to bring in the main course. It was curiously comforting to see her, albeit very much on her best behaviour, po-faced and straight-backed and, just for once, assiduously *not* catching my eye.

Christopher Jarvis was deep in conversation with Georgina. This provided my opportunity to express my admiration of Suzannah's paintings to the artist herself. But I was concerned to strike the right note – to allow that I was far from being an expert, but that my compliments were nonetheless considered and heartfelt.

'I visited the Sumpter the other day,' I said. 'I was tremendously impressed by it all. But yours was the picture that stayed in my mind.'

'Really?' She gazed at me, her pale eyes moving over my face as though whatever I said she would be able to read the truth anyway. 'You liked it?'

'Enormously. But it was disturbing, too.'

'I hope so.'

'You obviously intended it to be.'

She thought about this for a moment, glancing over her shoulder towards the garden. 'I don't know that I intended to disturb anyone else, but to find an expression for what was disturbing me.'

This begged an intriguing question which I forbore to ask, saying instead:

'And I saw two others in one of Mr Jarvis's back catalogues.'

'Which were they?'

'"The Garden" and "Summer Nineteen Twenty-Seven".'

She gave a slow nod, remembering. 'That dog was one of my best sitters.'

'He was very fine, I noticed.'

'Did you recognise Georgina?'

'No.' I glanced across the table. 'I haven't met her till today.'

'Anyway, it would have been surprising if you had, she was scarcely visible. And sound asleep. It was weather like this. I imagine everyone in the house was snoozing except for me and the dog, and he didn't stay awake for long.'

'You captured all that so well.'

'And "The Garden"?' she asked.

I was rather thrilled that she should be so interested in my opinion, and warmed to my theme. 'Where had everybody gone?' I asked. 'That was what I wanted to know. All those houses and gardens and not a soul in sight, as if they'd all been spirited away.'

'Yes,' she agreed, her eyes on my face.

'Except for one.'

'That's right.'

It was clear I was to be offered neither explanation nor insight. 'Anyway,' I said, 'it was wonderful when I found out that the artist was you.'

'Hadn't Christopher told you that?' she asked, and when I shook my head, said in a low voice: 'That's so like him.'

'Is it?'

'Playing games with us all.' Even though she had kept her voice down, and Christopher Jarvis was still turned towards his god-daughter, I was anxious in case he heard us, so I made no comment.

The salmon had been served, and looked delicious. Having so signally failed with the artichoke soup, I was determined to try and eat at least some of it.

I'd no sooner got the first mouthful in when Edward Rintoul leaned across, chewing and swallowing before saying:

'So you like her work, do you?'

It irritated me that he'd not only been listening, but had no qualms about advertising the fact. But I was determined to be polite.

'Enormously,' I said.

'You know she's working on me at the moment?' he announced in a self-satisfied manner.

'Yes, you told me.' I couldn't resist it: 'I've seen.'

'That's more than I've been allowed to do,' he said grumpily. 'She showed you?'

'I had to take something up to Suzannah's room.' It seemed only polite, since we were discussing her so freely, to use the artist's name. I turned towards her as I said it, but she had joined in the conversation with Jarvis and Georgina and was paying no attention to us.

'I shan't ask any more,' he said. 'Suffice it to say that it wasn't my idea. She asked to paint me. Must have something to do with my noble bearing and god-like good looks.'

I smiled, and began to eat, keeping my eyes on my plate to discourage further conversation with Rintoul, and to avoid looking at John Ashe. I did not want to meet his eye, or draw attention to myself in any way. When I'd eaten a little less than half I put my knife and fork together and listened to Georgina, who was telling amusing stories about high jinks at her finishing school. Christopher Jarvis, who clearly adored her, laughed loud and long and even Suzannah smiled, widening her eyes incredulously. It was all very normal – Georgina was so youthful and lively. The phrase 'a breath of fresh air' had never seemed more apposite. I was quite content to be on the sidelines, an inconspicuous member of her audience.

But I had reckoned without Amanda's conscientiousness. With the arrival of the strawberries (handed round by Dorothy), Paul Marriott tapped my arm and indicated that our hostess wanted to say something to me. What with the heat and the company, her cheeks were pink and her eyes shining; I'd rarely seen her so animated. It was obvious John Ashe's appearance didn't dismay her in the least.

'Pamela, are you all right? Are you being looked after?'

'Yes, thank you,' I said. 'I'm having a wonderful time.'

'Of course she's all right,' put in Rintoul in his boorish way. 'She's seen my blasted portrait! I told her she was luckier than me.'

'Poor Edward!' laughed Amanda. 'You feel very much at a disadvantage, don't you?'

'I do,' he said petulantly. 'But I can't say I wasn't warned, so I've only myself to blame.'

John Ashe's eyes hadn't left my face during this exchange. Now he asked:

'Tell me, do you have far to come to work each day?'

It was a perfectly straightforward question of the party small-talk variety but, just as when he'd thanked me earlier, something in his tone made it seem startlingly personal.

'Not very,' I said. 'The bus journey's only half an hour, and I have a short walk either end.'

'Whereabouts do you live?'

For some reason I didn't want to tell him, but I could hardly say as much. 'Near the Tottenham Court Road.'

'The very heart of town.'

'I suppose so.'

'There's a nice restaurant near there,' said Marriott. 'Bernardino's – do you know it?'

'I'm afraid I don't.'

Ashe was still gazing at me. 'How do you spend your time, Mrs Griffe? When you're not working?'

'Poor girl!' laughed Amanda. 'What a question! Why should she tell you?'

'She doesn't have to,' he said mildly.

'There really isn't anything to tell,' I said. 'I live a quiet life.'

The moment I'd said this I wanted to take it back, to swallow the words that made me sound insufferably dreary. I thought of Matthew, and it was as though everything – those words, these people, this place – was a betrayal of him, and of our love. My eyes prickled ominously. Fortunately no one seemed to notice my predicament, and Ashe accepted my answer without comment.

'If you had one wish,' he said. 'What would it be?'

'May I have a moment to think about it?'

'By all means.' He inclined his head politely, but Amanda and Marriott laughed, as though I'd said something clever.

'Let's see . . .' said Amanda. '*My* wish would be for order – yes, order and serenity.'

'That's two,' pointed out Marriott.

'I'll allow it,' said Ashe. 'It's a composite single wish.'

'Either that,' went on Amanda, 'or for Pamela to stay here for ever.'

'Hear that?' Ashe gazed at me. 'How does it feel to have made yourself indispensable?'

'Humbling,' I said. 'And rather frightening.'

I saw Amanda's expression change to one of agonised apology, but as she began to reassure me Ashe cut across her.

'Why should it frighten you?'

This time I chose my words carefully. It was extremely important to me not to utter a single syllable that didn't convey exactly what I meant. 'Because no one wants to feel that they'd be doing harm by leaving a particular person or place.'

Marriott clapped his hands slowly. 'Very well put.'

'It was such a silly thing for me to say,' said Amanda.

'Not at all,' I said. 'It's only a game.'

'Have you had enough time to consider?' asked Ashe who, I was beginning to realise, never lost sight of his objective.

'Yes.'

'So what do you wish?'

'To know what I want,' I said. I was pleased with this answer, and it seemed to satisfy the others, too; particularly Ashe, who inclined his head again, this time in courtly acknowledgement. I was elated.

'Yes,' he said. 'Precisely. A person who knows what she wants will never waste energy on something she doesn't. And so is more likely to realise her wish.'

'Steady on,' said Rintoul, who'd been listening in as usual. 'Knowing what you want isn't the same as getting it.'

Ashe looked at him coldly and remained silent. Marriott said: 'But it's a great deal more sensible to ask for the wherewithal rather than the thing itself. Remember "The Monkey's Paw"?'

'Oh heavens, yes!' exclaimed Amanda Jarvis. 'I was absolutely petrified . . .' She put her hand to her throat and closed her eyes at the mere memory of it.

The conversation turned to plays, and having precious little to contribute I concentrated on my strawberries.

When lunch was over, I remained behind in the dining room to help with the clearing away. Both the Jarvises put up a token objection on the grounds that today I was a guest like everyone else, but they were sufficiently intuitive to realise that I might have my reasons for offering, and so gave in gracefully.

The afternoon had clouded over and it was cooler; Christopher Jarvis suggested that they might have coffee served in the garden.

'Edward and Paul can put the umbrella up,' he announced, 'under Amanda's supervision. And I'll fetch the very acceptable cognac I've been keeping for the occasion. Ladies, you know where to go . . .'

Georgina left the room first and could be heard going up the stairs two at a time. On her way out Suzannah paused next to me as I stacked the plates.

'I'm so glad we've got to know each other,' she said. 'I don't have many friends.'

I said, truthfully, that I was glad too. But for the life of me I couldn't make out whether she meant that she didn't know many people – hardly surprising, since she avoided company – or whether those she did know didn't like her, which would have been even more surprising. Most surprising of all was that she should count me among her friends after such a short acquaintance, most of it in company.

John Ashe was the last to go. Rintoul and Marriott were already struggling with the giant parasol out on the grass beyond the window. He studied one of the pictures on the wall and asked, without turning round: 'Will you be joining us?'

'I don't know. I'll give Dorothy a hand with these first.'

'This must have been a strange couple of hours for you.' He turned to me. 'An occasion at which you must have felt neither fish, flesh, fowl nor good herring.'

He meant no offence, and I took none. 'It was a bit like that,' I conceded. 'But I've enjoyed myself.'

'Well done,' he said. 'It was a pleasure meeting you.'

He went out as Dorothy came in. She dodged exaggeratedly out of his way as if he were a ten-ton lorry, and made a face as she pushed the door to after him.

'Old ugly mug!' she exclaimed in a rather too-carrying stage whisper which made me wince. 'It's horrible, why doesn't he cover it up?'

It was then I realised that for the past half an hour and more I had scarcely noticed John Ashe's disfigurement.

The afternoon grew darker and darker. By the time we had cleared away the lunch things and tidied the dining room, the temperature had dropped and a scudding breeze had got up, nosing at the doors and windows and churning the branches of the trees. Suzannah came indoors and went up to her room, and Marriott went home, but the rest remained in the garden beneath the umbrella, which shivered and bellied in the wind.

I congratulated Chef, who accepted my compliments laconically.

'There's a lot left over.'

'It's the heat, it affects people's appetites,' I said.

Dorothy undid her pinny. 'That and having to look at Mr Gruesome Gob. It's enough to put anyone off their food.'

'I found it hard to begin with,' I admitted. 'But I found I got used to it.'

She shuddered. 'Anyway, Chef, you ought to be glad there's leftovers, less work for you tomorrow, eh?'

Shortly after that the two of them left. I wanted to go myself, but knew it would be rude to do so without making my farewells and thanking the Jarvises. The storm that had been stalking Highgate Hill for the past hour was very close now, snarling and flashing, though there wasn't yet any rain. Like seamen in the age of sail we fought to get the umbrella down again and ran back into the house as the first drops began to fall. Rintoul was despatched to hail a cab for Georgina, and she asked me if I'd like to share.

'I'm meeting some friends at the Cadogan,' she said. 'It's off Piccadilly, is that any good to you?'

I asked if she would drop me off at Heal and Son in the Tottenham Court Road, and when the cab arrived we prepared to leave together. Rintoul went upstairs to sleep it off, but John Ashe appeared to be staying for a while. He stood in the drawing-room doorway to say goodbye.

'We'll meet again,' he said, shaking my hand. 'I'm a pretty regular visitor here.'

Georgina kissed his good cheek. ''Bye, Uncle Ashe.'

During our taxi ride the rain came down in torrents, surrounding us with a hissing curtain of water, riven by shudders of thunder. Georgina's high spirits were undimmed.

'Wasn't that fun? Their parties are always such good value.'

'Did you know everyone there?' I asked.

'Not Paul whatsisname . . . or you. But everyone else. Ashe isn't really my uncle, by the way. He and Uncle Chris are great chums and Aunt Amanda adores him, but no one's related. It's just that I know him too well to call him Mr Ashe, but John would be too familiar.'

She was such a voluble, straightforward girl that I asked her directly: 'How did he get those terrible injuries?'

'Oh, in the war, like everyone . . .' She waved a dismissive hand. 'He was out east with Uncle Chris.' She glanced at me. 'Did you find it frightfully off-putting? I forget – I'm so used to it I don't notice it any more.'

'I found the same.'

'In fact –' she leaned towards me with a wicked, confidential grin – 'I think he's rather attractive.'

When we reached the Tottenham Court Road it transpired that Christopher Jarvis had given her the taxi fare, but I absolutely insisted on paying my share.

The next morning I woke refreshed for the first time in a fortnight. It had stopped raining and the window admitted a cool, watery sunlight. The sky was patchy with high cloud. There were puddles on the pavement and the gutters ran with water. Even the sound in the streets was different – brighter, sharper, more resonant, as if a thick dust had been cleared away.

I got up early and arrived at Crompton Terrace at nine o'clock prompt. I felt invigorated, both by the change in the weather and the fact that the long-awaited lunch party was over. It had been a trial, yet I had not only survived but enjoyed a good deal of it, and even emerged with some credit.

But the storm which had cleared the air so wonderfully had exacted casualties. The last baby swallow lay on the floor of the porch, bedraggled and dead. And not just dead but crushed, flattened as though a heavy boot had trodden it underfoot. Very gently I collected a handful of leaves and moved it to the shelter of the periwinkles which romped around the edge of the front garden.

Chapter Eight

'Your mother's not well, Pammie,' said my father. He was speaking on the public telephone, but I could hear the fear right through the loud, stilted voice he was using. 'Can you come?'

I realised as I replaced the receiver that I'd been guilty of thinking my parents indestructible. As far as I could recall they'd neither of them had a day's illness. They were always there, always the same, as sturdy and immutable as a pair of standing stones. Since Matthew's death I'd grown steadily away from them, so that our relationship was reduced to one largely composed of duty, tinged with a slightly wary affection. For my part, I'd taken them for granted.

Now, the fear I'd heard in my father's voice shot through my selfish independence like lightning. My parents were not indestructible. They were elderly, and shaken, and needed my help.

It was a Friday night when he called, so at least I did not have to get in touch with the Jarvises; or not yet, anyway, I had the weekend to take stock of the situation. Once I got over the shock I rallied a little. After all, a couple with such strong constitutions, who had always enjoyed good health, were bound to be thrown by illness. Very probably it was nothing, a routine complaint of some sort. And if it made us all more aware of our situation, that could only be to the good.

Dad had been very insistent I come right away. 'She'd like

to see you, have another woman about the place,' is what he'd said, but I was pretty sure it was he who wanted me there. I put some things in the scarcely used small suitcase I'd bought to go on honeymoon and set off. There was a flower stall on the corner of the road near the bus stop; the man was packing up for the day but I bought a bunch of pink and blue stocks, scented country garden flowers for my city-bred mother.

I used the journey across London to try and adjust my frame of mind. It was so hard, these days, to clear it of Crompton Terrace, its occupants and atmosphere, and to focus on anything else. Going home was like travelling to a foreign country: one I had visited in the past, but which was no longer familiar. I had to remind myself of the country's language, landmarks and customs, and also of my place in it, and how the natives would receive me. To them I was Pammie, the daughter they loved but had never fully understood: first the tomboy whose company my father had enjoyed; then the brainy grammar-school pupil; then – for an eye-blink – Matthew's bride; then the stoical young widow they didn't know how to treat; and finally, over recent years, the rather daunting career-girl who mixed (especially now) with the kind of people they could scarcely imagine, and whom they regarded with the gravest suspicion.

As I drew closer to my destination I hoped and prayed that I was right, and my mother's illness wasn't serious. 'Burning up' was how my father had put it – burning up and 'making no sense'. The doctor had seen her and prescribed aspirins, fluids and bedrest but she was no better, Dad said. Perhaps the fever would have broken and she would have turned the corner by the time I got there . . . I knew my prayers for Mum's welfare were essentially selfish because I couldn't bear the prospect of disruption to my new life. That was where all my energy and interest lay; I didn't have *time* for a domestic crisis.

I rebuked myself for my callousness as I walked up the road. This was a Friday evening; there were no other calls on my time between now and Monday morning – more than two clear days. I must – I *must* – devote myself to whatever needed doing here, and with luck it would all be over and dealt with by then.

The door opened as I approached, and there was my father. He looked ten years older than when I'd last seen him – smaller, stooped, disarrayed and altogether less sure of himself: a man whose certainties had been swept away. His cheekbones were flushed with spots of pink, like clown's make-up on his haggard face.

'Hello, Dad.' I kissed him, but he was too distracted to respond. By the time I stepped back he had already closed the door.

'She's upstairs,' he said.

I put my little case down in the hall, a hostage to fortune, and climbed the narrow stairs like an *aristo* ascending to the guillotine. My father followed, but not closely. Everything in his manner said that as of this moment he had handed over to me.

On the landing another realisation hit me. I had not been inside my parents' bedroom since I was a child. I raised my hand to tap on the door, but my father said: 'Go on in, she won't know the difference.'

The first thing I noticed was the unaired, slightly sour smell of sickness. On this fine evening the window was tight shut. A fine haze of dust lay on everything, not more than two days' worth, so little as to be negligible in most places but like an awful warning in this usually spotless house. Everything else was the same – the Scottish landscapes hanging from the picture rail against the trellis-patterned wallpaper; the glass-topped dressing table with its oval mirror; the fancy empty scent bottle which was only for show, and the ivory-backed hairbrush which had belonged to my maternal grandmother, and with which I'd occasionally been threatened (but never struck) as a child. There was the heavy dark wardrobe, too big for the room, and the square rug in a shade of speckled pink that matched that of the shiny eiderdowns. Between the beds was a cheap cupboard like a hospital locker, scarcely more than a plywood box, on which stood a brass lamp with a pink pleated shade, my mother's spectacles, and a glass of orange squash. There seemed to be dust floating on the orange squash as well.

My mother's bed was nearest the door. She lay on her back, with her head to one side, her hands on the eiderdown curled into loose fists. Her face bore a sheen of sweat. Beneath her open mouth the pillow was slightly damp. I could hear the ragged whisper of her breathing. She wore a sprigged cotton nightdress; her hair was in its thick, loose night-time plait. Normally rather a formidable woman, at this moment she looked like an odd, elderly child.

'You see?' said my father from the doorway.

'At least she's sleeping peacefully.'

He wagged an impatient finger towards my mother. 'You feel her.'

His restless, slightly accusing presence was getting on my nerves. 'Look, Dad,' I said, 'why don't you make us both a cup of tea—'

'She won't touch it.'

'I meant for you and me.'

'If you like.' He was still looking past me, his eyes fixed anxiously on his wife's face.

'I do. I'm gasping, Dad.'

'All right, all right, I'm going . . .' He trudged off down the stairs.

I went to the window and opened it a few inches at the top. This part of south London was flat, and I fought down a real sense of claustrophobia at the unending vista of roofs. My mother made a little sound, opening and closing her mouth as if tasting something. I jumped, and then sat down on the edge of the bed and took her hand, another thing I hadn't done since I was little. In spite of all the housework, she took a pride in her hands and the skin felt smooth, but it was hot, and the palm was sweaty. Her wedding ring had become rather tight and didn't look as if it would come off. Thinking it might be uncomfortable, I tried to loosen it, twisting it gently back and forth.

'Hello, Pam.'

She was looking at me. With her eyes open, the childishness was banished, and it was a relief to feel the familiar, penetrating stare. I at once released her hand.

'Mum – how are you feeling?'

'What are you doing here?'

'I came to see you.'

'Did your father ask you to?'

'No,' I lied. 'He mentioned you were poorly and I wanted to come.'

She tried unsuccessfully to raise her head and look out of the door. 'Where is he?'

'Making me a cup of tea. Would you like one?'

She shook her head, eyes closed and lips pursed at the very thought. 'No thanks. I can't take anything at the moment.'

'Do you feel sick?'

'Not sick, but not keen, if you know what I mean. Not at all keen.'

'You should drink, though,' I said. 'Shall I get you some fresh squash?'

'Water'll do. I'll try that.'

I heard my father's footsteps on the stairs as I took her

glass to the bathroom. When I returned he'd put the familiar lacquered tea tray, with its picture of the King and Queen, on the dressing table. He had moved the padded stool to one side and was sitting on it at a safe distance from my mother; he looked as uncomfortable as a circus elephant perched on an upturned bucket. He waved a hand at the tray.

'You be mother for now.'

I put the glass of water on the bedside table. When I'd poured us both a cup, I took mine and went to sit on my father's bed.

'Would you like some help with that?' I asked her.

'No, no, I'll get round to it . . .' Her tone was snappish, but her eyes closed once more as she spoke. I was beginning to understand my father's consternation: there was something fundamentally *wrong* in her debility. This was not how his wife, my mother, was supposed to be. It was as if we'd fallen victim to some cruel trick.

Her lips parted and I could hear that whispering breath again.

I tried to keep my voice light. 'Did the doctor say he was going to drop by again?'

'Tomorrow. Unless—' He stopped, twitching his shoulders as if shaking off the unwelcome thought. 'Unless we need him before that.'

'What did he think the matter was?'

'He couldn't say. Some infection. Thought it might be to do with her waterworks, but she hasn't gone in ages.'

'Perhaps that's it . . .' I recollected something about kidneys getting silted up, which had always sounded horrible. 'I think we ought to see to it that she drinks plenty of water.'

He shrugged helplessly. 'You try then.'

'Next time she wakes up.'

The evening seemed interminable. My mother dozed, my father fretted. Because I was anxious now myself, I found his agitation even more irritating. I made us corned beef, potatoes and carrots but we neither of us did much justice to it. When we'd washed up the supper things I went back upstairs, suggesting that he sit down and read the paper, at least try to relax. He put up a show of reluctance, but did as he was told.

My mother's eyes were open when I went in, trained on the door for my arrival.

'What've you two been up to?'

'I made us some supper. Not up to your standards, I'm afraid. Dad did eat some,' I added, before she could ask. She stared at me. I couldn't make out whether the stare was one of disbelief, or because she hadn't been listening and was planning her next sally. Either way I wanted her to stop, so I asked:

'Would you like something now, Mum? I could make you a little sandwich with the crusts off—'

'I will do, I will do,' she said, but her tone said not to bother her with it.

I glanced at her glass of water. 'You ought to drink. Do you need some help to sit up? I could—'

'Pam.'

Her voice wasn't loud, but she had summoned all her authority to stop me in my tracks.

'Yes?'

'How is he?'

'Dad?' I was so relieved I almost laughed. 'He's fine, Mum. Really. But he's worried, and he's lost without you. He'll be back to his old self once you're feeling better. So we must look after you and—'

'I need to go.'

'Now?' I asked stupidly.

'Give me a hand. Quick. I need to go.'

With a tremendous effort she got her head and shoulders

off the pillow, propped herself on her elbow and tried feebly to kick the bedclothes back. Belatedly galvanised into action I helped her, removing the bedclothes and pulling down the skirt of her nightdress, more for my benefit than hers because I didn't want to see anything I shouldn't. Her legs were smooth and white but very thin, with no shape at all – two straight sticks, and her feet (of which, like her hands, she had always been proud) were small and narrow.

Supporting her with one arm, I reached with the other hand under the bed for her slippers. As I did so I caught sight of a chamber pot, decorated with bluebirds – a welcome sight, since there was no upstairs lavatory.

'Mum, the po's here.'

'I want to go down.'

'But it's right here, and if you're—'

'Stop all that and give me a hand.'

She was tall, the same height as me even when she was barefoot and I was in shoes with a small heel. Though she kept her head up she leaned heavily on me; the end of her long plait tickled my arm, and her skin was hot to the touch. Her breathing rustled stertorously and the small puffs of air coming from her mouth smelt sour. As we hobbled to the top of the stairs my father appeared at the bottom. His hair was on end and one side of his face was red. He'd been asleep.

'What's going on? What's she doing out of bed?'

'We're going to the lav,' I said.

'There's a thingummy under the bed.'

'I know that!' I said, at the same time as my mother snapped: 'I'm coming down, thank you!'

'All right, all right . . .' He waved his hands, thoroughly moithered. 'Do you need help?'

'No thanks, Dad – well, you could go and make sure the doors are open.'

'I'll do that.'

He disappeared and we descended the stairs, very slowly, my mother getting both feet on to a step before attempting the next one. She was a fit, upright, vigorous woman as a rule and it was dreadful to see her so weak. She also seemed to be in pain, giving the occasional little grunt. I wished I'd been more insistent on staying upstairs – I'd been an obedient rather than a responsible daughter – but now that we were committed to this *via dolorosa* I determined at the very least to call the doctor when she was back in bed.

When we finally reached the bottom she was gasping for breath. My father was hovering nervously by the door of the front room. He took a hesitant step towards us, but my mother, determined to keep him at arm's length, flapped a hand and actually managed to say, quite forcefully:

'No, Gerald . . . No!'

His devastation at this rejection would have been comic if it hadn't been so maddeningly pathetic. They were a pair, I thought, both helpless and equally difficult to help. And here I was, stuck in the middle . . .

The privy was in a lean-to by the back door, absolutely freezing in winter, but thank heavens it was a fine warm evening. My father had thrown every door wide, and taken the precaution of propping the privy door open with a brick. I was quite certain that no matter what her condition my mother would want the door closed, preferably with me on the far side of it.

However, I was spared that decision because when we were halfway across the kitchen she doubled over with a high-pitched howl of extreme pain, followed by a spattering sound as her bladder voided itself on the tiles. I heard my father wailing, 'Oh God, what now? God in heaven, what's going on, what's she doing?' I ignored him till I'd lowered my mother, still moaning, on to a chair, where she folded over like a rag doll; then I spoke loudly and fiercely.

'Dad, listen!' He blinked. His eyes, taking in the large, sour-smelling puddle on the floor, were 'O's of horror.

'Dad!'

'What?'

'Go and call the doctor. Now.'

'But what's happening, what shall I say?'

'You can see what's happening! Mum's had an accident. But she's got a pain at the same time, and he needs to look at her.'

'What if he can't come?'

'He'll come as soon as he can. Dad – go. Please!'

At last, he went.

'Don't forget money!' I called after him. He didn't reply, but patted his jacket pockets absent-mindedly. His legs were wobbly as a drunk's as he headed for the front door.

When the door had closed behind him, I pulled another chair alongside Mother's and sat down with my arm across her shoulders. She was shuddering slightly, which I took to be either pain, or fever, but when she lifted her head I saw that she'd been crying. Was there to be no end to the shocks?

'I'm sorry,' she said. 'I'm so sorry, Pam, look at this mess, it's disgusting . . .' She shook her head and covered her face with her hands. Where her nightie was wet it was also stained with blood. And flecks of blood, microscopic clots, floated in the urine on the floor. My head swam. No matter how much it bothered her, the mess could wait. My first responsibility was to look after my mother.

'There's nothing disgusting about it,' I said.

'But you've got to – got to –' she could barely force the words out – 'clear it up.'

'It won't take a moment, and anyway I don't mind. Think of all the times you did it for me when I was little.' I pressed on before she could upset herself further. 'Now then, Mum, the doctor's coming. Before we get you back up to bed, do you need to go again?' She shook her head. 'And do you promise that if you do, you'll use the po?'

'I suppose I'll have to.'

'It would be best.'

'What about all this?' She plucked at her nightie with her finger and thumb. 'I can't see the doctor like this.'

'Don't worry, we'll get you changed and clean.' I patted her shoulder awkwardly. I was shamefully uncomfortable in my role as nurse. The thought of seeing my mother naked appalled me. 'Does it still hurt?' I asked.

'No. But when it starts to come—' Her mouth clamped in a thin line at the memory. 'It was like a knife.'

'Do you think you can manage the stairs? We could go into the front room – draw the curtains—'

'I can manage.'

I helped her to her feet. She felt cold and clammy now, and looked pale. It took us a long time, and my father returned as we were halfway up.

'How is she?' he asked.

'The cat's mother . . .' she muttered. 'How do you think?' She could often be curt, but never rude. There was no dealing with them. None of the old rules and customs applied.

'Doctor's coming,' he told me. 'He'll be about half an hour.'

He stepped on the first stair and stood there looking up at us. His face was red. If my hands had been free and there'd been a bucket of cold water to hand I'd have thrown it over him.

I had a brainwave. 'Dad – Mum needs to change her nightie. When we're ready, would you do that? You know where everything is.' I saw the panic on his face and hastened to outline the alternative. 'While you do that, I can be cleaning up downstairs.'

'Right you are,' he said humbly.

*　　*　　*

Dr Mayes was young and hard-pressed but calm and respectful, too. That, and the fact of having a person of authority in the house, meant that for a while my father regained a good deal of his old poise. Mayes spent a quarter of an hour with my mother, and then came downstairs to talk to us.

'Has she had a fall, Mr Streeter? Mrs Griffe?' he asked.

I said not that I knew of. My father shook his head. 'She's not doddery you know. She's not long turned sixty. A few years younger than me. I was sixty-seven in February,' he added in case Mayes had missed the point. 'And fighting fit.'

'You certainly look it. And I wasn't implying for a moment that your wife was infirm, she's a fine strong woman, but I believe she may have sustained bruising to the kidneys.'

'Does my wife say she fell over?'

'Not in so many words, no.' The doctor's air of quiet authority was nibbled by tiredness. He pushed his fingers through his hair. 'But you never know—'

'Then she didn't.'

'I'm not suggesting that she lied, Mr Streeter. Simply that she's proud. Anyway, it's pretty clear there's some sort of damage in that area.'

Deflated, my father sat down. 'Is that bad?'

'It is for her – as you've seen. From what both you and she have told me, Mrs Griffe, she's passing a small amount of clotted blood, and that's immensely painful. In fact, I suspect she's been in more pain over the last thirty-six hours than she's let on. Proud again, you see.' He directed an encouraging smile at my father.

'So what can you do for her?' I asked. 'Should she go into hospital?'

A look of absolute terror came over my father's face at this suggestion. Mayes understandably turned away from it, and towards me. 'Not necessarily. I don't believe the injury is serious – she was able to walk, and so on – and the bleeding will, quite literally, pass. I've given her something for the pain, and I shall leave some more with you to give her if the going gets tough during the night.'

'What do you mean?' asked my father, who was now white as a sheet.

'I mean that she probably will have more pain, particularly when she passes water. It's essential she drinks plenty. She may have been avoiding drinking because she's worried about the consequences, but I can't emphasise too strongly that that's counter-productive. The more liquid she takes, the more rapidly and easily everything will be resolved.'

'It's hard to get her to do what she doesn't want to, Doctor,' said my father. 'Phyllis is a stubborn woman.'

'But Dad,' I intervened, 'she's not stupid, either. We have to talk her into it.'

'Better you than me . . .'

'Between the two of us.'

'That's the spirit.' Mayes sat down and opened his bag. 'Now I'll leave you with a small amount of the medicine, and a prescription for you to take to the chemist tomorrow – there's a pharmacy open at this address . . .'

While he wrote the prescription my father went and stared out of the window with his hands in his pockets. Mayes put the piece of paper on the side table next to him, with a small bottle on top of it.

'There you are. I'll call again tomorrow morning.' He closed his bag and stood up. 'If she's no better we'll consider what to do.'

'You're going then,' said my father.

'I'm afraid so. Twins on the way in Ethelred Road.'

'You mustn't miss that whatever you do.' I knew it was

fear that was making my father sarcastic, but poor Mayes didn't deserve it. I smiled and accompanied him to the front door.

'You mustn't mind him, Doctor,' I said quietly. 'It's not like Dad to be rude, he's worried to death.'

'Don't worry, Mrs Griffe, I understand. It's a very common reaction and I'm used to it. You look after your mother and I'll see you soon.'

When I went back into the front room my father had picked up the medicine bottle and was staring at the label at close range, his glasses pushed up on to his head. I felt suddenly exhausted.

'Dad, I think I'll go to bed.'

'But Pammie.' He put the bottle down and lowered his glasses. 'What about your mother?'

'I'll pop in and see her first. And we'll be much more use to her if we're upstairs. Will you lock up?' There was no response, so I said, 'Remember to take the medicine up with you, and a spoon.'

I tried not to feel cruel as I left him standing there like a lost dog in the front room. There was nothing the matter with him. He was a grown man whose wife was ill. He had a responsibility towards her. I told myself that however wretched he felt it was only right he should discharge that responsibility, and he'd never forgive himself afterwards if he had not done so.

This was how I justified my retreat to the tiny second bedroom I'd occupied as a child. There was a third bedroom, a holy of holies called 'the guest room', but it was never used, and I would not have dreamed of doing so now. As far back as I could remember its pristine chenille bedspread, rag rugs and twin pink towels had been disturbed by no human hand but my mother's.

My narrow bed was crisply made up as always, with a

lavender bag on the pillow. On the table under the window stood a square mirror on a stand and a matching china vase and dish. There was a white-painted chest of drawers and two double hooks on the back of the door. I opened my case, put my nightie and book on the bed, my wash things and brush and comb on the table, and my dressing gown on one of the hooks.

Then I went in to see my mother. As I crossed the landing I could hear my father rattling bolts downstairs.

'Mum? How are you feeling?'

Her eyes were closed, but she hadn't been asleep, because as soon as she heard me she opened them and answered distinctly.

'Better since the doctor came. He gave me something.'

'Good.' I sat down on the side of the bed. 'He's left us some of that medicine, so you can take it if you need to during the night. And Mum, you have to drink.'

'I know, I know,' she said impatiently, but this time, with Dr Mayes' authority, I was disposed to be firm.

'Really, you must. Why don't you drink up the water that's there, and I'll fetch you another glass.'

'I don't want it, Pammie.'

Here we go, I thought. The last thing I wanted was a battle with my mother, but after my spirited words downstairs I was determined to stick to my last.

'Think of it as medicine,' I said. 'You may not want it, but it'll do you good.'

Her mouth tightened sceptically. 'So you say.'

'Not me, the doctor. Water's the most important thing.' I decided to take the unprecedented step of understanding her. 'I *know* you don't want to have to go – I know it's painful and horrible, but that's what will make you better.'

Her mouth pursed even more, and she turned her head

away. For one awful moment I thought I'd overstepped the mark, but then she turned back and hoisted herself on to her elbow.

'Give me a hand, then.'

As I filled the glass in the bathroom, my father came up the stairs. I heard him say my name in a loud whisper.

Irritated, I turned and replied in a normal voice: 'What is it?'

He beckoned furiously.

'What?'

'I want a word!' he mouthed.

'Wait a minute, then.' I took the glass in to my mother and put it on the bedside table. 'I'll be next door if you want me,' I told her. She nodded.

'I took a silly tumble,' she muttered. 'But he's not to know, he'd fuss.'

When I came out, my father had retreated to the hall, and I had no alternative but to join him.

'Dad, what is it, we're both tired—'

'Will you sleep in there?'

'I beg your pardon?'

'Ssh!' Frowning at me to keep my voice down, he backed into the unlit front room. 'You're good with her, you know what to do, she'd much rather you were close by. Another woman and so on.'

'Dad!' I didn't even try to conceal my anger. 'You're her husband, you should be there. You're the one she's used to, the one she—' I hesitated and then said it – 'the one she loves.' He grumbled sheepishly. 'You are!'

'She loves you too.' It was odd the way we were using that word as a weapon.

'Of course, but she'll want *you*.' Although by no means sure this was right, I was determined not to let my father duck his responsibilities. 'If everything stays the same,' I went on, 'it'll be a comfort to her. What's she going to think if you move into another room?'

He was considering his answer when there came a scream from upstairs and I flew back up, two at a time.

We had been deluding ourselves to imagine we would get any sleep. When I look back on that night it is as a vision of hell. My mother's pain, my father's panic, my own clumsiness, the unaccustomed mess and noise – it was as if devils had been let loose in that usually spotless and orderly house.

All night long, my mother was in agony. She groaned and gasped, and couldn't keep still. Sometimes she walked about, her arms clutched over her abdomen; sometimes she kneeled up on the bed, grasping the headrail. Occasionally she stood leaning with one hand on the dressing table, the other arm wrapped round her waist, swaying and moaning. She baulked at the medicine, but drank water like a woman taking poison; I was shocked by her suffering and lost in admiration for her dogged courage. She passed urine flecked with blood three times, each time agonisingly; the third time the blood was less noticeable; the time after that it was almost clear. At five o'clock, with a summer's morning already lighting up the curtains, she climbed into bed and fell asleep, looking more dead than alive.

My father was sitting on the chair on the landing. He must have been exhausted, but he sat bolt upright, rigid with misery, his face even whiter than hers. From time to time I'd given him the pot to empty, covered with a hand-towel to spare him the worst of it. Other than that there'd been precious little he, or either of us, could do, and he had been unable to bring himself so much as to cross the threshold of the bedroom.

The sudden silence must have petrified him. Without

getting up, he tried to peer past me through the half-open door.

'What's up?'

'She's asleep.'

'How is she?'

'I think she may be over the worst of it. But the doctor's coming again later. He'll know.'

'Thank God!' He seemed to collapse, as if there had been a stick up his back and it had been suddenly removed.

'I'm going to bed,' I said. 'In there, with Mum, don't worry. I'll get my things. And you ought to sleep as well, Dad, while you can.'

'Yes, you're right. Quite right.' He hauled himself to his feet. I dreaded what he was going to say next, but there was no escape.

'Pammie – thank you. You've been a tower of strength and I've – well – I've not been.' There were tears in his eyes. 'I'm ashamed of myself.'

'Don't be, Dad. I understand. Get some sleep, and you'll be right as rain when she wakes up.'

'Very well . . . all right . . . I just wanted you to know.'

I went over to him and kissed his cheek as if he were a child. Although it was morning, I said: ''Night, Dad.'

'Night-night.'

I forgot all about my things in the small bedroom. I just took off my shoes, skirt and blouse and got into Dad's bed. The pillow smelt faintly of the stuff he put on his hair, but the sheets were smooth and fresh. All I could see of my mother was the top half of her face, and one hand holding the edge of the bedclothes. There was no pleasurable drifting off. Sleep hit me like a sledgehammer, bringing instant unconsciousness.

The sound of the door knocker woke me. I experienced a

moment's wild disorientation, with no idea of where I was, or why, or what the time was. My mouth felt dry and my eyes itchy.

I scrambled out of bed and pulled on my outer clothes. To my relief, my mother made a little sound in her sleep and rolled her head on the pillow, but didn't wake. I ran down the stairs and opened the door.

Dr Mayes looked even more weary and rumpled than I felt.

'Good morning. How's the patient?'

'Asleep.'

'And the night?'

'Terrible.'

'I'm so sorry, for her and for all of you. But you coped.'

'We did.'

'Congratulations. It can't have been easy.' Catching sight of himself in the hall mirror he grimaced, straightened his tie and flattened his hair with his palms. 'I'd have been here sooner, but the second twin took her time.'

I'd forgotten that while in this house we'd occasionally felt close to death, he'd been ushering in new life. 'How are they?'

'Mother and babies all doing well. But she's done it five times before, which is more than I have.'

'You're new to the job?'

'Six months. But don't worry,' he added hastily. 'I'm pretty confident of this diagnosis.'

'We have perfect faith in you,' I assured him. 'She's suffered horribly in the last few hours, but it all went as you predicted, and she does seem better.'

'I'm so glad.'

'And you had no need to apologise for being late – your knock on the door woke me up!'

'Good – well, actually no, that isn't quite what I meant.' We both laughed. It felt good to do that, and I relaxed for the first time in over twelve hours.

'Look,' I said, 'would you like a cup of tea? My parents are both asleep and I certainly want one.'

'I can't tell you how welcome that would be.'

He followed me into the kitchen although my mother would have been appalled at a guest, especially a doctor, seeing her private domain, and sat at the table while I made tea and toast. Because he was a medical man and unlikely to be put off his breakfast, I described the events of the night in more detail, and he nodded in satisfaction.

'That's what I hoped. She may have a little more discomfort, but nothing to what she's been through. She needs to keep on with the fluids, though.'

'She was very good about that,' I said. 'It was the medicine she wouldn't take.'

He looked aghast. 'You're telling me she had no pain relief?'

'She refused. There was nothing I could do.'

'Of course not . . .' He shook his head in amazement. 'They're made of stern stuff, that generation.' This seemed to remind him of something: 'How about your father, how's he?'

I smiled. 'Recovering. At a rather slower rate than her, I suspect.'

'Poor man, I do feel for him,' said Mayes with obvious sincerity. 'These things are almost as bad for those who have to stand by and watch.'

I almost said something caustic about that being just about all he *had* done, but stopped in time. This was to protect myself more than my father: Mayes was so nice, and honourable, and I didn't want to appear in a bad light.

'Right,' he said, putting his cup down. 'Shall we?'

I went into my mother's room first and woke her gently as I knew she'd hate to be caught asleep with her mouth open. Even so she was flustered, and we took a minute to plump her pillows and pin back the front of her hair. Then I showed in the doctor and left them to it.

The door of the small bedroom was ajar, and I put my head round. The curtains were still drawn, and in the half-light Dad's hunched form bulked large in the childish bed. His clothes, neatly folded, were laid over the back of the chair, socks on top; his shoes sat side by side beneath it. He was well trained; Mum would have been proud of him. I smiled fondly, remorseful over my own intolerance. When he woke, I would make a special effort, even spoil him a little if I could.

After a few minutes, Dr Mayes emerged. He pronounced himself pleased with my mother, and he himself looked a lot better than when he'd arrived. This was probably the result of his correct diagnosis and the improvement in his patient, but I liked to think it was due to the tea, toast and company, too.

'How long are you able to stay?' he asked.

I thought quickly. 'Until tomorrow night, anyway.'

'That's good. You've managed so well, and you obviously have a calming influence.' If I blushed he didn't notice, and went on: 'Is your father still asleep? Only I may not be back till Monday and I think I should have a word with him before I go.'

'He'll want to thank you, too,' I said. 'Go on in.'

I had no qualms about letting him in first – in fact I was pretty sure my father would react rather better to being woken by the doctor than by me. I followed Mayes in and drew back the curtains.

He touched my father's shoulder. 'Mr Streeter?'

There was no response. He put down his bag, and touched the shoulder again, this time giving it a little shake.

I laughed. 'I'm afraid he's out for the count.'

Mayes felt with his other hand for my father's wrist. The smallest movement, like the stirring of a mouse. But it carried with it an implication so dreadful that I turned cold and faint.

He straightened up slowly. Gently, he pulled the dis-arranged sheet over my father's shoulder, straightening and smoothing it as he did so. Only then did he look at me.

'Mrs Griffe,' he said. 'I'm so very, very sorry.'

Chapter Nine

If I'd thought the night of my mother's illness was hell, I was
wrong. That, I now saw, had been purgatory: horrible, but
uncertain – a time of waiting. The day of my father's death,
was hell. Not only had the worst happened, but it was a worst
for which none of us were remotely prepared: a thunderbolt.
And hard on the heels of shock slithered the crippling realisation that my mother's life and mine would never be the
same.

It was hard to say whether it was worse for her, whose life
had scarcely altered in decades, or for me, who had only
recently tasted the heady wine of change and from whose
lips the cup might now be dashed. I tried, oh how I tried,
not to see my parents' tragedy in terms of my own welfare,
but the unwelcome and unworthy thoughts kept butting in,
adding guilt to unhappiness.

Thank heavens for Dr Mayes. He may have been young,
and new to the job, but his instincts were impeccable. While
I broke the news to my mother he went downstairs, out of
earshot and filled in the death certificate, describing the cause
of death discreetly, not as 'despair' or 'shame', but simply:
'heart failure'.

Seeing my mother's face when I told her of her husband's
death was like watching something die all over again.
Disbelief, horror and distress bloomed and were stifled in a
second, reabsorbed to be dealt with privately. I held her hand,
but it was heavy and inert; what little energy she had was

not for me. Too late I understood my father's earlier sense of helplessness. Only last night, a few hours ago, he had been here. I had snapped at him and ignored him, and seen him as a nuisance – and now he was gone. And at some point while the sun rose on his self-imposed banishment, his heart, worn out with worry and fear, had simply stopped beating. It had failed him, as mine failed me now. I couldn't, wouldn't, comprehend the finality of it: that his life, and his part in ours, was finished.

My mother and I had both been lost in our own thoughts. Now she retrieved her hand from mine, as though I had had it long enough.

'Where is he?'

'Next door. In my bed. He's very peaceful, Mum.'

'I should go and see him.'

It was a statement, but a fearful one: there was a question in her voice as well. I sensed and understood her ambivalence.

'Then do, if you'd like to,' I said. 'But for your own sake, Mum – it won't matter to Dad, he knew how much you cared about him.'

For once it seemed I had said the right thing. Something in her gave a little and her face softened.

'I think I will,' she said.

I helped her out of bed, and took her arm for the few painful steps between the room she had shared for so long with my father, and the childish one for which – and in which – he had left her. I glimpsed Dr Mayes down in the hall but he saw what we were about, and withdrew once more into the front room.

'Don't go,' my mother said to me. 'Don't leave us.'

I stood in the doorway, but I couldn't bear to watch, or to listen. I turned away and bowed my head, with my hands over my ears. Worse than the prospect of witnessing any intense emotion was that of witnessing none at all. My mother's feelings for her husband had been buried so deep and for so long that she might not be able to bring them to the surface even now. And why should she? No one, least of all my mother, could emote to order. But I did not want to see – or for her to think I had seen – what she might consider a failure on her part.

The seconds crawled by.

'All done.' She touched my arm. 'It's all right, Pammie. He's all right now.' She used his name for me, as though with his death it had passed from him to her.

By the time she was back in bed she was breathing heavily, and trembling a little. I made her drink some more water, and asked if she'd like something to eat.

'Maybe I should,' she said. I smoothed the bedding and lined up her slippers – anything to avoid looking at her as she struggled with herself, and her guilt about eating when her husband lay dead.

'Perhaps a honey sandwich.'

'With the crusts off,' I promised.

'Is Doctor still here?'

'He's downstairs.'

'What does he say? About your father?'

I realised that I didn't know. 'Would you like to talk to him again?'

'Not today.' Her voice had been steady, but now it began to quake: 'Maybe you could ask him – how long – when will they take him away?'

'Don't worry, Mum,' I said. 'I'll find out.'

Dr Mayes had contacted the local undertakers on our behalf.

'They're a very sound firm,' he said. 'None better to look after your parents.'

It was nice to hear them called that – a couple, together

still – and for the first time I thought I might burst into tears. Perhaps noticing this, he continued gently: 'When they come, Mr McEvoy will speak to you about arrangements. Remember they're experts, you won't have many decisions to make. Except – well – budget, obviously.'

'We've got the money for it,' I said, sounding sharp because I was trying not to cry.

'Of course. Other than that, be sure to look after yourself, and your mother. If you'd like something to help you sleep . . .'

'No thank you. We'll be fine.'

He closed his bag and snapped the clasp. 'I'm sure you will, but let me know if you change your mind. She'll want to be up and about soon, but keep her there till tomorrow if you can. I'll call again.' He held out his hand and I shook it. 'Goodbye for now.'

McEvoy and Sons came to collect my father at eleven o'clock that morning. My mother kept her door closed; she had said her goodbyes. They were the soul of professional tact and kindness, but I was still glad that she could not see the shrouded stretcher being manoeuvred down the stairs and nearly coming to grief when next door's cat ran across the front step, nor the small crowd of neighbours and passers-by assembled in the street to watch it being loaded into the van and borne away.

Mr McEvoy expressed his sympathy only once, and then moved on to practical matters, for which I could not have been more grateful. His manner was gentle, but formal. I arranged with him for the funeral to be on Thursday, at the Wesleyan chapel where Matthew and I had been married. This was subject to the chapel and its incumbent being free that morning, but Mr McEvoy claimed to be privy to the calendars of all the local churches and said that he would enter it in his own diary, and would wait to hear from me again when I'd spoken to the minister. He then excused himself on the grounds that I'd have a lot to do, and went to accompany my father for his final sprucing-up.

The van pulled away, and I closed the door. As I stood in the narrow hallway, bereft and paralysed, I could no longer avoid hearing the only sound in that otherwise silent house: the terrible sound of my mother weeping.

I may well, as Mr McEvoy said, have had a lot to do, but I didn't want to do any of it. What I wanted was to flee. It took a full two minutes, and all my resolve and self-control not to go out into the street and walk away, as fast and as far as I could. If it hadn't been for my mother, I probably would have done. But her sobs – so deep, wrenching, and elemental, in a voice so unlike hers – acted like the links of a chain that held me fast. In the end I pulled myself together, and opened a few windows. I should probably have kept them shut and drawn the curtains, but it was good to let in some of the normal, sunny, un-grief-stricken air.

By the time I went up to her she had stopped sobbing and we neither of us mentioned it. She had finished her glass of water and I filled it up for her. Soon after that she needed to pass water, which she did with a little discomfort, but only the most residual, rusty trace of blood. She washed her face and hands unaided, and then got back into bed while I helped her with her hair. We unplaited and brushed it, and she wanted to coil it up in her usual daytime style, but she was tired and I couldn't manage that to her satisfaction, so she had to be content, for now, with a tidier braid. While all this was going on, I told her about my provisional arrangements for the funeral.

'You have been busy,' she said.

'I'm sorry, Mum, I hope that's all right. I didn't think you'd want to wait too long.'

'No, no. No time like the present.'

'Mum—'

'There are things we need to decide. Hymns and whatnot. Not that your father ever went to church. The last time was your wedding.' Realising what she had just said she glanced at me and I saw again, for an instant, the turmoil below the surface.

'Oh Pammie,' she said. 'We're both widows now.'

A little later she took a nap and I walked up to the chapel. The minister's wife, distracted but affable, answered the door of the manse in an apron and heard the news of my father's death with businesslike sympathy: Gerald Streeter was a stranger, and it was all in a day's work for her. Her husband was out, but she checked his diary and pronounced Thursday clear and us booked in.

'Can he call on you later?' she asked.

'Yes – or tomorrow would do.'

'Not for him,' she pointed out briskly. 'It's his busy day.'

On the way back I did some shopping. I was nervous about cooking for my mother, and selected very simple fare: a couple of chops, some mince, vegetables and the makings of macaroni cheese. I also stocked up on various dry goods. I supposed, with dread, that I should have to lay on some kind of funeral tea on Thursday. How many would attend? That again was up to me; my parents had not had a wide circle of friends, and very few relations, but I would have to let the neighbours know, and Dad's former colleagues at the Speedwell works.

The last time I'd concerned myself with provisioning an event had been the lunch party at Crompton Terrace. Another world, but one, I reminded myself, that had a claim on me.

With all that had happened it was hard to believe that only yesterday I had put in a day's work there with no inkling of what was to come.

When I got back, to my consternation, but not entirely to my surprise I found my mother out of bed, pale and perspiring, attempting to get dressed. Nothing would deflect her from her intention to come downstairs, so I rallied round and half an hour later she was parked in a chair by the net-curtained window in the front room. I couldn't deny that it was consoling to have her there, a sign of normality. But of course things were not normal – everything we said or did, every move we made and mouthful we ate, reminded us of that. God knows why, but neither of us would cry in front of the other, so the quiet room throbbed and grew heavy with our unshed tears. Once or twice I went into the back-yard and wept and wept, and when I got back it was plain she'd been doing the same, but still we soldiered on with our pigheaded, unnatural charade. It was too soon to talk about Dad – to remember this and that, to look at photographs or revive old times. We didn't know what to do, or how to behave, so we simply trudged along, eyes down, both of us trying not to think of the weeks, months, years ahead and what they meant.

A little note dropped through the letter box, the first of many to arrive over the next few days. The messages, so kindly meant, were mostly rather stilted: 'Your great loss' . . . 'condolences from Wilf and me' . . . 'blessings at this diffi-cult time' . . . 'please accept our sympathetic thoughts' . . . Still, my mother seemed scarcely able to believe people's kind-ness, and read the notes over and over, taking them as a sign of her husband's excellent character, and the esteem in which he was held.

'You see?' she murmured, holding up the single page like evidence. 'You see?'

About four o'clock she became tired and dozed off. One of the neighbours, Mrs Coleman (she of the stillbirth all those years ago) knocked on the door, and I took the opportunity to explain, in a lowered voice, that my mother hadn't been well herself, and wouldn't be up to seeing anyone till Monday at the earliest. I also told her the date and time of the funeral, knowing that – good, gossipy soul that she was – the information would be speedily disseminated up and down the street. She asked if there was anything she could do and I took the opportunity to mention that a cake for Thursday's tea would be gratefully received. I was pretty sure this hint would result in at least half a dozen cakes, but what did it matter? The local ladies wanted to help and my own baking, learned at my mother's side in the months after Matthew's death, was rusty with disuse.

When she'd gone I shook my mother's shoulder gently, and told her I was going up to the phone box.

There were dozens of people I had to get in touch with, but they would have to wait till tomorrow. I couldn't help it – I called the Jarvises. The phone rang for some considerable time.

'Hello?' She sounded slightly breathless.

'Mrs Jarvis? It's Pamela. I'm so sorry to bother you at a weekend.'

'Pamela! Not at all . . . I was upstairs.' I could imagine – one of her afternoon rests.

'It was only to say – I ought to tell you—' Infuriatingly, my voice broke.

'Hello? Pamela? Hello?'

I cleared my throat. 'I'm here.'

'What is it? You sound rather blue . . .'

I knew I had to speak quickly, firmly and to the point if I wasn't to dissolve. 'Mrs Jarvis, my father died last night. I must stay down here with my mother till after the funeral, so I shan't be in until next week.'

'Oh my *dear* . . .' I could picture her face, contorted with concern for me. 'I'm so terribly sorry. What – I mean was he . . . ?'

I rescued her. Usefully the balance of our relationship dictated that I was the incisive one.

'It was very sudden, and very peaceful. He died in his sleep.'

'But such a *shock* . . . For you, and for your poor, poor mother.'

'Yes. She's not been very well herself, so you can imagine. I must stay here for a while.'

'Of *course* you must. Don't even *think* of coming back until you've done all you can for her. Christopher and I both understand perfectly, at least he will when I tell him, I know.'

'I'm sure Monday week will be fine. She has good neighbours. But if anything should happen to make it later than that, I'll let you know.'

'Thank you, but don't worry about us, we shall miss you of course, my dear, but we'll just have to muddle along as we used to do. Could we – could you let me have your address and telephone number so we can be in touch? I feel sure Christopher . . . we both would . . .'

I explained that we didn't have a telephone (promising myself to rectify that soon) and gave her the address. As I was about to ring off, she said: 'Oh, Pamela – this may not be quite the time, but compliments are always so nice I think I'll tell you – you made such a hit the other day. John Ashe in particular was terribly taken with you. But anyway, I only mention that as the tiniest thing when you're going through so much. We shall all be thinking of you . . . Goodbye, my dear . . . goodbye.'

When I'd replaced the receiver I remained standing there in a kind of trance. Hearing Amanda Jarvis's voice had brought that world rushing back, and its sights, smells and sounds enveloped me. At this time in the afternoon Chef would just have arrived and he and Dorothy would be gossiping in the kitchen . . . Amanda, her rest interrupted, would have gone to the office to tell her husband my sad news . . . he would be sitting between the desk and the window, the ankle of one long leg resting on the knee of the other . . . Edward Rintoul would be lying on the grass with his hat over his eyes . . . And upstairs in the breathless heat of the attic, Suzannah would be steadily covering her wall with all those faces collected in her head.

The swallows would surely have gone. But the shy, secret nightingale – perhaps she'd still be there.

I closed my eyes and prayed: for my father's soul, my mother's healing and my own future. I was overwhelmed by a sense of the distance separating my parents' house and the Jarvises' high on its hill in Highgate – a distance far greater and more unbridgeable than the miles and miles of London that lay between. But something that Amanda Jarvis said had spun a single spider thread across the void. The mention of John Ashe's name touched some deep, dark spot in my mind, far beneath my sadness and confusion; and the knowledge of his approval was like the most seductive whisper.

'Excuse me!' There was a sharp rap on the glass, and a woman's cross face outside. 'Are you finished?'

I returned to the house where my mother was still sleeping, her head nodded forward and her hands lying on top of the note in her lap.

At six o'clock the minister, Mr Holland, came round. He was not the same one who had married Matthew and me, but a brisk, rather bitter man who had either obeyed the wrong calling or been disappointed in it since; it was hard to tell. Underpinning every remark he addressed to us was the implication that because we had been non-attenders, and therefore non-believers, all these years, we had no right to expect too much. He hadn't known my father, and had only limited time available to get to know us. I heartily disliked him, the more so because both Dr Mayes and the undertaker McEvoy had been the soul of Christian kindness. I was worried that the unpleasantness which slunk just below the surface would upset my mother, but maybe it was fortunate that she was worn out, and also too taken up with mastering and concealing her own feelings to be much troubled by anyone else's.

He made some perfunctory notes on my father's life and career, evincing not the slightest interest in what sort of man he'd been. My mother, even now, would never have strayed on to such personal ground so it was left to me to say what a hard-working, honourable and devoted husband and father he had been. Holland nodded, closing his eyes as much as to say yes, yes, yes, all the usual things.

When it came to hymns, my mother chose 'The Lord is my shepherd', which Holland noted down with a slight smirk and an: 'Oh yes, an old favourite.' I decided it was time to make a point.

'I'd like to have "Who would true valour see",' I told him. 'My husband and I had it at our wedding. We were married at the chapel, you know, in nineteen eighteen.'

'Before my time,' said Holland.

'Long before,' I agreed. 'It was a lovely service. Your predecessor made us so welcome.'

He was a seasoned campaigner and I had no idea whether the shaft hit home, but I felt better for saying it.

When he'd gone I made us some macaroni cheese, and persuaded my mother to return to bed. She looked terribly pale and drawn; she needed rest, and, I was sure, the privacy to weep. When she was tucked in, in a clean nightdress with a bow at the neck, I was suddenly overcome by tenderness for her and leaned forward to kiss her on the cheek. As I did so I felt her give a little gasp and her hand clutched at my shoulder fiercely, the fingers digging in, as if she were falling and I was the nearest available branch. I kept very still until she removed the hand, and then smoothed the bedclothes unnecessarily to allow her time to compose herself.

'The doctor said he'd call again,' I reminded her. 'He'll probably want to see you.'

'That's all right,' she said, 'I shan't be asleep.'

'Can I get you anything for now?'

She shook her head. 'Except, if you don't mind –' she wagged a finger in a brusque, run-along gesture towards the dressing table – 'pass me that, would you?'

'What?' My hand hovered over the few items there.

'The picture – that's it.'

I handed her their wedding photograph and at once, as a pretext for having requested it, she began polishing the glass with her sleeve.

'I'll do some housework tomorrow,' I promised her. But she was polishing away, lips pursed, and didn't hear me.

It was only eight thirty and a fine, bright evening when Dr Mayes arrived, but I had fallen asleep in the chair. My tousled appearance gave me away, because he said:

'I'm sorry – I disturbed you.'

'I must have dropped off.'

'You've had a terrible shock, and that's physically and emotionally exhausting.' As always, the kind words slipped beneath my defences and the tears welled up. He didn't comment on this, but asked gently: 'How's your mother doing?'

'As well as can be expected, I think. She doesn't say much.'

'I don't imagine that's her way.'

'No.'

'And you?'

'Me?' I said. 'Oh, I'm fine.'

'There are a lot of practicalities to attend to, aren't there? But perhaps – people have said – they at least provide a kind of diversion. Something to occupy the mind.'

I agreed. 'It would be far worse to have nothing to do.'

'Is she expecting me?' he asked. 'I'll go up and see her if I may.'

'She is,' I said, 'please do.' But I still went up the stairs first so that I could announce him.

I needn't have worried. My mother was sitting up against the pillows, neat, composed and dry-eyed. There was no sign of the wedding photograph.

'The doctor's here, Mum.'

'I know.'

'Good evening, Mrs Streeter.'

I left them, and paused on the landing, confronted by the closed door of my own bedroom. Sooner or later, tonight perhaps, I would have to sleep in there again, in the bed where my father had died. Such was my mother's influence that the guest room never entered my mind. Briskly, I opened the door. Someone, I supposed it must have been one of McEvoy's men, had stripped the bed, folded the bedclothes and placed the sheets and pillowcase on the chair.

At first I thought: How dare they? But almost at once I was grateful to them. They knew what they were doing. It must have been obvious to them that this was not my father's usual room, and that my mother wasn't well. That one small act was an invaluable service, rendering the place impersonal – awaiting its next occupant rather than recalling the last. I picked up the sheets to take down with me, and left the door open as I went, to let my father's last breaths drift out and be absorbed into the air of the house.

Dr Mayes wasn't long; he joined me downstairs almost as

soon as I'd put the sheets in the cardboard laundry box in the kitchen (the use of a local laundry instead of Mrs Budd for the 'upstairs linen' was one of my mother's few indulgences).

'I must congratulate you,' he said. 'Physically, she's maintaining the improvement. In spite of everything.'

'She did it all herself,' I said dutifully, though I couldn't help being flattered.

'True, she's a strong woman, but you enabled her to. She's fortunate to have you.' Oddly enough, it was he who blushed a little as he said this.

After a couple of minutes during which he asked me politely about the funeral arrangements and so on, he announced it was time for him to go.

'My supper will be waiting,' he said. 'And I must say it will be very welcome.'

'Whereabouts do you live?' I asked.

'Not far. I lodge in Elm Road with the senior partner and his wife. I'm very comfortable. Mrs Cardew looks after us extremely well.'

I absorbed this information as I saw him to the door. 'Thank you, Doctor. Will we see you again?'

'Bound to. Yes, I shall definitely look in in a day or two. Sooner if there's any problem.'

We said goodbye. This time I didn't close the door at once, but watched him climb into his dilapidated little car, and waved as he chugged away.

The days between then and the funeral were strange, a period in parenthesis. It appeared not so much that time stood still as that it behaved differently. The individual hours crawled by, filled with the sort of small domestic and filial tasks to which I was unaccustomed and against which, shamefully, I chafed. But each evening, when I looked back on it, the day seemed to have passed in a blur.

In addition, as my mother's physical condition improved her behaviour changed. She took refuge, as always, in domestic activity. All her returning energy was poured into arrangements for the funeral, and it became pretty clear that if we weren't to be at each other's throats I had better let her take over. She would certainly have tried to do most things herself, but I was worried that she might suffer a relapse, so I submitted to a barrage of orders and instructions – shopping, cooking, cleaning. Oh, the cleaning! I had forgotten how houseproud she was. I realised how used I had become to Amanda Jarvis's *modus operandi*, and the independence it gave me. I frequently had to retreat to the kitchen, or even the backyard, and make a conscious effort to ungrit my teeth and breathe deeply. Tasks like registering the death, which took me out of the house for half a day, felt like time off for good behaviour. I counted the days till the funeral would be over, and the resumption of the status quo. On other occasions I would suddenly be overcome afresh by the fact of my father's death. I remembered happy childhood times when I'd been his tomboy companion – the golf lessons, the jokes, the sense of an affectionate alliance which my mother couldn't quite understand. The status quo could never truly be resumed. Everything from this point forward would be different.

It was wonderful to receive a letter from Amanda Jarvis, with an additional paragraph in her husband's handwriting. They had never known my father and they barely knew me yet they managed to strike exactly the right note, formal but friendly and understanding. They made a point of asking me to pass on their good wishes to my mother, but I did not at first show her the letter. Would she feel patronised, slighted even, by this articulate expression of sympathy from strangers?

I decided that I was complicating things unnecessarily. A

kind message was a kind message, after all. And the truth was I felt a sort of proprietary pride in the Jarvises' *savoir faire* and ease of manner, I wanted her to see that the people I worked for, though labouring under the disadvantages of being well-off and 'artistic', had instincts at least as sound as the next man's.

I watched her face a little anxiously as she read. It gave nothing away, but as she handed the letter back to me, she said gruffly: 'That was nice of them. Will you tell them I shall be writing when all this is out of the way.'

I was pleased, for all our sakes, that I had shown it to her.

I sent postcards to the tiny handful of my parents' relatives still extant – my mother's unmarried sister in Eastbourne, an uncle and aunt in Bristol, and a distant male cousin whose reputation suggested that the address we had for him would be years out of date – and to the Speedwell factory. Midweek when Mrs Coleman called again I invited her in, and brokered a rather one-sided exchange between her and my mother.

This made me realise how long it had been since I spoke to Barbara, and that evening I walked up the road and telephoned her. Her reliable, laconic affection was a tonic.

'God, I'm sorry,' she said. 'It must be ghastly. How are you?'

'Soldiering on.'

'How long will you be down there for?'

'Until the weekend. I'd like to get back to work on Monday, provided my mother's all right.'

'You must miss it.'

'I do.'

There was a brief pause during which I could picture Barbara puffing on her cigarette. She ended the pause by saying: 'She will be all right, you know.'

'I hope so.'

'She's got to be on her own some time.'

'I know, but—'

'She may even welcome it.'

It was so like her to turn things round, and make me look at them differently. I experienced only the most fleeting sense of injury before realising that she was very probably right.

The funeral was less upsetting than I'd anticipated. Twenty-five people came, including my mother's sister Auntie Nell, Dr Mayes, Barbara, and dear Mrs Budd, and the presence of so many provided the dignity and feeling which I'd worried the occasion would lack. In the event Holland's impersonal delivery did not matter at all. Most of those present took a pretty dim view of the clergy and had no expectations in that direction. He was simply a functionary, doing a day's work. We were the ones who mattered. On the short walk to the cemetery for the burial the sun was warm on our backs.

McEvoy and his men could not be faulted, and my mother was splendid – handsome, grim-faced and dry-eyed throughout. Mrs Coleman and her crack team had been in that morning, so a magnificent tea was laid out in the dining room, and I had done more polishing in six hours than in the rest of my life to date.

My parents' house had never seen so many people. There were more present than at our quick wartime wedding. All the effort had been worthwhile. I had never fully appreciated the value of 'a good send-off', and the paying of 'last respects'. Now, I did. Respect was what this occasion accorded my father. Affection, too, of course, but mostly respect: a recognition of his unwavering honesty and industry, and the downright decency that had dictated the course of his steady, well-spent life. Men I didn't know told me what a splendid chap 'Gerry' had been, and women referred to him as 'a perfect gentleman'. I was no great believer in an afterlife, but

I did hope that he was here, with us, and able to hear the affection and esteem in which he was held, and that wherever he was he would feel no remorse about that last awful night. The unprecedented panic on the eve of his death was the measure of my father's character: it had been terrible because I had never, ever, seen him anything other than calm, solid, and dependable. My mother was strong, but she had a temperament, not to mention a temper. Almost to the end, my father had been for her what Matthew would have been for me: a rock.

I made sure my mother sat down as much as possible, and allowed other people to come to her. I was only too happy to be kept busy, making tea and handing food. When things were well underway I went out to the kitchen to charge the teapot, and Dr Mayes followed me.

'Mrs Griffe – excuse me—'

'Oh, Doctor – hello.'

'I just wanted to say goodbye. I can't stay, I'm afraid.'

'Have you had something to eat?'

He patted his stomach. 'More than my fair share I suspect.'

'Thank you so much for coming today,' I said. 'It meant a lot to my mother, and to me.'

'I wanted to come.'

The two of us stood there, facing each other uncertainly, neither of us willing to end the exchange. I knew what I wanted to say but, modern woman though I affected to be, I hadn't the courage.

Thank heavens Dr Mayes was brave enough to end the awkward silence.

'You're planning to leave soon, aren't you? To get back to work?'

'At the weekend. All being well here.'

'I'd be sorry to think I might not see you again,' he said. 'I wonder whether you'd like to meet some time – either down here if you're visiting your mother, or I could come to you.'

'I'd like that very much.' I smiled for what felt like the first time in ages and saw my own happiness and relief reflected on his face.

'Do you have a telephone?' he asked.

'There is one in the house where I live. Here.' I took the shopping-list pad and pencil out of the drawer by the stove and wrote down the number. 'Just ask for me.'

'I will.' He took the piece of paper, studied it, and put it in his breast pocket. 'I definitely will. And by the way, my name's Alan.'

'Pamela.'

'I know – I mean, I heard.'

We laughed, a little embarrassed but extremely pleased with ourselves.

'Right,' he said, 'you have guests to look after, and I must get going.'

'Yes.'

'Goodbye then. Or au revoir.'

'Au revoir.'

He nodded at the kettle, which was steaming steadily. 'No need to see me out.'

I continued to smile as I made more tea, and sliced another of the cakes which I had been keeping in reserve. My heart was lighter and my spirits higher than they had been for days. I was still smiling when I returned to the front room, because I knew how tickled my father would have been to think that on this day of all days his widowed daughter had got herself a new beau, and a professional man at that.

By early evening when the guests had gone my mother was worn out. I was grateful to the relatives for having tactfully turned down her offer of a bed for the night. For now, what she needed was what she would have too much of in the weeks and years to come – peace and quiet and an early night. I tried not to dwell on the thought that with the funeral over she faced the bleak, inescapable fact of her husband's absence, and her own loneliness.

I let her help clear away the tea things, though she was weaving with tiredness, and then insisted she go up to bed.

At the foot of the stairs she paused, leaning with one hand on the newel post, and said: 'Thank you, Pammie. He'd have been pleased with that.'

'I think so.'

She put one foot on the first stair. 'Back to normal tomorrow.'

Her stoicism squeezed my heart. 'There's no rush, Mum.'

'Oh yes.' She took another step. 'Oh yes . . .' And another. 'You've got your life and I've got mine.'

When I'd washed up I had a couple of the leftover sandwiches and, greatly daring, a small glass of sherry from the decanter in the dining-room cupboard. It was thick, dark and sweet, and had the effect of making me first euphoric and then delightfully sleepy. When I went in to say goodnight to my mother she was sitting up in bed rereading the various letters she'd received. The wedding photograph stood on the bedside table.

I bent to kiss her cheek. 'Goodnight, Mum.'

'You can take that sherry with you if you want,' she said. 'It's no use to me.'

There were no flies on her. I told myself I was a grown woman and had no need to apologise for drinking a thimbleful of sherry in my parents' house at the end of a long day.

'Nor me,' I said firmly. 'And you should keep it anyway, it'll come in useful for guests.'

There was the merest sceptical pursing of her mouth, which I was glad to see. I was about to go, when she said: 'The doctor's a nice young fellow.'

'Yes,' I agreed.

'Do you like him as much as he likes you?'

She was in the mood for plain speaking, so I obliged her. 'Yes, I do.'

There was a microscopic pause. 'No harm in that,' she said.

I went to bed in the little room with this endorsement ringing in my ears, and fell instantly, deeply asleep.

Chapter Ten

It was one of the charms of Seven Crompton Terrace that when I was there I could be a different person, or at least that version of myself I chose to present. The Jarvises knew very little about me, so there was no need for deception.

On my return to work, the Monday after the funeral, it was a relief to assume once more the uncomplicated status of valued employee, and to escape my mother's all-seeing eye. My admiration for her, though, was boundless – when I left on Sunday evening she could not have made my departure easier. She waved me off as matter-of-factly as if I'd been down there for the usual Sunday dinner, though both of us knew that would never happen again.

Not only at my parents' house would things never be quite the same. My telephone conversation with Amanda Jarvis, and the subsequent letter from her and her husband, had created between the two worlds a connection, however slight, which had not existed before. And then there was the prospect of seeing Alan Mayes again some time soon, not in his professional capacity but as a friend.

Most tellingly perhaps, the mention of John Ashe and his approval of me had hovered on the edge of my consciousness for days, like a cat in the long grass. I despised the warped vanity that allowed it to do so. I had not liked Ashe, and intended to avoid him in the future, so his opinion of me, good or otherwise, could be of no possible consequence.

I was disappointed to find both the Jarvises out on the

morning of my return; in fact to begin with I was even a little insulted that at least one of them hadn't thought to be there to receive me back. But naturally there was a charming note of explanation on my desk.

> *Dear Pamela,*
>
> *I'm so sorry we have to be out today. We would have liked to be there to welcome you back, but duty calls in the form of lunch with an American painter at the house where he is staying in Kent. Let's hope it will prove to be a worthwhile jaunt, and that we'll soon be exhibiting his work at the Sumpter – he would be quite a catch! I'm leaving a very short list of calls and letters for your attention, but none of them are urgent – I'm sure you won't be averse to a quiet day after the difficult time you've been through. Amanda and I hope your mother is continuing to bear up, and we look forward to seeing you tomorrow.*
>
> *Yours,*
> *Christopher J.*

Mollified, I went through to the kitchen to say good morning to Dorothy (and, if I'm honest, to catch up on the happenings of the past week) and almost bumped into her coming the other way.

'Hello!' she said. 'I'm sorry about your father. That's horrible.'

I agreed. 'It was so completely unexpected. But he didn't suffer, he went in his sleep.'

'Best way. Chef's off today – cup of tea?'

'I was thinking of some coffee.'

'Coffee it is, then. How's your mother?' she asked as we went into the kitchen.

'Wonderful, considering. She wasn't well herself, you know. That was why I went down there.'

Dorothy paused, her hand on the cupboard door, an expression of appalled fascination on her face. 'You mean *she* was ill, but *he* died?'

I nodded.

'Blimey . . .' she breathed. 'That's awful. What was it then, heart attack?'

'Probably.' I didn't mind her robust interrogation, in fact her directness was invigorating, like a rough towel. 'That's what's on the death certificate.'

'Broken heart?' she suggested.

'No, she was over the worst, she was going to be all right . . .' I considered the proposition. 'Broken spirit, perhaps.'

She shook her head sympathetically as she stirred the grounds. 'Shame, isn't it?'

'A great shame, yes.' At that moment I could have hugged Dorothy. In her own way she was a sophisticate: the simplicity of her approach made everything else simpler.

'There,' she said. 'Nice cup of coffee. Think I'll join you.'

I didn't even think of dissuading her. We both knew that, for now, normal rules did not apply. We were employees, and friends, who found ourselves on our own and who had much to discuss.

'So,' I said, 'has anything been happening that I should know about?'

'Hm, let's see. Mr Rintoul's picture's nearly finished, and he's gone to France for a week, so today it's only you and me and her upstairs. Haven't seen her yet this morning, but then it's early.' She took a sip for dramatic effect before adding: 'Our Mr Ashe was round again last week.' She raised her eyebrows pointedly over the edge of the cup.

'Oh yes?' I asked cautiously.

'Oh, yes. I don't know, of course, but I think he took a shine to her.'

'Who? Suzannah?'

'Mrs J went and fetched her and they were chatting in the drawing room on their own for half an hour or more.'

It was on the tip of my tongue to ask what they'd been talking about – I was sure Dorothy would have made a point of cleaning the hall at the time – but I managed to stop myself, and said instead: 'Did they only meet for the first time at the lunch party?'

She laughed, eyes wide. 'I don't know, do I?'

'You might have done. You know most things around here.'

'That's true,' she conceded. 'Put it this way, I never saw them together here before. Anyway, they're thick as thieves now.'

I thought about this when I was back at my desk. I was aware of an unexpected and unwelcome pang of something awfully like jealousy. Surely, I reflected, it was I who had made an impression on John Ashe? Amanda Jarvis had made a point of telling me as much. Suzannah Murchie's name had not been so much as mentioned, and yet here was Dorothy telling me that she and Ashe were 'thick as thieves'. I despised myself for this reaction, but there was no denying it.

At about midday Dorothy tapped on the door and put her head round.

'Nothing else doing here, so I'm off. They said I could, but thought I'd better tell you.'

'Thanks, Dorothy.'

'It's the two of you, then.' She pulled a face that stopped just short of a wink. 'Be good.'

I heard her leave by the front door, something she would not have done had the Jarvises been at home. It was a tiny demonstration of independence: she did it because she could.

By a quarter to one I'd completed the list of tasks, and done a little discreet tidying. I decided to go up to the village as I usually did, buy a sandwich and an apple, and perhaps walk along to the edge of Hampstead Heath and have my lunch there.

Since the storm had ended the long spell of oppressive heat the weather had settled into a more typically English pattern of sunshine and cloud. Not that it made much difference to me – my head had been down and my nose to the grindstone, although I'd been glad of the blessing of sunshine at my father's funeral. Today it was lovely to be high up, above London and my cares, and I sat with my back against a tree and ate my picnic in a mood of slightly melancholy contentment. Afterwards, though I had nothing in particular to do, and knew the Jarvises wouldn't mind if I left, I decided to go back. I told myself that this was because I should be there to answer the telephone, but in truth I was reluctant to leave. The house in Crompton Terrace was where I felt most alive, and I was glad to be back. Before clambering to my feet I closed my eyes for a second and begged forgiveness of whoever was listening for my treachery.

There were very few cars in Crompton Terrace at the best of times, so I noticed that someone in the road had a new one, or had visitors. A sleek, black monster, capacious as a hearse, was parked near the gate of Number Seven. A uniformed chauffeur leaned back in the driving seat, his cap over his eyes. On the end of the bonnet perched a golden bird. Perhaps one day, I told myself fancifully, I would have a car like that . . . I was reminded of Alan Mayes and his dilapidated jalopy. All that seemed very far away and long ago, but I hoped I'd hear from him.

As I went in, I looked up at the swallows' nest. It was empty, and a tiny spider had slung its web across the angle between it and the beam, a sure sign that the occupants had flown. I supposed that demonstrated the cyclical nature of these things, but I was sad the birds were gone. It seemed to mark the end of something not just for them, but for all of us.

The house was quiet, with that air of suspended animation peculiar to empty places that are normally busy. Even the small sounds of my own movements made me self-conscious. I stayed in the office for a while but became fidgety in the unnatural silence and decided to go out and see if there was anything I could do in the garden. I left the study and garden doors wide open so that I could hear the telephone if it rang, and went outside.

Not surprisingly, there was plenty that needed attention. Nobody had done anything since I'd last been out here, but that suited me fine. I fetched the small fork and the clippers from the lean-to and busied myself with weeding. I was completely happy grubbing about, and seeing the effects of my labours growing in my wake. Once or twice I glanced up at the attic window; it was open but I didn't see anyone, and I had by now become used to Suzannah's reclusive habits. There was even something companionable in the sensation that we both belonged here and were going about our respective business, she up above, painting her mural, and I down here, pulling up weeds.

While in the garden I went up to the end and stood in the deep shade beneath the trees. The nest was still there, but I saw no sign of the nightingale. But she wasn't a bird of passage like the swallows; this was her territory and I felt sure she was in the branches somewhere, silently watching me.

I must have been at it for an hour when I stood up, about to go in to the kitchen to get myself a cold drink. But at the same moment someone came down the stairs, and walked swiftly along the hall to the front door. He opened the door and for a brief moment I saw, silhouetted against the afternoon light, the unmistakable figure of John Ashe. The door closed. He had come and gone so quickly I almost rubbed my eyes, unsure whether I'd really seen him. I forgot about the cold drink, ran into the office and peered out through the window, just in time to see him climbing into the back seat of the shiny black car I'd admired earlier.

I watched the car pull away. When it was gone I found that I'd been holding my breath. I took a great gulp of air. My legs were trembling as though I'd been running. Now, I needed the drink. I went to the kitchen and ran myself a pint of cold water from the tap, drinking it down in one and pouring myself some more.

Of course I couldn't be sure where Ashe had come from, but after what Dorothy had told me it seemed almost certain he had been at the top of the house, with Suzannah Rose Murchie. The thought made me shiver. I had thought I was alone, but for her, and now . . . Suddenly, I wanted nothing more than to get out of the house. I put the garden tools away hurriedly, stuffed the weeds into the dustbin, washed my hands at the sink and collected my things from the office. As I opened the front door I thought I heard something – and as I closed it I glimpsed a figure at the foot of the stairs. I heard my name spoken softly. Only Suzannah, surely, and yet my heart was in my mouth as I ran to the garden gate.

The woman from the house opposite called 'Good afternoon!' but I don't believe I answered her, and her surprised expression told me how strange and wild I must have appeared.

At the top of the hill I spotted a cab and hailed it – an unheard-of extravagance, but the privacy it afforded was worth every penny. Even the cab driver gave me a curious look after I blurted out my address.

I sat back and closed my eyes, trying to regulate my breathing. I knew my panic was completely unfounded.

There was no reason on earth why John Ashe should not visit a young artist in whom he had an interest. Even if that interest were not purely professional, he and Suzannah were both adults and it was no business of mine what they chose to do, or where. The house wasn't mine, I had no responsibility for it, or for them. But my skin continued to creep at the realisation that while I had been busy in the garden, they had been together up there . . . And so quiet, so very, very quiet.

I was still spooked when I got back. When Louise popped out of her door she made me jump, and my hand flew to my mouth.

'Did I give you a fright? I've got no make-up on yet, but I didn't know it was that bad!'

'No, it wasn't that . . . Of course it wasn't!' I laughed nervously. 'I was in a world of my own.'

'You're early. Want to come in for a bit?'

'All right – why not.'

Her cluttered room felt womanly and comforting. I sank down gratefully in the chair.

'Are you all right?' she asked. 'You're a bit pale. But then you've been having a lousy time.'

'I think I'm just tired,' I agreed. I didn't want to go over past events again, so rather than enlarge on them I batted a question back to her. 'You said you had a new job – how's it going?'

'*Wonderful!*' she said, fumbling for cigarettes in the pocket of her kimono. 'I can't tell you. A bit tiring, being up most of the night and doing the other job too, but it's such fun and the money's so good I may give up Maison Ricard altogether.'

'Tell me about it.'

'Well.' She took a drag and swung her legs up on to the bed. 'The club is called the Apache – have you heard of it?'

I shook my head.

'You will,' she assured me. 'Everyone knows about it, but *not* everyone can get in. It was a stroke of genius on Piggy's part to make it exclusive right from the start.'

'Piggy?'

'The manager. Charles Swynford-Hayes. That's what he's known as among friends and in the press – we lowly employees wouldn't use it to his face.'

'So who is allowed in?' I asked, more to keep her talking than out of any real curiosity – my interest in and acquaintance with nightclubs was nil. 'Only the very rich?'

'No – that's the great thing. It could be anyone – you, me, the candlestick-maker. Piggy decides. But nobody boring.'

'Not me then,' I said. 'That's a relief.'

'Pamela, you are not boring! Anyway, the result is the most fabulously exciting and unexpected clientele. It's like the most exotic party you can think of every night. And no one's allowed to pull rank. No one!' She made a face to indicate the extreme importance of those she was referring to. 'Piggy calls it the most exclusive democracy in London.'

Her enthusiasm was infectious. 'It sounds absolutely petrifying.'

'I don't know about petrifying – pretty humiliating though, if you're Lady Vere de Vere and you're refused entry!'

'It must be. What about you – what do you do?'

'I'm a hostess.' She held up her hand. 'And before you say a single thing there is absolutely nothing shady about it.'

'I didn't think for a moment that there was.'

'You don't fool me, darling. Anyway, it doesn't matter. There isn't. I'm a cocktail waitress, really, with extra responsibilities. Looking after people generally – bringing them their orders, making them feel at home, dancing with gentlemen when required, being decorative . . .' She wriggled her toes. 'All things I've trained for.'

'Piggy must be thrilled to have you,' I said. 'And you say he's paying you well?'

'Pretty well, but the tips are the thing – just for doing what any girl with an ounce of sense would do at a party.'

'You underestimate yourself,' I said, laughing to show there was no offence taken. 'I've got a couple of ounces of sense but I could no sooner do that job than fly!'

'No,' she agreed, 'and you wouldn't want to. You'd be a fish out of water, you'd hate it. But it's right up my alley, I can tell you.'

I was truly pleased for her, and the conversation went a long way towards calming me down. And then, just as I was leaving, she clapped her hand to her head.

'Oh God, I nearly forgot, I meant to say it to begin with – you've got a message.' She went to the mantelpiece and took a small piece of paper from beneath an ashtray. She smiled as she handed it to me. 'He sounded nice.'

The smile invited confidences, but there were none I chose to give. Instead I thanked her, and went upstairs before reading it.

Alan Mayes – call him before 6 or after 9. There followed a number. I glanced at my watch: it was five thirty. Taking the piece of paper and coins from the tin on the chest of drawers I went down to the hall, tiptoeing past Louise's room so as not to attract further attention.

As the phone rang the other end I pictured the senior partner with whom Alan lodged – large, waistcoated, slightly intimidating, not particularly keen that his young assistant engage in too much social activity – and prepared myself accordingly.

So it was a surprise when Alan himself answered.

'Alan? It's Pamela.'

'I was hoping it would be – I ran to pick it up. Hello. Listen, I can't talk for long because of evening surgery. But I'm free on Thursday evening, and I wondered whether I could see you?'

'That would be lovely,' I said.

'It's a pity we're on opposite sides of town, but shall we meet in the middle – say under the clock at Fortnum's at about six? Then we can go for a walk in the park, or the pictures – or anything really, depending on the weather. I shan't inflict my car on you first time in case it puts you off.'

'I'll look forward to it. But I might not be there dead on six.'

'Don't worry. I will, and I'll wait for you.'

'Fine.'

'Look, Pamela, I'd better dash. Thanks so much for calling back, see you soon.'

''Bye.'

On the way back up I encountered Louise crossing the landing from the bathroom, her head swathed in a towel.

'Did you get hold of him?'

'I did.'

'I don't know, you disappear for a week to attend your ailing parents and come back with a beau – it's outrageous! Whatever were you doing down there when you should have been playing the dutiful daughter?'

'He's a doctor,' I explained.

She hooted. 'So it was eyes meeting across the patient's inert form— sorry. Sorry, Pamela, that was—'

'Don't worry,' I said. 'You're right, it was something like that.'

'Anyway, I'm pleased. You deserve it.'

Oddly, it wasn't so much Louise's minor lapse of taste that upset me as her last remark. Why did I 'deserve it'? Was I such an obviously dull, worthy, undemanding young woman? I wished now that I'd appeared a little less wide-eyed and self-deprecating about her nightclub. I reminded myself that if she had even an inkling of the people I mixed with in Crompton Terrace, and my thoughts about them, she would have been astonished.

But this little irritation didn't last for more than a moment. Hearing Alan's voice, and knowing I was to see him, had gone a long way to restoring my balance after the shock of seeing John Ashe. I had not had even the most innocent friendship with a man since I'd been widowed. The only men I'd known had been colleagues, none of them had attracted me, and if any of them had taken a shine to me I hadn't noticed. Nor, to be fair, had I missed male attention. I had got used to my single, independent status, and to carrying a torch for Matthew, to whom no one else compared. Now I saw that comparisons were odious: Matthew had been who he was, my first and special love. That did not mean I should measure all other men against him – I did myself and them a disservice by denying their uniqueness. Perhaps it was significant that I had not at any stage compared Alan to Matthew, but simply accepted him for himself.

I looked forward to Thursday.

Another party was in the offing at Crompton Terrace. Christopher Jarvis had pulled off a coup, the modish American artist was to exhibit at the Sumpter in the autumn, and the Jarvises were going to entertain him before he returned to New York, the weekend after next. Oddly, although they anticipated having fifty guests, there was less fuss than there had been over the luncheon. I had the impression that this was the kind of thing they did fairly often; it did not involve complicated negotiations with Chef but simply the ordering in of quantities of champagne and the ingredients for Manhattans and dry Martinis. They also (via me) hired the services of a barman, Buck, who would see to the drinks on the night, and a jazz saxophonist who I gathered was a friend. A select few, including the American artist, would go out to dinner afterwards.

Once more I was invited, but in a more casual way. I declined politely. Better to hold back: I didn't want to be thought of by anyone as a hanger-on, though I did wonder if John Ashe would be there and if he would notice my absence.

Georgina arrived to stay on the Tuesday. Her youthful presence was like that of a bird, chirruping and whooping and flying about the place. I was a little underemployed and spent quite a lot of time in the afternoons out in the garden. I discovered an ancient, rusty lawnmower at the back of the shed and brought it back into commission with the aid of a can of oil purchased in the village. I had never mowed a lawn in my life, but I no longer felt self-conscious about taking on these tasks. Here, unlike at my mother's, there was no sense of experts looking on. If the Jarvises noticed what I was doing at all they were frankly admiring and delighted, since it accorded with their view of me as an absolute treasure. Also, the 'lawn' – which scarcely merited the title – was such that whatever I did to it could only be an improvement.

One afternoon when I was up at the end of the garden tearing bindweed away from the roots of the shrubbery, Georgina came out to see me and was duly impressed.

'You are a Trojan, Pamela – I swear this place has never had so much attention.'

'I like doing it,' I said truthfully. 'Just so long as everyone realises I'm no expert.'

She chortled. 'They wouldn't know the difference!'

I thought it best not to enter with her into even the gentlest criticism of my employers, and asked instead: 'How long are you staying?'

'I'm not sure . . . To be honest I'm at a loose end, and I'd so much rather be here than at home. Mummy and Daddy are sweet, but they're desperate to see me engaged. I think they hoped I'd come back from Switzerland with prospects in that direction. If I'm hanging about down there I have to face their enquiring looks at breakfast every time I go to a party. Honestly, Pamela, it's like something out of Jane Austen. And all the men are idiots so there's no encouragement I can give them, poor things. The men *or* my parents.'

'I see . . .' I shook my head. 'Yes, it must be difficult.'

'By the way,' she said, 'I'm sorry about your father.'

'Thank you.'

'I sometimes think about one of mine dying,' she went on cheerfully, 'and try to imagine what it would feel like.'

'Very, very sad,' I said.

There was a reflective pause. 'On the other hand,' she said, snapping a twig off one of the shrubs and pulling off the leaves one at a time like a child with a dandelion clock, 'it would be even more frightful to feel nothing.'

'True.'

'That's what bothers me – that I might not feel anything. I'm not sure I've ever felt anything. Not properly. Not *passionately*.'

This I did find surprising. I stopped yanking at the weeds and straightened up stiffly.

'Georgina – I'm sure you have.'

'You're being nice,' she said, throwing the twig away and folding her arms. I sensed that it was not a compliment, and tried again to reassure her.

'You don't strike me as an unfeeling person. Quite the opposite.'

'Well, no, I'm not . . . I don't think I am.'

'And don't take this the wrong way, but you're very young. You've hardly had time to experience strong feeling. Perhaps –' this only occurred to me as I spoke – 'you've simply been happy. What's wrong with that?'

'Nothing, I suppose. But it's not as if I go about thinking, "I'm happy! I'm happy!"'

'People don't. If they're fortunate it's their everyday condition.'

'Pretty dull, don't you agree?' she said glumly.

'If you were miserable for some reason it wouldn't seem dull, believe me.'

It wasn't intended as a dig, but she was a nice girl, and she blushed. 'No. I'm sorry.'

'That's all right.' I decided to end the conversation before it became too personal. 'All I'm trying to say is, don't worry. You've got your whole life before you and I bet it will be packed with highs and lows of every kind.'

She brightened up, and laughed. 'I tell you what, let's meet up in ten years and compare notes!'

As she wandered off in the direction of the house, I reflected that I had been eighteen – about the same age as Georgina was now – when I had been wed and widowed in the space of two weeks. I could not remember ever having been as carefree as she was most of the time, but when it came to powerful feelings, I had certainly had my share.

At about four o'clock I tidied up, washed my hands and returned to the office. Christopher Jarvis closed the newspaper he'd been reading and swung his feet down off the desk like a schoolboy caught skiving.

'Pamela! Have you been out there subduing nature again?'

'Trying to.'

He gazed at me admiringly. 'Is there nothing you can't do?'

'I'm no gardener, but I enjoy it.'

'We really should employ someone . . .' he remarked contentedly. 'Now then, I don't have anything else for you to do, and I'll let you go in a minute, but first there's something I want to ask you.'

I pulled out the chair from behind my desk and was about

to sit down, but he jumped up. 'No, no, don't let's be formal. Please –' He motioned me towards one of the safari chairs and sat down on the other himself.

The truth was I felt much less at ease here than I would have at the safety of my desk. It was altogether too unusual.

'Don't look so worried,' he said teasingly. 'It's nothing in the least unpleasant, far from it. I think my wife told you that our friend John Ashe was very struck with you when he met you the other day.'

'I can't think why.' My nervousness had made me sound tart, and I scrambled to regain lost ground. 'I mean, I'm flattered, but we hardly spoke.'

'He's a student of human nature,' explained Jarvis. 'Prides himself on it. Anyway, to get to the point, he happened to mention that he was looking for some part-time secretarial help in his business, and as you're if anything rather underemployed here I wondered whether you'd like me to mention your name.'

I clenched my teeth to prevent my jaw from dropping.

'I've said nothing to him, I hasten to add, but I'm pretty confident that if I were to do so the job would be yours. It would only amount to a couple of half-days a week, and it wouldn't affect your salary here – after all, you're ours first and foremost!'

Disconcerted as I was it still struck me that Jarvis had given the matter a good deal of thought for a man simply putting in a preliminary word. I ceased to worry about how blunt I sounded.

'I don't know the nature of Mr Ashe's business.'

'Oh, he's an entrepreneur . . .' Jarvis waved expansively. 'Nightclubs, dance halls, theatres, that kind of thing. Quite an empire and a considerable fortune built up since the war. He's a true self-made man. A remarkable individual, actually.'

'And he doesn't have a secretary?'

'Apparently not.' Jarvis smiled. It was just as well he chose
to find my spikiness amusing. Another employer might not
have been so tolerant. 'Or not at the moment. As I say, he's
unusual, he doesn't conform to the way of the world.'

Clearly, I was supposed to find this reassuring. 'I see.'

'So. What do you think? Shall I have a word?'

'I don't know,' I said. 'I haven't been here for long—'

'And here you shall stay, believe me! I assure you the very
last thing we want is to lose you, we've no intention of doing
so. But I'm conscious of the fact that Amanda and I don't
use you to your full capacity, and this, I'm sure, would be
interesting work – and paid well above the going rate.'

'I'd like to think about it,' I said.

'Well of course you would. And as I say, this is just between
us at this stage. Look on it as a tip: you can act on it or leave
it, and no harm done. But do give it serious consideration.'

'I will.'

He got up. I was being gently dismissed, and I needed no
second bidding. Trying not to appear as flustered as I felt I
straightened my desk and picked up my bag and jacket.

As he held the door for me, Jarvis asked: 'How is your
mother?'

It seemed to me that over the past few days people used
this question as a kind of lightning conductor, to absorb the
electricity of more contentious topics.

'Pretty well. I'll be visiting her at the weekend.'

'She's fortunate to have such a good daughter.'

I didn't answer. When, I wondered, would people realise
that to be reserved was not necessarily an indication of virtue?

All evening, my head whirled. Whatever Christopher Jarvis
said, I could not help thinking that he had not made the
suggestion unprompted. It was true I *was* flattered. And

pleased, too, that I hadn't been completely superseded by Suzannah Rose Murchie in John Ashe's estimation. Whatever reason he'd had for visiting her on that silent Monday afternoon, slipping in and out of the house like a ghost, it looked as though I had only to give the word to become his trusted assistant.

Whether I wanted to or not was another matter. I told myself that Friday, the day after tomorrow, marked a perfectly acceptable time limit for my decision. Unless pressed I would mention nothing about it until then. Apart from anything else I wanted to enjoy the pleasurable anticipation of my meeting with Alan Mayes.

Christopher Jarvis must have thought the same thing, for he didn't touch on the matter. It was a day humming with what was left unspoken. When I encountered Dorothy in the kitchen at lunchtime I was aware, for once, of having secrets she would have given her right arm to know. But I might have guessed that her intuition about certain things wouldn't let her down.

She and Chef were enjoying a smoke on the back step, but when she saw me she came in at once.

'Not up the village today?'

'I'm not hungry.'

She leaned on the kitchen table. I could feel her eyes running over me speculatively. 'Not like you to lose your appetite,' she said slyly. 'Why's that then?'

'I've no idea.'

'You know what they say, don't you?' She cocked her head in an attempt to catch my eye.

'No.'

'It's one of the symptoms of love.'

'Or of an upset stomach,' I countered tartly.

'Aah . . .' she commiserated, not entirely seriously. 'Come to think of it you have lost a bit of weight.'

'Do you think so?' I glanced down at myself reflexively and realised at once that this small gesture of vanity had fuelled her suspicions.

'Of course,' she said instantly, backing off like the crafty monkey she was, 'it could be the stress and strain.'

For the life of me I couldn't think what I might have said to anyone who might in turn have said something to her. Or was I simply so transparent? These days I seemed surrounded by people who presumed to know me, or what was best for me, better than I did myself.

Fortunately, Alan wasn't one of them. When I saw him standing beneath Fortnum's clock I experienced an easing of mind and body. Perhaps he did too, for he saw me coming and waved, and by the time we were standing face to face we were both smiling broadly.

'Hello,' he said. 'You've no idea how much I've been looking forward to this.'

'Me too.'

'Now then – what would you like to do?'

'I'm in your hands.'

'Then why don't we go for a walk in the park, and find somewhere for supper afterwards? The pictures are fun, but it might be nice to talk . . . What do you think?'

'I agree.'

As we walked together up Piccadilly towards St James's I recalled what I'd said to Georgina about happiness – that you only valued it, or even noticed it, when for some reason it deserted you. This evening I recognised the calm comfort of happiness because for a little while I had missed it.

We strolled around the lake and sat watching the ducks, our faces to the evening sun. During this time we talked about what we could see: the fine weather, the city, the other people, the dogs, the ducks . . . the kind of film we might go to on another occasion. After about an hour, instead of retracing our steps we left the park on the north side and headed for a restaurant Alan knew in Victoria. I hoped he wouldn't feel obliged to overspend since I was pretty sure I earned more than him, and it was too early in our friendship to discuss such things, but it turned out to be a cheerful, unfussy chop-house, within the means of a junior practitioner and serving the sort of simple well-cooked food that suited us both.

'I hope this is all right,' he said, as we sat down at a table in the window.

'It's a real treat,' I replied truthfully.

'I'm not well up on restaurants, but they do you very well here. Have whatever you like,' he added expansively.

We ordered: sausage and mash for him, lamb cutlet for me, and a small carafe of red wine. Sitting face to face, rather than walking side by side, our conversation inched very gently on to more personal ground. I learned that Alan was the same age as me, the youngest of three brothers, born and raised in Scotland, his mother's country, and that as boys they had enjoyed sailing with their father, a retired merchant navy captain. He described his mother as 'the most contented person I know', and I wondered what that must be like. One of his brothers had been badly damaged by the war, losing an eye at Ypres and suffering shell-shock which had left him nervous and depressed; the other had survived the war unscathed as an army mechanic and was now married and doing well in motor industry in the Midlands. He himself had joined up on his eighteenth birthday but seen no action before the armistice. His army career had been about as brief as my marriage, but his older brother's experience had inspired him to take up medicine. After the war he'd trained at St George's and been a houseman for a while before joining Dr Cardew's practice which, in spite of long hours and low pay, he loved. That, I told him, venturing a compliment, must be why he was so good at it.

'I try,' he said. 'But I'm still learning. What about you? I do know of course – forgive me, but your father mentioned – that you're widowed.'

I smiled. 'Don't worry. I didn't think you were a seducer of married women.'

His own smile was fleeting and anxious. 'I take it – the war?'

'Yes, only a month before the end. We'd just got married. A lot happened in a short time.'

'I'll say. How awful.'

'But we were so happy. I have only good memories of our time together. It's like a beautiful thing that I keep because of the pleasure it gives me – not a millstone of misery that I can't shake off.'

I felt I'd summed things up about right, and he obviously thought so too, because his expression became less anxious.

'And since then you've been independent?'

I approved of his choice of words. It made me sound spirited and free rather than dutiful and downtrodden. I told him about secretarial college and my various jobs since, making him laugh out loud with my stories about the publishers.

'You're wicked! I bet they didn't know there was a viper in their bosom . . . But it must have been fun, what made you leave?'

'A combination of things. My boss was a bully, and I saw an advertisement that intrigued me. So for the past few weeks I've been working for Mr and Mrs Jarvis – he owns the Sumpter Gallery in Bowne Street.'

'I'm sorry, I haven't heard of it. I don't go to exhibitions – lack of time rather than interest. And I'm shamefully ignorant.'

'So am I. But if you'd like to I'll take you some time. It's terribly interesting and I know one or two of the artists who are exhibiting there at the moment. Because I've met them at the Jarvises,' I explained hastily, in case he took me for some mock-modest expert on modern art.

'That would be splendid. I think I need a patient, sympathetic guide for my first time.' Something about what he'd just said caused our first moment of mutual awkwardness. Whether either of us blushed I don't know, because for a second we avoided one another's eye.

'Anyway,' he went on. 'You enjoy working for these Jarvises. It obviously suits you.'

'It does. No two days are the same, and they are charming people, the complete opposite of my last boss. They trust me to get on with things, they don't breathe down my neck, they're appreciative. They even invite me to their parties.'

'Is that where you met the artists?'

'Yes, although one of them lives in the house . . .' I postponed describing Suzannah Murchie until he had seen some of her paintings. 'All in all it's proved an excellent move.'

He offered me some more wine. I refused, but my cheeks were already warm, and my inhibitions sufficiently loosened to say: 'Actually, there is the possibility of another job if I want it.'

'You mean instead of, or as well as?'

'As well as.'

He frowned slightly. 'How would that work?'

'It would only be a few hours a week, and Christopher Jarvis would maintain my salary at the same level. I trust him to do that because he was the one who suggested it.'

'Curiouser and curiouser.'

'I'm not sure what to say yet,' I said. 'The person I'd be working for hasn't spoken to me himself. But Mr Jarvis knows Mr Ashe is looking for someone, and is pretty sure if he put my name forward I'd be offered the job.'

'So you're simply trying to decide whether to apply.'

'Not apply exactly . . .' It was hard to convey to him the subtleties of my exchange with Jarvis. 'I'm not sure there's anyone else being considered at the moment.'

'Two jobs sounds a lot to me,' said Alan. 'I have enough trouble coping with one. But you're obviously tempted. What would you be doing?'

'I'm not entirely sure . . .' I caught his incredulous look. 'Not at this stage. I know Mr Ashe is a businessman, he owns nightclubs and things like that. I think I'd be helping out with the clerical work.'

'Hmm. You want to watch out he doesn't have you pushing overpriced watered-down champagne to unsuspecting customers.'

I thought of my conversation with Louise, and laughed. 'No chance of that!'

'What about him – this Mr Ashe? Have you met him?'

'Yes, at one of the Jarvises' lunch parties.'

'And what's he like?'

I hesitated. There was so much I could have said, but this wasn't the right moment.

'He seemed nice enough. He's got a scar on his face from the war, which makes him look rather frightening, but he was very civil and friendly to me, when he didn't have to be.'

'I'm not surprised.' Alan had been gazing at me intently, and his voice was lower and softer than before. 'He has good taste.'

We parted outside the station, where he could catch a train and I could get on a bus.

'I've enjoyed this so much,' he said. 'Can we do it again soon?'

'Yes, please. Thank you for a lovely dinner.'

'Well . . . homely. But it's the company that counts.'

We hovered. A handshake was too formal; anything more, too soon.

'Will you be coming down to see your mother?'

'At the weekend. Saturday night to Sunday night. Do drop in if you're passing.'

'I will if I may. And if you think she wouldn't mind.'

'We'd both like it.'

As he moved away, he said, 'None of my business, but I think you should take that job – nothing ventured nothing gained!'

When I arrived next day the Jarvises were out somewhere with Georgina, and not due to reappear until teatime, according to Dorothy. She and Chef had been given leave to depart early, and in the early afternoon the house settled into a ticking, pregnant silence. Outside it was overcast and a half-hearted drizzle spattered the windows. I settled down to type out copy for the autumn catalogue from Christopher Jarvis's careless, squiggly handwriting. I had no idea whether Suzannah Murchie – with or without company – was in her eyrie. When I heard footsteps on the stairs it was as much to break the silence as anything that I opened the study door and went out.

'Hello.'

'Oh, hello.' She didn't seem in the least surprised to see me, but then she had the advantage of me – she'd probably seen me arrive. She came along the corridor towards me. 'I'm going mad up there. I thought I'd come down and listen to some music.'

'Good idea.'

'How about you?'

'Mr Jarvis left some typing—'

'I mean, would you like to keep me company?'

I mumbled something about needing to take a break, but

she seemed to take my assent as read, and walked past me into the drawing room and over to the gramophone. She took half a dozen records in paper covers from the shelf below and began looking through them.

'What shall we have?'

'I don't mind.'

'Classical? Or the other?'

'You choose,' I said. I was sure she'd decide anyway.

'This is lovely . . .' She took a record from its cover, put it on the turntable, wound the handle and lowered the needle. 'Listen to this.'

It was ballet music, Saint-Saëns' 'The Swan'. The swooping, swooning melancholy of the melody filled the room. Suzannah took a cushion off the sofa and lay down on the floor with her cheek pillowed on it, eyes closed. Feeling rather awkward and a great deal less at home I sat on the end of the sofa. But the beauty of the music seemed to enter my bones and in a minute I relaxed and leaned my head back.

I thought she might have gone to sleep, but when the record ended she got up and removed the needle. While she made her next selection, I asked: 'Have you completed Mr Rintoul's portrait?'

She nodded. 'Bar a few finishing touches, but I like not to look at a picture for a while before I do those.'

I couldn't resist asking: 'What about the surprise?'

She sat down on a chair with the records on her lap. 'It'll be finished when I move on. Which will be fairly soon.'

'You're leaving?' I realised how accustomed I'd become to her presence up there.

'Yes. I only ever intended to stay here while I painted Edward.'

'Where are you going?'

'Well . . .' She looked at me with those still, clear eyes as if assessing my trustworthiness. 'I've taken another commission, so I may find myself a room somewhere near my sitter.'

'Are you allowed to say who it is?'

Her eyes remained on me, steady and stern, as if exacting a pledge.

'John Ashe,' she said.

I was preparing to leave when Christopher Jarvis returned, and came into the study.

'Pamela, are you off? How did you get on with the catalogue?'

'I've done most of it, the pages are on your desk.'

'Thank you so much.'

'Mr Jarvis—'

'Yes?'

I didn't even have to take a breath. I had rarely been so sure of anything.

'About working for Mr Ashe —'

Chapter Eleven

My mother disliked being under an obligation. When I next saw her, the first thing she said after accepting my filial kiss was:

'There was no need for you to trail all the way down here, Pam.'

'I wanted to,' I replied, not quite truthfully.

'I'm quite all right.'

'I'm sure you are,' I said. 'But I wanted to see for myself. You know what a worrier I am.'

Both she and I knew no such thing, but my remark had the desired effect, that of putting all responsibility for the visit fairly and squarely on my shoulders: it was my unnecessary worrying, not any need of hers, that had brought me down here.

She looked pretty well, but tired. That wasn't surprising. The house positively gleamed; she must have relished bringing it back under her control after its period of relative neglect at my hands. To my amazement she had even begun the process of clearing out my father's things. His clothes lay in neat piles on what had been his bed. Knowing how she hated clutter, I asked if she was managing to sleep.

To my further astonishment she told me: 'I've moved into the guest room. It's a nice room and it's never been used to speak of.'

'No . . . Well, good idea,' I said.

'One thing we could do while you're here,' she said a touch

defensively, 'is finish the job. The Sally Army'll take away any stuff that's going, and that room could do with a good spring-clean.'

My heart sank, but I reminded myself that I'd come here to be useful. She'd made a wonderful plain stew for supper that night and we sat and ate it together at the kitchen table. One of my mother's unwritten rules specified that only women, and not more than two at that, could eat in the kitchen, which is why she would have been appalled at my allowing Alan Mayes to eat his toast there. Conversation was a little stilted – we missed Dad's presence almost more in this state of returning normality than we had in the wake of his death, when my mother had been ill. To ease things along, I said:

'Perhaps we'll see Dr Mayes.'

'You tell me.'

'He said he might drop in to see us some time.'

'To see us, or to see you?'

'Both, Mum.' I took the plunge: 'But as a matter of fact he and I did go out together the other night. Just a walk and some supper, it was very enjoyable.'

'Good.' She placed her knife and fork together neatly. 'Well, it's a good thing you left that sherry behind after all.'

There were no clothes left to sort; she had been through all of them. Everything was laundered, ironed and folded, even his socks and handkerchiefs. She was keeping his good overcoat to give to Mrs Coleman's eldest son; I couldn't believe he'd want it, but it was a kind thought, not to be discouraged. The rest we divided into two, for the Ex-Servicemen's Mission and the Salvation Army. I walked up to the telephone that night after supper and called both organisations; both were happy to collect on a Sunday after-noon. I didn't offer to deliver the coat to the neighbour; we left it hanging, spotless and mothballed, in the wardrobe.

Next morning my mother announced that we'd better get on, and took me upstairs to what had been their room.

'If you don't mind,' she said, 'I want us to go through his drawer.'

She took the bottom drawer from the bedside locker and laid it on the bed nearest the door, the one not covered in his clothes. If I needed assurance that it had been a good idea to visit, this was it. Here, I suspected, was one job she had been putting off. The contents had been Dad's private cache, and she didn't know what she might find there, so my presence would have a steadying effect.

'Heaven knows what all these bits and pieces are . . .' she murmured, stirring them with her hand. Beneath the vaguely disparaging tone I sensed her trepidation.

'Let's go through them one at a time, and see, shall we?' I said. 'Then we can decide what to do.'

I found this collection of my father's possessions heartbreaking, and could well understand why my mother had been steeling herself to go through them. They held no surprises or revelations, but their very mundaneness provided a portrait of Gerald Streeter's life. There were his old army cap badge, buttons and shoulder tabs; some newspaper cuttings about his firm, and about the war; snapshots of my mother in an old leather wallet; a smart brush, comb and clipper set she had given him years ago and which he'd obviously thought too good to use; a yellowed ivory shoehorn; a packet of stiff collars and the studs to go with them; a box of cuff links; a dog-eared leather-bound prayer book and Bible that had been his mother's, with her name in the front; an engraved silver propelling pencil and half-hunter watch, both presents for long service at work; a folding travel clock with a cracked crocodile-skin cover; a magnifying glass; an ordnance survey map of Kent; and, most moving of all to me, two poems I had written for him as a child of about ten, in the days when we'd been very close, a kind of unholy alliance which must have driven my mother mad.

'Hm,' she said with a little jerk of the head, reading. 'I remember these . . .'

'I do, too,' I said, 'but I didn't know he'd kept them.'

She didn't look up. 'He thought the world of you.'

To smooth the moment, I read the one I held aloud.

> '"My father has big feet and hands
> And brissles on his cheeks,
> He's like a giant when he stands
> And makes the floor go creak.
> But he is not an oger
> Althow he might well be,
> The very best of fathers
> Is what he is to me."'

I wanted to cry, but managed instead to pull a sceptical face. 'Talk about sucking up . . . What's that one about?'

'Birds,' she said, handing it to me. 'Here.'

If the first poem had been my young self's attempt to curry favour with my father, this one made a stab at a more philosophical vein. I refrained from reading it aloud.

> The birds hop about in the backyard
> And eat all the crumbs from the ground
> They peck and they flutter and chirrup
> And leave all their droppings around.
> [I could hear my mother's voice in that line]
> Their babies are scraggy and naked
> The cat eats them up for his tea,
> But as soon as the birds take off on the
>   wing
> They sing, 'Look at us, we are free!'

'Quite the poet,' said my mother. 'He'd definitely want me to keep these.'

I noted the choice of words, and hoped that her feelings weren't hurt. I wanted to say that if I hadn't given her any poems it didn't mean I loved her less, but that would have been more than she cared to deal with, and would only have embarrassed us both.

I handed the poems back to her. 'Do whatever you like with them, Mum.'

We put the brush and comb, the collars and studs and the shoehorn with the clothes on the bed. The rest of the things we stashed tidily in a tooled leather stationery box on the shelf at the top of the wardrobe, just above his best coat. Then, while my mother made shepherd's pie for lunch, I found an album with some empty pages in the cupboard under the stairs, and sat at the table to stick in the snapshots of her. She pretended to have no interest in them, and to be simply indulging me, but when I asked her for information for captions I could tell she was pleased.

'What? Oh, that's Margate. God in heaven, look at my dress.'

'You look lovely, Mum.'

'I look like a dog's dinner, but it was the fashion.'

'Where's this?'

'That's me and your father at the works Christmas do. About twenty years ago. Alfie and whatsername, Ena, she liked a drink. Good heavens, I haven't seen any of that lot for years . . .'

The Salvation Army came while we were still washing up, and the Mission hot on their heels, which was a good thing – it left us no time for reflection or changes of heart amid the general to-ing and fro-ing. I was still out on the pavement and my mother still in the kitchen when Alan's Morris chugged up.

'You've come at exactly the right time,' I said. 'We've just said goodbye to Dad's things.'

'That's a horrible job.'

'Come in, Mum would love to see you.'

He took my hand briefly. 'You too?'

'Me too.'

He was perfect with her. 'Mrs Streeter, how are you? I've got a free afternoon. Is there anything at all I can do?'

'You didn't come round here to work on your afternoon off.'

'No, well, I admit I came to see you and Pamela, but as I'm here . . .'

'I can't think of anything.'

'Does anything need doing outside?' I asked her.

'No,' said my mother firmly. 'If you feel like a bit of fresh air why don't you take yourselves for a walk, and I'll have the tea made when you get back.'

When the door had closed behind us we couldn't help laughing.

'I think we've been given our marching orders!' said Alan. 'Quite literally.'

'She means well. It's her way of giving us her blessing – telling us to go out and enjoy ourselves.'

'Thank God it's not raining. Where shall we go?'

'I know: take me for a spin in your car.'

He gave me a doubtful smile. 'I hope you know what you're letting yourself in for.'

'It gets you about.'

'Yes, but I'm not fussy.'

'Neither am I. Do let's. Please.'

'I give in.' He opened the door for me and gestured like a chauffeur. 'I'll take you on a tour of the area, featuring the houses of the sick, the halt and the lame, and those with child or just delivered, how's that?'

The car was fine. True, it was a hard ride, and bumpy, and smelt slightly of petrol, but I'd never ridden in a private car before and I couldn't have liked it more. Encouraged by my genuine enthusiasm Alan became confident and voluble. This, after all, was his domain, the one looked after by his practice, and his running commentary displayed as much pride in it and its inhabitants as any country squire.

'That's the twins, remember? Doing fine I'm happy to say . . . In there's Mr and Mrs Dromgoole, what are the chances of one chronic hypochondriac marrying another? Ah, this'll interest you, the young woman in that flat over the shop is completely blind, but she helps run the shop and looks after four children, I never cease to be amazed . . . Now up here we're coming into private patient territory, they're mostly Dr Cardew's, but occasionally I help out . . .'

After half an hour he pulled over at the top of a hill and switched the engine off. 'This do for a minute?' he asked. 'Only I have to be chary of the petrol, the patients depend on it.'

There was something intimate about sitting side by side in the car with its associations of lovers' lane, or perhaps the back seat of the cinema. The window was already open, but out of shyness I wound it down to its fullest extent. On either side of us lay the open spaces of a sports field, and at the foot of the hill the rooftops of south London stretched away towards Kent and the coast. I had a sudden flash of sensory memory, of Pevensey – the clear coastal light, the salty tang of the air, the sound of the sea on the shingle, the texture of the sheets and of Matthew's skin on mine—

'What a wonderful view,' I said.

'I think so.'

I could tell from his voice that he was not looking at the view at all, but at me.

'Pamela—'

'Yes?'

'I just want to say how much it means to me to be with you. I hope we can go on doing this – seeing each other.'

'Of course,' I said. I looked at him now. 'As often as you like.'

'And you?' He took my hand. For a shy young man, his own hand felt warm and firm, not in the least tentative. 'Do you like?'

I nodded. 'I do.'

'Because I realise,' he said, keeping hold of my hand, 'that you have been through some of the most difficult times a woman can go through, and I don't just mean in the past couple of weeks. I'd understand if you told me to go away, I really would. But if you don't, I'd like to – well – keep you company . . .'

Suddenly, he seemed a little flustered, as if he might have said too much, and released my hand. Even after such a short while, I missed its warmth.

'I can't think of anyone whose company I'd rather keep,' I said.

As we drove back to my mother's house we were quiet, but the air sang with our unspoken feelings.

He stayed for tea, and endeared himself further to my mother by carrying the tray and eating two slices of her cake with evident appreciation. When he rose to leave it was a testament to her approval that she allowed me to show him out.

On the doorstep, he said: 'I forgot to ask – did you decide whether to let your name go forward for that other job?'

'Yes,' I said, 'I did. And I am.'

'Well done!' He beamed, and leaning forward kissed me on the cheek. 'I'm sure you won't regret it. Next Wednesday?'

'Next Wednesday it is.'

As I rejoined my mother I felt sure she must be able to

see, like a postal stamp, the place where he'd kissed me. But all she said was: 'If this keeps up I can see I shall have to get back to baking once a week.'

That night in bed I was overwhelmed by such a mixture of emotions – sadness, elation, longing, remorse, hope – that I wept. I wept long, but not inconsolably. My sleep, when it came, was deep and peaceful and I woke feeling shiny and fresh as a rain-washed morning in the sunshine.

'Mr Ashe will be coming to the party,' said Christopher Jarvis. 'I know that you're not able to join us, but he suggests that if he were to arrive early, you and he might be able to have a talk before you leave.'

I agreed to this arrangement, although I was secretly disappointed not to be meeting Ashe sooner. I was worried in case my resolve, given too much time, would waver; and I would have liked to be able to tell Alan about it when I saw him on Thursday. But there it was; I would have to possess my soul in patience.

As for Dorothy, she seemed to have abandoned, or forgotten, any interest she might have shown in my social life. Of course she had only been teasing; she had no way of knowing that she was right, or that a little persistence now might have yielded results. Still, it was frustrating to have to keep silent on the matter just when I was in the mood to talk about it – she would have made such a wonderful audience.

Then I remembered that I did not have to endure the frustration. I had available an equally good listener, who had the added advantage of being an old friend. On Monday night I telephoned Barbara, and arranged to meet her the following evening for high tea at our usual Corner House; or at least what had been 'usual' during my time at Osborne's. It was a little odd to be going back there now, and I was jumpy, half expecting to bump into the dreadful Max, who would doubt-less bear a grudge against me to his grave.

I arrived first, and so had the doubtful advantage of being able to see Barbara as she arrived, before she saw me. She was drably neat as ever, and terribly thin. The collar of her jacket stood away from her neck, and the jacket itself hung on her like a sack. I entertained the brief, unworthy thought that the tailors wouldn't continue to want an employee who looked so poorly tailored herself.

But she was plainly pleased to see me. 'Pamela – I don't need to ask how you are.'

We touched cheeks; hers was very cold. 'And you?'

'Not bad. Shall we order? Then we can talk?'

We both chose an omelette, with tea for her and coffee for me. As soon as the waitress had gone she lit a cigarette.

'So what are they feeding you on up there in Highgate? Caviar and strawberries?'

I laughed. 'Not exactly.'

'The last time we spoke,' she said, with a hint of reproof, 'your poor father had just died.'

'I know. I shouldn't be so happy.'

'I don't see why. I'm sure he'd be delighted.'

'That's what I think.'

'Come on then, out with it.'

I told her about Alan – the sort of person he was, my feel-ings about him, and what he had said to me. By the time I'd finished we'd seen off the omelettes and were on a second round of tea and coffee. Barbara listened, as always, intently and impassively.

'I can tell you don't need my opinion,' she said, 'but for what it's worth he sounds like an all-round Good Thing.'

'He is.'

'And I'm so glad.' She put out a hand and squeezed my forearm. 'I really am.'

I knew her too well not to detect the small shadow in her face and manner, but I couldn't so much as guess at its cause. I had never known how she spent her time outside those rare occasions when we were in each other's company. She was not so much secretive as uncommunicative. As time went by it had dawned on me how privileged I was to have been her confidante all those years ago. I was a poor sort of friend to her but then, I asked myself, did she have any others?

Perhaps not, because suddenly, and with typical abruptness, she said: 'I said I wasn't bad. That's not true. I'm in a rotten state.'

'Oh, Barbara . . . Why? What is it? Can you tell me?'

'I can, but we shan't be much further forward. I'm just not happy. Unhappy, and lonely, and –' she frowned – 'paralysed.'

'How do you mean?'

'I don't seem able to change anything. I don't know how. I've lost the use of my will the way some people lose the use of their legs and arms.'

I was dismayed by her hopelessness; not just for her but for myself, as though the condition were contagious and might infect me.

'Of course you haven't,' I said. 'You may feel that way, because you're down, but you only need to change one thing – one small thing – and you'll begin to feel better. You'll realise you can change other things too.'

She shook her head. 'You're talking as if I'm like you, and I'm not.'

'We wouldn't be friends if you were. I rely on you, Barbara! You're my touchstone.' I hadn't known this till I said it, but it was true.

'You don't say?' She managed her dour, sceptical smile. 'You do pretty well, considering.'

I ignored this. 'How are things at work?'

'The same as ever. I'm invisible. I'm that funny old thing—'

'Barbara, you are not old!'

'That funny old thing who comes in every day rain, shine or head cold, who never takes holidays, and who gets the job done.'

'I bet you're more precious than rubies.'

'Precious?' She turned away to consider this, the hand holding her cigarette masking her face. 'It would be comforting to think so, but no. It would be *very* nice to be precious . . .'

'Everyone is to somebody,' I said, and immediately regretted my fatuous complacency.

'I'm certainly not, to anyone. I'm not complaining, it may well be my fault, but it's a fact. And to be fair I've been perfectly content with the situation till—' She bit off the end of the sentence and I heard her sharp intake of breath. 'Actually, Pamela, I do know why.' She turned her face towards me and for a second or less I glimpsed the bottomless, black depths of her misery. My hands flew to my own face to cover my dismay.

'I do know why,' she said again. 'I want my baby. My baby was precious, and I would have been precious to him. I want him and I miss him.'

'Oh, Barbara,' I whispered, 'my dear, dear Barbara!' But I was at a loss, and she was drifting down, and away from me.

'I did a terrible thing . . . terrible.'

'You did what you thought was best,' I said.

She swung her head back and forth, not in denial but like an animal trying to rid itself of pain. 'I gave away my life.'

The waitress came over and asked if we'd finished. I told her we had, but as she stacked our things on a tray she gave Barbara a funny look. It wasn't her fault, she was only a young girl, she couldn't know that right here, among the teacups and toast crumbs and warm, inconsequential chatter, a person's world was unravelling.

I felt fiercely protective of Barbara. 'Come on,' I said, 'I'll take you home.'

I expected at least a token refusal, some semblance of unwillingness, but when I took her arm she rose and followed, and stood next to me like a child as I paid at the till. Out in the road I hailed a taxi, banking on there being enough money between us to pay for the fare.

When the driver asked, 'Where to?' I realised I had no idea.

'Wait a minute,' I said. 'Barbara – where do you live?'

She gave an address in Waterloo – not too far away, thank God – and I relayed it to him. In the back of the taxi I held her hand, sandwiched between both of mine as though we were about to play a child's game, except that hers felt heavy and lifeless.

'You mustn't think of going to work tomorrow,' I said. 'Do you promise me you won't?'

'What else would I do?' she asked.

'Rest. Go to the doctor.' I realised neither of these alternatives sounded especially tempting, but they were all I could think of. I simply didn't know what she would normally do for pleasure or what her life consisted of. 'Now I know where you live I'll come down and see you tomorrow evening,' I added, though my heart sank. It seemed every time my life took off, something leapt, caught my tail feathers, and dragged me back down. But that, I reprimanded myself, was no way to look at the plight of a friend.

As we went up the Strand and round the Aldwych she seemed to rally a little and even displayed something of her old sardonic humour.

'I feel like a drunk being taken back after a hard night. You don't need to do this.'

'I want to.'

'I'm sorry, Pamela.'

'Don't be. I'm so glad you confided in me. I want to do anything – anything – I can to help.'

'You're a brick, but I'm a lost cause.'

'I am not a brick,' I said, a touch impatiently, 'I'm your friend. And it's not like you to be defeatist.'

She looked out of the window, saying so quietly that I only just heard: 'You don't know what I'm like.'

When the taxi pulled up, Barbara was sufficiently recovered to offer to pay half, and I didn't demur. The house was a YWCA hostel, about as homely and welcoming as a commercial hotel. When we'd settled up, she said: 'I'm sorry, Pamela, but I'm not inviting you in.'

'It can't be that bad,' I said. 'If it is, you shouldn't be here.'

'It's perfectly adequate. And as the oldest inhabitant I get preferential treatment – no curfew and extra marmalade.'

I couldn't tell if she was joking. 'I'd like to see where you live.'

'This is it. Honestly, thanks for coming down here, but I'd rather keep things separate.'

It felt as though, having been vouchsafed a glimpse of her desolation, a heavy door was being slowly but firmly pushed shut in my face.

'What can I do?' I asked. 'There must be something, surely.'

'No. Really. I have these bad moments and I'm just sorry that this one happened when it did.'

'I'm not. We've known each other for so long, you don't need to protect me from these things.' This sounded pretty hollow, even to me. Over the years, in spite of what I knew, I had hardly been the model of the concerned friend. I tried desperately to think of something that would, however belatedly, lodge in her mind and convince her of my seriousness.

'Barbara!' I grabbed her hand, which was unresponsive as before. 'Barbara. You're precious to me.'

She left her hand in mine for a second as she looked at me, trying to gauge the weight of this declaration.

'If you say so.'

'You are. You *are*.'

'Thank you.' I couldn't tell whether the thanks were genuine or mocking. With her hand on the door, she said: 'Don't come down here again, will you? I shall be fine now. Let's meet up again in a while and you can tell me all about everything.'

'All right . . . Barbara—'

'Promise?'

There was a fierce panic in her voice which subdued my better judgement. 'Promise.'

'Goodbye.'

'Goodnight.'

I was the only person at the bus stop. As I waited I couldn't help thinking of Barbara, also alone, in her room in that bleak hostel. Some friendship! I very nearly turned back, to knock on her door and demand entry. But we had entered into a pact, and I was bound by it.

The next day was fine and I was due to see Alan in the evening. The shadow cast by my meeting with Barbara, like any shadow, grew shorter as the morning went on. Stoic though she was, she was only human. Over the years she had reached an accommodation with her past, but it was only to be expected that from time to time that accommodation would break down. What she had said to me was clearly true – she was used to these lapses, and could recover from them quickly. Why, by the time she said goodnight she had regained her composure and was once more, typically, keeping me at arm's length. She knew where I was. What more could I do?

It was appalling how easily I soothed my conscience and set Barbara and her troubles aside. There were plenty of other things to think about. Edward Rintoul, never one to pass up hospitality, had returned to attend the party. The small fourth bedroom on the first floor which, Dorothy informed me, had been used as a boxroom since Christmas, was being brought back into commission for his benefit.

Dorothy had spent most of the previous day clearing it, under the supervision of Amanda and with her not very effective assistance. She complained to me about this when I went to the kitchen to make coffee for the Jarvises and myself.

'They never say no, that's their trouble. They say yes, and then wonder how they're going to manage it. All very well and fine, but it's muggins here who has to do the work.'

'They're very hospitable,' I pointed out. 'They don't like to turn people away.'

Chef, who was setting out cold meat and cheese on platters for lunch, had obviously had enough of Dorothy's grumbling for one morning and took the unprecedented step of agreeing with me.

'And a good thing too, or we might be out of a job.'

'Don't be daft!' snapped Dorothy. 'You think those two want to do a hand's turn for themselves, visitors or no visitors?'

'Stop bellyaching, girl.'

'That's rich, coming from you – trailing in here with a face like a slapped arse day in day out!'

'You watch your tongue, young lady, I don't have to put up with that kind of talk!'

I was witnessing a boiling-over of feeling that threatened to be extremely messy, and stepped in to avert it.

'I'm sure they appreciate what you – *all* of us,' I added tactfully, 'do for them.'

Dorothy's answer was to heave a seismic, put-upon sigh. She and Chef exchanged a look in which venom and mutual understanding were equally mixed. But in spite of her moaning I knew she liked being here, and would have found

most other households not nearly exciting enough for her
lively curiosity, quick intuition and gossipy tongue.

'Anyway,' I went on. 'Suzannah won't be here much longer.'

'Don't I know it. And it'll be no picnic clearing up that
attic.'

'Let's hope the Jarvises like the mural.'

'They're in it, aren't they?' she said, as if that was enough.
'They won't care. People'd rather be in any picture than none
at all, it's like the papers.'

I thought it prudent to move the subject away from our
employers. 'Do you know where she's going?'

She shrugged. 'Search me. Mr Ashe has been calling,
sniffing around, perhaps he's dragging her off to his lair.'

'She is going to paint his portrait. She told me.'

'There you are then. Good luck to her. You wouldn't catch
me cooped up alone with old monster-chops, I can tell you.'
She shuddered theatrically. 'He gives me the creeps.'

That evening, Alan and I went to the cinema. Halfway through
the film he put his arm round my shoulders, and when we
walked down the street afterwards we held hands. At the end
of the evening we kissed, and I wanted it never to end.

I didn't think of Matthew until I was in bed, and then only
briefly. My thoughts were no longer tinged with remorse, but
wholly peaceful. He had been a blessing then, and he still
was. As I fell asleep I framed the words to him in my head,
like a sort of prayer: 'Thank you.'

The next morning I woke feeling buoyant, carried on a wave
of happiness from the evening before, and excited anticipation over my meeting with John Ashe. I fretted a little over
what to wear – not that there was a great deal of choice –
but put a stop to that by telling myself that this was nothing
more than a job interview, and I should look neat and

businesslike. Besides, something told me that John Ashe would see right through any affectation. Whatever he had approved of in me, it was unlikely to have been my fashion sense.

This was just as well, because the house was busy with party preparation and I had almost nothing to do in the office, so I spent most of the day helping Amanda Jarvis with the flowers and furniture-moving, and tidying up the front garden, none of them activities designed to improve a *soignée* appearance.

While I was trimming the hedge (Christopher Jarvis had acquired a few more tools to encourage me) Dorothy came out to polish the door knocker and letter box.

'You going this evening?' she asked.

'No,' I said, 'not this time.'

'Lucky you, I've got to stay. Did they ask you?'

'They did, and it was very kind of them, but I can't go.'

'Mmm . . .' She flicked at a cobweb with her duster. 'Now why would that be?'

I didn't answer, stooping to assess the level of the top of the hedge with a frown of deep concentration.

'You could go home, you know,' she said. 'There's nothing doing here. I would, if I had a date. They won't mind.'

'Probably not,' I replied, 'but I might as well make myself useful.' I straightened up and stretched my back. 'You must be pleased the swallows have flown, Dorothy. No more mess to clean up in the porch.'

'I suppose I should be grateful for small mercies . . .' She folded her arms and looked up at the deserted nest with its shroud of cobwebs. 'Poor little blighters. One look at old uglymug and they were off.'

The party was due to begin at six. I came in from the garden at half past four, washed my hands and combed my hair, and sat at my desk nervously pretending to work. I could hear people's voices: Georgina's piping tones, Amanda's cooing, Edward Rintoul's staccato growl, Christopher's calm drawl. Dorothy's muttering and humming as she went about her business. No Suzannah – she was probably staying in her eyrie till the last moment, and who could blame her?

At five fifteen the doorbell rang. I heard Christopher Jarvis say, 'I'll answer that!' and then there was a brief exchange in the hall before he opened the door.

'Pamela, Mr Ashe is here.' He stood back and Ashe entered.

I got to my feet.

'Hello again,' said Ashe. I remember a curious handshake, firm but not fully engaged. My own hand was not gripped, but encircled – elegantly trapped, like a bird in a cage.

'I think,' said Jarvis, 'that the best place for the two of you is in here. The other rooms have been taken over, rather.'

'The ideal setting for a business discussion,' said Ashe, glancing around. As he did so, his unmarked profile was towards me, and his scarred side reflected in the mirror opposite. For a split second there seemed to be a third person in the room, and my skin crept.

'I'll leave you to it then,' said Jarvis. 'Would you like Dorothy to bring some tea?'

'Not for me, thank you,' I said.

'Nor me,' said Ashe. 'But if you had any of that exceptional malt . . .'

Jarvis nodded and withdrew. Ashe sat down on the sofa, but did not invite me to take an easy chair, for which I was glad. I felt both safer and more confident behind my desk.

'I'll cut to the chase,' he said. 'I understand from Christopher that in principle you'd be interested in doing a few hours' work a week for me, and that they could spare you.'

'That's right,' I said. 'But of course I've no idea what sort of work needs doing, or whether I'd be qualified for it.'

'I'll be the judge of that.' He had a calm, neutral way of speaking, though his eyes were piercing. He uses his voice like a mask, I thought.

'Anyway,' he said, 'the work's perfectly routine. Correspondence, filing and calls, the sort of thing you're used to here – though perhaps a little less interesting.'

'Could I ask who's been doing this until now?'

'I had a full-time secretary, but there wasn't enough for her to do. And I like to have the place to myself most of the time. In contrast to your present employers; they like nothing better than a crowd, as I'm sure you know.'

At this moment there was a tap on the door and Dorothy came in bearing a small salver with Ashe's whiskey, a jug of water and a glass. On her way out she pulled a face of round-eyed, open-mouthed astonishment, which I ignored.

'I hope you don't mind this,' he said. 'It's not my habit to drink at teatime, but . . .' He took a sip, closing his eyes for a moment as he savoured it. 'This will probably be my only one. There's far too much champagne in my line of business.'

This was my cue to ask: 'Could you tell me a little more about that – about the business?'

'I own half a dozen clubs in London. Nightclubs, I suppose you'd call them, although a couple of them are no more than fashionable bars. I own a good deal of property for rent, as well, but the clubs provide my main source of income. I should tell you that there would be occasions when I'd ask you to call at one or other of these places on my behalf.' He must have caught something doubtful in my reaction, for he added: 'During the day. Checking books, that sort of thing. Dealing with junior staff, you wouldn't mind that, would you?'

'I don't know, I've never had to do it.'

'Christopher says you practically run things here.'

'He exaggerates.'

'Probably. But your *sangfroid* is one of your more evident characteristics.'

'Shall I need that, then?' I asked. '*Sangfroid*?'

He answered the question with a rhetorical one of his own. 'It's a useful attribute in any walk of life, don't you think? As to hours, I was thinking in terms of two afternoons a week. But there can be considerable flexibility, to suit you and your work here.' He tilted his head slightly, in a way both quizzical and collusive. The impression given was that we were engaged not in negotiation but in a ritual whose outcome was a foregone conclusion.

I bridled slightly. 'That is important. I wouldn't want to inconvenience Mr and Mrs Jarvis, who've been so good to me.'

He inclined his head in silent agreement. 'And of course I shall at the very least match what they pay you. That would be only fair since your work for me would in effect be overtime.'

I realised for the first time how much more I would be earning. Ashe sipped his whiskey before taking another step in the ritual dance.

'My office is in Soho, by the way. I assume that wouldn't be a problem.'

'No.'

'You yourself live in Fitzrovia, I believe?' I'd never heard the term before, but he went on: 'Sometimes called north Soho. We're practically neighbours.'

'When would you want me to start?' I asked. The question was intended as another ritual move, but I heard at once that was not how it sounded, and Ashe was quick to draw the inference.

'So – you'll take the job?'

'Yes.'

'Good. Here's what I suggest.' He drained his glass and

put it down. Ritual over, he was brisk. 'Come down and visit
the office next week one afternoon when you've finished here
– say Wednesday at six o'clock – and then you can begin the
following week.'

'Yes. Thank you. I will.'

'Good.' He rose. 'I must say, Mrs Griffe, it's a pleasure to
meet a woman as incisive as yourself.'

Once again he held out his hand; once again my own was
encircled. It was the oddest thing. I was not held or restrained
in any way, and yet I couldn't help feeling that if I attempted
to withdraw my hand precipitately the jaws of the trap would
snap shut.

It was a ridiculous notion; the handshake was brief and
businesslike. He took a card from his breast pocket and laid
it on my desk. 'My address and telephone number. If for any
reason you can't make the agreed time, just let me know.
Otherwise I shall look forward to seeing you next Wednesday
evening.'

The door closed behind him. I picked up the card, and
read the few words that were to change the course of my life.
Ashe Enterprises, 12 Soho Square, W1.

I left almost at once after that. I didn't want my departure
to coincide with the arrival of guests, nor did I wish to engage
in conversation about the interview with any other members
of the household, especially Dorothy, who would be beside
herself with curiosity.

On the way up the road I passed the great black motor
car, which Amanda had told me was a Hispano-Suiza,
belonging to John Ashe. Like its owner, or more probably
by association with him, it had a presence far beyond the
smooth, heavy planes of metal and chrome. The gilded bird
on the bonnet was a stork in flight: not, it seemed to me,
the friendly, baby-carrying stork of popular children's stories,

but a creature strange and fierce as a pterodactyl, its angular wings mantling prey, its long, predatory beak poised to stab. The car's rich leather interior was like a cave. As I glanced in I half expected to see some other strange creature lurking in its depths. But I saw only the young driver, whose dark gaze met mine calmly, as though he were used to the curiosity of passers-by.

And yet, there was no mistaking my excitement – my own feet had wings as I headed for the bus stop.

Chapter Twelve

That Sunday I went down to see my mother again. I knew she was under no illusion as to the dual motive for my visit, but that was all to the good: her telling herself that I was only there to see Alan prevented the hated sense of obligation and made things easier for both of us. And with the long and unusual hours that he worked it made sense for me to do the travelling from time to time.

It rained heavily in the afternoon; we went for a drive as before and parked at the top of the hill. There was no view this time. Instead the windows streamed, like bead curtains, all around us as we talked. No longer embarrassed by intimacy, we sat as close as the Morris's front seat would allow. He told me for the first time about his interest in psychiatry.

'I love general practice, it's what I've always wanted to do. But the more patients I come into contact with the more I realise that some of their worst ills aren't the ones they've ostensibly come to see me about. Honestly, Pamela, you'd be amazed how many sad and desperate people there are.'

I thought, with a twinge, of Barbara. 'I believe you.'

'The war left its legacy, of course. But one can't always find such a directly attributable cause. And people are ashamed of their unhappiness because they feel there's no reason for it. And there are difficulties with children, or parents, or between man and wife. Some of my patients have physical symptoms which I *know* have psychological roots. But it's hard for me, and for them, to talk about it. I don't like to meddle in an area where I have no qualifications for fear of doing more harm – and apart from their natural reserve and embarrassment they're loath to unburden themselves to the junior partner, a young whippersnapper like me. They'd rather see Dr Cardew, who probably delivered them, let alone their children, and who will take them at face value and give them a bottle of pink stuff. Don't misunderstand me, Pamela, he's a good doctor and a caring man, but he's an orthodox physician through and through. No one's going to get any uncomfortable insights from him. But as things stand there's so little I can do.'

It was the most passionate I'd seen Alan. Looking back I think that was the moment I began to love him.

'So what *will* you do?' I asked. 'If you continue to have these convictions it doesn't sound as though general practice will suit you.'

'No, you're right. It would be downright unethical to hold the views I do and ignore them. But I can scarcely let them loose on my patients with no clinical training or experience to back them up. I'm thinking of retraining, but it's a big decision with all sorts of implications. Not least forfeiting my hard-earned salary for a good few years.'

'That doesn't matter,' I said. 'You must do it. The loss of income may be inconvenient, but that's nothing to the regrets you'd have if you didn't follow your instincts.'

He took my hand in both of his and looked down at our joined hands so that what he said next felt like a promise entered into together; a mutual vow.

'Then I shall. Your opinion means more to me than anything. Things may take a little while—'

'It doesn't matter how long it takes.'

He stroked the back of my hand. 'You wouldn't mind keeping company with a hard-up, hard-pressed medical student?'

'No,' I said, and couldn't resist adding: 'And from next week I shall be earning more, so we'll still be able to go to the pictures.'

'You're starting? With the mysterious Mr Ashe?'

'I am.'

'That's tremendous – congratulations!' His pleasure in my small achievement was delightful, but I simply wasn't used to such overwhelming approval.

'We'll see how it works out,' I said cautiously.

'It'll work out wonderfully . . .' He stroked my cheek, his eyes shining as our faces grew closer together. 'Dearest, dearest Pamela . . . we're both of us starting on a great adventure.'

The party, I gathered, had been a success. Dorothy was full of it – the music, the boozing, the dancing, the 'necking' as she called it. In spite of her best efforts the drawing room still smelt of smoke, three glasses had been broken, and some caviar had been squashed on the seat of the brocade sofa.

'Dirty beggars,' she said, clearly delighted. 'One thing though, somebody's backside is going to look even worse. You should have been there,' she added. 'It was quite an evening.'

'It sounds it.'

'Your Mr Ashe was the only sober one there.'

'He's not mine, Dorothy. And he doesn't like champagne, apparently.'

'Told you did he?' she asked, with a mock-innocent expression. 'Over the whiskey?'

'Yes, as it happens.'

'Come on then,' she said, hoisting herself on to the kitchen table and folding her arms expectantly. 'That's enough secrets. What were you and him in such a huddle about?'

'We weren't in a huddle. It was purely business. I'm going to do some work for him.'

'Ooh, I see!'

'There's nothing to see, as you put it. He mentioned something to Mr Jarvis, and they can spare me for a few hours a week, so . . .' I made a vague gesture to indicate what an incredibly trivial and everyday matter it was. But that didn't fool Dorothy.

'Rather you than me,' she said, screwing up her face. 'I hope he's paying you double to sit looking at that all day.'

'He's paying me more than adequately, and it won't be all day,' I said.

'You won't leave us, though, will you?'

'Certainly not.'

'Good.' She slipped down off the table and opened the cleaning cupboard. 'Because this place has been a lot more organised since you got here.'

I knew Dorothy well enough by now to understand that this was her way of saying she'd miss me.

'Don't worry,' I said. 'I'll still be keeping an eye on you.'

She grinned cheekily. 'Not this afternoon, you won't. I'm off early in loo.'

I hadn't expected to see John Ashe again until our meeting on Wednesday, but he called at Seven Crompton Terrace late on Monday afternoon. Christopher Jarvis was in town at the gallery, and Amanda had gone with him to do some shopping. I came back from posting letters in the village at about five, and the Hispano-Suiza was parked outside the gate in the space where the Riley normally stood.

When I got inside the house was very quiet and there was no sign of the visitor. I was about to leave anyway, and could hear Chef in the kitchen, so I popped in.

'Goodnight, Chef.'

''Night, Mrs Griffe.'

'Oh by the way —' I pretended that this inconsequential matter had occurred to me quite randomly – 'is Mr Ashe here? I saw his car outside.'

'He came to collect her.' Chef jerked his head upward, indicating the top of the house. 'She's moving out today.'

I had received due warning, but it was still a surprise, which I did my best to conceal. It struck me as odd that Suzannah should be leaving when the Jarvises, her hosts for the past few months, were not present. As I emerged into the hallway I heard slow footsteps on the stairs and John Ashe's uniformed driver appeared. On the couple of occasions I'd seen him before, sitting at the wheel of the car, I hadn't really noticed his appearance. Now I saw that he was an exceptionally handsome young man – dark-haired and olive-skinned, with wonderfully lustrous eyes. Elegant in his dark green breeches and jacket, he was tall but quite slim, and struggling to carry a large, battered suitcase in one hand, and a paint-stained canvas holdall in the other.

'Good afternoon, madam.' His voice was soft, with that precise diction that often accompanies the suppression of a regional accent. He obviously wasn't aware of my lowly position in the household, and I didn't correct him. His deference was charming.

'Good afternoon – are you going out with those? Let me open the door for you.'

'Thank you, madam.'

I opened the front door wide, and did the same with the gate. He carried his burden out to the car, opened the boot and loaded it. I went to the office to collect up my things. I heard Ashe and Suzannah come down, and the driver met them in the hall and relieved them of Suzannah's easel, art folders and cloak. I couldn't imagine how they would fit it all into the car, even such an impressively large one.

I emerged from the house as the driver was getting in behind the wheel. He had resolved the space problem by putting the folders and easel in the foot well of the front seat, the easel propped up like an angular, skeletal passenger. Suzannah sat in the back seat on my side, next to Ashe. Her face, small and pale in its cloud of silvery hair, was turned to the window, but she didn't appear to see me. My last sight of her was that pale face, seeming to float in the darkness of the car like a will o' the wisp as she was borne away.

That evening I tried ringing Barbara, but got no reply. Now that I could picture the large, dour hostel where she lived I found the persistent unanswered ringing an unbearably lonely sound. Surely, I thought, there must be others in the building, why didn't they pick up the phone?

First thing next morning I asked Amanda Jarvis whether I might make a short phone call, for which I would pay.

'A very old friend was taken ill the other night,' I explained, 'and I haven't been able to contact her at home. The place where she works might be able to tell me something.'

'My dear, you must,' cried Amanda. 'Set your mind at rest, do . . . Use the telephone in the drawing room, why don't you.'

'I shan't be more than a minute.'

'Be as long as you like!'

She was kind as always, but I anticipated only the briefest exchange with Rice and Claydon, a somewhat stuffy organisation which wouldn't approve of personal calls in office hours. I tried, without actually lying, to sound as much as possible like a business caller.

'I wonder if I might speak to Miss Chisholm.'

'I'm afraid she's not here,' said the thinly civil male voice. 'May I ask who this is?'

'Pamela Griffe. I work for Mr Christopher Jarvis at the Sumpter Gallery.'

'Can I be of any assistance? Does Mr Jarvis have an account with us?'

'Not at the moment, no . . .' Considering that this line of questioning could only end in confusion and embarrassment, I came to the point. 'When will Miss Chisholm be coming back?'

'Tomorrow I believe. She's not been well.'

'I see,' I said, as unfeelingly as possible. 'In that case I'll catch up with her in due course.' He began to speak again, but I cut him off with a brisk: 'Sorry to have troubled you,' and hung up.

'How is your friend?' enquired Amanda Jarvis as I emerged.

'Better, apparently. Thank you for letting me use the phone. How much do I owe you?'

'Not a thing, my dear . . . I'm glad all's well.'

My conscience wasn't entirely clear after this conversation, but it was sufficiently salved for me to indulge in some retrospective self-justification: Barbara had always been secretive, and regretted her lapse; I had called and received no answer; her indisposition had not been severe or protracted; she would be back at work tomorrow. I promised myself that I would arrange to see her again soon.

Dorothy was busy at the top of the house all morning, spring-cleaning the recently vacated spare bedroom. Suzannah herself had left a letter for the Jarvises directing them to the 'present' she had left for them, and they expressed great excitement about the mural. They were certainly unusual – I could detect not the smallest hint of dismay at having one of their walls painted over in this way. They even invited me up to the attic at lunchtime to admire it, which I was able to do quite naturally since I hadn't seen it in its completed form.

'So many people!' I exclaimed. 'Do you know them all?'

'More or less,' said Christopher. 'They're excellent like-nesses, but there are one or two I don't recognise, so they must be friends of hers she's thrown in for good measure.'

'Pamela . . .' Amanda took my arm and led me closer to the mural. 'Have you seen yourself?'

'Oh good heavens!'

It was the last thing I expected. My hands flew to my face and my cheeks burned. I was towards the bottom right-hand corner of the painting. Above the neat white collar of my blouse my face was serious, a little severe even, except for a hint of humorous disapproval around the mouth. I suspect it was the face I wore when addressing Dorothy.

The Jarvises were both smiling indulgently at my discom-fiture. 'She's definitely caught you,' said Christopher Jarvis. 'Or should I say one aspect of you.'

'Pamela's much prettier than that,' said Amanda sweetly, 'especially when she smiles.'

'It's true she hasn't flattered you,' said her husband. 'Unlike her latest patron, whom for what I assume to be sound commercial reasons she's treated most diplomatically.'

I saw what they meant. John Ashe was on the far right of the painting, his clean profile presented to us, with the effect that he seemed to be turning away from everyone else.

The person closest to him, at his shoulder, was me.

That evening Louise knocked on my door on her way out to work. She was at her most dazzlingly glamorous, and I told her so – but not that we were now fellow employees.

'It's my uniform,' she said airily, smoothing the turquoise lamé over her slim hips. 'I could hardly turn up in a wool two-piece.'

'I suppose not,' I agreed. Round her neck was a long string of cultured pearls, loosely knotted at the nape so that the

loop hung down her bare back. Her hair was now an extraordinary pinkish-red that owed nothing to nature, its sleek
finger-waves glossy as satin. Several inches of gossamer
fringing shimmered at her hem, dipping to just above the
knee on one side, slithering high enough on the other to reveal
a flash of lace stocking-top.

'That's a beautiful dress,' I commented admiringly. 'Where
did you get it?'

'Darling, isn't it? Madame let me borrow it. No end of
rich people come into the club, and I'm a sort of walking
advertisement.'

She was certainly something, though I couldn't help
wondering what the Apache's lady customers would make of
quite such a sumptuously turned-out hostess. Louise arrayed
in Madame's finest was not so much decoration as competition.

'Anyway,' she went on, 'I only popped in to say hello, and
to find out how you were.'

'Thank you, I'm fine. I hardly like to ask you in in that
outfit, but if you'd like something to drink—'

'No.' She held up perfectly manicured hands. 'No. But
quickly –' I could tell she was coming to the real reason for
her visit – 'how's the doctor?'

'He's fine too.' I tried to be non-committal but my face
must have given me away. Her own lit up as she took my
wrist and squeezed it.

'Pamela, I'm so pleased!'

'It isn't anything, really, we're just getting to know one
another.'

'Don't be silly, it's written all over you!'

'What is?' I asked, beaming.

'*It!* You've never looked better, honestly.'

'Really?' I glanced self-deprecatingly down at myself, then
at her.

'Yes! Anyway, forget all this!' She flicked at the sparkling material. 'Anyone can look good in an expensive dress. You know what the best beauty treatment is . . .'

'No.'

She leaned towards me and I was enveloped in a wave of flowery scent.

'*Love!*'

Later that evening Mrs Dent knocked on the door and said there was a young man on the telephone for me. The tone in which she conveyed the information suggested that I was displaying the first signs of an unsightly and contagious condition which, unchecked, would romp through her other tenants and bring her establishment into disrepute.

'Try not to be long,' she said as I flew down the stairs ahead of her. 'It's getting late.'

'I can't be long,' said Alan, 'but isn't it tomorrow that you're to visit Mr Ashe's office?'

'That's right, after work.'

'I managed to change my evening off – why don't I meet you afterwards and you can tell me about it?'

'Could you? But I don't know how long it'll take . . .'

'Never mind that. Probably about an hour. Tell me where you're going to be, and I'll make sure I'm somewhere within spotting distance when you come out.'

'All right.' I gave him the address, and warned him jokingly: 'It's Soho, remember, be careful!'

He laughed. 'Don't worry, I'll beat off the loose women. Must dash – 'bye!'

As I put the phone down Mrs Dent was just closing her door. By the look on her face I could tell that my last remark had confirmed her darkest misgivings. I managed to get halfway up the stairs before bursting into laughter.

*   *   *

Next day Christopher Jarvis asked me to accompany him to the gallery in the afternoon.

'A few things need doing down there,' he said, 'and since you have to be in town anyway, I thought this might suit us both.'

Again I sensed the lightest web of conspiracy, of being eased along a preordained path, but told myself it was nonsense. My employers were never anything but kind and charming, and all Mr Jarvis was doing now was proposing a plan for our mutual convenience.

To my delight, we drove there in the Riley. As we roared down Highgate Hill with the top down, and the hot summer wind combed through my hair, my heart fluttered and strained in my chest like a flag – this was another of those moments which three short months ago I could never have imagined. I couldn't help wondering what the groundlings on the pavement made of us. Would they guess that I was no more than this handsome man's secretary? Or would they suppose I was his sister, wife – mistress? I tilted my chin up and adopted the slightly glazed, haughty half-smile that I had seen on the faces of smart women in sports cars.

'Not too blowy for you?' he asked, voice raised over the rush of air and engine.

'No – no, not at all!'

'Good! Some women worry about their hair, you know.'

'Not me!'

He turned and grinned. 'One more way in which you differ from the herd!'

All in all the drive made me feel so wonderful that I never wanted it to end, but when we reached the Sumpter and I looked at myself in the cloakroom mirror I was confronted with the awful truth. I did not look wonderful, I looked a fright; my hair was in wild disarray, my face reddened by sun and wind, and there were salty snail-tracks on my cheeks where my eyes had watered. The passers-by would not have been impressed.

I restored order to my appearance with comb and cold water and joined Mr Jarvis in a rather more realistic frame of mind than the one in which I'd zoomed into town. The afternoon's work centred around the imminent changeover from the current exhibition to that scheduled for the early autumn. But as usual I wasn't given overmuch to do and worked quickly, so there was time for me to become more familiar with the gallery's hinterland of offices, storage rooms, delivery bay and reception area and to take another look at the current exhibition which had so impressed me on my first visit. Since then, I noticed, many of the paintings bore the yellow sticker denoting that they had been sold. These included 'Nobody' by S.R. Murchie. I was pleased for Suzannah, of course, but sad that the picture would be going who knew where. Because I had met the artist so soon after seeing her work for the first time, I felt proprietary towards the painting, and resented its departure. It seemed unfair that it should go to someone whose only qualification for owner-ship was that they were rich enough to buy it – some shrewd, wealthy individual who was probably acquiring the paintings of this rising young artist as an investment. I refused to believe that the painting's new owner understood it as I did. Mine was an arrogance born of ignorance, soon dented when Christopher Jarvis joined me as I stood gazing at 'Nobody'.

'Suzannah's work speaks strongly to certain people,' he said.

And I'd been presumptuous enough to think it only spoke to me! Still, the 'certain people' helped preserve a sense of exclusivity. 'Yes,' I said humbly. 'I can see that.'

'Your new employer has bought this one. And the others you liked, that you saw in the back catalogue.'

I don't know why I should have been surprised. After all,

John Ashe had liked what he saw enough to commission a portrait.

'So Suzannah's doing well.'

'Quite well, and I'm pleased to have played a small part in her success, so far as it goes. But she's not yet quite established in the art world's consciousness, and she's a slow worker, which can have one of two effects – either everyone goes wild for her and people fight like mad dogs over every picture because there are so few; or they get bored with waiting and start looking around for the next new thing.'

'She worked hard all the time she was staying with you,' I pointed out.

He never seemed to mind my uninformed comments. 'Oh, she worked hard, but what was she doing most of the time? That mural. Which, charming though it is, is scarcely a saleable commodity. It may even detract from the value of the house in years to come. Not everyone wants an entire wall covered in portraits of unknown people by an obscure artist.'

'I should absolutely love it,' I said.

'Ah, but Pamela,' he touched my shoulder confidentially as he used my Christian name. 'You're not typical. You liked Suzannah's paintings right away.'

My self-confidence fully restored, I glowed.

At the end of the afternoon I set out for Soho. Christopher Jarvis offered to drive me, but I elected to walk. For one thing I wanted to shake off that lingering sense of being manoeuvred between these two clever, enigmatic men; and for another I needed the time to myself, to adjust to the meeting with John Ashe. After that, I reminded myself, Alan would be waiting for me; but as I drew closer to Soho Square his image seemed to retreat before me until it was as distant as the dark side of the moon.

I felt very prim and buttoned-up – not to mention nervous – walking through this part of London, even on a sunny summer's afternoon. The place was off duty at this time of day, but it gave off an air of an alley-cat indolence, watchful and knowing, that made me self-conscious in my neat suit and sensible shoes. I had allowed more than enough time, and moved at such a pace that I arrived with ten minutes to spare. Not wanting to hang about aimlessly, though goodness knows I'd have made an unlikely streetwalker, I filled the spare time with two brisk circuits of the square, eyes firmly on the pavement.

Ashe Enterprises at Number Twelve was so discreetly advertised that I might have missed it altogether had it not been for John Ashe's car parked outside. The door to the building was in a deep, narrow recess, and Ashe's brass plate one of half a dozen on the wall next to it. I pressed the bell and a moment later his voice, from a speaker nearby, told me to push the door and take the lift to the second floor.

He was waiting to greet me as the lift door opened. In contrast to his usual sombre, immaculate turnout he wore no jacket and was collarless, his tie loosened and his shirtsleeves held back with brass bands. A suggestion of dark hair showed at the neck of his shirt. All this made him seem younger, but the scars, in contrast, stood out more fiercely.

He held out his hand. 'Mrs Griffe. How nice to see you. And punctual to the second.'

'I hate to be late.' I slipped my hand in and out of his as swiftly as I could.

'No difficulty in finding me, I hope?'

'None at all.'

'Come in and look around.'

He opened wide the door behind him, and stood back to let me enter.

My face must have been a study. The offices of Ashe Enterprises could not have been more different from what I had expected. Almost unconsciously, I'd imagined a rich, dark, pre-war heaviness, redolent of masculinity and wealth. But this room was more like the Sumpter Gallery – spacious, brilliant with light, empty. The few items of furniture were severely attenuated and modern, the walls bare except, oddly, for a long strip of mirror, about three feet deep at head height on either side. There were no pictures, nor any books that I could see, but I supposed a low white cupboard along the wall beneath one of the mirrors must contain some of the files, ledgers and papers generally associated with running a business.

There was a moulded steel desk and a matching chair with its back to the window overlooking the square. Ashe's black jacket hung over the back of the chair. The surface of the desk was empty apart from a telephone and a framed photograph facing away from the room. In the centre of the room four more chairs, in sculpted white leather, smooth as seashells, stood grouped about a low, glass table bearing the single, startling splash of colour. In a matte black cylindrical vase three extraordinary scarlet blooms – tall, thick-stemmed, and vivid, their waxy petals open like mouths – revealed sooty-tipped orange stamens. I had no idea what sort of flowers they were; they looked strange enough to have come not just from another country, but from another world.

If I had felt out of place in the streets of Soho, I felt even more so here.

'What an unusual room,' I said.

'I hope so,' he replied. 'Do you like it?'

'Yes . . .' I wondered of what possible interest my opinion could be. 'Yes, I do.'

'I like peace, and order,' said Ashe, as if an explanation

were needed. 'Or at least the appearance of order. I suspect that you're the same.'

'It makes life easier,' I agreed. He smiled. The effect of the mirrors on either side of us was to remove all those little moments of privacy and secret observation normally present between people, particularly between people who don't know each other well. We were visible, to ourselves and each other, the entire time.

'For me, certainly,' he said. 'I'm baffled by people who are able to function no matter what the conditions. Your current employers are a good example of the genre. On the other hand they have you, now, to impose order.'

I wanted to say that I imposed nothing, but simply worked within the system like everyone else at Seven Crompton Terrace, but this was not the moment for self-deprecation. Let him think what he liked.

'Now,' he said, 'you'd like to see where you'll be working.'

'Thank you.'

He led the way back on to the landing, and opened a door on the right, opposite the stairs.

'Here we are.'

My office was also sparsely furnished and immaculately tidy, but here the resemblance ended. For one thing it was tiny, not much bigger than my childhood bedroom at home. For another it was utterly plain and functional without the smallest flourish of the style so evident next door. A slatted blind hung at the window; there was a clock on the wall, two filing cabinets, a waste-paper bin, and a revolving chair at a desk which faced out of the window. The typewriter was new, as was the telephone. Spotless, serviceable corded carpet covered the floor. It looked as if it had just been fitted out, as if no one else had ever worked there.

'Will this be all right?' he asked.

'Absolutely.'

'Is there anything else you think you'd need? I believe in giving a person all the tools necessary to do the job.'

'I shan't know that until I start,' I said, and immediately rebuked myself for sounding peremptory. 'I mean, I can't imagine that there is anything.'

'But you'll let me know?'

'Of course.'

He showed me out again.

'And over here are the usual necessities.'

These were a cloakroom and a tiny kitchenette, both neatly and unexceptionally appointed, like the small office, in the same neutral colour scheme and with identical slatted blinds. I noticed a fourth door on the landing, but it was closed, and he didn't so much as mention it.

Back in his own room he pushed the door to and invited me to sit down. The leather chairs were surprisingly comfortable, and their slight backwards tilt gave me no option but to sit in a way that made me feel, as the Riley had earlier, like a different woman – elegant and poised.

Ashe must have thought the same, for as he sat down opposite, he remarked: 'You have good legs.'

I suppose I should have been shocked, or at least taken aback. Strangely, I wasn't, but not being sure of the appropriate response, I said nothing. He displayed again that hint of a smile, as if his view of the world had just been confirmed to his satisfaction.

'How remiss of me,' he said, 'I haven't offered you anything. Would you care for a drink of any kind?'

I should rather have liked a cup of tea, but the thought of him making one for me in the narrow kitchenette was too uncomfortable. 'No thank you.'

'In that case,' he said as he leaned back, opening his arms briefly before letting them rest on the chair, 'do you have any questions for me?'

Though I'd had cause to feel afraid of Ashe on more than one occasion, I sensed that in small matters he was not easily offended. Best to know now, anyway – I backed my intuition.

'Yes,' I said. 'Mr Jarvis told me that you'd bought several of Suzannah Murchie's paintings. Will you hang them here?'

'I haven't decided,' he replied. 'I doubt it. I like to keep things simple here, as you've noticed. In my house in Kensington, probably.'

'I hope you won't mind my mentioning this, but I hear she's to paint your portrait.'

'You heard that, did you?' I detected, for the first time, a silky coldness in his manner. 'Who from?'

'Suzannah herself.'

'Did you.' He opened one hand. 'Then it must be true.'

There was no reproof in the words themselves and yet I was, unmistakably, rebuked. I had overstepped the mark. Complacently, I had believed I'd got the measure of him, and what I could and could not say with impunity. Now I saw that I knew nothing, not even what it was that I'd done wrong. But I would have given my right hand to have the last two minutes over again.

He sat very still, his gaze on me, hands relaxed where they rested on the sides of the chair. I realised I could not apologise – to say 'sorry' when he'd offered no reproof would be as good as saying, 'I am a crass, foolish young woman', and I wasn't about to do that.

Instead, I got up. 'Mr Ashe, it's time I was going. Thank you so much.'

He waited for a moment before rising. That moment before he stood was the most exquisitely judged slight.

Now he was once more the gentleman, opening the door, showing me to the lift, waiting beside me in silence. When it arrived and the door opened, there was no farewell handshake, but he said pleasantly enough:

'I look forward to seeing you next week, then.'

'Yes. Goodbye, Mr Ashe.'

'Goodnight, Mrs Griffe.'

As the lift swayed slowly down to the ground floor I closed my eyes in a mixture of relief and shame. Everything had been going so well; my intuition, surely, had been sound, until that moment of icy disapproval.

And suddenly it washed over me: what it was I had done wrong. That white, empty, elegant room was a mask, just as Ashe's soft voice and civil manner were a mask. But I had presumed to know what lay behind them.

I'd behaved as if I knew him, and John Ashe did not care to be known.

When I emerged on to the pavement, I was temporarily disorientated. I stood there, trying to collect myself. Remembering my arrangement with Alan, I glanced at my watch. I had only been in the building for half an hour, much less time than predicted. I would probably have to wait for him, but where? The garden in the centre of the square looked inviting, but there were two tramps weaving about on the grass, sharing a bottle. A man wandered past and brushed heavily against me so that I staggered. He turned and snarled something at me, his face blurred and angry.

'Pamela!' Alan was at my side, a little out of breath. 'You beat me to it – I'm so sorry.'

'We were quicker than I expected.'

He put his arm through mine, and it was so welcome. 'How was it?'

'Fine.'

'I hope you don't mind my saying but you look a bit peaky. Would you like to find somewhere to sit down?'

'No, I'm all right. Let's just walk.'

'If you're sure. Tell you what, let's head down in the

direction of the Embankment. It'll be lovely down by the river this evening. If we want to we can always hop on a bus.'

We set off at an easy pace, falling naturally into step. I was steadied by Alan's arm, and his presence. I no longer felt stiff and out of place. We were just another young couple strolling through the summer streets. As I relaxed, I began to see that my faux pas with John Ashe had not been so terrible; perhaps had not happened at all. He was an odd, unsettling man and I had been thrown off balance. In future I would make sure always to err on the side of caution.

Alan squeezed my arm. 'How are you?'

'Better.'

'Good. I knew you weren't right the moment I saw you. It's my job, remember.'

To reassure him, and myself, I said: 'The place was terrifically smart – very different to where I work in Highgate.'

'You said that was, sort of, colourful and chaotic?'

'Chaotic's a bit strong. But certainly not highly organised. This is so tidy and clean you could eat your breakfast off the floor as my mother would say. I couldn't see one piece of paper.'

'Sounds a bit off-putting. Not too tidy? You'll be able to work there?'

'Oh yes, I'm sure I will.'

'And this chap Ashe – he'll be a fair employer?'

I considered this. Whatever else he might or might not be, I was convinced of one thing.

'Very fair,' I said.

We were approaching Cambridge Circus and I suddenly caught sight of the road sign.

'Romilly Street!' I exclaimed. 'A girl from my digs works here. At a place called the Apache Club. It's one of John Ashe's.'

'Can't say I've heard of it,' said Alan, 'but then I wouldn't have.'

'Nor me, until she told me about it. It's madly exclusive.'

He slapped his brow. 'Damn – and I was thinking I could take you there!'

'Do you mind if we find where it is, just out of curiosity?'

'Lead on.'

We walked down the street one way and back the other, without success.

'No wonder it's exclusive,' said Alan, 'no one can find it.'

'I know it's here somewhere. Wait there.' The proprietor of a small newsagent and tobacconist was out on the pavement, pushing back the awning over his window preparatory to shutting up shop.

'Excuse me,' I said. 'I'm looking for a place called the Apache Club.'

'Isn't everyone, miss?' he asked. He had a gentle world-weariness rather like Chef's.

'Are they?'

'I'm not surprised you haven't spotted it. That's the idea, if you get my meaning.'

'So – where is it?'

He pointed in a westerly direction. 'Thirty yards, other side of the road, doorway next to the flower shop. Not open for hours yet.'

'I realise that.'

'Nothing to see.' He shook his head. 'Looks like a bit of a dump. Beats me why they're all mad for it.'

I said, by way of explaining my own interest: 'A friend of mine works there,' and at once, as so often, wished I hadn't. The man's eyebrows rose.

'Does she now?'

'Anyway—'

'Used to be a church there, you know.'

'Really?'

'Funny idea, having a nightclub where people were buried.'

'I suppose so . . . Thanks, anyway.'

'What was all that about?' asked Alan. 'Is he a member or something?'

I had to laugh. 'No!'

'Well, you said it was exclusive . . .'

'Come on, it's just along here.'

The man had been absolutely right – there was nothing to see. Like John Ashe's office the entrance to the Apache was almost anonymous and not just discreet but drab. Next to the buckets of flowers, still out on the pavement on this fine evening, a flight of steps scuttled down to basement level. We peered over the railings. The door at the bottom was painted black. On the ground in front of it, picked out in small brass letters in the concrete, was the word 'Apache'. The window was obscured by a black wooden screen.

'What does your friend do down there?' asked Alan.

I thought of Louise in her backless turquoise lamé, a bird of paradise in that dark, secretive box of a place. 'She's a sort of waitress.'

'Accent on the "sort of", I bet.'

'It's perfectly respectable and above board,' I said without much conviction.

'Pull the other one, Pam. It's a dive. I bet someone's watching us through a peephole.'

'This isn't America! Anyway, there's probably no one there yet, I don't imagine it gets going until after nine o'clock at night.'

He put his arm round me. 'No place for a GP on call, I fear.'

His hand on my waist was warm; it made me conscious of my figure in a way I hadn't been for years. And hadn't John Ashe told me I had good legs?

We walked all the way to the Embankment. And as we perched on the wall watching the river traffic slip by in the sunshine, we kissed again. I might never be a bird of paradise like Louise, but I could feel my dowdy feathers dropping away, one by one, and my truer, brighter colours showing through.

Chapter Thirteen

Not only the surroundings made my work for John Ashe different. As he had implied, this was not a situation in which it was up to me to order things. Everything was already perfectly ordered, and my sole responsibility – for the time being anyway – was to arrive punctually, sit down quietly at my desk and do the job exactly as it was set out for me.

After the uncomfortable moment during my first visit I was not going to run even the tiniest risk of being thought over-familiar. I was determined to be the reserved, dependable, discreet person who had attracted his interest in the first place.

A list of the copytyping, correspondence, and calls to be made, in Ashe's tall, racing, black handwriting, would be waiting on the desk. On my first visit he pointed out that they were listed in order of precedence, and should be undertaken as far as possible in that order. He always greeted me civilly, delivered dictation – in my office, not his – and then left me to get on with it. In this respect he was like Jarvis, except that when Ashe retreated to that big, white room and closed the door he seemed to disappear off the face of the earth.

I learned that the Apache Club was his, but knew better than to mention Louise.

I didn't know what silence was until I went to work in Soho Square. The passers-by, the policemen, the newsvendors, the traffic, the tramps in the garden, seemed to occupy another dimension; or more accurately I did, looking down at them from the stillness of the second floor. At Seven Crompton Terrace when the house was empty, or almost empty, the silence was of a different kind – the house itself seemed to breathe, and pulse, and seethe with life even when I was the only person in it. Here, where I was never alone, the silence was palpable, as though a muffling hood had been thrown over the rooms. The brass plaques testified that there must have been other people besides us in the building, but I never heard them. The occasional slow, muted grinding of the lift moving between floors only emphasised the dense hush. It made me self-conscious about the simplest thing like coughing, going to the lavatory, or filling the kettle, so I tended not to do them, and to emerge after two hours with a full bladder, a dry mouth, and for some reason a ravenous appetite. I always left the office empty as I had found it, and John Ashe invariably saw me out with the utmost courtesy.

Everyone was eager to know how I was getting on, and their curiosity confirmed my sense of going where few had gone before. In a way it was a pity to disappoint them, but professional ethics apart, there was so little to tell.

Dorothy met me, duster in hand, the moment I came through the door the morning after my first stint at Ashe Enterprises.

'Well?'

'Well what?' I replied, removing my hat as I went into the study.

She followed. 'Don't be like that! What's it like?'

I didn't bother to conceal my smile. She enjoyed being teased as much as I enjoyed teasing her. 'Just a job, you know . . .'

'No I don't! Spoilsport – give over.'

I sat down and began taking the cover off my typewriter. 'Truthfully, Dorothy, there's nothing to tell. I took dictation, typed letters—'

'Who to?'

'Dorothy!' I laughed at her sheer cheek. 'You know perfectly well I wouldn't dream of telling you that!'

'No harm in trying. Was he there all the time?'

'No, he was in his own room next door.'

'Anyone else come? Pick up any snippets?'

'No!' I said, rather more firmly. She was incorrigible, as well as insatiable. 'I didn't, and I'm not going to.'

She shrugged. 'What a waste. If I could do that –' she nodded at the typewriter – 'I'd be in there, I can tell you.'

'I dare say. Look, Dorothy, I must get on.'

'If you say so.'

She made to leave and then paused, counting off the names on her fingers: 'So madam up top's gone; Mr Rintoul's gone too, what a surprise; Miss Georgina's gone home. It's like the grave round here. I wish someone'd offer me another job . . .'

With this shaft she closed the door and continued with her dusting, humming as she went. Given her powers of observation and her quick brain she was wasted in domestic work, but the thought of her acting as someone's personal assistant, charged with discretion at all times, made the blood run cold.

Christopher Jarvis dressed up his own curiosity as professional concern. 'Having as it were put you in the way of this extra work,' he said urbanely, 'I do hope it's all going well.'

'So far,' I said.

'I have a feeling the two of you are well suited,' he remarked, adding as though I might have leapt to some other conclusion: 'Professionally speaking.'

'We seem to understand each other,' I agreed.

'Excellent. What do you think of the office? The height of fashion, isn't it?'

'Mr Ashe's is. Mine's functional and none the worse for that.'

Jarvis glanced around, one self-deprecating eyebrow raised. 'Makes a change, I dare say . . .'

'It's different.'

'And life would be dull if we were all the same!'

I was being pressed, albeit charmingly, for an opinion, which I was not going to venture. To deflect his interrogation I asked a question of my own.

'You will let me know if these hours are inconvenient, won't you?'

'They aren't, in the least.'

'Both Mr Ashe and I appreciate that my job here must come first.'

'Don't worry,' said Jarvis. 'If there's a conflict of interests at any time I'll have a word with him.'

It was on the tip of my tongue to ask, 'What about me?' but I stopped myself. He had meant nothing by it, and I was their employee after all.

Amanda Jarvis inclined more towards the giving than the eliciting of information. Neither she nor her husband were ones to pull rank, but it was as if my job at Ashe Enterprises put me in a different position vis à vis her – one of slightly greater equality. It was a case of 'to them that hath': I knew more, so I could be spoken to more freely.

'I've never been to the office, of course,' she said, 'but I believe it's very different from the house in Piedmont Gardens.'

'Is that the one in Kensington?'

She sighed, one hand on her cheek in awed reflection. 'It's magnificent! A palace . . .'

'I think he's going to hang the picture there, the one he bought of Suzannah's.'

'I expect so. He's got a valuable collection, you know.'

'He's a connoisseur?'

'Oh yes. Christopher's rather put out at Ashe having bought

all three. It's much better for the artist at this stage if their
work is spread about, seen more widely, to get people talking.'

'I suppose so.'

She shook her head, contemplating something in her mind's
eye. 'I don't know what Felicia thinks of all the stuff he buys,
considering she's not interested herself.'

'Felicia?'

'His wife. I don't believe you've met her; she came late to
our last party, but you weren't there.'

'No.'

'You're bound to encounter her some time. Oh, Pamela
. . .' Amanda breathed reverentially, 'be prepared – she's the
most beautiful woman in England!'

This exchange stayed with me for some time. I don't know
why I should have been surprised that John Ashe was married.
Of course, a wealthy, middle-aged businessman was bound
to have an attractive, capable wife to run his house and help
him entertain, to be a social asset and an adornment, the
presiding goddess of hearth and home. Far more unusual
had he been a bachelor. But everything about Ashe was
unusual. Try as I might I could not picture Ashe the married
man, taking breakfast and dinner *à deux*, submitting to the
rule of domestic and social arrangements, keeping another
person apprised of his whereabouts. And as for sharing a bed
with 'the most beautiful woman in England' – no wonder that
in spite of his fearsomely damaged appearance he exuded
such unshakeable self-assurance. Here was the stuff of the
redemptive fairy tale, yet I could not bring myself wholly to
believe in the essential nobility and selflessness of this twen-
tieth-century Beast. Felicia Ashe, I considered, must be a
remarkable woman in more ways than one. Either that, or a
stupid one.

Summer crawled on. It was late July and the Jarvises were

due to take off for Italy, where they had friends who owned a large house near Siena. Georgina would be going with them and not for the first time I wondered what her parents made of it all. But she had said herself that they were desperate for her to become engaged, so perhaps they saw this jaunt with her godfather as an opportunity to meet the right young man.

Christopher Jarvis encouraged me to take some time off while they were away.

'It's going to be busy at the gallery in September, but thanks to you we're pretty well ready for the off. You deserve a holiday.'

'Thank you. But what about the office? If there's no one here—'

'Don't worry, it's the silly season, and I'll make sure to tell everyone who matters that we're not around.'

At Ashe Enterprises there was no talk of holidays, and having only been there for a short while I would not have dreamed of asking. I had begun to find the silence less oppressive, and to feel, if not exactly at home, at least more at ease. I was also increasingly aware of the nature of John Ashe's business and the people he was dealing with.

What emerged most clearly from the correspondence and calls with which I dealt, and letters already filed, was my employer's power. Not simply the authority of the boss, the man in charge, but the inbuilt, intractable, absolute power of a man who inspired fear. I sensed it in the urgent, careful, somewhat overwrought tone of his subordinates. They were plainly terrified of him, though in my hearing he never used anything but the coolest, simplest, easiest language. His communications were never effortful, because they didn't need to be.

One particular exchange was typical. The manager of a place called the Calypso in Bredan Street near Berkeley Square wrote to Ashe concerning the cost of the champagne

currently served in the club. There was, it seemed, an issue
of how much it was reasonable to charge the customers.

'. . . while we must, of course, maintain the standards to
which our patrons have become accustomed,' wrote the
manager, 'the price of the champagne we offer has risen to
such an extent that I am unsure if it is any longer reasonable to charge those patrons a corresponding price. I therefore wonder whether, with your approval, we might not
consider ordering a less expensive label, for a trial period at
least . . .'

This tentative suggestion, tinkling with trepidation, padded
out with an obsequious preamble and a final paragraph that
was the typewritten equivalent of a nervous grin, met with a
reply which took less than ten seconds to dictate:

'. . . if our patrons are accustomed to the best champagne
then we had better not disappoint them. If they are not, and
can't afford it, they need not remain our patrons. Yours
sincerely etc.'

I couldn't help feeling sorry for the wretched recipient.

Apart from the normal business of the clubs, there were
two other organisations with which John Ashe had dealings,
whose function and identity were a mystery to me. They were
Libellule – 'Dragonfly' – of Paris, which maintained a London
office in Belgravia; and Ben Dimarco Associates of Ninety
Dean Street, only a few hundred yards from Ashe Enterprises.
I believe they were suppliers of some kind, because the correspondence tended to concern the delivery and condition of
orders, identified only by a date and reference number.
Communications, unlike those of the unfortunate nightclub
managers, were crisp and businesslike on both sides,
exchanges between equals. Once, I had occasion to place a
call to Mr Dimarco on Ashe's behalf. The voice on the other
end was softly accented and charming, a voice that contained
a smile and invited one in return.

'Excuse me – who am I addressing?'

'It's Mrs Griffe – Mr Ashe's secretary.'

'Welcome, Mrs Griffe!'

'Thank you. I'll put you through.'

The only other employee I saw, albeit very occasionally, was Ashe's driver who I found out was called Parkes. I wasn't entirely happy calling this pleasant and dignified young man by his surname, but he never invited me to do otherwise and like 'Chef' it soon became a habit. Not that we spoke much. From time to time when I left the building at six o'clock he would be waiting outside in the Hispano-Suiza, or polishing the glossy metalwork to an even higher shine with a shammy leather. Sweetly, perhaps because he considered it rude to demote me after his original mistake, or because he had noticed my wedding ring, he continued to address me as 'madam'. This made me feel a little older and grander than I was, and I'm afraid I rather played up to it. Our exchanges were confined to small civilities, the currency of goodwill between strangers.

'Good evening, madam,' he would say. 'How are you this evening?'

'I'm very well thank you, Parkes. The car looks splendid.'

'She's a beautiful car. I look after her.'

'You do. Keep up the good work.'

'I will, madam.'

'Goodnight.'

'Goodnight, madam.'

I would have called Parkes 'beautiful', except that it seemed an inappropriate epithet for a man. His skin was smooth as velvet, his eyes large and dark as a deer's; he had the kind of curly black hair usually given by artists to the god Pan, and a wide, sculpted mouth; when he permitted himself an unrestrained grin, his teeth were perfectly white and even.

I was always left reflecting that John Ashe, in spite, or perhaps because, of his disfigurement, had surrounded himself with beauty: his car, his chauffeur, his clothes, his office, his 'palace' of a house, his art collection, not to mention his fabled wife.

I didn't, of course, include myself in this litany of loveliness. I filed myself under 'functional'. I considered that now I was becoming a fixture in Soho Square Ashe in all probability scarcely noticed me. But I was wrong. One afternoon when he came into my office to dictate letters, he said:

'Was that your young man I saw you with the other day?'

'That depends,' I said. 'Where did you see me?'

'A perfectly fair question. In the square outside my window.'

I was suddenly hot and flustered. 'Yes, it was.'

'He waits for you very faithfully. He was on the seat in the garden for a quarter of an hour before I realised he was there for you.'

This observation was left to hang, and for me to comment on, which I chose not to do. Ashe stood next to me, leaning on the cabinet, ankles crossed and arms folded.

'What does he do?' he asked.

'He's a doctor.'

'M-hm.' He made it sound as though this was what he'd expected. 'Where does he do his doctoring?'

'In south London.'

'So it's a long journey for him.'

'He's used to it.'

'He must be devoted to you.'

The word 'devoted' sounded slightly odd in his mouth, as if it were a term he had never used before, and of whose precise meaning he was unsure. I said nothing.

'Right,' he said. 'Shall we make a start?'

Next time Alan met me I gave my head a little shake as I walked towards him, and linked my arm through his rather than exchanging our usual kiss.

'What's up?' he asked. 'Secret police after us?'

'No, but Mr Ashe saw us last time.'

'So? What does it matter?'

'It doesn't, really – but I don't like to think of us being watched.'

'Perhaps it cheers the old boy up.'

This idea of Ashe being a sad, lonely individual who gazed indulgently at courting couples made me smile, as it was intended to.

'Anyway,' said Alan, 'let's not talk about *him* . . .'

My mother on the other hand, when I next saw her, was keen to talk about everyone, in order to be horrified by what she heard. I'd hoped that now she was on her own she might make some closer friends among her neighbours, but after the flurry of activity surrounding my father's death, and his funeral, she had returned to her former aloofness. As a result I felt more than ever obliged to visit as regularly as clockwork, and when I was there to submit to a barrage of questions. I was her link not just with the world at large, but with parts of it as foreign to her as Timbuktu.

She listened with thrilled disapproval as I told her about Ashe's car, and driver, and the champagne party with the jazz musician, and the state of the back garden at Crompton Terrace. House-proud woman that she was, she was particularly keen to know how Suzannah's mural had gone down with the Jarvises.

'No!' she exclaimed. 'What did that poor woman say when she found her guest-bedroom wall all covered with paint?'

'She was delighted,' I said. 'They both were.'

My mother shook her head in a positive ecstasy of shocked disbelief, and relieved herself of a torrent of platitudes. 'Well I never, would you believe it, there's no accounting for taste . . .'

'Yes,' I went on, determined to give her full value while we were on the subject, 'the only thing that concerned them was whether some future owner of the house would paint over it and blot it out.'

My mother bridled. 'I would, I can tell you.'

I decided it was time to move on. 'You'd like Mr Ashe's office. It's absolutely spotless. The main office is all white, and not a thing out of place.'

'All white? I'm not sure I'd care for that.'

'With big mirrors on either side. I try not to look.'

'You've got nothing to be ashamed of, Pammie.'

I took this somewhat faint praise as a compliment. Such was the store she set by cleanliness and neatness that almost nothing else mattered. Other people's children were always judged by these exacting criteria: 'lovely, clean, well-turned-out youngsters' was her most ringing endorsement, whereas 'a scruffy lot' condemned the relevant offspring to outer darkness. When she said I had nothing to be ashamed of she meant that I was clean and neat, all that was required of a nice young woman in my position. Outstanding good looks were somehow suspect, as though the person concerned were trying to pull the wool over the eyes of ordinary, decent people. Make-up, especially noticeable make-up, was 'muck', and fashionable clothes 'showy'. Anything truly showy in the dress line was 'common', which meant tarty. I couldn't think of a single one of my new circle of acquaintances whose appearance would have met with her approval, particularly Louise . . . Heavens above! It was fortunate that she was unlikely to encounter any of them.

There were two people, however, who met her exacting standards.

'How's that friend of yours,' she asked, 'that tall girl, who works at the tailor's?'

'Barbara.'

'That's the one. She came to your father's funeral which was very civil of her, I thought.'

I couldn't help wondering what my mother would have thought if she'd known that Barbara had committed the unpardonable sin of getting herself in the family way (always how it was expressed – the girl 'got herself' into the mess, the man was rarely held responsible). But Barbara's secret was safe with me.

'She was quite ill a while ago. I believe she's better now, but I ought to get in touch with her.'

'You should,' said my mother. 'Especially if she's been poorly.'

The simple truth of this tweaked my conscience. She was absolutely right. I resolved to go and see Barbara the minute the Jarvises went to Italy.

The other person who came up to scratch, thank heavens, was Alan. She didn't actually say so – in her book that would have been to invite trouble – but her manner made it plain that he had been placed under the heading 'suitable'. True to her word, there was always a cake in the tin, and the 'visitors'' sherry was regularly replenished.

Some Sunday afternoons, if the weather was nice, Alan would leave the Morris outside my mother's, and we'd go for a walk. Quite often we went via the churchyard and visited Dad's grave. It didn't feel in the least morbid to do so, but friendly and peaceful. It was nice to go there with Alan, who in a very short time had instinctively understood what made my parents tick. We'd buy half a dozen blooms from the flower seller on the corner, fill the metal container at the tap in the corner of the churchyard and arrange them in it. If the sun was hot we'd treat the place as a park and sit down in the grass with our backs against the stones. Dad would have liked it – company for him.

On one such afternoon, as he tried to fire plantain heads

at a stone angel, Alan said: 'I've made a start, Pam. I've applied for the Diploma in Psychiatry.'

I was taken aback, even a little awed to have played a part in this big decision.

'Well *done*,' I said. 'When would you start?'

'Next year. That's if they'll even have me.'

'Of course they will!'

'Nothing's guaranteed. Since the war it's become an increasingly popular area. But I'm fairly optimistic. I've got a good clinical record and my time in general practice should count in my favour.'

'Where would you be?' I asked.

'That's the thing . . .' He popped another plantain. 'Missed again. I'm afraid I'd be in Edinburgh.'

'Never mind,' I said, without hesitation, 'it's not that far away.'

'No, but – we shan't be able to do this sort of thing.'

I was buffeted by a small, delayed shock wave, and it made me brusque. 'We may not have Dad's grave or Mum's cakes, if that's what you mean, but we can still see one another. I make more money now, I can come up on the train to see you, you must have times off, I've never been to Edinburgh, they say it's magnificent—'

I stopped in my tracks. He was looking straight at me, his expression deadly serious. 'I love you, Pamela,' he said. The words were so short and plain, and timeless.

The trouble was I couldn't find my own voice. Seeing me struggle, Alan got to his knees and put his arms round me. My face was against his heart and I could feel its steady rhythm.

'I do,' he said again. 'And that won't change, wherever I am.'

I nodded against him. I didn't have to say anything. We understood each other.

★   ★   ★

The Jarvises went off to Italy and the house in Crompton Terrace was locked up for four weeks. On my last working day before they left there was nothing much to do in the afternoon once I'd been out shopping for last-minute things for Amanda. I tidied the garden and had a cup of tea with Dorothy, who had all kinds of plans.

'I'm going to my auntie's in Brighton,' she told me. 'I always have a good time down there.'

I realised how little I knew about her life. That was the secret of her success – she picked up all sorts of information about other people while giving away nothing about herself. I didn't even know where she lived, but in this holiday mood she was happy to tell me.

'Archway,' she said. 'Just down the road. I walk here most days.'

'Do you live with your family?'

'Do I!' She pulled a face. 'Mum, Dad, and my two younger brothers. My sister's married to a butcher, they've got a shop and two babies, rather her than me! She's only two years older, but she knows exactly what the rest of her life's going to be – can you imagine?'

I admitted that I couldn't and we spent a moment in gloomy, self-satisfied contemplation of such a fate.

'But my auntie's a one,' Dorothy went on with a twinkle. 'And my uncle. If I ever get married I'll do it like them.'

'How is that?' I asked.

'No babies, for a start. And lots of fun. Just 'cause you get married doesn't have to mean no fun.'

I thought quite carefully about this. 'But shouldn't things change a little when you marry? You can't just go on pretending you're not, surely?'

Dorothy shrugged. 'Not pretending – but it doesn't have to be a prison. Anyway, you tell me. You've done it.'

'Not for very long,' I reminded her. I wasn't offended by

her question; this was no longer a sensitive subject between us. 'We only had a honeymoon.'

'That's what I want!' she declared triumphantly. 'One long honeymoon!'

I had my plans, though they weren't very adventurous. I rather envied Dorothy; it would have been nice to go to the seaside, or to another part of the country, but I wasn't entirely free. I would spend the few days at either end of each week in London, so as to be on the spot for my work for Ashe. And the middle period, from Thursday to Tuesday, staying with my mother. That way Alan and I could see plenty of each other, and I would have time to track down Barbara, too. I also wanted to see more of Louise and find out more about the Apache Club.

As it was, I saw Louise rather sooner than I bargained for. On the first Tuesday evening after the Jarvises' departure, I stepped out of the lift at Twelve Soho Square and almost bumped into her. She looked, as so often, almost too glamorous for six o'clock in the evening – 'showy', in fact – in a low-necked pink suit and an amusing little hat, in darker pink trimmed with pleated satin ribbon. I don't know which of us was the more astonished. We both said each other's name simultaneously, and then:

'What are you—?'

'What are you doing—?'

I was discovered anyway. 'I work here.'

'What a coincidence. Who for? I've got an appointment with someone called –' she consulted a business card – 'John Ashe.'

'Second floor,' I said. 'He's the man I work for.'

'No!' She frowned. 'But I thought you were up in Highgate?'

'I am. This is just part-time – two hours twice a week.'

'You're so full of surprises, Pamela!'

'So are you! By the way,' I asked cautiously, 'have you met him before?'

'At the Apache. Yes, I know, ghastly, but you get used to it, don't you?'

'What time's your appointment?'

'Six o'clock.' She looked at her watch. 'Jeepers.'

'You'd better go up. He likes punctuality.'

''Bye! I'll tell you all about it!'

As I walked away I pictured Louise, a pink, exotic bloom in Ashe's austere office. An unaccountable anxiety slithered in my stomach. Perhaps the journey from the subterranean black box to the empty white room was not as great as it seemed.

But the next day Louise was buoyant. I went down to her room at five thirty when I heard her come back from Maison Ricard.

'How did it go?'

'Marvellous! You are lucky, Pamela, he is *such* a fascinator!'

I confess this was not the reaction I'd expected, and I needed a moment to think about it, asking tamely: 'You think so?'

'*Yes*! Don't you?'

I paused again. I was indeed fascinated by John Ashe but not, perhaps, in the way that Louise meant.

'He's an interesting man,' I conceded cautiously. 'What were you seeing him about?'

'Oh, doing some different work: reception, bar management – you know he owns the Apache? Silly question, of course you do. For some reason, he's trying to woo me away from the frank stares of the customers . . .'

'And did he succeed?'

'Not yet.' She slid me her most alluring and sagacious smile. 'I'm not stupid, he can keep right on wooing for a bit. And make it worth my while . . .' She raised an eyebrow. 'If he does his stuff I can pack in Madame and all her works. I shan't need to borrow any more gowns.'

'Louise,' I said, not caring how prim it sounded. 'You know he's married, don't you?'

'I'd have been astonished if he wasn't. They all are. And I saw the photograph, my *dear*!' She flapped a mock-languid hand. 'She looks far too cut-glass to give a man like that a good time.'

This remark made me realise how different was Louise's relationship with Ashe, however recent, from mine of several weeks' standing. In all that time I had never ventured far enough into the white room to be allowed a glimpse of the photograph on the desk, whereas in the space of one short meeting she had been made – or had made herself – sufficiently at home to have studied it. I couldn't help but feel mortified, and my mortification made me ungenerous.

'Be careful,' I said. 'You hardly know him.'

'True,' she said. 'But I know men. No need to worry, darling, I can look after myself.'

When, at the weekend, I mentioned all this to Alan, he laughed.

'It sounds as though Mr Ashe has met his match.'

'What do you mean?' I retorted irritably. 'I get along with him perfectly well. He doesn't walk all over me, you know.'

'I do know, but that's different. From what you've told me you and he have a sound business relationship based on mutual respect.'

'He told me I had good legs!' I snapped.

Alan laughed even louder as he put his arms round me. 'Not so different then! You must introduce me to this chap some time.'

In the end I laughed, too – but as for introducing him to Ashe, I swore I never, ever would.

Though at first I'd envied Dorothy her holiday at the seaside, the few days each week I spent in south London while the Jarvises were away were sublimely happy. My mother was pleased, in her fashion, to have me there and to have someone to look after, and I was able to see Alan every free moment that he had. We talked and talked, and as we talked we grew closer. I realised how much I had missed real intimacy with another person. I should have liked to be more intimate still. Our kisses had undergone a sea change; no longer the culmination of a romantic friendship, but the precursor to something more. I left behind that residue of widow's guilt, confident that my happiness with Matthew would lead to even greater happiness now. We wanted to get married, and discussed how it might be managed. Conscious of his responsibilities, he fretted more than me.

'Perhaps I should abandon this psychiatry idea,' he said as we sat in a tea shop near the surgery. He thrust his hands into his hair in an attitude close to despair.

'Don't do that, you mustn't do that,' I said, pulling at his wrist and taking his hand in both mine. 'You know how much you want to, and you might never forgive yourself – or me – if you gave it all up.'

'I haven't got it yet,' he said ruefully.

'But you will have, and you must go all out to make a success of it.' Something Dorothy, of all people, had said, popped into my head.

'Marriage shouldn't be a prison,' I said. 'We don't have to be like everyone else.'

'But what about money? It'll be damn close to a prison if we find ourselves on bread and water.'

Now it was my turn to laugh gently at him. 'It won't come to that, or anything like it! If we're married I shall be living in Edinburgh, too, and I shall find work. I'm good at that.'

'You are, but . . .' He grimaced in frustration. 'How can I be kept by my wife?'

'Very easily, if you let me. And there's no shame in it. Quite the opposite – when you're consultant psychiatrist to the crowned heads of Europe I shall lounge about and spend your money like any other pampered wife of a distinguished man, never you mind!'

He smiled, and was soothed for the time being, but I knew how much he worried. It seemed a pity, when we were so happy, and so full of anticipation for the future, that our pleasure in each other should be spoiled by the dead hand of convention. No one would ever have taken me for a rebel, but in this respect I was: the prospect of working while my husband studied for three years did not strike me as either odd or unsuitable, but highly desirable, not to mention practical. I accepted that love might very well be eroded by penury, and if in our case we could easily avoid it, what possible reason could there be to do otherwise?

I wasn't too insistent. Alan's anxieties were honourable ones, and there was time in hand. The last thing I wanted was to impose on him an idea with which he wasn't comfortable, and which would only, if he acceded to it under duress, see us starting out on the wrong foot. If necessary I could (though the prospect was terribly hard) wait. The other side of me, the non-rebel, the patient, industrious, 'deserving' Pamela, was good at waiting. But I hoped – oh, how I hoped – that it wouldn't come to that.

My mother caught a sniff of something in the air. She'd have had to be deaf, blind and stupid not to, and she was none of those things, especially not the last. One evening I cooked our supper and, greatly daring, I persuaded her to join me beforehand in a small glass of sherry. It was virtually unheard of for the two of us – two women, on our own, at home – to partake of alcohol, in the front room, too, and it gave the evening a real sense of occasion which helped smooth the path for my cooking. After two or three sips her cheeks grew quite pink.

'You're seeing a lot of Alan, then.'

I agreed that I was.

'Reason you came down here, I expect,' she said, quite without rancour.

'Part of the reason.'

'Killing two birds with one stone. And very sensible. I'm not complaining, it's nice to have you here, Pammie.'

I found myself hoping she wouldn't regret this effusion in the morning. But there was more to come.

'It's nice to be here. And I'd have come anyway, Mum.'

'Your father and I used to worry about you, you know.'

I'd had absolutely no idea. 'What for?'

'It's been such a long time since Matthew died, and you're only a young woman.'

'That's true – but I haven't been unhappy all that time, Mum. Not once I got over it.'

She turned her head away slightly, as if peering out into the street, but I knew she wasn't.

'Takes a while, I dare say . . .'

'Oh, Mum!' Aided by the sherry, it flooded over me: how recently Dad had died, that she had been ill herself when it happened, how well she had coped, how little burden she had placed on me considering, and how far from selfless it was of me to come down and see her. I went over and put my arm round her shoulders. They felt very stiff, and her head remained averted, but there was the smallest glistening on her cheek, and when I kissed her I tasted the tears.

'It does,' I said, 'it takes ages. But it will get better, I promise. And you and Dad had a good marriage. That makes it harder to lose him, I know, but it'll be a comfort too. All those years you were happy together will make a difference when the sadness begins to go.' I squeezed her shoulders gently. 'I promise.'

Her still, silent struggle for control was awful for her, and for me too. On top of everything else it must have been incredibly hard for her, in this one sad area, to be the less experienced one. But there was nothing I could do about that, and after what seemed a long time, she put up her hand to pat mine: I was acknowledged, thanked, and dismissed.

I returned to my chair, trying to think of a way to change the subject smoothly.

'Can you keep a secret?' I asked.

This caught her attention. It was not the way we spoke to each other; we were not playful. This, to her mind, was the sort of question uttered between friends rather than mother and daughter. Quick as a flash she was back in control, and looking at me, sharp-eyed.

'It depends,' she said firmly. 'I should certainly hope so.'

'Don't worry, it's nothing bad. Nothing that will trouble your conscience, Mum. Just that Alan may be moving to Scotland next year.'

'Scotland?' Her surprise was genuine, and gratifying – I'd succeeded. 'Whatever for?'

'To take a course in psychiatry at the medical school in Edinburgh.'

'What about Dr Cardew?'

It was so like my mother to see all this in terms of leaving someone else in the lurch.

'Well of course, if Alan's accepted he'll give plenty of notice and Dr Cardew will be able to replace him.'

'I see.' She beat busily at her skirt with the palm of her hand brushing away non-existent crumbs. 'And what do you think of this idea?'

'I think it's splendid.' For some reason I felt a lot depended on her response.

'That's the main thing,' she said. She sniffed: 'Had you better check that oven?'

I was smiling as I went to the kitchen. For the first time in my life I could see my mother as an ally.

The following Tuesday I spent an almost unprecedented afternoon window-shopping. As a general rule all I asked of clothes was that they be serviceable, inexpensive and inconspicuous. 'Neat but not gaudy' was my motto; in that regard I was my mother's daughter. Today I felt slightly different. When it came to fashion I would never be in Louise's class, but I felt a sudden inclination towards a little more colour, and prettiness.

A gulf still yawned, though, between inclination and execution. I was out of practice. I wandered, gazed, and yearned, and became first dazzled, then confused, by the choice. How did anybody do it? How did Louise, or Georgina – let alone someone like the legendary Felicia – arrive at their stylish and glamorous toilettes? There were simply too many decisions involved. But I was determined to buy something, however small, to start the process.

After two hours I spotted the brilliant-blue kid shoes. They glowed in the centre of the window on a little plinth all to themselves, like a kingfisher among sparrows, royalty among footwear. I didn't stop to consider their lack of practicality, or what, if anything, in my neat, plain wardrobe, would do them justice. I simply coveted them in the way I had coveted things as a child. Where the shoes led, the rest of my wardrobe would surely follow. And it was clearly meant to be, because although they were the last pair (there had only been three, the assistant told me), they were in my size! I felt like Cinderella as she kneeled before me and the first shoe was slipped on to my right foot as softly and sweetly as if it had been made for me. Wearing both of them, I walked to where I could admire myself in the long mirror. They were perfect – the delicate, waisted heel, the T-bar with its tiny seed-pearl trim, the elegantly elongated toe ... I was transported.

'They look *very* well on you,' said the woman. 'Madam has a nice slim ankle if I may say so.'

Oh you may, I thought, you may! For it was true – hadn't John Ashe already commented on my legs?

The one thing I had omitted to ask was the price, but by that time I had as good as bought them, and handed over the three pounds with as much insouciance as I could muster. After all, I reasoned, I might well have bought several cheaper things that afternoon, and altogether they would almost certainly have cost me five pounds. Louise, who was rapidly becoming my touchstone in these matters, would have thought nothing of it.

As I left with the box under my arm I had to restrain myself from giving a little skip of elation. But having spent so success- fully and extravagantly once, I had to resist the temptation to do so again. The shops which two hours ago had appeared so exhaustingly overstocked seemed suddenly crammed with things I might want to buy. In the space of that heady few minutes in the shoe shop I had undergone a Jekyll-and-Hyde transformation from self-effacing novice to devil-may-care profligate. It was exhilarating but alarming. Seeing that it was already four thirty I decided to avoid temptation by going straight to Ashe Enterprises. I was sure John Ashe wouldn't mind my being slightly early; it was lateness he didn't care for.

By the time I reached Soho Square I was hot and foot- sore, and couldn't wait to reach the cool seclusion of my little office, and the promise of a long drink of cold water. In the lift I leaned back and closed my eyes. So it was almost like a dream when, on the second floor, the doors rattled back to reveal a strange young woman.

I had never seen another soul in the place. Even Louise's visit had been timed to coincide with my departure. And this girl was not waiting for the lift, she was moving across the landing from the direction of Ashe's office. I had time to take in a tall, slim figure in loose black trousers and a scarlet satin jacket, a long black scarf tied round her head. Bare feet, I noticed. Brown skin.

My arrival obviously startled her, too, because she paused for a second, half turned away as if shy.

'Oh! Hello.' Her voice was quite deep, but no more than a whisper.

'Good afternoon,' I said as I stepped out.

'I'm just . . .' She pointed in the direction of the room which was usually kept closed. The door was ajar. 'Excuse me.'

She disappeared into the room and closed the door. I went into my office, put the shoebox under the desk, hung my hat on the back of the door and went to the kitchen for a glass of water. I let the water run over my wrists for a moment to cool me down. I could hear a faint murmur of voices from the other room. I wished now that I had not arrived early. I had interrupted something; I was out of place. I hoped this wouldn't mean a black mark against me in John Ashe's book.

Back in my office I pushed the door to, opened the window and removed the cover from the typewriter. I had nothing, as yet, to do. I sat very still, catching my breath. Ten minutes later I heard the internal door close, light footsteps, the soft clank of the lift doors.

When John Ashe did come in he was, thank goodness, calm and pleasant, and I detected no hint of criticism. On the contrary, he said: 'I'm sorry to have kept you waiting; I was conducting an interview.'

'No, I was early.'

'You've been shopping, I see.' He nodded in the direction of the shoebox under the desk. Not much got past him.

'Just looking, really.'

'But you bought some shoes.'

'Yes.'

'Good. May I see?'

'I suppose . . . yes.'

I picked up the box and undid the ribbon. When I removed the lid the shoes were like two bright birds nestling in their bed of soft, white tissue. My heart pattered in agitation. I felt foolish, vain – exposed. But before I could collect myself, John Ashe leaned forward and removed one of them, holding it up before him and turning it this way and that as though it were a rare vase.

'These are beautiful. Exquisite.'

'Thank you.' There seemed nothing else to say. Except, perhaps, to take credit: 'They caught my eye right away.'

'Yes . . . yes . . . they would do.' He set the shoe down on the edge of the desk and I put its companion next to it. We gazed, he with an expression of sophisticated appreciation, I somewhat anxiously. I was overwhelmed – by my extravagance, by the presumptuousness behind it, by the situation.

'You must wear them often,' he said.

'I don't know,' I replied. 'They're party shoes.'

'Do you attend many parties?'

I found it hard, as always, to assess the weight of this question. Was I being patronised? His tone had been one of neutral, polite enquiry. Since I was scarcely in a position to take offence, I thought it best to be truthful.

'No,' I said.

'No.' He showed neither dismay nor approval, but

commented thoughtfully: 'Still, it's a pity when beautiful things don't get used.'

'I'm sure an opportunity will come along.'

'With your young man, the doctor, perhaps.'

'Perhaps.'

'Until then,' he suggested, 'you could wear them here, any time you like.'

I couldn't tell if he was joking. 'I don't think so, Mr Ashe.'

'Ah, well.' He shrugged. 'To business.'

The shoes were returned to their box and we dealt with the correspondence. When he went back to his own room I began typing, but made a far from perfect job of it and kept repeatedly having to erase mistakes. I was finding it hard to concentrate. Now that he had seen them, the blue shoes had assumed a significance far beyond their worth.

And there was the young woman who had been here earlier. . . For minutes on end I gazed out of the window, searching my mind. But try as I might, I could not remember where I had seen her before.

Chapter Fourteen

Louise was reticent about her meeting with John Ashe. Like
Dorothy, she was more interested in eliciting information
from me than confiding any of her own, but her interrogation only served to confirm how little I knew. She shook her
head in exasperation at my lack of enterprise.

'Pamela! You probably spend more time alone with him
than his wife!'

'I very much doubt that.'

'You very much doubt – listen to yourself! You know, if
you played your cards right you could be his trusted confidante. That's what happens to the secretaries of powerful
men. I've read about it in books.'

'It's not going to happen to me,' I said.

'You're such a saint,' she complained, lighting up. We were
in her room, between my return from work and her departure.

'No I'm not. I don't want it to happen. I don't want him
to confide in me, even if it was likely, and I certainly don't
want to confide in him.'

She leered, narrow-eyed, through her smoke. 'You protest
too much, darling.'

To prove my point, but also to get it off my chest, I said:
'I've never even seen the photograph of his wife.'

'But it's standing there, on his desk!'

'I've never had occasion to go to that side of the desk. In
fact I've hardly been in the main office since my first day.'

'Be a bit nosey, can't you? He's not there all the time, surely.'

'He is. And anyway, I've told you, I don't want to be nosey.'

'*I* do,' she said. 'I am.'

'Well, good luck. Let me know if you find out anything.'

'I might. He likes me!' She prinked, in a self-parodying way. Then her manner changed completely as she leaned towards me, gesturing fiercely with her cigarette. 'He likes me, but he doesn't respect me. He respects you.'

'Louise! I'm his part-time secretary.'

'Nevertheless. A man like that doesn't respect – certain kinds of women. I don't care, it's not his respect I'm after. But you – he could be putty in your hands.'

I laughed and shook my head. I was only half-flattered. I had heard what she had been too polite to say: that it was pretty women John Ashe didn't respect. But I had good legs, and a pair of kingfisher-blue kid shoes, and he had admired both. I wasn't all I seemed, any more than he was.

More time had gone by and I had not been in touch with Barbara. Now that I knew she was well again it was too easy to keep putting this off, but as my mother had said it was only right and proper to make the effort to see a friend who'd been ill.

The hostel was a long way away and clearly embarrassed her, so I decided to call in on the tailor's in Jermyn Street. My unannounced arrival at its hallowed, masculine portals would almost certainly be unwelcome, but I calculated that if I arrived there just before one they could hardly stop her taking her lunch hour with me.

It was a grey, drizzly day, and I put on my mackintosh, also grey. The blue shoes had thrown the dullness of the rest of my wardrobe into sharp relief. Until now, the utilitarian mackintosh had fulfilled its function perfectly – it was capacious, and it kept the rain off. Now it seemed down-right ugly. On an impulse, I stopped and bought an umbrella with bright blue and pink panels. Carrying it, even furled, put a swing in my shoulders and a snap in my stride. I was beginning to see what all the fuss was about.

I arrived at Rice and Claydon at five to one. It was another of those establishments of which I had encountered several in recent months that proclaimed its exclusivity through self-effacement. Nothing could have looked duller or less inviting than the frontage in Jermyn Street with its window empty but for an unremarkable City suit and its unpainted door, beside which a small notice advised me to 'Ring and await admittance'. 'Await', forsooth! Perhaps it was due to keeping company with more unconventional and relaxed people these days that I found such pomposity irritating.

The door was answered immediately by a youth in dark trousers and the light-coloured jacket that went with his junior position.

'Good afternoon, miss. Can I help you?'

'I'm a friend of Miss Chisholm. I wondered if she was free, whether I might have a word with her.'

'Oh – er – I don't know. What's your name, miss?'

'Mrs Pamela Griffe,' I said pointedly.

The lad went scarlet. 'Sorry, madam.'

'That's quite all right,' I said in a clipped tone, as if the poor lad had actually put his foot in it.

'I'll go and see for you.'

'Do you think I could come inside while I wait? It's raining.'

'Um—' He glanced over his shoulder, thoroughly moithered. 'I don't see . . .'

'Thank you.' I stepped in and shook my umbrella. The interior of the shop stretched away, twilit and mysterious, like the temple of some arcane sect of which the bolts of cloth, dummy figures, and catacomb-like shelves of patterns and papers were the votive objects. I had some sympathy with the youth – even I could tell I was out of place.

'I'll wait here,' I said.

He hurried away and was met, towards the back of the shop, by a tall man in pinstripes. They conferred. First the youth, then his superior, glanced in my direction before the youth disappeared, and the older man advanced on me with a measured stride. If he intended to intimidate me, he failed: recent experience stood me in good stead.

'Mrs Griffe, I believe?' It was the same thinly supercilious voice I'd heard over the phone on several occasions.

'That's right. I'm a friend of Miss Chisholm. I was passing, and I wondered if she was free to join me for lunch.' I was careful not to frame this as a request, but a straightforward enquiry as to Barbara's availability. After all, I was not this man's employee; I had every right to consider myself his equal.

'So I understand.' He looked down his long nose at me. A hand gestured dismissively: 'Richard is finding out.'

'Thank you.'

We stood in silence 'awaiting' Richard's return, side by side, but separated by an unbridgeable gulf. After an inter-minable time – probably thirty seconds – Richard reappeared with Barbara, buttoning her jacket, in his wake. I noticed that she was still dreadfully thin, her eyes sunk deep in blue-grey sockets. She addressed her employer first.

'Mr Rice, is it convenient for me to take my lunch break now?'

'We seem to be quiet. Shall we say –' he consulted his watch – 'a quarter to two?'

'Yes of course.' Finally, she looked at me. 'Hello, Pamela.'

'Hello,' I said. 'Shall we go?' I wanted to sweep out, and sweep my friend with me. I hated to see her so wan and put-upon. The tailors were lucky to have her.

Out on the pavement it was raining in earnest, and I put my umbrella up. It bloomed like a big, brightly coloured flower over our heads.

'Where shall we go?' asked Barbara, hunched up close to me. Only then did I realise that I had no idea. This was an expensive part of town and one I didn't know well.

'What do you usually do?'

'I bring a sandwich!'

'Let's do that, then!'

She gave me a pale shadow of her special look, but this afternoon I was in charge. Splashing along under the umbrella, we scurried back to the top of the street where I'd seen a baker's that sold rolls. I bought two, and two Eccles cakes, for a shilling.

'Where to now?'

'In there?'

She nodded towards a church, whose noticeboard bore the slogan 'Down on your luck? Come in and tell the Lord. A problem shared is a problem halved. Tea and a biscuit free. Prayer beyond price'. It was one of the many places catering for the increasing number of derelicts and down-and-outs, the human detritus of the war that littered the city – depressed, demoralised, homeless, and out of work. We weren't down on our luck, or not in the way that they meant, but I told myself that a church was a place of sanctuary for everyone, not just the indigent, so they weren't going to turn us away.

Inside, the candles were lit, and several people sat in the pews, not worshippers but patrons of the tea-and-biscuit table in the transept, from which a queue snaked down the south aisle. Some were obviously tramps, others threadbare but respectable, still – just – holding their heads up on the slippery slope to destitution.

'This'll do,' I said. I folded down the umbrella and led the way to a pew beyond the north aisle, away from the queue. 'There. A roof over our heads, a place to sit, space and privacy – perfect!'

I could hear myself sounding somewhat overenthusiastic about what, by any standards, came under the heading of any port in a storm. We sat down with our picnic, and I offered Barbara a roll, which she absent-mindedly broke in half and stared at as if unsure what to do next.

'As a matter of fact,' she said, glancing around, 'I often come here.'

'Oh.' I couldn't help being disappointed. My resourcefulness had been well and truly put in its place. 'I must say you surprise me.'

'I don't see why. It's perfect, you just said so yourself.'

'Yes, but – I don't know. It's not very you, somehow.'

Head averted, she murmured something which I could not hear.

'I beg your pardon?'

'I said, you don't know what is me.'

'Perhaps not.' I was nettled, and afraid I sounded it. 'But I am trying. That's why I'm here.'

'Very decent of you.'

It appeared I could do nothing right. Our almost untouched picnic lay on the pew between us, the symbol of my folly . . . I took a deep breath, and asked myself, what would Alan do? The answer was clear: he would not substitute self-pity for sympathy.

'I've been worried about you,' I said. 'After last time, and what you said.'

'You don't want to take any notice of all that. I was sickening for something, I wasn't myself.'

'How are you feeling now?'

'Fine. A bit tired.'

'You look it.'

'That's encouraging.' Her mouth twisted in a small, wry smile.

'I'm sorry, that was tactless. I just want to say, look after yourself.'

'If I don't, no one else will.'

'Exactly. For a start, you should eat something. These look good, come on.'

I ate the whole of my ham roll in the time it took her to nibble uninterestedly round the edge of hers. I would have eaten an Eccles cake, too, but her lack of appetite made me self-conscious. We talked about a girl we had been at college with, whom Barbara had bumped into in the street.

'She behaved as if we were old friends,' said Barbara. 'I was mystified.'

'It was a long time ago.'

'Not so long that I don't remember I had only one friend at that place. And it wasn't her.'

I was hugely gratified and touched by this, but knew better than to make too much of it at a moment when the balance between us was uneven. Instead, I asked: 'What's she doing now?'

'Married. Three children. Lives in Godalming. She was up for the day to buy school uniform at the Army and Navy Stores for the eldest boy who was with her.' Barbara stretched out her long, bony fingers and examined them. The backs of her hands were spotted with small scabs and scars. 'You and I are strange, unnatural beings, Pamela.'

I wasn't having this. 'We are not! Unusual we may be, and thank God for it.'

She seemed not to have heard me. 'He was a nice boy as a matter of fact. About twelve. Red hair, freckles, took his cap off when he said hello . . .'

'I should think so too.'

She looked at me directly. 'How is your man friend? Alan.'

'Very well.'

'Do you think you'll get married?'

I didn't want to tell her, but it would have been wrong to patronise her by lying. 'Yes. Eventually.'

'You see?' she said. 'So you're not unusual, in spite of your brave words.'

'No,' I said briskly, 'and I want a cup of tea, with lots of sugar. Are we allowed, do you think?'

'I always do,' she said, 'but since I'm not quite a tramp yet, I give them something for it.'

Her melancholy would have been almost comical, but for the fact that I'd glimpsed its dark depths once before. No amount of self-deprecation could fool me. We walked over to the south aisle and joined the queue for the urn. At the entrance to the transept a side door stood open; a notice with an arrow and the words: ATTENDED NIGHT HOSTEL IN CRYPT pointed down the flight of stone steps. I thought this was a good use of a city church, and said as much. Barbara agreed.

'I've no time for holy joes,' she said. 'Vicars and do-gooders have been precious little use to me when it mattered. But at least this lot are doing something constructive.'

There were three people behind the table, a vicar and two cheerful, well-spoken middle-aged women who might have started their lives in the pages of an Angela Brazil story. I began to explain myself but presumably they recognised Barbara, because they smiled, poured and waved us through. I put a threepenny bit in a saucer on the end of the table.

Back in our pew, Barbara looked at her watch. 'Mustn't be long, I'm due back.'

'They're stingy with their time.'

'Time is money!' She raised a finger, parodying her employer. 'Actually they're not that bad. They've put up with me all these years.'

'They're lucky to have you,' I said staunchly.

It was still raining outside and we half-ran down Jermyn Street, huddled together under my cheerful umbrella. Our feet got wet just the same. When we arrived at the door I said:

'Let's meet up again next week.'

She examined my face for signs of duplicity. 'You don't have to do this, you know.'

'Barbara. Would you like to?'

'Might as well.'

'I'll meet you here after work on Tuesday then.'

'All right. 'Bye.'

'See you soon.'

When I glanced back her gawky figure had broken into a run.

'You did the right thing,' said Alan when I told him about this. 'Try and keep in touch even if she is grumpy. She obviously needs you.'

'I don't know about that. But I will.'

'Good for you.' He held my face between his hands. 'I love you.'

That was one of the nice things about Alan – that he believed in, and brought out, the best in me. No wonder love, as Louise had said, was considered a good beauty treatment. Those in love recreated themselves in the image of their reflection.

One evening after supper I did something daring. I took the bus to Highgate, and walked down the hill to Crompton Terrace. It was nine o'clock on a beautiful night: sweet-smelling, balmy and still. There was no one watching, and even if there had been they would have recognised me, and known the Jarvises were away, but even so I stopped and looked around before opening the gate.

I went in, closing the gate behind me without a sound, and walked round the side of the house into the back garden. The deckchairs were stacked against the wall, but I took one and set it up on the grass, arranging it on its lowest notch. When I sat down, I lay back, legs stretched out, and gazed up at the stars. Not a soul knew I was here, in this sequestered garden high on the hill above London. Its peace and privacy were my secret. It was bliss.

And then, after a few minutes, the nightingale began to sing. The sweet, liquid notes bubbled and trickled like a spring. The only living creature who did know I was here was singing for me alone. I listened, spellbound, for I don't know how long, to this private recital. When the song eventually melted away, the silence rang in my ears. I felt warm, relaxed, comforted. The nightingale had told me she was safe.

The Jarvises were due back the following Tuesday. I had been deputed to go up to Crompton Terrace on the Monday, collect a key from the people over the road, and generally make sure that all was well for their return. I was to admit Dorothy, too, to put a welcoming shine on things and air the beds. In other words, I had been placed in charge. They were very trusting, and I was very aware of my responsibilities as I turned the key in the lock.

The house felt a little stuffy and neglected; I could have sworn it was pleased to see me. I went round opening windows, and the back door on to the garden. Here, as at the front, nature had once more asserted itself – the grass was long, the weeds rampant and the first few dry, premonitory leaves had fallen.

Perhaps I shouldn't have done, but I looked into each room. After all, the Jarvises had asked me to check that all was well. The top attic was neat, and bare, and stifling hot.

I could scarcely breathe up there, and pushed open the back casement window as far as it would go. A dead bee lay on the windowsill.

With Suzannah gone, the mural appeared even more striking, as if, separated from its creator, it had taken on a life of its own. As I stared at it my heart beat furiously and my head swam; I felt a little faint. Telling myself I must have taken the stairs too quickly in the heat, I sat down on the edge of the bed to recover. This time I saw a curious prescience in the painting, as if Suzannah instinctively knew of connections and associations yet to be. Why, otherwise, had she seen fit to place me, of all people, at John Ashe's shoulder as he turned his back on everyone else?

When I'd caught my breath, and my balance, I went back down the stairs, and went at once, without hesitation, into the Jarvises' room − I had no feelings of guilt, after all I was simply checking and airing it according to my brief. It was pleasant and light, the beds covered with white broderie anglaise, a painted linen chest at the foot, colourful cushions at the head. The walls were painted china blue, and there was a pretty light wood armoire with mirrored doors opposite the window, to my right. Facing me, and ajar, were the doors to the bathroom and Christopher Jarvis's dressing room. I opened the window on to the garden, and peeped into the dressing room. In contrast to the main bedroom it was plain, austere and masculine. Jarvis's ivory-backed brushes and shoe-horn, bearing his initials in silver, lay on the chest of drawers, and there was a framed pen and ink sketch of Crompton Row, signed by Paul Marriott, over the bed. On an impulse I pulled back the bedspread, leaned over and sniffed the pillow. It exuded Jarvis's scent. This, undoubtedly, was where he slept.

'Hello! Mrs G, you up there?'

It was Dorothy. She must have taken the chance of coming in through the front door.

'Coming, Dorothy!'

We met in the hall. She hadn't yet put on her apron and cap, and wore a cotton dress patterned with strawberries. She herself was like a strawberry, rosy and ripe after her holiday. Her hair was soft and untidy, a little fairer than before, and her skin lightly coloured by the sun. I saw for the first time that Dorothy was a beauty.

'You look very well,' I said. 'Did you have a good time in Brighton?'

'You could say that.' She smiled coquettishly. 'Fancy a cuppa?'

When we were sitting with our tea at the kitchen table, she said: 'He was called Jimmy.' And then, as if this needed explaining: 'The good time I had – Jimmy Doyle.'

I knew Dorothy had plenty of admirers; she made casual references to one or other of them from time to time, but something in her manner told me this one was different. She was smitten.

'Does he live down in Brighton?' I asked. Of all the things I wanted to know about her new boyfriend this intrigued me least, but I was hoping that given an opening Dorothy would tell me more.

She shook her head. 'Over the water. He's Irish.'

'So he was on holiday too?'

'Working on the pier. On the funfair. I took one look, and thought, "That's for me." He's the handsomest bloke I've seen outside the cinema, and wicked as sin. All the blarney in the world.'

I said drily: 'Which didn't work on you, of course.'

'I let him think so! Mind if I have a smoke?'

They weren't allowed to smoke in the kitchen, but given

the general tenor of our conversation it would have seemed
unnecessarily pompous to enforce this rule especially with
the Jarvises themselves not due back till tomorrow.

'Carry on.'

She fetched cigarettes and matches from her bag, and lit
up. 'Truth is, I'm stuck on him.'

'I can tell,' I said. 'But if he's down in Brighton . . . Will
you see him again?'

'Every chance I can. I'll save. It's not far on the train and
you can do it in a day.'

'And I suppose he could come up to town as well.'

'Not really. It's still high season, and weekends and
evenings are his busiest time. I don't mind.'

It was silly – Dorothy was far more a woman of the world
than me and could, as she'd often remarked, look after
herself, and yet I experienced a sudden wave of almost
maternal tenderness and anxiety on her behalf. I could all
too clearly picture Jimmy Doyle, the darling of the dodgems,
black hair, merry brown eyes, soft brogue, blarney and all,
and it was not a picture that nourished hopes of fidelity. I
didn't for a moment doubt that he had fallen for Dorothy
– what red-blooded young man wouldn't? – but in his life
there would be Dorothys galore, a continuous, ever-changing
parade of them, some not so pretty, some prettier, but all
his for the taking.

I tried for a light, teasing tone. 'Careful you don't make
things too easy for him!'

'Play hard to get, you mean? No . . .' She tapped her cigarette on the saucer. 'Not this time. I want to be with him
while I can. He goes back to Ireland at the end of the season.'

'You're going to miss him.'

She shrugged, then sighed. 'I will, yes, but what can I do?'

I wanted to say 'forget him', but it would have been too
cruel, and anyway, Dorothy said it for me.

'It's a case of forget him now, or forget him later. I may as well make the most of him while he's around.'

I was overcome with admiration for her strength of feeling, her fatalism, her confidence in her chosen course. A kind of nobility shone through in Dorothy's attitude towards this young man; a heroic acceptance that her brief period of bliss would have its price, but one she was prepared to pay. There was nothing else I could say.

'And what about you, then?' she asked. 'Been up to no good down there in Soho?'

'Ah,' I said. 'That would be telling.'

The Jarvises came back from Italy, and August gave way to September. The difference between one month and the next was no more than a name, a single tick of the clock, but as always I felt the change in the air. No matter how hot the sun – and that September was very hot – I had a sense of the curtain slowly closing on summer.

I wasn't sorry to see it go. It had been a long one, and I liked autumn. The sharper air and shorter days concentrated the mind. London was more itself in autumn and winter. Already I felt more energetic, in anticipation.

Not everyone shared my feelings, but Amanda Jarvis did. I had never seen anyone so pleased to be back from holiday. Both she and her husband looked well and rested, but she had found the extreme heat unbearable.

'I can't understand how anyone lives in a climate like that!' she confided in me. 'It's like a furnace, from dawn till dusk, day after day . . . They close the shutters to keep the house cool, but what's the point of hiding away in the dark all the time? If I went outdoors I had to sit under a tree and even that was too much. Christopher and the others went swimming, which I should have liked to do, but the sand and the rocks were too hot to walk on . . . It's so lovely to be back, and you've looked after everything beautifully, Pamela.'

'We only came in yesterday,' I pointed out, giving Dorothy her due as well. 'And very little needed to be done.'

'Still, it gave us peace of mind knowing you were around. We've come to rely on you, is that awful?'

This was the sort of question, typical of Amanda, to which there was no appropriate answer. I could scarcely agree, but neither could I tell the truth which was that no, it was not awful, but it might be unwise. Instead, I smiled politely and asked what she'd like me to do.

Naturally there were house guests expected. The American artist, Bob Sullivan, was coming over for the launch of his exhibition. The small bedroom was being kept free for Georgina; though she had been commanded to report back to Wiltshire following the Italian holiday it was not expected she'd remain there long. Edward Rintoul would be using the attic room to work in for an extended period. I didn't know why they put up with it. He had his own flat, and was surely quite successful enough in his field to have his own studio, too, either there or elsewhere. The only possible reason he came here was to take advantage of the Jarvises, and batten on their good nature. I found him tedious and boorish, but they were endlessly, indiscriminately hospitable. I was glad that much of my time would be taken up with work at the gallery.

My mother, though she complained of the heat, was not looking forward to the turn of the year. I sensed her foreboding, and could understand it. In her changed circumstances how she must have been dreading the long, dark, lonely evenings. And though she liked to keep herself to herself, there was a difference between fending off unwanted visitors and having almost none to fend off, which I feared might happen with the onset of winter. I tried as gently as possible to encourage the idea of fostering friendships. The best way to do this was to compare her circumstances with less favourable ones elsewhere.

'You're lucky to have such nice neighbours,' I said. 'I don't even know everyone in my house, let alone in the ones on either side.'

She gave the little rabbit-like twitch of her nose and mouth which only politeness prevented being a sniff of disparagement. 'I don't like too much to-ing and fro-ing.'

'At least you have friends nearby. People you can ask round whenever you want.'

'I wouldn't call them friends, exactly.'

'Mum – people were kindness itself when Dad died.'

She bridled. No taint of indebtedness was going to attach to her. 'I'd do the same for them, they know that.'

'But why wait for a sad occasion? Or any occasion? You could have someone in for a cup of tea any time.'

'I could,' she said, allowing the possibility but denying the likelihood. And that ended the matter.

'I don't know what she imagines will happen if she invites another person over the threshold,' I said to Alan, in some exasperation. 'She's her own worst enemy.'

'She's never less than welcoming to me,' he pointed out. 'She likes you.'

'And thank God for it! One thing's certain, she's not going to change just because we want her to. She's an independent, strong-minded woman, and you're very like her, Pam.'

'I'll try and take that as a compliment.'

'That's the idea.' He put his arm round me and kissed my temple. 'But you're quite right, she is going to feel isolated. We shall have to make a special effort.'

I was touched by his use of 'we'. I thought of Dorothy and her elusive Irish boy, and recognised once more how right she was to pursue her quixotic passion, and how fortunate I was to have love, and to hold it. Not a year ago my life had been airless and dull – becalmed. Now, there was wind in my sails, and on my face. I was by no means sure where I was going, but the voyage was exhilarating.

He did not expect to have a reply to his application for the Edinburgh course until September when the academic year was underway, and then an interview and a written exam would follow. We had decided that to make any plans before we knew the outcome of all this would be to tempt fate. We were absolutely confident of our feelings for each other, and of our shared future. For the second time in my life I made the mistake of imagining there was plenty of time . . . If I could go back, I would not have allowed our being together to depend on other things.

I would not have waited. And it would have been a whole different story.

In the world of John Ashe, I was beginning fully to understand the nature of my relationship with my employer. He presented me with a mask; there was no pretence that it was anything else; my job was never to question or examine the mask, and to turn a blind eye to whatever I might occasionally glimpse behind it. What was required of me was not so much discretion as a selective blindness. He knew I was no fool, that I would catch on to the terms of engagement without them having to be explained. What was neither acknowledged nor spoken of could be deemed not to exist.

This strategy worked, to the extent that I was spared having to confront, or make judgements about, the less savoury aspects of Ashe Enterprises. But Ashe was right, I was no fool, and I could not deny their existence. The clubs that he owned prospered, but it was the people he owned who maintained the 'palace' in Kensington. His empire consisted not of bricks and mortar, but flesh and blood, and was founded not on cash, but on human weakness.

It became increasingly obvious that Louise was one of these. Since her visit to Soho Square there was no denying that she flourished as the green bay tree. She had given up the job at Maison Ricard, but showed no sign of missing the borrowed finery – on the contrary, she appeared in an endless array of sumptuously elegant gowns, always set off by a fur stole, or satin wrap, and the sort of jewellery she could not possibly have afforded herself. On top of this an extra sheen enhanced her appearance, a poise and polish which money could not buy. She had moved to another level. I did not care to think how.

She was happy, though; she positively sparkled. And when she discovered my nascent interest in fashion, she decided to take me in hand.

'Let's go shopping!' she cried. 'And buy you a dress to go with those scrumptious shoes.'

I demurred, invoking a general unwillingness to overspend on something I might never wear, but she sucked her teeth in impatience.

'That's the old Pamela talking. I want to go shopping with the new one.'

In truth I was in transition. Not still a dull grey cygnet sculling along at the rear, but not yet a swan, either, spreading its wings in the sunlight. Perhaps I needed a creature like Louise, already in gorgeous flight, to pick me up and help me fly.

On the Saturday morning in question she instructed me to wear new stockings and the blue shoes. When we set off, she hailed a cab in the Tottenham Court Road and asked to be taken to Maison Ricard. I was appalled.

'Louise – we can't go there!'

'Why not?' She was insouciant. 'I know them, and they have lovely things.'

'For one thing you've just left and they might not

appreciate you returning in as a customer. And for another I shan't be able to afford a thing!'

'Believe me, they will be delighted to see me. Madame's a frightful old hypocrite, she knows I mix with more money these days than she'll see in a lifetime. She'll practically force us to take something even if she has to give it away.'

'But *I* don't mix with money,' I protested.

'Who do you work for?'

'It's not the same.'

'She's not going to know that.'

'Louise – look at me.'

'Hmm.' She did so, eyeing me up and down expertly. 'Not so long ago I might have agreed with you. But these days, there's something about you . . . Don't worry, I shall have no problem passing you off as a rich man's plaything.'

Her devil-may-care mood was infectious. What did I have to lose? When we arrived, I played along shamelessly, on the grounds that Madame and her cohorts didn't know me from Adam and were most unlikely ever to see me again. It was true, they did have lovely things, but most of them were quite unsuitable. Even masquerading as something I was not, I refused to be traduced, to be cajoled into buying something that had no place in my life.

There was one dress though – a silvery-blue moss crêpe, bias-cut, with cap sleeves and a skirt that brushed the knee . . . a dress that seemed to flow round my body like water slipping over a statue . . . a dress that I fell in love with. The blue shoes might have been made for it. I stared, wordlessly, at my reflection in the mirror, quite overcome at my transformation. Madame's aide-de-camp was saying something which I could not hear, but Louise appeared at my shoulder, and whispered in my ear:

'That's the one.'

'Do you think so?'

'You know it is.'

'Yes, but Louise—'

'Ssh! Leave it to me.'

Ten minutes later we left the shop, and I owned the dress of my dreams. Louise had not only negotiated a favourable price with Madame, but insisted on paying half. I protested vehemently, but quite apart from the fact that the sepulchral hush of Maison Ricard was no place for a vigorous altercation, she was quite simply, and charmingly, intractable.

I resumed my protests less self-consciously outside, but she was having none of it.

'I'd have paid for the whole thing if I thought you'd let me. It was my idea and I press-ganged you into it.'

'I'm not that feeble. I didn't have to buy it.'

'But you might not have done if I hadn't hovered like Satan at your shoulder, breathing temptation in your ear.'

This was such a vividly accurate description of what had taken place that I had to smile, and then we both began to laugh.

'Let's go to the Ritz!' cried Louise. 'And have a glass of champagne!'

This time I didn't argue. She was unstoppable, and I was the owner of a beautiful dress which I knew suited me down to the ground. We sat in the hotel's marbled halls like two high society ladies, sipping our champagne and discussing the other patrons, making up for what we didn't know with shameless flights of imagination, and laughing like drains at our own cleverness. My mother would have been appalled.

Louise and I laughed rather more that afternoon than Barbara and I did at the Laurel and Hardy film we saw on one of our now regular Tuesdays. She was morose and withdrawn, and my own laughter died in my throat next to this grim, silent presence. I couldn't help feeling a little impatient with her – couldn't she make at least some effort? She did nothing to help herself, or to improve her circumstances. She moped. Compared to Louise, Barbara was a dour and unrewarding companion.

She might have been reading my mind. 'I'm sorry,' she said, as we parted company at her bus stop. 'I'm not much fun.'

'It doesn't matter,' I said, adding hastily: 'And anyway, you're not.' But we both knew it was too late. I had agreed with her.

'Let's meet again next week and I promise to be jollier.' She framed the last word as though it were some strange-tasting substance in her mouth. 'Agreed?'

I did agree, but as I walked away I had to face the bleak fact that I no longer wanted to see her. She had been a friend, but was becoming a duty.

On the Thursday, my next session at Ashe Enterprises and my next meeting with Alan, I took my courage in both hands and wore the new dress and blue shoes. I was at the gallery all day, helping Christopher Jarvis take receipt of the American pictures, but at half past three I retreated to the cloakroom and got changed. I hoped to slip away unremarked but I'd underestimated my employer's antennae for such things. The moment I emerged, he swooped on me.

'My word, is it Mrs Griffe?' He took my hand and then stood back, as if about to dance with me. 'May I say you look quite charming?'

'Thank you.' I brushed at my skirt self-consciously. 'It's new.'

'New it may be, but that dress has been waiting for you all its life. I hope Ashe appreciates it.'

'I'd better go.'

'Yes indeed, you run along. Well I never . . .' I felt his eyes following me as I walked out. I lifted my head and lengthened my stride, but I couldn't quite bring myself to swing my hips as Louise did.

When I arrived at Twelve Soho Square, Parkes was emerging from the lift.

'Afternoon, madam. Just taking something up.'

'Good afternoon, Parkes.'

I felt his appreciative glance scanning my dress, my shoes, the *toute ensemble*. 'Going somewhere this evening, madam?'

'Possibly.'

'Have a nice time.'

'I will.'

He was, I knew, being a shade too familiar, but it didn't trouble me. Parkes was so young, and handsome, and soft-spoken, it was impossible to take offence. He was how I imagined Dorothy's Jimmy Doyle – able to charm the birds from the trees. To charm and be charmed was something new for me, and like sweet wine it coursed through my veins and made me quite light-headed as I rose in the lift to Ashe Enterprises.

As I emerged John Ashe was in the room to my left, and the door stood open. On seeing me he came out, smiling and unhurried. He turned to close the door behind him, and I heard the click of a key in the lock. But those few seconds were enough for me to gain an impression of a room dark and rich as the other rooms were pale and plain; a space like an animal's mouth, silky red and black and fleshy pink, with something in the centre which I could not make out – a mysterious monolithic object, draped in black cloth.

I could tell, as we went into the small office and I prepared to take dictation, that he had noticed the way I looked, but rather to my disappointment he said nothing. I began to think that our exchange about the shoes had been an aberration, one of those things I should banish from my mind and never refer to again, even in my own head. But two hours later, as I was about to leave, he came out of the white room.

'Mrs Griffe, I have to tell you – you are a picture of elegance.' He inclined his head slightly in a manner both courtly and knowing, as if in acknowledgement of an understanding between us. 'Have a pleasant weekend.'

'Thank you. Goodnight, Mr Ashe.'

'Goodnight.'

Outside, Alan was waiting for me in the usual place. He rose, smiling, but had learned not to greet me too warmly while we could still be seen from the building. This time, however, whether due to the clothes or the compliments or both, I was seized by the impulse to show off, and flung my arms round his neck.

'Hey! This is nice!' Baffled but delighted he returned my embrace, I planted my mouth on his and for a long moment we were fused together. When we separated he was almost gasping.

'What a treat! And Pamela, you look wonderful! Where on earth shall we go that will do justice to you?'

'Anywhere,' I said, 'anywhere at all.'

As we walked away, with Alan's arm about my waist – a waist that seemed smaller, somehow, in that sleek, cloud-coloured dress – I glanced up at the window and saw John Ashe staring down at us. In spite of the distance between us, our eyes met. He didn't move. It was I who looked away, but I could feel the intensity of that stare, like a pinpoint on my back, all the way along the pavement until we turned the corner.

Edward Rintoul and Bob Sullivan had arrived at Crompton Terrace over the weekend, and the house was full of booming male voices and heavy footsteps. Sullivan was in his early thirties, a handsome, fair-haired, open-faced man, with brilliant blue eyes, who looked as if he should have been playing baseball rather than painting. His appearance served to remind me all over again, as the 'clerks' had done, that creativity, like lightning, was no respecter of persons. It could strike anyone, anywhere. The only artist of my acquaintance who looked, to me, as an artist should, was Suzannah. I wondered where she was, and how she was faring. She and I had gone to work for Ashe, in our separate ways, at about the same time. It would have been interesting to compare notes.

One impression I received very clearly at that time was of the strong feelings Christopher Jarvis had for Sullivan. He quite simply adored him. His eyes shone when Sullivan walked into the room, and rested on him every second he was there. He smiled even more readily than usual and was exceptionally appreciative of beauty, elegance, the comforts and adornments of life. It was obvious that all his senses were heightened and intensified. He radiated happiness, which made him a pleasure to be with. Even Amanda seemed in no way diminished by his feelings, but enhanced – he was much more attentive than usual, and she prettier as a result. Try as I might, I could not equate his behaviour with the 'muckiness' so darkly referred to by Darblay. I noticed no sign that his feelings were reciprocated; Sullivan demonstrated nothing that was not consistent with a normal, relaxed, social friendship. It was an instance of unrequited love being strangely complete in itself.

I would never have mentioned this to Dorothy, but she could be relied upon to do so, and without making any bones about it, either.

'Sir's cheerful then, with his new beau.'

'Dorothy!'

'Don't say you haven't noticed, Mrs G, not much gets past you.'

I mumbled something and she gave me a sardonic look. 'Who cares, as long as he's happy? She doesn't seem to mind, never does, so why should anyone else?'

We left it at that. For all Dorothy's cheeky talk, she had lost her holiday shine, and looked tired. When I asked her about the weekend's trip to Brighton, though, her face lit up with a gentle glow quite unlike her usual bright, saucy grin.

'We had such a lovely time. And Jimmy's boss gave him a couple of hours off in the middle of the day so we went on the beach and had a paddle, and an ice cream.'

'I'm glad,' I said. But her remark brought home to me the fact that Dorothy was undertaking the regular train journey to the south coast with her hard-earned money to keep company with a young man who was working most of the time; and whose work consisted, by its very nature, in advertising his attractions.

She held something out to me. 'Want to see a picture?'

'Yes please, I would.'

It was one of those posed photographs you could pay for in a booth on the pier. The two of them had poked their heads through holes in a board in order to look like a couple in Edwardian dress, riding on a tandem. Dorothy was in a well-corseted top and striped bloomers, her delight and hilarity plain to see. But between bowler and stiff collar I saw that Jimmy Doyle was not the curly-headed, dark-eyed Irish boyo of my imaginings but had pale hair and eyes, a narrow, fine-boned face, and a secretive smile. It was the face of a young man altogether more subtle than my preconception, and all the more disturbing for that.

'That's nice,' I said. 'You were having fun.' I held out the picture, but she didn't take it.

'So what do you think?' she asked.

'I told you – it's very good of you.'

She sucked her teeth impatiently. 'Never mind me – what about him, Jimmy?'

I wanted to say: What does it matter what I think? But didn't wish to appear dismissive. I knew I could often be unintentionally brusque and this was one – perhaps the only – occasion when Dorothy was vulnerable to offence or, worse, injury. To please her, I took another more considered look at the photograph, and then laid it on the table between us.

'You were right,' I said, 'he is handsome.'

'Not what you thought, though, eh?'

Even with her heart laid bare, she was bright as ninepence. I had to admit it:

'No.'

She picked the photo up and gazed at it. 'He's one in a million.'

'So are you, Dorothy,' I said.

'Me?' She laughed incredulously. 'Give over!'

To spare her embarrassment, I didn't pursue it, but I did hope she would remember.

'What do you do,' I asked, 'when he's not free?'

'I help out,' she said proudly, adding with a touch of her old dash: 'He smiles at the girls, I smile at the boys. He says I'm a real asset.'

'I'm sure you are! He should give you a percentage.'

'I wouldn't take his money,' she said. 'I like doing it, so it's cheap at the price.'

What a treasure Dorothy was, I thought, and what a wonderful wife she'd be for some lucky fellow. I could only hope that Jimmy Doyle, who held her heart in the palm of his faithless hand, appreciated what a gem was in his possession, or had any idea what to do with it.

The next day, Tuesday, I arrived at Ashe Enterprises to find

John Ashe about to go out. I don't know why I should have been surprised, except that it was unprecedented. I had become used to an almost unvarying routine – settling myself at my desk, his emerging from the white room shortly afterwards, the twenty minutes or so spent on dictation, even the silence while I got on with my work which, while I could never have described it as companionable, no longer unsettled me.

'I'd like it if you could give me some more of your time this evening,' he said. I noticed that, though polite, this was not framed as a request.

'Of course,' I replied.

'I have to catch a train at five thirty, so I'll be brief if you don't mind. When you've finished here, there are some books that I'd like collected from two clubs. Pick them up after six o'clock if you would and deliver them to my home address in Kensington. My wife's in and will be expecting you. Take a taxi for the evening and please go home in it afterwards. You can charge it to me.'

Ashe was never less than calm and courteous, and seldom if ever raised his voice, but this was the closest he'd come to being curt. I knew that outside circumstances and not I were the cause of the curtness, but even so the 'if you would' and 'please' were the merest token civilities. I had my orders.

'I've written down the various addresses for you, and left them on your desk.'

'Thank you.'

'Good. I'll see you on Thursday as usual, then.' He made to leave, but turned in the doorway. 'I'm not expecting anyone. Simply lock up when you leave.'

When he'd gone I leaned over my desk to look out of the window. The Hispano-Suiza, which had not been there when I arrived, was drawn up outside. The black bodywork and silver chrome gleamed like silk; the stork's beak was a golden dagger in the sun. I saw Parkes get out, and a second later Ashe appeared. Parkes opened the rear door, stood smartly while Ashe climbed in, closed it softly but firmly, and returned to his place behind the wheel. The car glided away.

I sat down. The place became even more silent now that I was the only person here, but the silence was quite different. Before, it had always been stifling and intense, as though Ashe's presence weighed heavy on the atmosphere. This evening it was thinner, lighter – it breathed, like the rare emptiness of Seven Crompton Terrace. I picked up the piece of paper on the desk and read the addresses: the White Flamingo Club, Greek Street; the Apache Club, Romilly Street; and finally Hall House, Three Piedmont Gardens, Kensington. The names I was to ask for at the nightclubs were Mr Miles Easter and Mr Charles Swynford-Hayes respectively. So I was going to meet Piggy! And, very probably, Felicia.

I put the paper down. The time was ten to five. Only a few letters lay on my desk, all requiring no more than standard replies. Like a sleepwalker, without conscious decision, I got up, went into the hall, and turned the handle on the door of the white room. It was not locked. I opened it wide and went in. Everything was exactly as it had been the first time I saw it, except for the flowers. The snarling red blooms had been replaced with huge waxen lilies whose sweet scent was quite overpowering. I had no idea who changed the flowers; it was not something I'd been asked to do. Perhaps Felicia arranged for them to be brought, or one of Ashe's other female visitors.

I crossed to the desk, and round to the far side. My legs shook slightly with the guilty thrill of what I was doing. Slowly, I pulled out his chair, and sat down. Only then did I look up at Felicia.

The photograph was one of gauzy, film-star perfection.

Felicia seemed to be sitting below the camera and to be leaning slightly forward and upwards, to emphasize the length of her swanlike column of throat with its choker of pearls. Her sleek dark cap of hair formed an elfin point on her forehead and a smooth curl on one cheek. On the other side it was swept back to reveal a small, perfect ear from which hung another pearl in the shape of a teardrop. Her eyes were large and heavy-lidded, her closed mouth a cherry-dark Cupid's bow, her expression cool and curiously blank. She might have been any age from eighteen to thirty-eight. Felicia Ashe was a hothouse plant, gorgeous but cultivated, unnatural, and – in her photograph at least – without a scintilla of self-doubt. Even though I could, in a split second, have leaned forward and turned the photograph on its face, I would never have done so. I wouldn't have dared. And when I finally looked away, I felt as if I were averting my eyes not from a man-made object of paper, glass and silver, but from a real woman, who had stared me down.

I replaced Ashe's chair precisely as I had found it, smoothing the small indentation from its leather seat even though I knew he would not be back for at least a day. Irrationally I found myself thinking that whatever I did he would know where I had been and what I had done – that he had designed this still, white room to register every movement, every sound. My face in the mirrors looked hectic and scared – perhaps the glass concealed cameras and my gross intrusion would be recorded?

As I closed the door behind me my skin prickled with anxiety and I wiped my palms on my skirt.

There wasn't enough to do to fill the time between now and six o'clock, but I didn't like to leave my post early. I busied myself going through the already well-organised filing cabinet. At five to six, just as I was preparing to leave, the phone rang. The sudden, loud summons after more than two hours of silence was startling, and my heart was thumping wildly as I lifted the receiver.

'Hello – Ashe Enterprises.'

'Is that – excuse me – is that Mr Ashe's secretary?'

'Yes.'

'Mrs Griffe.'

'Speaking. Who is that, please?'

'It's Felicia Ashe here.'

'Oh!' Felicia's image rose up before my mind's eye. 'Mrs Ashe – hello. I was just about to leave.'

'Of course you were . . . I wanted to make sure you knew where to come.'

'Mr Ashe left an address. And he said I should take a taxi, so—'

'So you are perfectly in command of the situation. As you always are, I'm told.'

'I don't know about—'

'I'll expect you in about an hour, then, shall I?'

'Yes.'

'Goodbye.'

The phone her end went down with a click. I replaced the receiver. In spite of the coolly civil tone she had used, I knew I had been knocked about by Felicia: patronised by a past master. The effects of her assault were like little soft bruises all over me. As I covered the typewriter and prepared to leave the office I knew that she had not been in the least concerned about me or my ability to find Piedmont Gardens. Still less was she impressed by my organisational ability. She had been checking up on me; seeing that I was where I was supposed to be, and ensuring that I arrived on time so as to cause the least disruption to her smooth running life.

Because both the clubs were so close I decided to walk there, and pick up a taxi afterwards from the cab-rank on Oxford Street. The entrance to the White Flamingo was

easier to find than that of the Apache, only because it was
at pavement level. I rang the bell, announced myself to a
male voice over the intercom and was admitted. Inside there
was a narrow hallway with what I took to be a cloakroom,
currently shuttered, to my left, and ahead of me stairs leading
down to the basement. Above the brass handrail, the wall
was lined with a series of photographs of what I took to be
famous people, one or two of whom I recognised. The same
man's voice called:

'Come down, I won't keep you!'

I descended the stairs, which wound down in two long
curves. At the bottom was a low-ceilinged room elaborately
decorated in a tropical-island motif with palms, parrots on
swings and murals depicting vistas of improbably turquoise
sea and silver sand. The bar had a palm-thatch roof and
stacks of coconut shells. A little yellow-faced monkey scam-
pered around on the bar, attached to a stand by a thin chain
on its collar. I ventured a guess that later on, in the soft glow
of table lamps, the decor would be effective. But now, lit
harshly from above as two men set out chairs and ashtrays,
it looked vulgar. Mr Easter, a slim, dapper man in a striped
suit, walked towards me across the small dance floor, two
large books and a folder under his arm. He held out the
books, but when I took hold of them he didn't relinquish
them, asking instead:

'You are John Ashe's secretary, I sincerely hope? It's more
than my life's worth to let these go to the wrong person.'

'Don't worry, that's me. Mrs Griffe.'

I had no means of identification, but fortunately he took
my word for it.

'Fine, fine, fine . . .' He let go of the books and waved a
dismissive hand. 'There you are then. Now if you'll excuse
me I've got work to do, can you see yourself out?'

I excused his rudeness on the grounds that he was obvi-

ously nervous – not of me, but of what, or who, I represented.

It only took a few minutes to get from there to the Apache
Club, which was just as well because the books were heavy.
I was glad that Alan and I had located the entrance on that
earlier evening. Here, the door was opened by a stout man
in shirtsleeves. His fine, frizzy hair had receded to reveal a
great expanse of domed, freckled forehead, at present
covered with a sheen of perspiration.

'Good evening! Charles Swynford-Hayes. You've come for
the books.'

'That's right.' After my last experience I thought I'd better
identify myself fully. 'I'm Mrs Griffe, Mr Ashe's secretary.'

'I know, I know, I can see that.' His manner was as abrupt
as Easter's, and only slightly more genial. 'They're in my
office. Come through.'

There was no chance of the Apache being thought vulgar.
It was half the size of the White Flamingo, and even in the
semi-darkness looked rather shabby. Piggy's office was
stupendously untidy, but he must have looked out the relevant books earlier, because he was able to pick them up from
the corner of his desk and give them to me right away.

'Can I offer you something, Mrs Griffe?'

'No thank you. I'm going straight on to deliver these.'

'Soho Square or Piedmont Gardens?'

I wanted to ask what business it was of his, but it wasn't
my place. 'Piedmont Gardens.'

'Give my regards to the divine Mrs Ashe, won't you?'

He must have known that I wouldn't – couldn't – do any
such thing. 'Right,' I said briskly, not assenting so much as
announcing my departure. 'I must be off.'

Piggy came with me to the door and opened it for me,
but his gentlemanly gesture did not make me feel like a lady.
Something insinuating in his manner made me glad to get

away. Out in the street I reflected on the irony of this vain, unprepossessing individual making arbitrary judgements about who could or could not enter his poky little *boîtes*. Why did people put up with it? I could only suppose that it was an example of a place acquiring the value that it put on itself, since the policy obviously worked and the Apache was one of the most recherché clubs in town.

The knowledge that I would never in a million years want to get into such a place gave me a sense of power. That, and my particular connection with John Ashe, to whom both these men were answerable and of whom, I sensed, they were very properly in awe.

Piedmont Gardens was a square of opulent cream and white Georgian mansions, each with a flight of steps up to the entrance, and an immense pillared doorway. In the centre, protected by tall black iron railings tipped with gold paint, was the garden, an oasis of well-mown grass intersected by winding paths and shrubberies and shaded by immense trees. The Ashes' house was in the centre on the northern side of the square. Wisteria grew up from basement level and hung in cloudy ringlets around the windows on the upper floors.

I told the cab driver to wait, ascended the steps and rang the bell. Its silvery tinkle resonated in the spacious interior of the house. In my dull work clothes and clutching an armful of ledgers I must have looked more suited to the tradesmen's entrance. The door was opened by a liveried butler who greeted me with immense dignity and courtesy and proceeded ahead of me across the wide hall with its black and white tiles to the drawing room where Felicia Ashe was waiting.

My first reaction was: She's *not* beautiful.

My next: But she can make us believe that she is.

In that moment I realised that beauty is not only a gift of

nature, visible or invisible; nor even an artifice, the product of time, effort and money. It is also a talent – a charm, a spell, a conjuring trick. Felicia Ashe was thin as a boy and pale as a ghost, a wraithlike blank canvas to which had been added everything money, taste and confidence could provide. Her very voice proclaimed her power, for it was soft – a voice, I was sure, that never had to be raised because it commanded instant attention.

'Mrs Griffe . . . You found us. Do, please, put those down.' She indicated an exquisite marquetry table. There was something disdainful in the gesture as though she wished the unsightly, slightly dog-eared books to be set aside as quickly as possible.

'Won't you sit down?' she asked.

In many ways I would rather have left, but I didn't wish to appear rude, and I was hypnotised by Felicia Ashe. She had scarcely taken her eyes off me since I entered the room; there was something cold and snakelike about that unblinking stare.

I sat; or, more accurately, perched. The chair, with its curved back and stiffly upholstered gold brocade seat, was resistant and unwelcoming. My hostess draped herself lightly on the soft cushions of the sofa opposite and crossed her legs. The movement made a just-audible silken whisper.

'It's so nice to meet you at last,' she said. 'I've heard all about your efficiency.'

I made a self-deprecating sound, though I knew it had not, in her rules of engagement, been much of a compliment.

'You work for the Jarvises as well, I believe?'

'Yes,' I said. 'It was through them I met Mr Ashe.'

'Mm. I believe I was abroad for that particular lunch party. In Beirut.' She raised impeccably arched, plucked eyebrows. 'Do you know it?'

'Only by reputation.'

'Oh dear, you sound a little disapproving.'

'No, no, not at all – I believe it's a—' I floundered, and the eyebrows rose again. 'A very colourful city.'

'It is. If you ever have the opportunity, go. Now, tell me – how do you like working for my husband?'

She must have known how awkward this question would make me feel, but then she was not in the business of putting me at my ease.

'I like it very much.'

'There's no need to be polite, Mrs Griffe. You don't find him intimidating? Lots of people do.'

'No. A little, to begin with, but not now.'

'Now you've got used to his face.'

I felt a surge of loyalty towards Ashe, a loyalty that his wife was trying for some reason to undermine. I answered sturdily: 'Oh, that took no time at all.'

'How perfectly splendid,' she said. 'And is he a fair and reasonable employer?'

'Absolutely. I have no complaints.' This sounded somewhat half-hearted, so I added: 'I'm very happy in my work.'

'And how many people can honestly say that?' she murmured, before nodding in the direction of the books on the table. 'Had you been to any of those places before?'

'No.'

'A disobliging experience I should imagine – no, don't demur, there is nothing seedier than a nightclub in daylight. "A successful nightclub is like an experienced tart, best after dark." My husband's observation, not mine.'

I recognised that dangerous thing, an individual prepared on the face of it to 'slum', but who could and would pull rank at the drop of a hat. Felicia Ashe was trying to provoke me into an indiscretion, and I didn't want to give her the satisfaction. I said, almost too quickly: 'They were exactly as I expected.'

She ignored this. 'The best by far is the Calypso. The nastiest, and most exclusive, is the Apache. No one has the least idea what the qualifications are for admittance with the result that all kinds of people who should know better clamour to get in. Incredibly clever.'

'I can see that.'

Her black eyes rested on me. She was completely still except for the middle finger of her right hand which she tapped gently on the arm of the sofa. I gazed about the room. Seconds passed. She might have been reading my mind for at the very moment that I was about to say I must go, she stood up and pulled a bell-rope near the fireplace, dismissing me before I could dismiss myself.

'Well, Mrs Griffe, I mustn't keep you. I dare say you have things to do this evening.'

There was a lemony quality to her voice which trickled scorn on whatever paltry things I might have to do. The butler came back into the room.

'Canter, would you show Mrs Griffe out? And put those,' she indicated the books, 'in Mr Ashe's study.'

In the hall I glanced up. A gallery ran round the first floor, and I could see that the wall was covered in pictures. Presumably Suzannah's were among them. How bitterly I resented the paintings I'd so instinctively and profoundly admired being hung out of sight in this dreadful woman's house.

I'd never been so glad to get out of a place. I asked the cab to take me back to the Tottenham Court Road and went straight to a café where I consumed buck rabbit and strong tea with the appetite of an Alpine mountaineer. It was impossible to imagine Felicia Ashe eating it at all. Having met her I was sure that Louise's assessment had been right – she was not the sort of woman to keep a man like John Ashe entirely happy. But I was equally sure that she knew this, and that it was less than nothing to her.

There were many occasions over the years when I was to be forcibly reminded of Felicia's assessment of the Apache Club as 'the nastiest and most exclusive' in Ashe's portfolio. I came to know such things – and about such people – that it still makes my hair curl to think about. If my mother had had the least idea of my responsibilities it would have driven her into an early grave. A theatrical knight, a cabinet minister, even on one memorable occasion, an Anglican bishop – let alone pillars of society and glittering members of the *beau monde* without number – were among those whose reputations had to be rescued, at a price, by Ashe's weaponry of power and influence. A weaponry of which I was the agent. The suppression of unwanted scandal was the stock in trade of Ashe Enterprises and one of its greatest money-spinners. The fabled 'discretion' of the Apache Club's management was of a fairly loose weave. Mine was the real thing – cast-iron and rock-solid.

That day, and especially the meeting with Felicia Ashe, disturbing though it was, marked a turning point in my attitude towards my job. I hailed a taxi home without a qualm.

Back at the house, I staked my claim to the bathroom by putting enough coins in the slot meter for two baths, and running far more hot water than was allowed. I soaked for half an hour before I felt properly clean, and relaxed. Then I sat in my dressing gown and did some long-overdue mending. I darned stockings, and reattached buttons, and adjusted a hem that had needed doing for weeks. Much as I usually disliked sewing, the everyday practicality of the tasks soothed me and took my mind off the peculiarities of the day.

At nine o'clock, I went to bed and fell asleep almost at once. At three, I woke with a start, possessed by the idea that there was something of overriding importance that I had overlooked, and forgotten to do. But nothing came to mind, and by three thirty I was asleep again.

Chapter Fifteen

On Thursday John Ashe was back at the office. He thanked me for the extra time I had put in and made no enquiries about what I had done. It was business as usual.

I might have missed the short report on an inside page of Thursday's evening paper, if Georgina's return from junketings in Wiltshire had not been affected by the delay on the trains. But on Friday morning, in the naturally self-centred way of the young and fortunate, she was brandishing the page excitedly, keen to tell everyone what a 'nightmare' she had had getting into town.

'I should have gone in the car with Alex,' she told me excitedly. 'He was desperate to drive me, but I'm not interested and I told him so. Then of course I had to take the train, and this had to happen! I mean, poor thing, it's too awful, but why couldn't she have stayed at home quietly and slit her wrists?'

According to the report, the woman had 'hurled herself' on to the rails at the end of the Salisbury line platform at Waterloo. An onlooker was quoted as saying: 'She looked very neat and quiet, not in the least agitated, it came as a complete surprise when the poor creature jumped.'

I knew immediately. It came back to me in a sickening rush – what I had forgotten to do that evening, and why. But I still telephoned the hostel in the faint hope that I had leapt to a false conclusion.

'Yes,' said the woman on the other end, irritably. 'That was her. She hadn't been herself for months. We're having trouble tracking down anyone – are you a friend?'

I said, 'Yes,' but it felt like the worst sort of lie, weak and self-serving.

'Perhaps you could help out? It's not really our responsibility to deal with this kind of thing, and I've already had the police and what have you. I had to identify the body,' she added with a kind of grim pride.

'How awful for you.'

'Yes, well . . . If we could just get her room cleared for a start, we have a waiting list you know.'

'I'll come down,' I said. 'Tomorrow.'

'Can't you manage it before, only—'

'No,' I said, with a firmness I was very far from feeling. 'I'll be there on Saturday morning. Unless of course you manage to contact the family.'

'We won't have, because there isn't any,' declared the horrible woman triumphantly.

I pleaded with Alan to come with me and he managed to get time off between the morning and afternoon surgeries. He would have no truck with my self-recrimination. We sat on Barbara's bed in the hostel, while I wept and he held my hand tight, as if to stop me from drowning.

'It's awful,' he agreed. 'A tragedy. And you were friends. But it isn't your fault, and you mustn't tell yourself it is.'

'But if I'd remembered, if I'd been there—'

'She would have done this some other time. God knows I may never get the qualification, but I've learned enough about this sort of thing to know that it takes more than an outing with a friend to cure someone who's really ill. And from everything you've said she's been ill for years – nursing all that sadness from the past, bottling it up, being a loner.'

'I was the only person she told – about the baby.'

'She trusted you.' Alan squeezed my hand. 'People do, you may have noticed.'

'Yes, and I let her down!'

'Everyone forgets arrangements from time to time. Especially busy people, like you. She could have found some way of getting in touch – she could have come to you. She could have got cross with you, that's what most people would have done, and you'd have said sorry and there'd have been an end of it. Friendship takes two, Pam.'

I shook my head in despair. 'This was different. She wasn't well, so the responsibility was mine.'

'No,' he said. 'She had parents. Still has, for all we know. And other people who knew her and probably saw her far more often than you did. Her employers, all the people who live here, for heaven's sake.' He stood up and pulled me to my feet. 'Come on, Pam. We're here to do something useful now, and I don't have much time. Let's get it done.'

It was my father all over again, except that here there was pitifully little to sort out. Barbara's few clothes we packed in her case for the Salvation Army. Her wash-things we threw away. A childish brush, comb and mirror set with pink backs decorated with flowers I kept; I imagined her having been given them by her mother before the great falling-out. We went through her small shelf of books, of which a couple were library books, due for return. From the remainder I took *Palgrave's Golden Treasury*, because it contained a bookplate from her schooldays with her name on it – a reminder of a happier time. In the bedside drawer we found a scrapbook containing pictures cut from magazines and newspapers, even, I suspected, other books, since some were not photographs but illustrations. The pictures were of individual children – all boys – from babyhood to about seven years old. Each section of a few pages was headed by a year, written in black ink. It was a pretend photo album of Freddy, her lost son.

The police had rescued the handbag she had been carrying when she jumped, and we saved the harrowing task of examining the contents till last. I think I'd hoped that there might be some clue, the key to the mysterious forgotten hinterland of Barbara's life, but there was almost nothing. Perhaps that was the key – to an empty world. A handkerchief, spectacles (I never knew she needed them) in a hard grey case, a glass jar containing aspirin, a tortoiseshell comb, a train timetable and a tiny diary with its own pencil.

'You should look at that,' said Alan. 'It might tell us something.'

The diary too was almost empty. There were a very few appointments – 'Dentist', 'Library' – and the initial 'P' here and there, with a place and time. Only one other date was marked, with the name Freddy. Her son's birthday.

The only entry for the day she had died was the letter 'P'.

I sat there numbly, staring down at the diary. Gently, Alan took it from me. 'That's that,' he said. 'Nothing there.'

Arranging the funeral was not a lengthy or arduous business, but I felt better for performing a practical service for Barbara even this late in the day. There was more than enough in my savings to pay for a simple ceremony and the attendant costs, and I did so willingly. I supposed there would be financial affairs to be sorted out and hoped against hope that some long-lost mercenary relative of Barbara's would come forward at the last moment to deal with all that.

I knew she had not been in the least interested in organised religion, but it occurred to me that St Xavier's, the church where she and I had had our picnic on that rainy day, and where she was known to the people behind the tea urn, might be the right place for the rest of us to take our leave of her.

I went down on Sunday. The vicar was conducting morning service for about twenty people, but the omnipresent tea urn was still there, and the crypt open, and the pews at the back and sides were dotted with the church's regular weekday patrons, coughing and murmuring, waiting patiently for the religious observances to be over. I aligned myself with neither group, but loitered in the south porch until the service was ended.

The vicar, one of those who had been serving tea on my first visit, was a nice man, a shining advertisement for his faith. He heard the news about Barbara with genuine sympathy, but with a realism born of experience. He was only too happy that I had come to him.

'I'd be glad to take a service for her,' he said. 'Such an interesting woman. She was always welcome here.'

Just to hear him say that was, quite literally, a blessed relief. In a single sentence he had provided Barbara with a humane, adult, uncritical setting. She had not been entirely helpless in the face of her despair – she had found this place, and been accepted, and taken comfort from what she had found. It was almost enough to make one believe in a benign God and His self-sacrificing Son.

The service was on Tuesday at two p.m. The Jarvises willingly gave me the afternoon off, though I still intended to go into Ashe Enterprises later on. In the face of their sympathetic enquiries and expressions of understanding I couldn't bring myself to tell them about the connection between this event and the one which had made Georgina late the week before. I presented the funeral as a simple issue of duty.

There were only a handful of mourners present: myself, my mother (who had insisted on coming), Alan, Messrs Rice and Claydon from the tailor's; the warden and another woman from the hostel; and half a dozen habitués of the church, both helpers and visitors. Quite a number of the others sat round the edges as they had on Sunday, but I felt that their slightly restless presence gave the proceedings a much-needed vitality. Barbara had been a young woman, taken in the midst of life, and in the midst of life we were saying our farewells. We sang 'Who would true valour see' because it was one of the few hymns I knew, and I wanted to remember her not as lonely and put-upon but as courageous. With tears blurring the words on the page, I found myself remembering what Georgina had said, how whoever-it-was might have had the courtesy to stay at home quietly and cut her wrists. Good for Barbara, I cheered inwardly. No hole-in-the-corner stuff for her – she held up the trains!

The vicar summoned up a team of his regulars as pall-bearers and the small, plain coffin was carried unsteadily, to the accompaniment of groans and coughs, out into the small, crowded churchyard. There was just room for Barbara in the far corner.

Afterwards we remained in the church for a little while and had tea. The women had made a delicious chocolate cake, of which my mother approved. But she was silent and tight-lipped, discomforted by the occasion and her surroundings. Mr Rice made a point of coming over to me and saying what a loss Barbara would be to them.

'I confess we took her for granted, and knew very little about her.'

'Not only you,' I said. 'She didn't want to be known. I met her years ago, but most of her life was a closed book to me.'

'She will be extremely hard to replace,' said Mr Rice.

After that Alan, who had to be back for evening surgery, drove my mother home. I said goodbye to the others. The vicar went into the vestry and disrobed, appearing five minutes later to take up his place behind the urn while the usual queue formed. Wet clothing dripped and gave off a pungent smell. It was only three o'clock but the rain had intensified and it made the atmosphere dingy. The lights were on in the nave and the transept, and the altar candles had been left alight.

Nobody paid me any attention now; the normal life of the church was resumed, and I was glad of it. For the first time in a week I had the sense of a good job well done. Barbara would have been pleased.

Finding myself with time on my hands I went down into the crypt, not from any desire to gawp at those less fortunate than myself, but to see how things had been arranged down there. I imagined that at this time in the afternoon there were unlikely to be many customers, anyway.

I was right. The long, low room was lit by a single oil lamp and in the semi-darkness I thought at first that it was empty. About a dozen narrow wooden pallet beds were lined up, six to a side, each with two army blankets, one folded lengthwise to form a thin mattress, the other in a neat square on top. At either end of the central aisle stood galvanised iron buckets whose purpose I could guess at. Just inside the door, to the right of where I stood, was a table and chair, and a tall cupboard with a padlocked door. Two metal grilles in the ceiling provided the only ventilation – one to the church above and the other to the pavement outside – and the stairs down which I'd come. An overpowering smell of paraffin hung in the air, as well as that of some strong cleaning fluid, which was probably preferable to the alternative.

Not much to see, and I was about to turn back up the stairs when my eyes became used to the dim light and I noticed two other people in the room. In the bed furthest away on the right-hand, inner wall, someone lay beneath the blanket. He was a small, skinny man; his feet reached nowhere near the end and his shoulder stuck up above the edge of the blanket in a bony point. Next to him, on a low stool, sat a second man, a much more substantial figure in a dark overcoat, the collar turned up. He was leaning forward as if talking under his breath, or perhaps listening intently, and as I looked he stretched out a hand and touched the head of the man on the bed in a tender gesture that was almost maternal. Then he stood up. Ashamed of staring I turned to go, but not before I'd caught sight of his face in the faint light of the paraffin lamp. It was John Ashe.

I positively flew back up the steps and crossed the church just below the chancel without a second glance at the altar, before taking refuge, breathless and fearful, in a pew on the far side, tight against the wall. A moment later Ashe emerged. I was terrified that he would choose to leave by the centre aisle, and have to walk towards me. He nodded a goodbye to the vicar, and buttoned his coat. There were still a few men waiting for tea, and he paused by one of them, placing a solicitous hand on the man's shoulder as he spoke to him. Then, to my unspeakable relief, he stalked down the north aisle and was gone.

Like a child spooked by an invisible bogeyman I peered, and hesitated and peered again before daring to get to my feet. I felt like a spy, though God knows it was the merest accident that I'd seen him. I wondered if he had been down there in the semi-darkness of the crypt all the time, while Barbara's funeral was taking place up here. The thought made me shiver.

When I was absolutely certain he had gone I went back over to the tea table. There were only a couple of people left to serve and one of the women was washing used cups in a bowl of soapy water.

'Excuse me,' I said, 'I just wondered – the man who left just now, the one who was downstairs, I thought I recognised him, but I wasn't sure . . .'

'Mr Jameson, our philanthropist, really? Is he a friend of yours?'

'Oh. No, my mistake. I only saw him briefly and I thought . . . But I was wrong.'

'He comes here often,' she said, swilling the cups and setting them upside down on a spread tea towel to drain. 'He takes a special interest in the war veterans who've fallen on hard times. Listens to their stories, gives them food, tobacco, money even. But mostly time – he has all the time in the world for them.'

I knew I had not been wrong, that it had been Ashe, and yet she was describing someone very different from the man I thought I knew. I expressed my admiration and she warmed to her theme.

'Yes, he's pretty well responsible for us setting up the arrangement here, gave us the money for the furniture and extra lighting and heating . . .' She smiled. 'Ministering angels come in all shapes and sizes. Mr Jameson is ours.'

I left by the north door and went to say a last goodbye to Barbara, who in the shock of seeing Ashe I'd almost forgotten. My own small spray of flowers was dwarfed by Rice and Claydon's rather pompous wreath. She had no headstone yet, though I hoped to get her one, and her grave was a mound of fresh earth, marked by a simple wooden cross bearing her initials and the date, like someone fallen in battle. Which in a way she had been, though not of the kind to whom John Ashe was an angel.

I made particularly sure on this occasion not to arrive even a minute early. When I did get there everything was exactly as it always was, and Ashe his usual civil, quiet-spoken self. I'd half expected to notice some telltale sign of where he'd been and what he'd been doing, but of course there was nothing; not even the smell of the place hung about him. That black coat must have been shut away somewhere, until the next time.

Among the correspondence I typed that afternoon were letters to Charles Swynford-Hayes and Miles Easter, with appointments to call at Ashe Enterprises on Thursday morning.

From the peremptory wording of the letters I had the strong sense that the meetings would not be to their advantage.

Over the following days I felt completely exhausted – drained by everything that had happened. My tiredness was more than just physical, I found it hard to concentrate and was often close to tears. Fortunately no one at Seven Crompton Terrace noticed; they were far too preoccupied with the launch of the Sullivan exhibition, due to take place with fanfares and champagne the following Friday. Christopher Jarvis was like a dog with two tails and there was a lot of joshing, and drinking and laughter. Much of my day was taken up with associated matters: contacting those members of the press who had not replied, checking with the caterer, going back and forth to the gallery on various commissions. I felt as if I were sleepwalking through it all, and prayed I wouldn't overlook anything important. But Amanda, mindful no doubt of the death of my friend so soon after the loss of my father, was even sweeter than usual.

I don't know which of us was the more horrified when one morning she discovered me sitting at my desk, my coat still on, and my head in my hands.

'Pamela? Are you all right?'

I jerked up. 'Oh – yes, Mrs Jarvis, perfectly. I'm so sorry, I'm rather tired.'

'You must be, poor girl . . . so much has happened. Are you sure you should be here at all? We joke about you being indispensable, but we muddled along before, and can always do so again for a while, you know.'

'No, thank you, but I'd much rather be here,' I said truthfully.

On my desk when I returned from the village at lunchtime lay a large white envelope containing a formal invitation to the launch. It was addressed to me, but Christopher Jarvis impressed upon me in person that I was welcome to bring a guest.

'Your mother, for instance!' he suggested, with the delighted expression of someone who had been struck by a sudden happy and charitable thought. 'If you think she would enjoy it.'

'She might,' I said doubtfully. 'It's very kind of you.' I knew my mother would hate such an event, and had probably exhausted her limited social energies by attending Barbara's funeral.

'Or someone else, of course,' Jarvis went on affably. 'Just let us know the name of your guest by the day before, so that we can ensure that they're on the list.'

I hesitated. 'Could I perhaps ask my – my young man?' They didn't know about Alan, and I wasn't sure how to refer to him. I supposed he was my fiancé, but we hadn't as yet bought a ring. 'Dr Alan Mayes,' I added, to emphasise his respectable professional status.

Jarvis's face lit up. 'But of course! Nothing better. Let's hope he can come.'

But Alan could take no more time off and was on call that evening.

'Damn, what a pity, I'd have enjoyed being your escort – and meeting all these people I've heard about. Will John Ashe be there?'

'Probably.'

'Him especially.' He laughed. 'What an opportunity lost.'

I didn't know if I could face going on my own. Dorothy of course hadn't the slightest doubt.

'Go on, Mrs G, you must! I want to hear all about it.'

'Who on earth would I talk to?'

'Lots of people – anybody! Wish I could go, just let me at 'em.'

'*I* wish you could,' I said, 'instead of me. They'd adore you, I know they would.'

She flapped a hand at me. 'Go on, I'm far too common.'

I wanted to tell her she was one of the most uncommon people I knew, and perhaps I should have done. Instead I said: 'How's Jimmy?'

Her face quietened at once, and her voice became gentler. 'Not long now. He goes back to Ireland in a week.'

'You're going to miss him.'

She nodded, and busied herself at the sink. For the first and only time I sensed she was close to tears. Paralysed by uncertainty I did nothing, and then Chef was back in the kitchen and the moment had passed.

That evening Louise knocked on my door. She was in her kimono, the one she'd been wearing when we first met, with no make-up and a cigarette in her hand. In the other she carried an open bottle of champagne and two tumblers.

'Have you got time for a quick celebration?' It was clear from her manner that she'd already made a start.

'You know I have.' I checked my watch. 'But do you?'

She waved the bottle airily as she came in. 'What the hell, I can be late . . .'

With the cigarette between her lips she put the bottle and glasses on the mantelpiece, sloshed in a couple of fizzing measures, handed me mine and then flopped down on the bed as she would have done in her own room. I perched on the windowsill.

'What are we celebrating?'

She raised her glass. 'Well, old thing, I did it!'

She didn't have to explain. I knew at once what she meant: her conquest, if that's what it was, of John Ashe. I raised my own glass with rather less of a flourish.

'Come on, do!' exclaimed Louise. 'Say something, if it's only goodbye!'

'Congratulations.'

Even my half-heartedness couldn't dampen her spirits. 'It

was so easy! I told you that wife of his couldn't keep him happy.'

Here at least was a subject on which I could agree with her. 'I met her the other day, and I think you may right.'

'What?' Her mouth literally fell open. 'You did, you met the ice queen? What was she like?'

'As you predicted. Icy.'

'Jee-pers . . . I was only guessing, you know. Shooting a line as usual . . .' She took out another cigarette and lit it from the stub of the first. 'More, tell me more!'

'She's extremely elegant and glamorous, in a way. But I didn't like her. She was artificial and charmless and she patronised me.'

'Attagirl!' Louise shrieked and then added ferociously: 'The bitch!'

'But—'

'No, for God's sake don't let there be a but!'

'*But*,' I went on, determined to make my point, 'my guess for what it's worth is that they have an understanding. An accommodation, isn't that what people call it?'

'Don't get me wrong, I didn't suppose he was begging her, or anything,' said Louise airily. 'He's not the type. Just that I'm not surprised he looks for his pleasures elsewhere.'

Studying Louise, so worldly-wise and self-confident with her glass and her cigarette, her kimono parted to reveal long, slender, gleaming white legs, I wondered which of us could claim to know John Ashe better. In spite of everything I concluded, in all honesty, that I did. Louise was infinitely more experienced than I in the game between the sexes, its terms, its rules, its moves and how to interpret them. Ashe, I was sure, made her look like a beginner. They were worthy of each other's steel. But I had seen other sides of him; was gradually, albeit imperfectly, forming an impression of the whole man. There was plenty that I still did not know, and even more that I did not understand – but at least I recognised and acknowledged my ignorance and lack of understanding. Whereas Louise was sublimely unaware of how little she knew, as this ad hoc celebration proved.

'. . . still feel sorry for him,' she was saying. 'I can't imagine anything more ghastly than being stuck in a loveless marriage. Correction, a sexless marriage.'

'No.'

'Tell me!' She scooped her legs up in front of her, treating me to a flash of mouse-coloured private hair. 'Tell me – has he seen you in the dress?'

'Yes.'

'And, and? You're such a miser with gossip, Pamela.'

'He complimented me on it, eventually.'

'I'm very glad to hear it. You must wear it often. Change the way the world sees you.'

'I'm quite happy with the way it sees me,' I said. This wasn't wholly true; I had always been uncomfortable with Louise's assumption of my dull, virtuous respectability, and her assumption, too, of the role of Svengali to my blameless Trilby.

But tonight Louise wasn't interested in what I had to say. She was detached and buoyant, afloat on her own success.

'You know,' she said, 'I'm beginning to think that all my life I've been in training to become a rich man's plaything. I shouldn't in the least mind being set up in a pretty little flat in Mayfair and kept for best.'

'Is that what you expect to happen?' I asked. I was genuinely curious. I myself could think of nothing worse than the sort of pampered captivity she described with such relish, but it had nothing to do with prudishness. The passivity, the acceding to another's will which such a situation implied, was anathema to me.

'I'm not saying I expect it, but it's not impossible. I am his mistress, after all.'

I didn't like to say that the term 'mistress' implied an exclusivity which I was sure Louise did not enjoy. Instead I asked: 'What happens when he finds someone else?'

She shrugged. 'I'll find someone else too. I shall have had some fun, and enjoyed the attention. No hard feelings.'

'I can't imagine it.'

'But I have to, don't I?'

'I suppose.'

She looked as if she were focusing on me for the first time. 'Don't be disapproving, Pamela. Please.'

'I'm not.'

'We're friends, aren't we?'

I was touched, and not a little shocked by this. We were certainly on good terms, or she wouldn't have been confiding in me now, but whether we could truly be said to have a friendship based on half a dozen conversations and a shopping spree, I was doubtful.

'I think so.' I saw something like dismay in her eyes, and added: 'Yes, of course we are.'

'I'm not some poor little thing, you know,' she went on more spiritedly. 'I won't be taken advantage of, even by Ashe. Especially by him.'

'Good.'

'It's just so – so – *exciting*!' she said. 'Such *fun*! And if he's a bit of an unknown quantity that makes it more exciting and more fun. For the first time in my life I feel like someone special and important. People look at me and *know*, and they wonder . . . And I'm not going to tell anyone about what goes on. That's between him and me. Can you understand that?'

This time I could. It was the effect John Ashe had on those around him. His appearance, his secrecy, his wealth, his aura of utter, unforced power – they both repelled and fascinated us. It was as though Louise and I were working for royalty, who demanded fealty and complete discretion. We had been chosen by Ashe and we knew what was expected of us. But as to which of us was most secure in her position, I had no doubt: it was me.

'Louise,' I said, 'would you like to come to a party?' Her face registered a moment's doubt about the sort of party to which I would be invited.

'Everyone will be there,' I said.

She drew on her cigarette but I saw the gleam in her eye. 'When's that?' she asked. 'I'll check my diary.'

Charles Swynford-Hayes and Miles Easter were sacked. In the case of the former I was there, working at my desk while it was happening, but I heard almost nothing. The only voice I heard was Ashe's, and it was lowered. The whole thing took less than five minutes. Though Swynford-Hayes greeted me civilly enough on his arrival his departure was swift and silent. The lift door clanged shut on the eddying wake of his humiliation. Ashe's door remained closed.

The following week, when I typed out letters to the two men confirming their dismissal in barely two sentences I felt a guilty thrill of power by association. If Ashe was Jupiter, icy in his wrath, then I was his Mercury. Still I could not for the life of me reconcile this Ashe with the self-effacing philanthropist I'd seen in the crypt of St Xavier's and somehow the presence of another, more benevolent side to my employer made him still more forbidding. Once more I hoped, fervently, that Louise would be careful, for she was dealing with so much more than she, or any of us, knew.

There was no question of her arriving at the gallery with me, new dress or no new dress.

'You go on,' she said, 'I'm hopeless at getting ready.' But I knew the real reason was so she could make a late entrance, the effect undimmed by a less glamorous female companion.

I didn't in the least mind. I had told Christopher Jarvis she would be coming, and I wanted her to shine.

When I arrived, I left her name with the greeter on the door. I noticed at once that Ashe was not there either. The Jarvises welcomed me warmly and insisted that I enjoy myself.

'You're not working tonight, Pamela,' said Amanda.

I stood beneath Bob Sullivan's largest canvas, with my untouched glass in my hand, observing. The painting was entitled 'Desert Rocks, January 1928'. The purples, umbers and slate greys in which it was executed went well with my dress, but whatever the Jarvises cared to pretend, I was not like my fellow guests. I could not imagine ever knowing so many people or having so much to say. As the room filled up, the conversation became a positive roar. It was easy to spot the guest of honour, because he was a head taller than most other people, and there was a slight shift in the crowd as he moved around, carrying the focus of attention with him. It was like watching an animal walking through long grass. The crowd around him made up a vivid and eclectic mix. Many of those present – artists, presumably, or would-be artists, poseurs affecting an artistic manner – were dressed in an eccentric style that ranged from gorgeously bohemian to downright scruffy. Others, whom I took to be dealers or potential customers, were smart, the men expensively tailored and the women ruthlessly chic. A few individuals, who might have belonged to either group, affected a studied plainness, as if their sole object was to blend into the background; these I suspected of being critics.

This notion was more than borne out when John Ashe arrived, with his wife on his arm. She was like a dragonfly in blue and silver – brilliant, but frangible and inconsequential; he, plain and dark as ever, exuded a still, intense presence powerful enough to be felt across the room, and not just by me. For the first time, at their entrance, attention shifted momentarily away from the artist and his work. As soon as they'd been greeted by Christopher Jarvis they parted company, turning away from one another so that each was at the centre of a separate group. This might have resulted from long practice, or prior agreement, or just a natural social instinct, but it was very noticeable.

A voice beside me said my name: 'Pamela?' It was Georgina, her cheeks as pink as her georgette dress, and her eyes shining. 'Pamela, you look quite wonderful!'

'Hello, Georgina. So do you. What do you think of the paintings?'

She glanced at the one above me, and then mock-furtively from side to side before positioning herself between me and the rest of the room.

'Not much – too big and obvious. Like the artist.'

I laughed. 'I believe he's terrifically popular in America.'

'That just proves my point. Clever old you, though, to stand under this one, which goes so well with that beautiful dress.'

'It wasn't intentional,' I lied.

'Then it was a very happy coincidence. Do you like them? The pictures?'

'I do, quite. Not as much as Suzannah's, though.'

'She's here, you know,' said Georgina, putting her hand on my shoulder and craning her neck to see. 'Somewhere around . . . She looks *awful*.'

I felt a little spider creep of anxiety across my skin. 'In what way?'

'Every way imaginable – tired, thin. *Ill*, actually. I know she's older than me, but she's such a little waif, and there doesn't seem to be anyone to look after her.'

'Doesn't she have a family?'

Georgina shrugged. 'Who knows? If she does she's never mentioned them. She just always seems to be alone.'

'Or perhaps she's a loner,' I said. 'Which isn't quite the same.'

'Anyway, she makes me want to wrap her up in a thick rug and feed her sponge pudding and custard with a runcible spoon.'

'She was painting John Ashe's portrait, wasn't she?'

'Yes – she's finished, she told me. Wouldn't you absolutely love to see?'

'Perhaps we will. Mr Jarvis likes her work, maybe it will be displayed here.'

Georgina made a face. 'Not if he doesn't want to frighten the customers!'

'Surely,' I said, a touch pompously, 'you can't judge a painting by the appearance of the subject.'

'Not in the papers I dare say, but would you have that face hanging on your drawing-room wall?'

Oddly, I thought, I might. But it would have been much too complicated to explain why, so I let her rhetorical question go by as if I agreed. Besides, Georgina's attention was already elsewhere.

'Who in the world is *that*? She'll put Felicia's nose out of joint. Mind if I go and investigate?'

I looked where she was heading. It was Louise, of course; I felt proud of her. She wore the simplest column of white, with a cloud of maribou at the neck, a white and silver plume in her pinky-golden hair, and silver shoes. Knowing her predilection for show, she must have thought long and hard about the impression she wished to make. Aside from her youth, and the fact that she was unaccompanied, she might have been a high society belle from the very top of the top drawer. She had even softened her make-up, and smoothed her hair. She was quite lovely. Christopher Jarvis's face was a study; he could surely never have suspected me of having such a friend. Georgina was introduced, and was equally impressed.

All three of them looked my way, and Amanda pointed me out. Louise smiled, took a glass of champagne and started to make her way in my direction. I waited, relishing the sense that almost the entire room – covertly, of course – was waiting to see who the newcomer was acquainted with. Felicia Ashe was holding court in the far corner, her back to me, but one of the men she was talking to sent a predatory, greedily admiring glance over her shoulder. I couldn't see Ashe.

Louise had almost reached me when she was, inevitably, intercepted – and by Bob Sullivan himself, no doubt thanking his lucky stars for this God-given opportunity to flaunt his special status.

'Good evening, may I introduce myself? I'm Bob Sullivan.'

'Not –' Louise consulted her catalogue, she was such a pro. 'Not R.J. Sullivan himself? The artist we're here to celebrate?'

'The very same. And you are?'

'Louise Baron.'

'Louise . . .' He shook her hand slowly. 'I'm mortified that we haven't met before. How is it that you're here?'

'Oh, I'm just a hanger-on, really. My friend knows Christopher Jarvis. Here she is – Pamela, meet the artist, Bob – may I call you Bob? – Sullivan. This is Pamela Griffe.'

'We know each other,' he said, and added that it was a pleasure to see me, though I was far from sure how much of a pleasure since he must have been hoping to have Louise to himself. He had the easy, confident charm that Americans were famous for, but seeing the way he looked at Louise I felt sorry for Christopher Jarvis.

'Are you ladies enjoying the show?' he enquired. I said that I was.

'I've only just arrived,' said Louise, 'so I shall answer that when I've had a good look round.'

'Quite right!' he agreed. 'But if it's bad news, don't tell me, OK?' I had the distinct impression that he'd have been enchanted by whatever she cared to say. 'Champagne's good, huh?'

Louise took a sip, frowning slightly. 'It's as good as I'm used to, and I'm used to the best.'

'I bet you are!' Sullivan roared with laughter.

I hadn't seen John Ashe approach, but quite suddenly he was there, a dark background to Louise's white dress.

'Hey, Ashe,' said Sullivan, the easy manner appearing suddenly overfamiliar. 'Let me introduce you to these charming ladies.'

'Thank you. I know them both.'

'You do? Well I'll be!'

'Good evening, Mr Ashe,' I said. 'Would you excuse me?'

They scarcely noticed I'd gone, so wrapped up were they in their own reactions. I stepped aside, and turned half away to examine a picture on the wall, still close enough to witness the small scene that followed.

Somewhat mischievously, I had not told Louise that Ashe would be present. I justified it by telling myself that I'd not been absolutely sure. What I hadn't known, or suspected, was that Felicia would come too. After all, till now I had never seen them together, so I had got into the way of thinking that they led largely separate lives.

For a minute or two Bob Sullivan continued to boom away enthusiastically, but then Christopher Jarvis came and bore him off, under mild protest, to meet other people.

'I didn't expect to meet you here,' said Louise. I caught at once the different tone in which she addressed him – the quick, low, casual voice of a lover.

'Nor me. It's a very pleasant surprise.' In his voice, I could detect no difference. 'But then . . . you've met Mrs Griffe.'

'Yes.' I felt Louise look my way, and affected the closest possible interest in Sullivan's work. 'Yes, she and I live in the same building.'

'A small world indeed. Felicia – this is Louise Baron. It turns out we have acquaintances in common. My wife, Felicia.'

'How do you do.'

I couldn't tell if Felicia responded, but I did hear her say: 'Ashe, shouldn't we talk to the artist?'

'I've just met him.'

'But I haven't, and I don't want to stay long.'

'We'll find him then. Goodbye, my dear.'

A second later Louise was at my side. Even in the crush I could hear her shallow breathing and feel the furious heat emanating from her. With shaking hands she rummaged in her tiny bag for her cigarette case. The moment the cigarette was between her lips a lighter was proffered, but she only flashed a 'Thanks,' swift and brilliant as a blade, before turning back to me and hissing: 'Bitch!'

'It's only her manner,' I said. 'And she doesn't know you.'

'Then he's more of a bastard than I took him for. He behaved as if *he* didn't know me – you must have been listening, didn't you hear?'

'He was distant and polite. What did you expect?'

'*Something* . . . I don't know!'

'If it's any consolation,' I said, 'she was bound not to like you. She's used to being the most admired woman in the room.'

'Hm.' Louise sucked fiercely on her cigarette and snorted smoke through her nostrils like a dragon. 'Can't think why. She's a cold little china doll.' She rounded on me. 'Did you know they'd be here?'

'I thought he might be.'

'What were you doing? Did you want to see me humiliated?'

'No!' This was so far from the truth it took my breath away. But, unable to deny that I had been meddling, I now reproached myself for it. 'I thought you might like to see Ashe,' I muttered.

'I don't need your help to do that, Pamela. I can see him whenever I want.'

There was no mollifying her, and the man with the lighter was hovering with a smitten expression. 'Excuse me,' I said, 'I think I see someone else I know.'

I needed to escape, but as I moved away through the crowded room the last thing I wanted was to get tied up with Rintoul, or Paul Marriott, or even Georgina or the Jarvises. I did not belong here. In fact it was hard to say where I belonged any more. I felt small, and foolish and ashamed, faintly ridiculous in my expensive dress.

I had already decided to leave when I saw Suzannah. She was leaning against the wall near the door, arms folded, staring into space. Even when I was in front of her it was clear she couldn't see me. When I said her name she started, and I could tell it took a moment before she realised who I was.

'Hello.'

'It's Pamela. From Crompton Terrace.'

'Pamela, yes. I'm sorry, I was miles away.'

'How are you?'

'Pretty well,' she said. But Georgina had been right, she did look awful. Her pale orange hair was tied back in a scarf, her small, pale face was like a sick child's; her eyes were clogged with scurf at the corners, touched with blue shadows beneath. Her lips were red, dry and cracked. The tendons in her neck stood out and I noticed a hollow on either side of her collarbones. Her nails were bitten, the cuticles ragged.

'I'm rather tired,' she said, as if she'd known what I was thinking.

I asked if she had finished the portrait.

'Oh yes. In fact I don't have any commissions at the moment so why I should feel like this . . . Who knows? Perhaps doing nothing is exhausting. For someone like me who doesn't know where the next penny's coming from.'

'But your paintings are doing well, surely,' I said. 'There were several in this gallery when I first came.'

'Just because Christopher likes them doesn't mean they're popular. Unfortunately. But I don't want to court popularity, so . . .'

'Is Mr Ashe pleased?' I asked.

'He's got what he asked for.'

'And you? What do you think of it now you've finished?'

She hesitated, looking away as though weighing her words. It occurred to me that I was asking too many questions, that I was harrying her.

'He's an interesting subject and a good sitter.'

'I'm sorry,' I said gently, 'it's really none of my business. But I'm such an admirer of your work.'

She smiled wanly, and the smile made a tiny bead of blood appear on her lower lip. 'You're not a flatterer. So thank you. The answer to your question is that there was some compromise involved but the result is better than I hoped.'

'I can't wait to see it,' I said. 'You know I do some work for him – perhaps it'll hang in his office.'

'I've really no idea.'

I was beginning to understand that to Suzannah the picture was like a ship which she had built, but which had now sailed way out to sea, in the hands of others and bound on a separate and different course. It no longer had anything to do with her. But I couldn't help being fascinated and curious.

'Where have you been living?' I asked. 'Were you staying with the Ashes?'

'No, they have a little flat . . . But I'm moving out of there now. I'm coming back to the Jarvises for a while until I decide what to do.'

'But that's marvellous!' I cried. I could scarcely believe how pleased I was by this news. 'It'll be like before, when I first arrived.'

'Yes,' she said, so softly it was almost a whisper. 'Almost like before.'

I explained that I'd been on my way out, and said goodbye. As I left, I scanned the crowd once more. Louise was at the centre of a group of admirers, including Bob Sullivan. From across the room, John Ashe was staring directly at us, with such quiet and intense concentration that I had the strong impression – impossible of course – that he had heard every word we said.

Chapter Sixteen

It was odd that I should have felt so out of place that evening because, looking back, it was the occasion when I became enmeshed. Till then I had been a bystander, an onlooker and proud of it. I thought I could remain detached. But detachment was no longer possible: John Ashe had seen to that. I was not proud of the trick I had played on Louise, but I had felt compelled to prove that she was not as important to Ashe as I was myself. It was disturbing to think that this might have been not an aberration, but my true colours.

My mother, of course, seemed to sense it when I saw her at the weekend.

Her actual words were: 'You're looking very smart.' But I knew what she meant. It wasn't my new jacket and skirt she was alluding to: she could smell it on me, the difference – the subtle shift, as she saw it, in allegiance.

'I've been doing some shopping,' I said. 'So many of my clothes I've had for years.'

'It was all well-made stuff.' She crimped her mouth, turning my remark against me.

'I shan't get rid of them,' I said.

'It's up to you, Pam.' She was at her most maddening in this mood. 'Will you be seeing Alan while you're here?'

'This evening. I hope. When he's done his calls.'

She sighed, as if confronting a tedious but necessary duty. 'So what about this party, then? The American fellow?'

I'd mentioned the Sullivan launch to her some time before,

but it still struck me as interesting that she remembered, let alone enquired. I suppose that living on her own, with not enough to occupy her mind and with her good memory for events, she monitored my life much more closely than I imagined.

'There were too many people and too much noise,' I said. 'The paintings were quite nice, but not many people were looking at them. You'd have hated it.'

'I dare say. It was a pity Alan couldn't go with you, though.'

'He was working, but it couldn't be helped.'

'I'm surprised you wanted to go on your own.'

Now what was she implying? It was like one of those party games where obstacles are set out for inspection and then removed once the person is blindfolded. I was tiptoeing over, and round, objections which might or might not exist. I trod carefully to avoid them whatever they were.

'I had to, really, Mum. The Jarvises like me to be around, there are usually one or two things I can help with. And it's nice of them to include me. They don't have to.'

She didn't actually sniff, but she might as well have done. 'I don't see that it's all that nice if you're making yourself useful.'

'Anyway,' I said more spiritedly, 'I enjoyed it. It's interesting to go to these things. Different.'

'Oh, they're different I'm sure.'

This was the last straw. 'Mum – what is it?'

'What?' Immediately, she sounded defensive.

'What have I done wrong? My life can't stay exactly the same for ever, you know. And I don't want it to.'

'No, I can see that.'

'After Matthew died, you and Dad always wanted me not to mope, to get on and make something of myself, and that's exactly what I'm doing.'

Her expression softened at the mention of Dad. 'Pammie,

all I'm saying is don't change too much. You've got a very
nice young man there, that Alan. Don't lose him.'

'I'm not going to!' Even to my own ears my protest sounded
too loud and insistent – too sure, when I was anything but
sure. To cover my uncertainty I hit back at my mother.

'Stop concerning yourself with what I'm doing, and make
some friends of your own!'

She whitened with shock. 'I've got as many friends as I
need, thank you.' Her voice was tight with the effort of maintaining control.

'Of course you have, Mum, of course . . . I'm sorry.'

'And since when was it wrong for a mother to show a bit
of concern for her daughter?'

'It's not.' I shook my head, wishing I could put the clock
back five minutes. 'It's *not*.'

'I'm not saying anything against these people you work for
and their friends, I don't know them. But I know you, Pam,
and I don't want you losing out again.'

'Oh, Mum.' If we had been a different sort of mother and
daughter, or living at a different time, one of us, at this stage,
might have put her arms round the other. But it was a long
time ago, and we were who we were. We simply called a halt,
withdrew, and began again.

Our afternoon continued along the usual lines, though not
exactly as if nothing had happened, because it was there in
the corner of our minds like an object thrown down in anger
that no one would pick up. But we went through the motions
of normality, with me offering to help and being assigned
undemanding tasks, and my mother marching about as if it
were Monday morning, she had six mouths to feed, and the
mayor was coming to call. I longed to tell her to sit down
and read a book, or simply relax, or to come for a walk with
me, but I had muddied the water with my earlier outburst
and had no alternative but to keep the peace by playing

things her way. I did wonder, was she *always* so busy? Every
day, seven days a week? Or did she save up all this activity
in order not to seem at a loose end when I came to visit?
Surely no house needed to be cleaned so exhaustively all the
time?

By the time Alan came round at half past seven we were
both pretty much worn out especially since my mother, who
would normally have served and eaten tea at six, had postponed it in case he wanted some. Under the circumstances
I was loath to crush this hospitable thought, though our stomachs were rumbling when the bell rang.

'Good evening, Mrs Streeter,' said Alan. He always greeted
my mother first in her own house. 'How are you doing?'

'Pretty well,' she replied. 'There's an oxtail in the oven,
would you like to join us?'

I couldn't bring myself to catch his eye, but I needn't have
worried – he always managed to react in the right way.

'Oh, no!' He put his hand to his brow. 'I should have
guessed there'd be something delicious waiting here. But
surgery dragged on and I helped myself to a cheese sandwich before I left.'

'That won't keep you going,' said my mother comfortably.
'Never mind, it'll keep till tomorrow, if you'd like some lunch.'
She sounded quite unperturbed – there was no justice.

'Why not, that sounds splendid. You'll be here, won't you,
Pamela?'

'She'll be here,' confirmed my mother before I could so
much as nod.

Alan looked from one to the other of us, gauging the mood.
'I say, you didn't wait for me, did you?'

'Yes, but we didn't have to,' I said. 'Shall we go?'

'Stay and have a glass of sherry,' said my mother.

She had made it a straight fight, but Alan sidestepped it.
'Do you know, I think I should say no? I had a nip with

Dr Cardew a little earlier and that was enough to be going on with. But lunchtime tomorrow – that would be different.'

She let us go, like a lamb. When we were safely in the Morris I clapped my hands to my face in exasperation.

'She drives me mad!'

'She can't help it.'

'Of course she can. She's a perfectly intelligent woman who knows what she's doing.'

Alan started the car. 'Which is?'

Now I wasn't sure exactly what to say. 'She interferes,' I said lamely.

'Mothers do that. My mother used to. But now she's gone I miss being fussed over, and you would too if it wasn't there.'

'Maybe,' I said grudgingly.

'You would. Look, I'm going to buy you something to eat. After all, I deprived you of the oxtail, and food does wonders for the morale.'

He was quite right, an omelette and a cup of tea revived me and went a long way to restoring my sense of proportion. Afterwards we drove to our hill. The evenings were drawing in and dusk had already fallen, but the long view dotted and strung with lights was still pretty. Alan put his arm round my shoulders. My mother was right – I was lucky.

'So tell me about the party,' he said.

But I couldn't tell him, not truthfully. There was too much he didn't know already, too much that was complicated to explain, and which I scarcely understood myself.

'There's nothing to tell,' I said. 'You didn't miss anything.'

His eyes rested quizzically on my face, but he didn't press me. It wasn't his style. He wasn't to know that with those few words I took a small but irrevocable step away from him.

'What about you?' I asked. 'How's your day been?'

He told me, of course. He trusted that my interest was genuine, and paid me the compliment of replying in full measure. He didn't, like me, feel the need to keep things from me because they were too complex, or for fear I might not understand. I enjoyed his account of his day, but I appreciated even more the difference between us.

He left the important news till last.

'I've got an interview in Edinburgh.'

'Congratulations! So you're as good as in.'

'Not quite,' he smiled bashfully. 'But at least my application's not been turned down out of hand.'

I kissed him. I wasn't as excited as I might have been not long ago, but I was tremendously pleased for him.

'Will you come with me?' he asked.

'When is it?'

'At the end of the month. The last Saturday. It'll mean taking a day off to travel up there, but at least it's only one, with the weekend just after.'

'That ought to be all right . . .' I tried to remember if there was anything in particular in the diary for that day. 'I'll see.'

'Do try,' he said. 'It would mean such a lot to me.'

I saw in his eyes how much. It meant far more to him than to me. The truth was that I did not especially want to go. I was so caught up in my new life that I could not bear to leave it, even for one day, an important day, with the man I had said I wanted to marry.

'Of course I'll try,' I said. 'They're always very reasonable and I don't work for Ashe on a Friday . . . I'm sure it will be fine.'

'It's a lot to ask, I know. But it's a chance for us to be together.'

Suddenly I saw why this was so important to him – it wasn't only my moral support he wanted, but also the chance 'to be together'; the chance I, too, had once longed for. And this evening it hadn't even crossed my mind.

He was watching my face. 'Pamela? It is what you want,

isn't it? Because I'd hate to be rushing you into something you're not ready for. It's just that – you're the woman I love, and . . .'

He blushed, and gripped my hand in both of his. It was a moment of agonisingly awkward emotions for both of us, all the more awkward for me because I was caught between the strength of his feeling and the confused, divided nature of mine.

'Yes,' I said firmly. 'It is what I want. More than anything.'

He lifted my hand to his lips, laid it against his cheek. I felt him smile as he said: 'Your mother wouldn't approve.'

'She approves of you, though.'

'Only so long as my intentions are honourable. Not when they involve whisking her daughter away to satisfy my baser instincts.'

'What she doesn't know won't worry her.'

'I hoped you'd say that.'

'And anyway, it doesn't matter what she thinks. Not really. Not any more.'

'Precisely.'

I was being teased. He had the priceless ability to make me smile in spite of myself. He was a gem, and I knew it, which made everything a thousand times worse.

'I'll be there,' I said, 'I promise.'

With autumn approaching, the house at Crompton Row took on a different character. I think it was because of the changed light, lower and more mellow after the pale glare and deep shadows of that long, baking summer. I've always been susceptible to the seasons, their own pace, colour and character, and this year the turn of the year held a particular significance for me. It confirmed the shift that had taken place in my life. I had been working here for only a few months but those few months had seen me move into different territory. The garden – its trees, bushes, flowers and weeds, even its grass – was changing with me. The plants I'd trimmed, tended and subdued were dying back, retrenching for the winter.

'I haven't heard the nightingale for ages,' Amanda said. 'I do hope she'll come back.'

'She will,' I said, 'in the spring.'

Ashe had gone away for a fortnight, I didn't know where, and had told me there would be nothing to do in his absence, so my working week reverted to its earlier pattern and tempo. With the Sullivan exhibition launched, and due to remain at the Sumpter till Christmas, business was relatively quiet, and so was the house itself. Suzannah had not reappeared as yet; there were no other house guests. Bob Sullivan had gone back to America, and Christopher Jarvis was melancholy and listless as a result – he told me he and Amanda planned to go to New York for Christmas and it was pretty obvious he was counting the days.

I was so underemployed that I took to helping Dorothy with an out-of-season 'spring-clean'.

'Might as well,' she said. 'They don't care either way, but you've got to take your chance when you can around here.'

She always made it sound as though she liked nothing better than the opportunity to do extra work. I was pleased to see that in spite of Jimmy's return to Ireland she was looking well and pretty again, and I told her so one afternoon when we were on our own, sitting cleaning silver out on the terrace.

'Blimey, do you think so?' She swiped at a lock of hair with the back of her wrist. 'I must've been looking in the wrong mirror.'

She was agog to hear about the party, especially about Felicia Ashe, whom she had seen before at the house.

'She's got the most beautiful clothes and jewels I've ever

seen – like a queen. Imagine what it must be like having all that money!'

'She was glittering,' I conceded, and couldn't resist adding: 'but my friend Louise was the toast of the evening.'

'Good for her.' Dorothy gave me one of her searching looks. 'How do you know her, then?'

'She lives in the same building as me. But she's very pretty, and she works in the fashion business.'

Dorothy sighed. 'Lucky girl . . . How did she get a job like that?'

'I don't know. She's no prettier than you.'

She snorted with laughter. 'Says you! Mind you, any woman with a bit of money, and the time to spend it, can look halfway decent.'

'What about you, Dorothy?' I asked carefully. 'Are you enjoying life?'

'Me? Oh yes. You got to keep smiling, haven't you?' She was a dab hand at these catch-all clichés, which served her very well. And because I knew that beneath all the chirpy garrulousness she was quite guarded about her own affairs, I didn't press her further.

I didn't even know Suzannah had come back until I stumbled upon her, almost literally, in the garden. I had arrived one morning to find that the Jarvises had left early to spend the day with Georgina and her parents out of town. Dorothy and Chef were nowhere about. I unlocked the back door and went out. The air was quite cold and the leaves were beginning to turn. I shivered as I went over the clammy grass and along the stepping-stone path into the shrubbery. A little way in I stopped and turned; I liked to look back from here, to gain a different perspective on the house, especially with no one else about. Even if someone was in, this end of the garden was so secret one became invisible between one step and the next, and I wasn't sure anyone else ever came here but me.

So when I had the sensation of being watched, not from the house in front of me, but from the overgrown darkness at my back, my skin crawled. For a second I was caught between wanting to know who, if anyone, was there, and a childish fear of finding out. Telling myself not to be so foolish, I turned round.

To begin with I couldn't see anyone, but then I heard a voice say, softly: 'Hello.' I peered in the direction it had come from and now I could make out Suzannah, sitting in the corner of the garden between the wall and the largest tree, her knees drawn up and her skirt wrapped round them. She looked even more of a waif, like the abandoned changeling child of some Victorian fairy tale.

I laughed with relief. 'You gave me a fright!'

'And then you saw it was only me.'

'When did you get back?'

'Last night. But I can't stay.'

'I'm sure you could, for as long as you want.'

'That's the point. The Jarvises have been too kind already.'

She made a little movement to one side, an invitation to sit down. I did so without a second thought, in spite of my business suit.

'Look,' she said, 'it's still here.' With her left hand she parted the tangled ivy and dying greenery between the roots of the tree. I leaned round to see. She was right – the little nest, at least, was still whole and perfect although long empty.

'Will she come back?' Her voice was dreamy, the question rhetorical, addressed to herself as much as to me, but I answered her just the same.

'I'm going to find a bird book and look it up.'

She laid her cheek on her knees, her face averted, her hand still lying by the nest. Her voice now seemed to come from far away. 'The swallows won't.'

'I thought they always did. Once they'd found a good place.'

'This isn't a good place. Not any more. They were disturbed. They lost one of their young.'

'That must happen from time to time.'

'No.' She gave her head a little shake. 'They won't be back.'

A long silence followed. She was so still I thought she might have gone to sleep. Then she lifted her head and said more firmly. 'But she might, the nightingale. It's so secret here. And no one knows about her except me and you.'

'That's right. She's perfectly safe.'

We sat side by side, thinking about this, and drawing comfort from it. It was so strange – we could never truly be friends, there was too much dividing us and neither of us quite knew how to bridge the gap. And yet the possibility of friendship hovered over us like a benign spirit.

'What will you do next?' I asked eventually.

'I'm not sure,' she said, frowning slightly. 'I've got a lot of things to sort out. I don't have any work but I'm not sure I could manage any at the moment. I may have to go back to Ashe's, but I don't want to.'

'Then you mustn't.'

'We'll see.' She had all at once become much less like a child. She was so changeable, you never quite knew where you were with her. Not five minutes earlier I had wanted, like Georgina, to wrap, feed and protect her. Now she seemed the epitome of independence, a free spirit whom it would be impossible for anyone, least of all me, to mollycoddle.

'Still,' I said, 'this is a good place to have a rest and take stock.'

'I suppose.'

After a moment she kneeled and sat back on her heels, looking down at the nest. Then she covered it again carefully and got to her feet. I did the same. The spell of secrecy and intimacy was broken. We were both damp, and I brushed fussily at the seat of my skirt.

'Do you know what I wish?' she said. 'I wish that next spring she will come back, and that I'll come back too, and I'll hear her singing away, safe and well.'

Conscious of her new mood, I said nothing but in my heart I made the same wish, for all our sakes. The nightingale had become for us a sort of talisman, a harbinger of hope and peace.

By the time Ashe returned from abroad, Suzannah had gone again. Though it was entirely typical of her I was a little hurt that she hadn't told me she was going, or where. When I asked Christopher Jarvis, he was vague.

'I understand she's found accommodation with friends. You'll have noticed she's something of a gypsy, never in one place for long.'

'She didn't look well,' I said.

'You think so? My wife said that too, but I can't say I noticed. Perhaps we men just aren't so observant about these things. She's never been a girl to look in the pink at the best of times. Not like Georgina . . .' He began telling me about his god-daughter's new beau who might, as he put it, be 'the first real prospect'.

At the next opportunity, I tried Amanda. We had been doing one of our inventories of the kitchen and were sitting in the drawing room, finalising a list for the next week's orders and shopping. When we finished, I asked about Suzannah, and where she was living.

'I don't know, Pamela – I don't know and I wish I did.'

'Mr Jarvis said he thought she was with friends.'

'Well, that's what we tell ourselves. She flits about, you know . . . But she has very little money and no work so far as we can tell. I can't pretend I don't worry about her.'

'Couldn't she have an exhibition at the gallery?' I asked, astonished at my own boldness. 'Mr Jarvis admires her work, and so does Mr Ashe; it would probably do really well.'

'It might,' said Amanda doubtfully. 'But she'd have to produce such a lot, and she works very slowly and haphazardly. I was amazed she took on the commission for Ashe, and in such a limited time . . .' She frowned anxiously. 'Perhaps that's what it is, Pamela. Perhaps she's just worn out. Ashe is a dear, but he's awfully demanding. He wants what he wants when he wants it, if you know what I mean – well, of course you do, how silly of me . . .'

The strange thing was that I didn't, or not as it affected myself. The thought of Ashe as 'a dear' was pretty hard to take, but I had only once, personally, been the focus of his less obliging side. And I had merely picked up a sense of his anger, rather than witnessed anything he had actually said. As my employer I did not find him 'demanding' in the tyrannical way that Amanda meant. He was punctilious himself, and he liked efficiency and punctuality in those who worked for him, but he was not bad-tempered, impatient or unreasonable. In some ways he was easier to work for than the charming, disorganised Jarvises with their erratic life and poor timekeeping. But I knew only too well that there was a far, far blacker side from which I had so far been protected. I might be infinitely less worldly than most of the people I mixed with these days, but I was not so naïve that I'd failed to understand the real nature of Ashe's business. The nightclubs might well be successful, but not so profitable as to account for the wealth I had seen at the house in Piedmont Gardens. There was that other current that flowed, swift and dark, beneath the quiet orderliness of our working life in Soho Square, and the clue to its nature lay in the locked, red room.

Before coming to Ashe Enterprises I had only ever read the words 'vice' and 'prostitution' in the pages of a newspaper, but now I was almost daily made aware of their existence. Vice washed against the walls of the building like the effluent from an overflowing drain. I may have sat perched above it, typing away in my neat, sterile office, but it was there and I could not ignore it. It existed in layers, strata that fed off one another from the bottom up. In the gardens opposite were the drunks and the tramps, the pathetic human rubbish, roaring and reeling in their separate world. On the pavements and in the doorways were the traders, the frontmen and women who murmured and cajoled, whose sidelong glances and inviting gestures seemed to brush against me in the street like cobwebs every time I walked to work. Beyond them huddled the dingy burrows and basements and backrooms where the first, lower, levels of business took place; where money changed hands for services which I could only imperfectly imagine. This was the area to which I was sure Ashe's nightclubs belonged, for all their glamour and exclusivity. The books I had carried to his house were the official record of an elaborate and sophisticated deceit. Some small flaw, oversight or lapse in the deception had led to the summary dismissal of two men. I had begun to realise that Louise, by becoming Ashe's latest mistress, had committed herself to the process, however willingly – her body was not her own any more.

Away from Soho Square, in Mayfair mansions, home-counties manor houses and distant, glittering yachts, lived the rulers of this world, the fat spiders at the centre of their webs – motionless, but sensitive to every movement and nuance of change in their territory. Anything out of place, and a single quick, decisive movement would ensure that it never happened again.

I flattered myself I was safer than most, but only because my area of responsibility was so close to the top, and therefore the risk that I tacitly accepted was greater. I also knew that none of this would ever be made explicit. I had been put on trust, and with every day that passed without questions asked, this complicity bound me to Ashe with hoops of steel.

I kept my eyes open. I noticed things. Once or twice when I arrived in Soho Square early, and was walking round to kill time, I saw Ashe talking to the tramps in the garden. And not just talking, but sitting down with them, passing them things, pressing them by the hand and on the shoulder . . . It was like that other time, the day of Barbara's funeral, when I'd come across 'Mr Jameson' in the crypt of St Xavier's. I did not find these contradictions in his character comforting, but I was fascinated and repelled by them as I was by his face.

The day before I was due to accompany Alan to Edinburgh, I made a discovery which meant that neither I nor Ashe could persist in the pretence of my ignorance. What was implicit became explicit in the most extraordinary way.

I arrived at the usual time, but possibly my watch was slightly fast, for when the door of the lift pulled back I heard Ashe's voice, talking on the telephone in his office. The door of the red room was half open as though he had left it either to answer or to make the call. Naturally I glanced in, at the same time as the person there moved forward swiftly to shut me out. It was the tall, striking, dark woman I'd seen before, quite naked apart from black silk stockings rolled above the knee, and a jet choker. Astonished as I was, my attention was caught at the same time by the woman's clothing, discarded beside the chair that faced the camera. For there on the floor were the cap, boots, gold-trimmed green jacket and breeches of a chauffeur's uniform. I had been right, on that first occasion, to feel I recognised the woman. It was Parkes – I saw the hostile, terrified animal panic in her eyes in the second before the door closed. My blood was thundering in my veins as I stood there in the hall, I felt as if I might faint.

It might have been more discreet either to retreat, or to have advertised my presence to Ashe, but I did neither; I couldn't think straight and my mouth was dry. Trembling with shock, my face cold, I tiptoed over to my room, removed my coat and hat, and sat down at my desk. I'd left the door ajar but felt too weak to get up and close it.

I was removing the cover from my typewriter with shaky fingers when the door of Ashe's office opened. He stepped into the hall, and paused.

'Mrs Griffe, are you there?'

'Yes, Mr Ashe.'

'I'll be with you in a moment.'

I heard the red-room door open, and close. No voices. In a moment the door opened once more.

I glanced behind me through my own half-open door. Perhaps I shouldn't have done. Ashe stood in the hallway. Beside him was Parkes, now in his smart lovat green uniform. Both were entirely composed – far more so than me.

'I'm sorry I was a little early,' I said. 'My watch—'

'Never mind.' He turned to Parkes. 'I shan't be needing you until seven.'

'Very good, sir. Good evening, madam.'

'Good evening, Parkes.'

Our usual simple, formulaic exchange was suddenly freighted with importance. She, Parkes, had asked for my silence. And I had given it. I could never deny, nor forget, what I now knew, but neither would I disclose it. I had taken one more step into the web.

Chapter Seventeen

At ten o'clock the next morning, Alan boarded the Edinburgh train at King's Cross. In spite of travelling with him, I felt alone, and that was strange, and confusing, as though I had become two people. Or perhaps as though I had always been two, but it hadn't mattered until now, when suddenly they were at war. I could not even say that it was a case of head versus heart, because both my head and my heart spoke for Alan, for the importance of this day in his life and, by association, in mine; of our future together, of which we had been so confident that there had been no sense of urgency. But some other, unwelcome, part of me refused to let me respond as I should.

Nothing about this long journey, the wonders of the Flying Scotsman, our purpose in travelling, excited or interested me; my every smile and remark was a sham. A short while ago Alan had been my haven, my happiness, my soulmate, and he remained the same good, generous, honourable man as before – it was I who had changed. I longed to feel as I had then, but I was powerless to turn the clock back. My self was like some adamantine machine set on its own course, beyond my control. Against my will, I was moving away.

In Edinburgh, the pathetic fallacy held good: autumn was further advanced. When we alighted from the train at six p.m. that Friday night the air was cold and the city's grey stones heavy with their dark, melancholy history. The castle, high on its great rock, seemed forbidding. I felt small, mean and foolish with my curtain-ring wedding band and my shabby overnight case. But in truth it wasn't the grandeur of my surroundings that shamed me, nor what we were about to do. What should have been a moment of pride, happiness and fulfilment was diminished by my own dishonesty.

It was impossible to combat what I couldn't understand. I think I hoped that by sleeping with Alan some alchemy would restore me to myself, and to him, that the deed would be father to the impulse. Only a year later and he, with his new knowledge, would have been able to tell me that this was impossible. How ironic that I was with the one man who might have been able to help me understand myself, who would have appreciated the need for me to go my own way until I found the right one. But I couldn't confide in him because I didn't know what to say, or how I'd say it.

He had been to some trouble, too, which I knew he could not afford. Heaven knows what he must have gone without in order to pay for my train ticket, book a room at a small hotel, and take us there in a taxi from the station. He wouldn't hear of anything else.

'I'm playing the gentleman for once, Pam,' he said. 'So indulge me.'

I did, because I had no alternative. 'Playing' the lady was exactly what I was doing. I had never felt less like one. As I stood at the hotel reception desk and watched Alan sign us in as 'Dr and Mrs Mayes', I thought of my mother, and what she would make of it all. Instinct told me that whatever rules of upbringing and conventional morality I was breaking by being here, she would disapprove of me far less for that than for my sickly infatuation with my other life in London. This, at least, showed (or should have done) evidence of proper and appropriate feelings; and Alan was indisputably her idea of the right man for me. Whatever our differences there was no doubt that my happiness was important to her. I even entertained the dreadful possibility that she might be beginning to live through me, a responsibility that would prove quite intolerable.

The woman behind the desk glanced uninterestedly at the signature, and barely at all at us. She told us our room number on the second floor, and that the bathroom and lavatory were left out of our door and at the end. She said that we should have checked out by ten o'clock next morning. We replied, like good, slightly nervous children, that of course we would. A boy appeared from the back of the hotel and offered to take our bags, but we only had such a small one each that we declined, a faux pas which probably marked us out for the novices we were.

There was no lift. I walked up the stairs with the heavy tread and even heavier heart of a condemned woman. Much, much later, when I was a very old lady, a song I heard on the radio declared that learning to love yourself was 'the greatest love of all' – the sine qua non of all other loves. It served to remind me of that evening in the narrow, dark house in Edinburgh, and how my hatred of myself amounted to a paralysis.

Alan unlocked the door and held it open for me. The room was about the size of my parents' bedroom, and dominated by twin beds with high wooden bedheads and shiny, brass-coloured eiderdowns. I made straight for the window opposite the door. It was closed and I tried to open it, without success.

'It's stuck,' I said.

Alan had a go as well, and also failed. 'Perhaps we're not meant to open it. Never mind, it's not stuffy.'

'But I need a little air,' I said. He would never know how much I needed it – I felt stifled, breathless, as if I would die of suffocation.

He kissed me. 'Then air you shall have. I'll go down and ask if there's someone else who has the knack.'

'Thank you.' I sat down on the bed.

'And you,' he said, placing his warm hand on the back of my neck. 'Just don't worry about anything. It's enough that we're here, together.'

The moment he'd gone tears oozed from my eyes. I was a widow, the survivor of a happy marriage, however brief — I had done all this before, so Alan could scarcely interpret my mood as one of maidenly anxiety. Perhaps it would simply appear as the natural diffidence of a respectable young woman in what was undoubtedly a risky and risqué venture. But that was not me, and never had been. I was in despair.

He returned with the youth, who hauled and shoved at the window for a minute or two and declared it jammed.

'Will it bother you much?' he asked. 'It's gonna be cold tonight.' He pronounced it 'toneet'.

Alan said it wouldn't. What else could he do? The youth hovered, clearly expecting a tip for his failed efforts, and on not receiving one beat a sulky retreat.

Alan sat down on the bed next to me. 'Never mind. We shall be cosy. I'm going to unpack my few things, make myself at home. I might nip along for a bath before the rush — or why don't you? That journey's a beast.'

'I'm all right,' I said. 'You do what you like.'

'Very well.'

I hadn't meant it to sound so curt, so dismissive. When he'd gone to the bathroom I took off my shoes and lay back on the bed, on the slippery eiderdown. I tried to relax but I felt as stiff as an effigy on a mediaeval tomb. Everything about this situation and my surroundings conspired to paralyse me.

When Alan came back and began at once to get dressed, talking cheerfully, and no doubt tactfully, of dinner, my relief was so intense that I almost bounded from the bed and set about smartening myself up. A reprieve had been granted.

In the hotel dining room we were the focus of indulgent glances from fellow diners.

'I bet they think we're newly-weds,' said Alan. He took my hand in both of his. 'Let's not disappoint them.'

The food was nice, but I couldn't eat. I wasn't hungry, and when I did get the food to my mouth it was hard to swallow, because my mouth was dry and my throat tight.

'I'm sorry,' I said, 'I seem to have lost my appetite.'

'It doesn't matter.' For the first time he allowed himself to look concerned. 'You are all right, aren't you? Because the last thing in the world that I want is to make you unhappy, Pamela.'

'No,' I lied helplessly. 'No, honestly, I'm fine. Just too tired to eat, that's all.'

'The sad truth is, I'm starving.' He laughed, and speared one of my roast potatoes. 'May I?'

My unhappiness was compounded by guilt. Alan, after all, was confronting the ordeal of a lengthy interview by the Admissions Board in only a few hours' time. I knew how much all this meant to him, and how much preparation he had done, though he had never groused or complained about it. Yet his concern was all for me, when it should have been the other way round. And all the time I had the oddest feeling of being watched. I recalled the evening when I had met Alan just after work, and had glanced up to see John Ashe looking down at us from his window. It was exactly as though he could still see us now, and, as before, only I was aware of him.

He had taken up residence in my head. Everything I did these days, I did in relation to him.

Our night together was disastrous. When we got back upstairs Alan began by saying that we both needed our sleep, and that there was no hurry about anything. But only an hour later desire got the better of him and he slipped into my bed. He was tender, but urgent, and I was wholly unreceptive. I didn't deny him, there was no sense in which he forced himself on me, but I was cold, dry and detached, longing for it to be over. That wish, at least, was granted – passion and inexperience made everything very quick. Afterwards he lay with his arms round me and his face tucked into my neck like a child, overcome by love and lost for words, while the tears seeped down my cheeks. Too late I managed to express some tenderness, or the sorrow which might be taken for tenderness, as I stroked his head and shoulders.

After quite a while of lying entwined but hopelessly separate, he kissed me once more and whispered: 'Thank you.' It was almost unbearable.

'Alan . . . please. Don't say that.'

'I know you didn't want to. You're so beautiful. I couldn't help myself.'

'Please, no . . . it's all right. I'm sorry.'

'There's no need.'

But there was, and we both knew it. When he'd gone back to his own bed the space between us became an unbridgeable black gulf. I don't know which was worse, proximity without closeness, or this bleak retreat into isolation. He was utterly silent – I couldn't even hear his breathing and had no idea whether he was lying there awake or had drifted into merciful sleep. The seeping tears became a flood and I cried and cried, without making a sound. When the tears eventually dried up there was no relief, just a bleak, desolate wakefulness. Remorse, disappointment, self-loathing bore me company and kept me awake. There were church bells nearby in the city, chiming the hours, and I heard all of them. Some time after four a.m. I must have fallen asleep.

The next morning we enjoyed none of the happy, relaxed intimacy that I recalled with Matthew. How could we, when it had been so awful? We were careful and polite. Alan took me in his arms and told me he loved me, but he didn't hold me too close. And I was glad that he didn't. I couldn't have borne to go through it again. It couldn't even have been called failure; everyone's fallible, and failure is forgivable. I could have accepted it, we both could, for hadn't we said we wanted to be together for ever? Love, expectation and goodwill would have overcome such a small thing. But it seemed that, for me at least, those essential qualities were no longer present. I was possessed.

Alan's appointment with the Board was at ten o'clock. Though the postgraduate Diploma in Psychiatry would be taught, and the residency conducted, at the Royal Edinburgh Hospital, the interviews were to be held among the splendours of the Royal Infirmary. It was a beautiful morning, the sky that thin, singing blue of early autumn, the air with a tang of heathery hills, the castle shining on its rock, the street sounds bright and resonant. Glittering gulls swooped over the distant docks at Leith. A lone hawk hovered high over the rooftops.

'Look,' said Alan, pointing as we left the hotel. 'Isn't that a beautiful sight? I'm going to call it a good omen.'

We'd left our bags behind the desk at the hotel. After the interview Alan planned to take a look round the Infirmary's School of Medicine. 'You can come if you want,' he said but I told him that I'd amuse myself. I had to be on my own, away from the place where all my sins were remembered.

We walked together to the big, grey building where the Board was to take place. Another, younger, man was walking in, his coat over his arm, his hat held nervously in both hands. Alan pulled a rueful face.

'There's competition. I mustn't forget that.'

'You have experience,' I reminded him. 'Don't forget that, either.'

'And you,' he said. 'I have you, don't I.'

It wasn't so much a question as a reminder to himself. I didn't reply. We agreed to meet at two o'clock, six hours before the London sleeper was due to leave.

'What shall we do with our afternoon?' he asked. 'Be sightseers, and go to the castle?'

But I wanted to see the castle by myself, to be all on my own high above the city. Perhaps I imagined that it would give me a new perspective, and restore a sense of order and proportion.

'What about taking a bus out of town, then?' he suggested. 'We could have a good long walk among the bonny banks and braes – or by the sea, on this lovely day?'

He embraced me, carefully, and went in.

I set out to walk to the castle. It was a long way, and fiercely steep, but I trudged up the narrow lanes and steep flights of steps, with my eyes on the ground, like one of those pilgrims who shuffle penitentially on their knees, mortifying the flesh as they approach the mountain-top shrine. I was already lightheaded from lack of food and sleep, but now I actually wanted to exhaust myself. If my body was worn out, I reasoned, perhaps my mind would tire too, and stop plaguing me. By the time I reached the entrance to the castle I was sweating, my back ached and my legs were quivering with the strain. But having paid my entrance fee I was determined not to stop until I'd reached the very top.

Nothing could better have suited my mood than what I found there, on the far north-eastern corner: the tiny, austere Norman chapel of St Margaret. I found out later it was the oldest building in the city, but I could have guessed that anyway. Even on this fine day the wind sighed around the ancient walls, but inside the stillness was palpable, like a smooth pebble, pressed and polished by centuries of prayer. I sat down opposite the stained-glass window. For the first time in twenty-four hours a kind of peace stole over me. An imperfect, threadbare, hard-won peace, but enough to calm me a little. I didn't exactly pray for Alan, but I did think of him, as I had once thought of Barbara, as if my thoughts could help and protect him. I'd read, and heard it said, that the hallmark of true love was the desire for the other person's happiness over and above one's own, but I realised they were weasel words. I wanted nothing more than Alan's happiness, but that was evidence not so much of love (though I still did love him) but of the need to salve my own conscience. I could no longer bear the responsibility for his happiness. My own feelings were trouble enough.

Still, it was good to be free, and alone, and to be experiencing unselfish, untwisted thoughts. And if I was far from Alan, I was even further from John Ashe. I experienced a childish sense of liberation. No one knew where I was. No one could find me. I need never go back! But then my physical exhaustion took over. I sat there as limp as a rag doll, gazing at the narrow oblong of blue sky framed by the window-space. The possibility of recovery, though remote, was more likely than that of escape. Stranger things happened. I thought of my parents: their lives had been different from mine, but that did not make them less dramatic in their way. They had had to reach accommodations, to adapt their natures. It could be done.

My eyelids had begun to droop when suddenly I heard a shuddering sound and felt a wind on my cheek. A bird had flown in through the door! Shocked into full consciousness I saw the creature – a sparrowhawk – sitting on the altar-stone. It was small but it had a ferocious presence: each foot boasted a fan of feathered hooks; its eyes were a brilliant yellow, fierce and cold as a snake's; the beak a wicked little killing-tool. As I watched it spread its wings and beat them, twice. I flinched, terrified of being trapped in this small space with the bird, but equally terrified of moving and perhaps causing it to fly wildly at me. But it seemed a great deal more composed than I was. For less than a minute we sat gazing at each other, I in terror, the bird with a speculative hostility. Then, as quickly and cleanly as it had arrived, it launched itself off the altar and through the half-open door without so much as brushing the sides with its wing-tips. All that remained was a single feather and a small browny-white deposit next to the crucifix.

My modicum of peace was shattered. Though every rational instinct told me that this could not have been the same hawk that had hovered overhead when we left the hotel, I was possessed by the idea that it might be, and that I had been followed. The chapel no longer felt tranquil and inviolate. The calm air seemed to shudder in the wake of the hawk's flight, and my heart was beating even faster than it had been when I arrived at the top of the steps. I got unsteadily to my feet, picked up the feather and attempted to throw it out of the window, but instead of being carried away by the wind it was whipped straight back in, brushing my face as it did so, and floated to the floor.

I left, or rather fled. Some more people were trudging up the steep hill, two men in dark overcoats, one in a scarf and hat, the other carrying a briefcase; they might have been academics. Goodness knows what they made of the dishevelled, white-faced, wild-eyed woman running and stumbling past as though her life depended on it.

Outside the castle entrance a bus stood waiting at the stop. It was empty, and the driver and conductor were smoking outside. In response to my query, the driver said:

'Not going for another quarter of an hour I'm afraid, miss.'

'I'll wait, if I may.'

'It's up to you.'

I boarded the bus and took a window seat about halfway

along the cab. I was trembling, but at least I felt safe. The two men were standing guard. No bird was going to fly into a bus. But I still found myself glancing around for the speck in the sky, the silhouette on the rooftop, the sudden shadow . . . and listening for the flitter and dart of swift wings.

For the first time I glanced at the little guidebook Alan had given me that morning. My eye was caught by a reference to the 'Castrum Puellarum', a sanctuary built on the castle rock by the Pictish Kings, where women and children could live in safety while their menfolk were at war. Nothing could have felt safer than St Margaret's Chapel when I first arrived there; and nothing more threatening than the same place when I fled.

Back in the city centre, I found a café and ordered cocoa and a buttered scone. Both were hot and delicious and I wolfed them down, filling the void. When I looked at my watch it was twelve thirty. Even allowing for delay, Alan's interview would be over, and he would now be looking round the medical school, while the Board – did what? Reached their decision? Discussed the morning's interviewees? Conducted still more interviews? Maybe his future was already decided.

I sat in the café for as long as possible, until it became clear my table was needed. Then I left and wandered about, killing time. The prospect of the rest of the day, and the journey home on the sleeper, seemed empty and depressing. I went into any number of second-hand shops, immersing myself in other people's possessions, other people's stories. I kept telling myself that I was surrounded by people who were in all probability going through far worse than me. All that I suffered from was indecision. I did not know what I wanted, and while I hesitated I had the sensation of doing harm, something I wasn't used to. I was a lost soul.

I had arranged to meet Alan outside the main entrance of

the Royal Infirmary. I arrived first, and stood on the pavement with the slight sense of exposure and awkwardness that one has when waiting for someone, as if anyone else knew or cared what I was doing. I could see why Alan wanted to study here; the buildings around me were almost as splendid as the castle, even the Infirmary looked baronial, its pavilions sprouting magnificent turrets and towers. A down-at-heel drunk reeled around nearby, his noisy and unpredictable behaviour creating a little no man's land around him. He wasn't trying to be offensive, and didn't know that he was – he simply couldn't help it. I had some sympathy for him, but stayed well out of the way.

Because Alan came along the road, instead of from the building, his arrival took me by surprise. I was looking the other way, and my nerves were so stretched that I probably looked quite scared when he put his hand on my shoulder.

'Pamela? It's OK, it's only me. I went to check the bus timetable, and there's one we can get that takes us down to the coast beyond the docks. We could have a walk in the sea air and be back this evening for the train.'

'What about our bags?'

'I took them over to the station and put them in a locker.'

His thoughtfulness overwhelmed me. 'You've thought of everything.'

'It was no trouble.' He looked at me searchingly, tenderly. 'In fact it was a pleasure.'

'Alan!' I remembered, suddenly, where he'd been. 'How did it go?'

'Pretty well – hard to tell, of course, but I think I put up a good show.'

'I'm so glad. Shall we go then?' I began walking down the steps. He fell in beside me.

'We don't have to, you know. Our time is our own.'

'No – no, I'd like to go,' I said, too sharply even to my own ears. Much better to have an objective, something to do and see, than to confront the challenging intimacy of 'our own' time.

At the foot of the steps the drunk suddenly lurched towards us. Alan didn't, like everyone else – as I did – move out of the way, but put out his hand and caught the man by the upper arm, to stop him falling.

'Whoah . . . Easy does it.'

For a second I could smell the man's sour odour, and see his eyes, uncomprehending and desperate but bright and wild, too, looking out from his scabbed and overgrown face like the eyes of a trapped animal.

'Spare a penny, sir?'

'Here.' Alan took some coins from his pocket and held them out in his open palm. To my astonishment, the man gazed at them, and having made a considered decision, took two – not the largest – and put them in his pocket, leaving the rest.

'Price of breakfast. Thank you, sir.'

'Good luck.'

As we walked away, I said: 'He could have taken all that money!'

'I suppose it was a risk, but one I was prepared to take. If you treat people like animals they behave like animals. If you treat them like human beings they behave accordingly. He's done his time in the trenches. I decided to treat him like a gentleman.'

'It's more than most people would have done.'

'But not because they're heartless, because they're intimidated. I understand that.'

'How did you know he was ex-service?'

'He's shell-shocked.'

'But drunk, too, surely.'

'With some justification, poor chap.'

This gave me food for thought; in particular, that the last time I'd seen someone displaying such spontaneous and unaffected gentleness to society's lowest of the low, it had been John Ashe. And yet two more different men than Ashe and Alan I could scarcely imagine.

We rode on the bus for an hour, to Leith and then east along the coast, and got off at the end of a long, austere, seaside promenade, having established that we could catch a bus back to the station at the same place in two hours' time.

The beach where we walked had no pretensions. The proximity of the docks had ensured that this was no longer a place where many visitors came; we had the gritty, dun-coloured sands almost to ourselves. But the afternoon sun made the Firth of Forth shine like pewter, and the long sigh of the shallow waves played in counterpoint to the steady crunch of our footsteps.

'I do love Scotland,' said Alan, 'and not just because it feels like home. It's uncluttered. Invigorating. If they'll have me I can imagine doing good work up here.'

'You must come,' I said. 'It's clearly the place for you.'

'And you?' he asked. 'What about you?'

'I walked all the way up to the castle,' I replied, as if that was what he'd meant.

He let it go. 'So the last thing you want is to be taken on another route march!'

'No – it's good to be by the sea.'

'Let's sit down when we get to the windbreak.'

In some ways I'd have preferred to keep walking, but it was true that I was tired. When we reached the windbreak Alan put his coat down and we sat with our backs to the knobbly wood and our faces to the sun. In the sparkling haze of the middle distance the jagged structures of the docks appeared like the spires of a mysterious citadel. A cormorant flapped across the surface of the water and came to rest on the breakwater opposite, holding its wings out to dry like some strange heraldic creature.

'Did you eat anything on your travels?' Alan asked.

'I had cocoa and a scone.'

'I saw a café up there. Shall I see if they do fish and chips?' I nodded. 'Can you be bothered?'

'I'd positively like to. While you were scaling the heights in the sunshine, I was sitting in a gloomy room being grilled by senior consultants. The more I move about the better.'

'Thank you.'

He got to his feet and I watched him walk up the beach, with that splay-legged gait people adopt when trying to gain a footing on shifting sand. When he reached the steps he turned and waved. I waved back, and he disappeared over the parapet.

I smoothed my hand over the lining of the coat on which I was sitting. On the side he'd vacated there was something quite bulky in the side pocket. Idly – I wasn't even all that curious – I turned that corner of the coat over, slipped my hand into the pocket and took out the object.

It was a small, black box. I opened it, and inside was a plain silver ring with a single diamond. I didn't touch the ring, let alone take it out. I just stared at it for a moment, and then replaced it in the coat pocket and rearranged the coat itself to exactly how it had been when Alan first got up. I had not had an engagement ring first time around – with Matthew there had been neither the time nor the money – and I had never thought about one since, until now.

Alan returned with a portion of fish and chips in newspaper and we shared it, afterwards washing our greasy fingers in the edge of the sea. When we got back, he picked his coat up and shook it. As he dusted the sand off I saw his hand hesitate for less than a second over the left-hand pocket, checking that the ring was there.

Walking back, he said to me: 'I'm so glad you came, Pam – it made such a difference knowing you were around, thinking of me.'

I couldn't answer, but squeezed his hand.

By the time the bus arrived the temperature had dropped sharply, and the warmth inside was welcome. What with that, the drone and rattle of the engine and my self-inflicted exhaustion, I soon fell asleep. In the brief period between my eyelids closing and unconsciousness I felt Alan's arm go round me and gently ease my drooping head on to his shoulder.

He understood me, even if he did not, could not, understand my reasons for behaving as I did. It was a measure of how much he loved me that he never showed me the ring. He must have embarked on the trip to Scotland with the intention of giving it to me and making our engagement official, but he had read the signs and, without the tiniest trace of recrimination or self-pity, had kept it to himself.

Our journey home on the sleeper sealed the unspoken pact we had made. Now, when everything must be 'shared' and 'talked through', it would be unthinkable for a couple who considered themselves close to have endured forty-eight hours in each other's company without discussing matters vital to both of them. But that was what we did. And we were close – perhaps closer for not speaking. Before going to sleep we lay together in the bottom couchette, Alan in his pyjamas and me in my cotton nightdress, wrapped in each other's arms. Wordlessly we communicated our deep feelings of forgiveness and understanding and tolerance and affection, and after a while Alan clambered up to his own bunk and we slept like children.

We disembarked on Platform Ten a little bleary-eyed, but outside the station it was a beautiful Sunday morning. We had undergone a long journey together in every sense and now we could feel our separate lives beginning to pull us apart, and began to speak at once.

'Pamela—'

'Please—'

We both laughed, and Alan said: 'Your go.'

'I was going to say please tell me the moment you hear anything.'

'You'll be the first.'

'Now you.'

'Oh, I don't know really. Just remember that I love you, and that you can call upon me any time. For anything.'

'Of course.' I felt a flap of panic. 'But we'll see each other this week, as usual?'

'I expect so,' he said, but I didn't miss his momentary hesitation.

We said goodbye and exchanged a hug – or half a hug, for we were still holding our suitcases. The church bells were ringing as we parted company, and a clatter of pigeons flew up towards the vaulted station roof.

Chapter Eighteen

Because it had been a hot, fine summer, autumn in England was long and glorious that year. The trees on the Heath, along the pavements, and in the gardens of Crompton Terrace became great bouquets of red, gold and amber, holding the rich, low sunlight as the days grew short. But as the glowing leaves drifted down to form dank brown floes in the gutter, it wasn't only the bare branches that were revealed. A pattern of events emerged, every bit as inevitable as the turn of the year.

Alan and I continued to see each other, but much less often. My mother was quick to pick up on the change that had taken place.

'Is everything all right between you two?'

'Yes, of course.'

'Only he doesn't come in and chat like he used to.'

'He's very busy, Mum.'

'He was busy before.'

'Well – he's had the interview, in Edinburgh, the one I told you about. He's waiting to hear from them, so naturally he's a bit preoccupied.'

She wasn't satisfied, but there was nothing else I could say. Gradually but inexorably Alan and I were letting one another go, and the process still felt too painful for me to want to discuss it with her.

My mother wasn't the only one. John Ashe had noticed the change as well.

'I haven't seen your young man waiting in the square for a while,' he remarked one afternoon as I was leaving.

'No – he hasn't been able to get away.'

'Not neglecting you, I hope.'

'No,' I said. And then added, I don't know why: 'It's rather the other way round.'

'I see.'

The lift arrived and he went to the door. But instead of opening it he stood blocking my way. I could smell his clean-linen smell, as dry, fresh and sweet as a laundry cupboard.

'Must you dash off?'

'No.' It was a reflexive answer which left me nowhere to go, and by the time my lips were forming a cautious qualification, he'd asked:

'Would you care for a drink before you go? To mark your emerging from the probationary period with flying colours?'

'I didn't realise I was on probation.'

He smiled and touched my elbow briefly to steer me back towards his office.

'Only in the most informal sense. Generally speaking I'm against mixing business with pleasure but in your case I shall make an exception.'

He led the way into the white room. 'Sit down, do. I have sherry or whisky.'

'Sherry, thank you.'

He opened one of the low, white cupboards and poured sherry for me, and a whisky for himself. He gave me my drink and sat down opposite.

'How do you like working here, Mrs Griffe?'

'Very much,' I replied.

'A bit different from Christopher Jarvis's place . . .'

'Yes.' I refrained from elaborating, even though he had done so himself in the past. Better to be dull than risk offence.

'As I've said in the past, he revels in a certain casualness. I prefer formality. It's a difference in style.'

'I realise that.'

'You will also have realised —' he stretched forward to put his glass on the table and as he did so his gleaming white cuff pulled back to reveal the black hair on his wrist — 'that my business is very unlike that of the Sumpter Gallery.'

'I know very little about it,' I said.

'Officially. But you're an intelligent woman, Mrs Griffe, and an observant one. You can't fail to have noticed that I deal with some fairly disreputable people.'

'I'm not sure I'd have used that word.'

'No, because among your other excellent qualities you're also discreet. Anyway, it doesn't matter. The important thing is that we work well together.'

I agreed. And I was undeniably flattered. The idea that Ashe and I worked 'together' was pleasing to me, as he intended it should be. So I was a little more than his employee, I was his colleague.

I was also a fool.

'Like many people with no special talent, I deal in human nature,' he went on placidly. 'Christopher Jarvis does, too, I suppose. We're both entrepreneurs in our different ways.'

Warily, I sipped my sherry. 'I can see that.'

'Of course, in Christopher's case he is dealing with artists, individuals who have a specific creative gift. But he has the ability to turn that gift into hard cash — by persuading others, with no such gift, that they are people of taste and discernment.'

'Like the Emperor's New Clothes.'

He didn't smile. 'That's an incorrect analogy. He's not in the business of inviting people to admire what isn't there, but of making what is there desirable. And he does so very effectively. In my case the exercise is just as complex and subtle but a good deal less respectable.'

'I see.'

He gazed impassively at me. 'If there's anything you want to ask, please do.'

I hesitated. He had taken me right to the brink, but no further. I was being offered a rare opportunity to satisfy my curiosity, but I also knew that there were right and wrong ways of doing so, and only Ashe knew which was which.

'I've often wondered . . . What happens in the other room here?'

My voice seemed to echo slightly, the words hanging in the air after they were spoken. John Ashe got to his feet. My face went sickly cold – had I got it wrong?

'Let me show you,' he said.

I rose, and followed him out of the office and across the hallway. The door of the red room was closed as always but not, on this occasion, locked. He opened it and held it back for me with his arm, so that I could go in first.

'There you are,' he said. 'My little photographic studio.

I entered, and felt a sharp jolt of disorientation, as though I'd just woken from a vividly realistic dream. Where was the sinister, voluptuous, red and black cave that I was sure I'd glimpsed before? Ashe was right – this was simply a photographic studio, as neat and plain as the other rooms on this floor. There were shelves and cupboards covering the wall next to the door, a low platform to the right, and a window opposite giving on to the central well of the building. Rust-red curtains hung at the window, but they were drawn back. A camera on a tripod stood in the corner, flanked by two stands with spotlights like round metal flowers blooming on their black metal stems. Besides this equipment there were two upright armchairs, one on the platform and one in the centre of the room, and a chaise longue against the left-hand wall, on which I could see a fringed crimson shawl, neatly folded, and a row of matching cushions. A round mirror hung above the chaise longue. The floor was simple polished boards. The overall effect was light and businesslike.

I waited, pretending to look round, until I was sure I wouldn't betray any surprise. When I turned back, Ashe was still standing in the open doorway, his broad frame filling the space, his hands in his pockets.

'So you're a photographer,' I remarked.

'Of a sort. For my own amusement.'

'What do you photograph?'

'People.' He took a step forward and the door swung gently half-shut behind him. 'Women. They interest me.'

I had the curious feeling that for reasons of his own he was disposed to answer anything I cared to ask. 'What kind of women?'

'Any. All. Beauty isn't a prerequisite. But naturally they have to be willing to be photographed.'

I thought of Parkes.

'You may have seen Parkes here once or twice,' he said.

I went cold. 'Yes.'

'You were shocked, I dare say.'

'No—' He tilted his head quizzically. 'Yes,' I said.

'It would have been astonishing if you weren't. But I can assure you that nothing happens here without everyone's full consent.'

I struggled for words. 'But Parkes is your chauffeur.'

'Certainly. And a good one. I don't care to drive.'

'I thought that – she – was a man.'

'That was the general idea.'

'Is she happy?' I asked.

'As far as I know,' he said, as though the question of her happiness had never occurred to him. 'I've had no complaints. She's well paid to do a job she enjoys. One of the conditions of her employment is that she assume a disguise, of sorts, during working hours.'

'But why?'

'Because it pleases me,' he said. His tone was silky, but implied: enough.

I would have left the room at this point, but he stood by the door. There was no indication that he was intentionally barring my way, but the polite 'Excuse me' required to make him step aside simply would not form on my lips. Instead I pretended that I had no intention of leaving, and affected a keen interest in the camera.

'Do you know anything about photography?' he asked.

'Not a thing.'

'Would you like me to take your picture?'

'No!' I snapped. And then, taking a hold of myself: 'No thank you. I dislike myself in photographs.'

'Most people do . . .' He strolled over and laid a hand on the camera. 'To begin with. Until they see what the camera's capable of.'

'I thought it was supposed never to lie.'

'That's true, in the sense that it can only record what it sees. But what people don't always appreciate is that it can be made to see in many different ways. It's the conduit between photographer and subject. It records a particular vision.'

Suddenly, I was absolutely terrified that he would insist on taking my picture. To divert attention from myself, I said: 'May I see some of your work?'

'I don't see why not. Sit down for a moment.'

I did so, being sure to choose the chair that was not on the platform. He took a folder off one of the shelves near the door, looked at it, replaced it, and repeated the exercise with a couple more before bringing one over and placing it in my lap.

'Help yourself.'

As I opened the folder he sat down on the other chair,

hands resting loosely on the arms, legs apart. I felt like an examinee with an invigilator. A moment ago he had all but read my mind with his mention of Parkes. I did hope he couldn't do so now. Whatever criterion he had used to show me this particular portfolio, it surely could not have been its inoffensiveness. I stared at the first one . . . the second . . . turned the pages quickly to see if there was to be any relief. My cheeks burned with embarrassment, and humiliation.

I closed the folder and laid it on the floor.

'You've grasped the idea,' he said.

'Yes,' I whispered.

'And what do you think?'

'I don't care for them,' I said. 'But then, they're not for me.'

'Quite. As I say, they're principally for me. And anyone interested in owning them, for whatever reason and for a fair price.' He got up and replaced the folder on the shelf. 'The negatives, of course, are beyond price.' I heard the door open and realised that he was standing there, waiting to show me out. 'Did you spot your little friend Louise?'

I pretended I hadn't heard him. I had not seen Louise, but I couldn't bear to think of her trapped in that vile book, like an animal in a zoo.

'She has nothing to fear,' Ashe said. 'It's those who consider they have a reputation who are eager to begin with and then have second thoughts.'

He closed the door with a soft click behind us. 'So much for Bluebeard's Chamber.'

If this was his idea of a joke, it was a bad one. 'I'd better be going,' I said.

'In that case, I shall see you next week.'

'Yes, of course.'

I entered the lift, but he held back the outer door for a moment. 'Don't be too hard on your young man, will you?'

I wanted to say that it was none of his business, but I was too shaken, and remained silent.

I stepped out into the street gulping for air, dark spots before my eyes. I braced my hand against the wall to steady myself. Parkes had been sitting in the car and now she got out and came over to me.

'All right, madam?'

'I will be . . .'

'Want to sit in the car for a moment, catch your breath?'

I looked into her face, which showed nothing but concern. I should have liked to sit down in the car's soft leather interior and ask her everything I wanted to know. But the thought that Ashe might be looking out of his window even as we stood there was so unpleasant that I managed to get my head up, draw a deep breath, and say: 'No, really – I'll be fine.'

She kept her hand on my arm for a second. 'Look after yourself.'

'Thank you.'

As I walked away her last words stayed with me, not because of their simple message, but because of the way they'd been spoken: without the usual 'madam', the charming deference, but straight and intense, as to a friend. I glanced over my shoulder and saw her standing by the open driver's door, watching me intently. Neither of us waved, but I felt the current of understanding pass between us.

Not long after that, Louise left her room on the floor below me. Before she went, she came up with some clothes she no longer wanted.

'Don't be offended, but if there's anything you'd like, you're welcome.' She tossed them down, a puddle of colour on the pale bedspread. 'Otherwise put them in the dustbin, I've finished with them.'

I thanked her, and out of habit began shaking out the clothes and folding them in a neat pile. Something sad struck me about these fine feathers of hers, summarily discarded, the more so because I could tell at a glance there was nothing in which I wouldn't have looked ridiculous.

'Where are you going?' I asked.

'I've got a flat in Sussex Gardens. Not far from the park. All to myself!'

'Louise . . . You must be doing well.'

'Not so bad, thank you. Better for not being with John Ashe.'

'That's over?'

She drew sharply on her cigarette with a toss of the head. 'Certainly is.'

'And you're— that didn't cause any trouble?'

She shrugged. 'Depends what you mean. I'm not working at the Apache any more. A nice clean break. But while I was there I met a sweet man, who adores me and been after me for ages, and all I had to do was send a speaking look in his direction . . .' (she demonstrated) 'so all's well that end's well!'

'Are you working at all?'

'No!' She darted her head at me teasingly. 'Oh Pamela, isn't that too awful? Shameful.'

'I didn't mean—'

'I'm just doing what thousands of married women do all the time, *including* that frigid bitch Felicia Ashe, which is precisely nothing, except of course to make Roly happier than he's been in the whole of his poor little deprived life.'

Her tone was no longer teasing, but quite savage – she could still be hurt.

'I do wish you well, Louise,' I said quietly. 'I shall miss you.'

At once she softened. I was forgiven. 'I'll miss you, too.

But we mustn't lose touch. What about you, are you still typing away for that arrogant monster?'

'Yes.'

'Rather you than me. Not that anyone with half a brain would employ me to do their typing!'

'I think you're right.'

We laughed; there was relief in my laughter. It appeared I had underestimated Louise, who had got out in time, with her head held high. Maybe she really could look after herself, as she was always telling me. There remained the matter of the photograph, tucked away where only Ashe could see it, but I did not intend to spoil the moment by mentioning that now. She was so full of hope and high spirits, perched on the end of my bed with one slim leg swinging beneath her.

'If I was a bad, wicked fairy, do you know what my wish would be?'

'No,' I said warily. 'What?'

'I'd wish that Ashe would conceive a mad, hopeless passion for you, to which you would be massively indifferent, and you would spurn him as you would a mongrel cur!'

This idea was so wonderfully ridiculous that we both began to laugh again, and continued to do so till we were breathless and clutching our stomachs.

'Yes, and pigs might fly!' I spluttered when I could speak.

'Oh, God!' Louise wiped her eyes with the corner of the bedspread. 'But it's not *that* strange when you come to think of it. I bet he's inflamed by your demure appearance and upright nature. In the popular novel, that's what would happen – think of Mr Rochester!'

'Well it's *not* going to happen in real life!'

'I do so want it to! I want you to be his nemesis, Pamela – nemesis in a neat grey suit!'

We parted happily, as friends, still laughing at the idea of me as an unlikely femme fatale. But almost imperceptibly our conversation had planted a seed which was already starting to take root.

In early November Alan returned to Edinburgh to sit his exam. At the end of the month he received a letter from the Edinburgh Infirmary, offering him a place at the School of Clinical Psychology. We could no longer avoid the issue of our future. We met in town on a Sunday, and went for a walk in St James's Park, following the long paths beneath a tracery of branches. The sky shone glassy blue but there was a bitter wind, and we kept our heads down.

He made it very easy for me.

'I do hope you'll be able to come and visit me, Pamela.'

'Try and stop me,' I said, and meant it.

'If it wasn't for you, I don't think I'd be doing this.'

'I'm sure you would. But I will come.'

We sat down on a bench by the water. At once a flotilla of hopeful ducks moved our way. Alan spread his hands apologetically.

'Sorry, chums, nothing for you . . .' He thrust his hands back in his pockets and said, still looking out over the lake: 'I hope you know how much I still love you.'

I nodded. I couldn't speak.

'That's why I can accept your not coming with me, for the time being, anyway. It would be torture for both of us if you weren't happy.'

I found my voice, but it was a poor, weak thing. 'I'm so sorry.'

'Don't be. You've never been anything but good for me. And to me. Even when you didn't feel like it. You probably don't want me to say this, but you're a truly good person – and you're not sure yet what it is you want. There's nothing wrong in that. What would be wrong would be for you to do something against your nature and instincts because you felt you had to.'

'That sounds like a charter for the selfish.'

'It wasn't meant to. Or at any rate, I couldn't be happy knowing that you weren't, so it works both ways. All that matters to me is that I keep your love, in whatever form it comes. If the price is that we spend time apart, and don't have marriage lines to tie us together, then it's a small one, and I'll pay willingly.' He smiled. 'In advance if necessary.'

Even as I wept, finally, on his shoulder, letting out all the doubt and tension of recent weeks in a slow tide of tears, I thought how incredible it was, and how undeserved, that in one short lifetime I had been loved by two such gentle, proud men. And how ironic that having been robbed of the first I was wilfully turning my back on the second.

'Don't cry, my darling . . .' He leaned his head against mine, and wiped my wet cheek with his hand. 'You mustn't cry. We haven't lost a thing. We've just rewritten the plan a bit, to suit us both.'

'I wish,' I began, 'I do so wish . . .' But I wasn't sure what I wished.

'Don't let's. I wish too, but it's a waste of time and energy. Look at us – here we are, close as anything.' He tilted my face towards his, and I saw that he was smiling. 'The worst thing is we'll be disappointing your mother, and we can handle her between us.'

We ate lunch in the little restaurant where we'd had dinner that first time and, as we came out afterwards, Alan said: 'Why don't we go and visit your friend Barbara?'

We walked back through the park, and then along Piccadilly and down Jermyn Street and Manns Place, to St Xavier's. In the corner of the churchyard we found the new grave with its simple wooden cross. I was slightly shocked at how quickly the grass and weeds had reasserted themselves, and we both

kneeled down and did some weeding, digging and pulling
with our cold, bare hands until the plot was tidy again.

Alan stood up first, dusting the mud off his trousers. 'Why
don't I nip up to the corner and get a few flowers, show the
flag?'

'Would you? That would be nice.'

'It would make both of us feel better, I suspect. Shan't be
long.'

I got up too, and as I was standing there, wiping my hands
on my handkerchief, I saw John Ashe standing by the church's
north door. He was wearing his big black coat, and carrying
his hat. His crooked face looked very pale and intent; it
seemed to be etched more distinctly than other people's –
over a distance of some fifty yards I could see it quite clearly.
My heart hurtled as I lowered my head and fumbled with
hankie and handbag, unsure whether he'd seen me or not.
When I glanced back up, he'd gone.

Five minutes later Alan came back with some shaggy orange
and white chrysanthemums.

'Not terribly inspiring, but it's the thought that counts.
Now then – something to put them in, I hadn't thought of
that. And unlike hospital, we can't ask a passing nurse.'

'They're bound to have something in the church.'

We went in by the north door. To our right we noticed a
big double-fronted cupboard. I looked around, but although
lights were on in the transept, and at the east end of the nave,
there didn't seem to be anyone to ask. Apart from ourselves
the only people were a couple of the usual patrons sitting,
hunched and patient, in the side pews. The cupboard door
wasn't locked, and inside we found plenty of vases, jam jars,
candlesticks and the like. None of them looked valuable, so
we selected one of the taller pots to take outside.

As we left one of the seated men turned round and I saw
that it was Ashe, and that this time there was no doubt he'd

recognised me. My skin prickled as we went out into the grey
shutting-down of the afternoon.

I didn't mention what I'd seen. When we'd filled the vase
at the outside tap and arranged the flowers in it as best we
could on the uneven turf, Alan said:

'Poor thing, she needs a headstone. Do you think she had
any relatives at all?'

'Only her parents, as far as I know. And she was estranged
from them.'

'Terrible, isn't it? How people can let that happen.'

'It was their fault, not hers,' I said, touchily, as though I'd
been accused of something. 'And I'm going to get her a headstone.'

In all the months I'd been employed at Crompton Terrace
Dorothy, in spite of her erratic timekeeping, had never missed
a working day. So when she was off sick for a week in mid-
November there was a noticeable gap in the life of the household. I asked Amanda Jarvis if she knew what was wrong.

'I'm afraid, I've no idea . . . Her young brother came round
with a note to say she wasn't well and would be back next
week. So I gather from that she's not been taken into hospital
or anything, it can't be too serious. Still, it's not like her.
She's such a sprightly, robust little thing, we're awfully fond
of her . . .'

And they depended on her, too. It was quite an eye-opener.
During that week I did a good deal of Dorothy's work as well
as my own. Amanda didn't actually ask me to polish the tables,
sweep the porch and do the washing-up but it was pretty clear
that if I didn't, nobody else would. Also, I had acquired a
reputation for initiative and reliability of which I was secretly
rather proud, so I did such chores as I had time for and which
caught my eye willingly, even happily. The activity deepened
my sense of being an essential part of the household, and was

the very antithesis of the tense, oppressive calm of Ashe's office. I didn't tell my mother who, in spite of her almost evangelical enthusiasm for order and cleanliness, would have been horrified to learn that her highly qualified daughter was doing another woman's dusting.

I asked Chef if he knew what was the matter with Dorothy.

'Search me,' he said, 'she was right as rain on Friday. What I do know is, the sooner she gets over it the better. I can't manage this kitchen on my own for ever.'

At the end of that week, on the Saturday, I went to the funeral director and ordered a headstone for Barbara. He presented me with the monumental mason's brochure, from which I selected the simplest model (still exorbitantly expensive), a plain slab of arched granite, with the letters 'Barbara Chisholm, Rest in Peace'. The funeral director asked me for her date of birth, and my inability to supply it may have contributed to the slight frostiness with which he told me that there was a long delay on this particular model of headstone, and that it was unlikely to be in place until February.

A new girl had moved into Louise's room during the week; there could scarcely have been a starker contrast. She was an accounts clerk at Maples, short and homely with a fuzz of curly hair and bright eyes behind round glasses. She was nice enough, but so commonsensical that within twenty-four hours it was I who felt like the newcomer. She created a system for organising the post in the hall, and another for ensuring that everyone got at least one hot bath a week. A doormat appeared outside her room. It was clear that there would be no more drinking, smoking and gossiping, let alone men being smuggled out of the building in disguise. Her arrival gave the whole house a different atmosphere. She brought the place to heel, and now I became the outsider, the woman from the second floor at whom the landlords looked askance.

I had changed. But so, too, had Dorothy. The following Monday she was already there when I arrived, mopping the floor tiles in the porch.

'Welcome back,' I said. 'We missed you.'

She stood with her arm resting on the mop. In spite of her exertions her face was colourless. 'That's not what I heard. I heard you did your job and all of mine, too.'

'Scarcely!'

'I'd never have bothered coming back if I'd known. Except I need the money.'

'I'm extremely glad you did. A fraction of what you get through in a day was far too much for me. Anyway, how are you? Properly recovered from whatever it was?'

She dunked the mop vigorously in the bucket and began swabbing again. 'Not bad. Getting there.'

'Because you shouldn't be doing that if you're not,' I said.

She didn't look up. 'Don't worry. It's all sorted out.'

I'd been told to mind my own business, and I did. But as I sat at my desk in Jarvis's office, listening to the familiar sound of Dorothy's footsteps up and down the hall, I was puzzled by her choice of words.

Whatever had been 'sorted out', the job was an imperfect one, because a couple of days later at four o'clock, when I was about to leave for Ashe Enterprises, Chef burst out of the kitchen in a state.

'Hey – Mrs Griffe! Can you come – it's her! I knew she wasn't right!'

The Jarvises were up in their room and hadn't heard. I didn't alert them immediately, but ran into the kitchen. Dorothy was on the floor beside the table, attempting to drag herself up, using the seat of a chair as a prop. Her face was a damp, greeny white and with each laboured breath she uttered a little moaning sound.

'Quick!' I barked at Chef. 'Help me!'

Together we eased her on to the chair.

'Fetch some water! Please.'

He brought a glass, slopping in his haste, and I held it for her. But she was already rallying, and took it from me.

'Thanks. That was pretty stupid . . .'

'Dorothy, we have to get you to a doctor. No, better than that, I'm going to tell Mr Jarvis what's happened and he can call for one.'

'No!' Her hand groped for my wrist, and then gripped it. Her fingers felt cold, but the grip was surprisingly tight. Because her skin was rough, it felt like a bird's foot clinging to me. 'No, there's no need. And don't tell anyone, either.'

Chef made an explosive sound of exasperation, half-sigh, half-snort, and went out of the back door. She pulled on my wrist, making me lean down to her.

'Promise? Pamela, you promise?' More than anything, her unprecedented, instinctive use of my Christian name alerted me to the importance of what she was saying, but I was in an impossible position.

'No, Dorothy, you know I can't, it would be quite wrong of me to make any such promise when you're clearly very unwell.'

'I know what's the matter with me better than any doctor. I'll be myself again in no time,' she said. And in fact I could see that she was beginning to revive; some colour was returning to her cheeks and her breathing had become more even.

'Tell *me*, then,' I said. 'You can't ask me not to worry and not to get any help unless you confide in me. It isn't fair.'

She looked up at me, and I could see how difficult it was for her to decide. She had let go of my wrist but now, having reached her decision, she slipped her hand into mine in a gesture that was trusting and confiding as a child's. I saw her glance anxiously at the back door, beyond which Chef was calming his nerves with a cigarette, and I leaned down again to be sure that only I could hear.

'I was expecting,' she said. 'But I'm not any more.'

'Dorothy!' How had I failed to guess? I tried to put my arm round her, but she stiffened. As if apologising for the rebuff, she gave my hand a squeeze before releasing it.

'All done and dusted,' she said. 'But I'm still getting some cramps.'

'Was it Jimmy's?' I asked.

She gave me a sharp, reproving look. 'What sort of girl do you take me for? Whose else would it be?'

'I'm sorry.'

'So you should be.'

'I mean, about the baby.'

'Yes. Well . . .' She placed her hand flat on the table and eased herself, slowly but quite steadily, to her feet. 'It had to be done.'

I heard these words uncomprehendingly to begin with and, after their full implication dawned on me, I was still knocked for six when Chef came back in.

'Feeling better, girl?'

'Yes thanks.'

'Thank Gawd for that,' he said in an ungracious, grumbling tone. But at least he had the good sense not to ask her to do anything immediately.

'Would you like to go outside for a few minutes?' I asked.

'Do you think that'd be all right?'

'I think some fresh air would be just the thing – it's what Mrs Jarvis would advise.'

As luck would have it, Christopher Jarvis, in his best suit, was coming downstairs as we made our way across the hall.

'Hello – Pamela, I thought you'd be gone. All well?'

I took charge. 'Dorothy's feeling a bit under the weather; she's going into the garden for a moment for some air.'

'Good idea. Dorothy, I'm so sorry. Not yet quite shaken off the illness?'

'Looks like it, sir. Nothing serious, though.'

'Mrs Jarvis will be down shortly, perhaps we could take you home?'

'That won't be necessary, sir.'

'Well, we're in your hands.' He looked at his watch, then at me. 'Hadn't you better head off to Soho Square? We can deal with things here.'

'It won't matter if I'm a little late,' I said. 'We're not that busy at present.'

The truth was, I didn't care. I sensed that my unspoken pact or understanding with Ashe had entered into another phase. I was unlikely to be dismissed for one instance of unpunctuality.

We went out into the garden. It was cold, and almost dark except for the light spilling from the house.

'Mind if I smoke?' asked Dorothy. She lit up and stood there with her arms folded. The red spark of the cigarette dilated and contracted as she drew on it.

'Who—' I began.

'My sister knows someone. I'm not stupid, I wouldn't go to a stranger.'

'But this person wasn't qualified.'

'She knows what she's doing.'

I remembered things Alan had told me. 'There's a risk of infection. You should be examined by a proper doctor.'

Dorothy snorted. 'Don't make me laugh. I may not have much of a reputation but I'm not going to ruin what's left.'

'I know one who'd check you over. Make sure everything's as it should be.'

She turned towards me. Even in the darkness I could make

out her incredulous expression. 'You mean, see your boyfriend?'

'He's a good doctor and he'd be completely discreet.'

'No thank you!' She shook her head. 'I'd have to be desperate! Still—' her voice softened. 'If I am, you'll be the first to know.'

John Ashe wasn't in the office when I arrived. The doors of his office, and the studio, were locked, but that of mine stood open and some letters lay on the desk. On top of them was a note in his immaculate handwriting – each letter stood separately, neat and elegant as a soldier, shoulder to shoulder with its neighbour.

> *Dear Mrs Griffe,*
> *You had not yet arrived when I had to go out. Please see to these. I'm not expecting anyone, but refer any queries to me tomorrow.*
> *Yours, John Ashe*

I was almost disappointed to miss the opportunity for the little scene I'd rehearsed, in which he would offer that steely hint of reproof and I would meet it with a confident composure.

It didn't take me long to deal with the correspondence, but I didn't leave at once. I sat there in the perfect silence of the empty office, conscious of my isolation. I had thought myself part of this other world, but I wasn't, any more than I was part of the one I'd left.

I was on my own. But not, I realised, lonely. And I experienced an extraordinary sense of something almost like power: an independence that had nothing to do with money. At that moment I knew that no matter what happened, I would never be like Parkes, or even Louise. I would never depend for my happiness on someone else, especially not a man. I had helped Barbara, albeit imperfectly and too late. I could and would help Dorothy if she would let me.

And then there was Suzannah, the most completely lost of all. I would find her.

Chapter Nineteen

John Ashe met my request for more money with his customary air of mild civility.

'Let me see,' he said. 'You haven't been here very long.'

'No,' I agreed.

'And I believe – you'll correct me if I'm wrong – that I am paying you more, pro rata, than your other employers.'

'Yes.'

'It's none of my business, of course, but are you also asking the Jarvises for a rise?'

'Not at the moment.'

'Then . . .' He opened one hand in enquiry. 'Forgive me . . .'

'They're not in a position to pay more.'

He displayed no reaction whatsoever to this, but I sensed my directness had done no harm, and went on: 'I have plans. I need more space to live in. And I want to save and invest some money in a business of my own.'

'In effect you're asking me for an increase in pay so that you can put in place arrangements which will enable you to leave.'

I could hardly deny it. 'I suppose I am. In the long term.'

'But then,' he said, as if speaking for me, and to himself, 'I couldn't expect you to stay for ever.'

'No.'

We were in the white office. Ashe was sitting behind his desk, I was standing before it, in a traditional senior–junior tableau which put me at a slight disadvantage. Now he rose and stood with his back to me for a moment, looking down into the square.

Without turning round, he asked: 'Might I ask the nature of the business into which you'd be putting these savings?'

'You may, certainly, but I'd rather not say.'

'Fair enough.'

I made a split-second decision. 'Except it's a charitable venture.'

'I see.'

There was a short silence. I felt quite calm, but curious. I believed I had read the psychology correctly; Alan would have been proud of me. The last time I'd thought that, I had been overconfident, and suffered the consequences, but I had learned a good deal since then. Ashe turned.

'Very well.' His face was unreadable, his voice light and matter of fact. 'I'm more than happy with your work, and your attitude to it. I am prepared to pay you a further two pounds a week.'

'Thank you, Mr Ashe.' This small formality – the use of his name – conveyed as much extra gratitude as I was prepared to show. This was business, and we both knew it.

'One word,' he said, 'about timekeeping.'

'I apologise for being late the other afternoon. A fellow employee at the Jarvises' was taken ill and I was helping out.'

'Commendable. But not, if you please, in my time.'

'It won't happen again.'

'In that case I shall implement the increase this week.'

I must have been more nervous than I realised, because in the lift on the way down my whole body seemed to roar back into life, or another gear: my heart, my breathing, hearing, everything was amplified. I had forcibly to contain a great shout of delight.

The car was parked outside and I expected to see Parkes,

and to exchange our usual pleasantries, which had taken on more meaning recently. But the uniformed figure reading the paper behind the wheel was a stranger – a heavy-set man with a thin, clipped moustache. He glanced incuriously at me as I hurried away.

I had to admire Dorothy: she was a strong, determined and resilient girl. Her physical health improved rapidly, but I sensed a protective shield formed by the scar tissue around her wounded heart. She was not quite so carefree and, though willing to gossip about other people, certainly not so ready to exchange confidences. Before, she had always delighted in drawing me out, or deploying her fiendishly accurate intuition at my expense – no more. It seemed as if, by exercising discretion herself, she was asking me to do the same, and I was happy to comply.

I did, however, ask if she knew anything about Suzannah. She shook her head, thoughtfully.

'After she went off with old ugly-mug Mr Ashe she only came back the once that I know of . . . I don't know what he did with her, but I hope she was well paid for it.'

I was struck by her turn of phrase. 'Why do you say that?'

Dorothy shrugged. 'She looked poorly, didn't she? Not that it means much in her case, she's such a peaky little thing. I reckon she weighs less than my niece, and she's only twelve.'

I had to admit this was true, and yet – 'You've seen her paintings, haven't you?' I asked.

'Only what she did here. On the flaming wall!' She rolled her eyes despairingly. 'And that one of Mr Rintoul. It looked like him, I'll give her that.'

'She's wonderfully talented. There are so many big ideas in that one small person.'

'Interesting, that,' agreed Dorothy. 'You can't judge by appearances.'

This was one of those occasions when the cliché served perfectly. But I was still left wondering, like Dorothy, what Ashe had done with Suzannah.

It was Georgina who, if she didn't precisely answer the question, at least told me where Suzannah was.

'Oh, she's staying at Edward Rintoul's while he's in Paris,' she said.'

'Does Mrs Jarvis know? She mentioned the other day how worried she was.'

'The answer to that is no. Suzannah doesn't want any fuss.'

'Fuss about what?'

I was at the bureau in the drawing room, and Georgina was on the sofa with her feet up, looking at a magazine. Now she got up and came over.

'Promise you won't tell?'

For the second time in a few days someone was trying to elicit a promise from me before I could properly make a judgement. But something in Georgina's manner, so loaded with secrecy and excitement, made me say: 'I promise.'

She leaned towards me, and whispered, 'She's pregnant!'

I felt dismay, and a queasy flutter of fear. But I was not surprised. Ashe had effected a change in me – educated, hardened, corrupted me, call it what you like. There was only one thing I wanted above all to know.

'Whose is it?'

'I think we can guess, don't you?' Seeing I wasn't to be drawn, she said: 'It has to be Ashe's, surely!'

'We don't know that.' This met with a grimace of disbelief. 'Is anyone looking after her?'

'I've no idea. Ghastly, isn't it?'

'How did you find out?' I asked.

'Edward told me she was going to be there, and I went to

see her. She's like this.' Georgina described, with her hand, a protruding stomach.

'But did she say anything about it herself? Did she say what her plans were?'

'She doesn't make plans, you know her. She's an artist.'

'Where will she go? How will they live?'

Before Georgina could answer, the door on the other side of the hall opened and Christopher Jarvis came out, marking the end of our conversation.

The address of Edward Rintoul's flat in Marylebone, off Baker Street, was on file in the office; I had typed out the odd letter to him. I decided to go straight round there after work. I knew that I was intruding, that I had no right to interfere, and that Suzannah might be angry, or simply not let me in. But Barbara's fatal despair and, more recently, Dorothy's situation, haunted me. Experience had shown that nothing came of nothing. Discretion had its place, but there were occasions, I reasoned, when valour was the better part of it, and this was one of them.

Looking back, a sort of madness afflicted me for those few weeks in the winter of 1929; but it was a necessary, beneficial madness, which set the course for the rest of my life. Without it, I'd never have found the courage to do what I did.

Rintoul's flat was a basement. He, or perhaps some previous owner, had set a large plant in a half-barrel in the area, and sinewy branches with a few desiccated hand-shaped leaves reached almost to pavement level. I went down the steps and knocked. The interior of the flat looked very dark, but after a moment the door was opened by Suzannah.

'Oh,' she said. 'It's you.' She walked away from the door, leaving it open, which I took to mean I could go in.

'I hope you don't mind,' I said, closing the door behind

me. 'I heard you were here and I was worried about you.'

'How did you know?'

'Do you mind if I don't say?'

I followed her into the large, dark room that I'd seen through the window. Inside, the dim winter light and the branches on the other side of the glass made it feel as though we were in a wood – or perhaps at the end of the garden at Crompton Terrace. It was also very cold, and I didn't remove my coat. Suzannah wore one of her long patterned dresses, the hem at the front lifted by her obvious pregnancy, a shawl round her shoulders. The room was untidy and uncomfortable-looking, half studio, half living room, with a table in the window, some unmatched hard chairs and a black stove, which in spite of the temperature was unlit. I got the impression that this was not a room in which Suzannah had bothered to make herself at home, but then perhaps she never did.

'Georgina . . .' she said, sitting down on one of the chairs.

I decided to neither confirm nor deny this. 'Would you like me to try and light the stove?'

'Is it cold in here? Yes, I suppose it probably is. One good thing about this condition is that it makes you warm. Do, by all means, carry on.'

She watched me with a kind of detached interest as I removed the lid of the stove and checked for fuel; some coal was in there.

'Matches on the table,' she said. I fetched them, and gathered up some sheets of paint-spattered newspaper as well. I rolled these into long spills, twisted them and stuffed them through the panel at the base of the stove. Handfuls of dust and grit fell on to the rug, but when I put a match to the paper it caught cheerily enough, and I blew, like a human bellows, on the clinker until it began to glow red.

When I replaced the panel, Suzannah remarked: 'How

clever you are, Pamela,' as though I'd pulled off some astonishing feat.

'We'll see.'

The stove, which needed clearing out, didn't draw that well but its small red glow cheered the room up, and there were some candles in saucers on the mantelpiece which I lit as well.

'That's better.'

'Thank you.' She was so calm, so – I searched for the word – fatalistic. Maybe that was a state of mind brought on by pregnancy. But there was as well a disturbing contradiction between her heavy, swollen stomach and her little white hollow-eyed face, made still smaller by her cloud of elfin hair that in this dim light looked almost grey.

'When is the baby due?' I asked.

'Soon. Two or three weeks, I think.'

I found her vagueness terrifying. 'Where will you go?'

She gazed at me thoughtfully, as if deciding how much to say. 'Into hospital, of course. It's been arranged. Then it will all be over. The baby has a home to go to.'

'You mean it will be adopted?'

She nodded, closing her eyes as she did so. 'Thank God! I'm so tired of it living inside me. I don't want to be a house any more.'

That was it, of course: she had expressed, in her odd way, what I had not been able to put my finger on – that she seemed invaded by her pregnancy, uninvolved. Occupied rather than preoccupied by it. Waiting, as she'd said, for it all to be over.

'What will you do then?'

'I shall be on my own. Completely on my own. That's what I want more than anything, Pamela. I shall go down to the seaside in Sussex, and eat fish, and walk on the beach in all weathers.'

'And paint?' I asked. 'You must paint again.'

'I might. When the time's right. When I'm ready.'

'You know we all think about you,' I said. 'Amanda in particular would like to know that you're well.'

She gave a little sigh. 'I can't imagine why. There's no need for me to be on anyone's conscience.'

'They're good people, Suzannah. They're fond of you.'

'Good people?' She frowned. 'Are they?'

'They seem so to me.'

'I like them,' she said. 'And they've been kind to me. But it's easy to be kind if you have no troubles.'

'Easy to be selfish, too,' I reminded her. 'And they're not.'

She didn't reply. I was glad I'd lit the stove, because I had the oddest feeling that without light, warmth, attention, company, she might simply fade away in this dingy, neglected underground place. It was now quite dark outside, and the impression of being in the middle of a wood was even stronger. All I could see of Suzannah was her three-quarter profile. It was eerie to think of John Ashe's child being so near, enclosed in that frail frame. I could picture it crouched fiercely in its hot, wet sack, ready to burst into the world.

'Where will the baby be going?' I asked. 'Do you know?'

She shifted in her chair and looked at me. She was so thin; her eye sockets were so deeply gouged with tiredness that her eyes were no more than a glint in the darkness. Like the drunk Alan had been kind to in Edinburgh, Suzannah seemed to look out from the prison her pregnant body had become. Her voice when it came was no more than a whisper. Afterwards, I knew what she must have said, but what I heard at that moment was:

'It will be ashes . . .' And it sounded like a curse being cast. I never saw her again.

When I told Alan about my plans for the future he was, as

I might have expected, overwhelmingly generous in his support and enthusiasm.

'It's a splendid idea, Pam. Truly it is. And *you're* splendid. Just so long as you realise you'll have to face down a lot of hostility and criticism. Unmarried girls with babies are no better than prostitutes as far as some people are concerned. For instance, I don't imagine your mother has much time for them.'

'She'll come round. It's losing you she can't forgive me for.'

'Ah,' he said, 'but you haven't lost me.'

It was true. If ever there was an example of love not altering when it alteration found, nor bending with the remover to remove, it was Alan, who would remain steadfast to the end. Indeed he seemed to love me even more for my quixotic ambition, and was unstinting with his help and advice.

'You'll need to have a good relationship with your local doctors,' he pointed out. 'And you'll want to know exactly where you stand legally when irate parents and boyfriends come banging on the door. You're also going to need strong locks, Pam, and an even stronger nerve. It won't be easy. And remember, sooner or later these girls will have to leave and stand on their own two feet in a society that doesn't think much of them. They must go, so others can come in. You'll have to harden that heart of yours sometimes.'

I blessed Alan for thinking me tender-hearted, when I'd been so hard on him. But perhaps Fate, or God, or whatever rules our destiny, did have my best interests at heart, because although I had turned my back on an adoring husband I had gained a faithful friend for life.

I was still a long way from realising the dream. Every week I saved the full amount of my increase in pay from John Ashe, but it was to be a long, slow process.

*   *   *

I say I never saw Suzannah Rose Murchie again after the meeting in Rintoul's basement. And it was true that I never saw her in the flesh. But one afternoon close to Christmas, when John Ashe was in Manchester – or so I believed – I found the studio door unlocked.

I went in and took down the folder of photographs from the shelf. This time, on my own and without his cruel scrutiny, I spared myself nothing. I turned each page slowly, and studied the faces of the women whose humiliation he had recorded. Because they *were* humiliated: even the most beautiful, the rich and famous (and there were several I recognised), grinning and posturing and imagining that they were in their glory, he had reduced to the level of his creatures. After the first few pictures I was no longer shocked by what I saw – this time I knew what to expect. What made my flesh creep with disgust and revulsion was the collusion of these women in their own debasement, and brutalisation. They thought they were playing, but they were playing on the end of a chain. Now I knew why some tribes consider that a picture steals a part of their soul. These pictures had robbed the women of all of theirs, and the worst of it was, they didn't know.

Only one or two had retained something, a kind of dignity, and they had done it by admitting their humiliation. Their sad-eyed acknowledgement, gazing back at me, made me want to weep. Parkes was one – a tall, beautiful sacrifice; where was she now? And Louise, in her way, another. Naked on all fours, back legs splayed towards the mirror behind her, she glared furiously, snarling, into the camera. Ashe had wanted a picture of a vicious bitch, and he had got one. But at least her rage was real, and not a self-regarding pose. She had got out.

Halfway through the folder I found an unsealed white envelope slotted between the pages. The envelope was crisp and fresh; I was sure it hadn't been there before. It contained another photograph, which I took out.

It was of Suzannah, naked, and taken not long ago. Her pregnancy sat on her stick-thin frame like a bulging parasitic growth. Her tiny breasts were pushed apart by its obscene bulk. There were no props in the picture – no drapes, jewels, plants, cushions – not even a rug on the floor. She sat on the edge of the wooden platform with her legs splayed, arms at her sides. I noticed with a pang that there were paint stains on her hands. Her head hung, though whether in shame or because she had been told to pose in this way it was impossible to tell. Her hair was dirty and wild. She looked abject. But the worst thing was that her protruding stomach had been used as a canvas. Someone, presumably Ashe, had painted a face on it, in the rudimentary way of a child: two dots for eyes, a larger dot for a nose, a straight slash for a mouth. The left-hand side of this face was covered in marks, wild scribbles of paint. For the first time I understood the full force of the word defaced. At the bottom of this obscenity the artist had scrawled the initials 'S.R.M.'

I replaced the photograph carefully in its envelope, and then between the same pages of the folder, exactly where I'd found it. Then I put the folder back on the shelf, among the others, and left the studio. I had been sitting there, looking at the pictures, for over an hour, without moving. The act of rising, and walking, made my head swim and I only just made the lavatory in time before I was very ill.

On Christmas Day I was staying with my mother. I gave her a pretty scarf she would never wear, but always treasure. She gave me lavender soap and talcum powder. We had a roast chicken, and my mother's special plum duff – one of my father's favourites which to my knowledge she hadn't made since his death. Our day was peaceful, orderly, restrained; and peace, order and restraint were what my soul craved.

Alan was on duty, but he came round to see us for tea in the afternoon. We all knew as we exchanged presents that we were saying goodbye. My mother had bought him handkerchiefs, with a narrow tartan border – an unprecedented flight of imagination for her. I had found a nice illustrated book on the history of Edinburgh, but it was the inscription I had laboured over. It needed to be valedictory, affectionate, *multum in parvo*. In the course of an hour I'd scribbled it many times on rough paper, before finally settling on: *To my dearest Alan, with my love, gratitude, and good wishes for the future, Pamela. London, Christmas 1929.*

The simple addition of the word 'London' had made all the difference. It confirmed our separation, and lent a sort of dignity to the message. When he'd unwrapped the book and exclaimed with delight, Alan read the inscription carefully, but I felt suddenly awkward, and busied myself folding paper so that I wouldn't have to meet his eyes when he looked up.

His present to me was an elegant purse and wallet combined, in chestnut leather. My mother, who could always spot quality, was impressed.

'That's very smart, Pammie.' She turned to Alan. 'I hope you haven't given it empty, it's bad luck you know.'

He smiled. 'I may be a Scotsman, but I'm the exception that proves the rule. There is a little something inside.'

I undid the purse section, and found a threepenny bit, and a small twist of tissue paper. I knew what it must be, so I left it there, and took out the coin, holding it up between my finger and thumb.

'There we are,' I said. 'Riches!'

I replaced the coin, and palmed the twist of paper. A few minutes later I took the teapot out to the kitchen for more hot water, placed it on the stove next to the kettle, and undid the tiny package. The little ring shone bright as a star, undimmed by inconstancy and rejection. Through the prism of my tears it looked even more brilliant.

I collected myself, put the ring in the pocket of my skirt, and filled the pot. When I re-entered the front room my mother was in full flow.

'. . . be sure to eat properly,' she was saying. 'You can't tend the sick on an empty stomach.'

'Don't worry, Mrs Streeter. There's an excellent canteen up there, I saw it with my own eyes, and I'm not entirely useless in the kitchen.'

'Then you're the first man who wasn't,' said my mother. 'Would you like to take some pudding away with you this evening? We hardly touched it.'

'Have I ever been known to say no?'

After tea Alan got out the cards and we played games for an hour. The fire glowed in the small hearth, the room was warm, my mother laughed and smiled and looked ten years younger. There was more comfort and security and goodwill in that room than would have been present at many other, grander, Christmas celebrations, and it was largely of Alan's making. Once I felt my mother's eyes on me and I knew what she was thinking – how could I have given up this man? But although I was sorry that I couldn't crown the season with an engagement for her sake, I was content. Alan and I were at peace, with ourselves and each other.

On the doorstep, we held hands – both hands, like children about to dance.

'Well, Pamela.'

'Thank you,' I said, 'for the beautiful ring.'

'It's always been yours. I thought you should have it anyway. Wear it sometimes, on whichever hand you want. Like a knight's favour.'

'I will.' I took it from my pocket and slipped it on the third finger of my right hand. 'There.'

He rubbed the ring with his thumb. 'How will you explain it?'

'I'll say it was a Christmas present from a dear friend.'

'That'll get them talking.'

By 'them', I knew he meant the people I worked with and for, the people in my other life. But he had no idea, how could he, what they were like, or the strangeness of the landscape they and I inhabited. Perhaps if he *had* known – about Suzannah, and Ashe, and the Faustian pact I had entered into, he might not have given me his ring. But then the ring was meant to be my talisman, as well as his favour: something to protect me whatever I did.

'Good luck,' he said.

'And you.'

'I want to hear all your news. Everything that happens. Perhaps when you start up your sanctuary there will be some practical help I can give.'

'That's a long way off,' I said.

His voice was very soft as he said: 'We're setting out on our adventures, aren't we?'

'Yes.'

He lifted my hands and clasped them together in both of his, holding them against his heart. 'I'm going now. If you look in the wallet, there's a note from me. It doesn't need a reply.'

He gave my hands a quick kiss, and was gone. There was no sign of the car; he must have come on foot. I watched for a moment as he walked away, but he didn't look back. Slowly, I closed the door and rested my head against it for a second, bracing myself for the kitchen, and my mother and her questions, spoken and unspoken.

But when I turned round she was standing behind me in the narrow hall.

'Mum . . . I didn't know you were there.'

'He's gone then, has he?'

'Yes. He'll have calls to make. People don't stop being ill because it's Christmas.'

'He's a good doctor.'

'I know that, Mum,' I said wearily. 'Shall we wash up?'

'I've done that, there was next to nothing anyway. Come and sit by the fire.'

I did as I was told. I had no energy for anything else. I sank down in the chair that had been my father's, where Alan had been sitting a few minutes ago; it still bore his imprint and his warmth. My mother crouched down and carefully placed a few more coals on the fire with the pewter tongs. Then she swept the hearth unnecessarily before sitting in the chair opposite. We both gazed at the fire with its hypnotic, pulsing red heart and the shoots of new flame that rose from the fresh coal. That was what a fire was for, I thought – not just for heat, but a focus for unspoken feelings. It dispelled the slight awkwardness between us. We didn't need to look at one another while we could look at the fire and see in its living glow the reflection of our own dreams and our regrets.

We sat for some minutes without speaking. My heart was too full to say anything and my mother didn't make me. The tension eased and dissipated. We were together, but wrapped in our separate and different silences.

When my mother first began to sing, it was to herself, and very softly, almost under her breath. But gradually, as her pleasure and her confidence grew, she sang out. Her voice was sweet, clear, resonant as a bell, as unlike her ordinary voice as it was possible to be. The song she sang was 'My love is like a red, red rose'; a Scottish love song that was also a lament. Where from? How? I sat spellbound, hardly daring to move in case the spell was broken.

'"And I will love you still, my love, till all the seas gang dry . . ."'

When she'd finished I didn't say anything right away, but let the easeful silence grow around us again. For only the second time in my life I prayed – for Alan, for my mother; for myself. And for Suzannah, whose baby must surely be born by now. I thought of all those cribs in churches and schools and church halls at this time of the year, with people clustering round them, polishing that harsh and brutal story with seasonal sentimentality. Whereas out there a sick, terrified girl had given birth to a baby she did not want, and given it away to a man she did not love.

'I was taught that song at school,' said my mother. 'And I never forgot it.'

'It's lovely,' I said. 'And you sang it beautifully.'

She fidgeted self-consciously, pulling at her skirt and patting her hair. 'I don't know what possessed me, I'm sure.'

'It's Christmas. People do sing at Christmas. Some of them do in church. You sing by your own fire.'

'Best place for it,' she declared.

In bed, I read Alan's note. It was very short, and simple. He told me, again, how much he loved and admired me, and that I could always rely on him. But there was no escaping the fact that, like my inscription in the book, it was a message of farewell.

The next day Mrs Coleman invited us round for cold cuts. My mother, of course, demurred, but I said we would definitely go, at least for a while, as I had to return in the afternoon.

'It'll do us both good,' I said firmly. 'We've been pretty solitary till now.'

'That's how I like it. Your father and I always had a quiet Christmas.'

I persisted. 'But now it's you and me, Mum. And I'd like to go, and I can't very well go without you.'

She did come, with much tutting and sighing. And of course when we got there the hospitality was so simple and delightful that she unbuttoned and enjoyed herself though I knew she'd never admit it. The Colemans had a little granddaughter, Jessie, aged two and a half, and I could see my mother was smitten. She would have made a wonderful grandmother – reliable, strict, but adoring and indulgent. Jessie seemed to sense this and spent a lot of the time climbing on to her knee and pressing sweets into her mouth. The sweets were red, so that by the end of the afternoon my mother's mouth looked as if she had applied garish lipstick while rolling drunk. Mrs Coleman gave Jessie a napkin and told her to wipe it off. It was a delicious reversal of roles that made us all laugh, and my mother – who had no idea what she looked like – took it in good part.

'Now Phyllis, are you going to the panto at the Masonic?' asked Mrs Coleman.

My mother shook her head. 'I'm not keen on panto.'

'But this is different, isn't it, Wilf? Mr Ormrod from the hardware shop plays the dame, it's the funniest thing you ever saw, such a great big chap in frilly bloomers and a poke bonnet!'

Mr Coleman agreed. 'He's a right Herbert in the shop, but put him up there in a silly frock and he knocks their socks off.'

Everyone joined in the general eulogising of Ormrod's Widow Twanky, and the upshot was that by the time we got out of the door my mother's name had been added to the party for the following Saturday. She grumbled furiously, but I took absolutely no notice.

At six o'clock I packed my night case and came down the stairs to say goodbye. She was waiting in the hall with my coat over her arm as she used to do with my father. It was a mark of respect which I didn't underestimate.

''Bye, Mum,' I said, taking my coat. 'Thank you for a lovely Christmas, and for my present.'

'Thank you for yours,' she said. 'It's in the top drawer with the lemon verbena.'

'Enjoy the pantomime. Remember little Jessie's taken a shine to you. Don't disappoint her.'

'We'll see.'

'And next time I come, you must sing again.'

'Good heavens, I shall do no such thing.' She pulled a wry, self-deprecating face. 'There's the neighbours to think of.'

I placed a kiss on her cheek and, greatly daring, accompanied it with a quick hug. It took her by surprise, and when I stepped back her cheeks were a startled pink.

'Dear me.' She made a brisk brushing movement with her hands. 'On your way.'

Arms folded, she watched me from the doorway, as I had watched Alan. But a little way down the street I did turn and wave, and she raised her arm in salute.

My past life had let me go, like the old, plain friend that it was, trustingly and without questions. It had presented me with freedom, without conditions. What I did with that freedom in my new life was up to me.

Chapter Twenty

After Christmas, Amanda Jarvis returned first from New York, full of the excitement of Manhattan and the pleasures of ship-board life. Her husband stayed on until well after New Year, ostensibly to visit galleries and see new work, but I was pretty sure the real reason had more to do with Bob Sullivan, a view confirmed by his morose and overhung appearance when he did get back.

Dorothy was unsympathetic. 'Till the next time. Won't be long, you wait and see. I don't know why she puts up with it.'

'Perhaps she loves him,' I suggested.

'Then she's even sillier than I thought, and that's saying something.' She caught my look and added. 'No, she's all right. There's not a mean bone in her body . . . I just don't understand it, that's all.'

I didn't either. But whatever the oddities of their marriage, the Jarvises still struck me as happier than many more orthodox couples. Perhaps, I thought, the capacity to allow the other person to be themselves, not to demand change as of right, was a greatly undervalued quality. It was one Alan possessed, although in our case it had permitted a different sort of freedom.

No sooner had the Jarvises returned than the Ashes went away. I received a note saying that the office in Soho Square would be closed, and I was suspended, on full pay, until the end of February, when John Ashe would be back in touch.

There was no indication of where they'd gone, or why, and when I mentioned it to Christopher Jarvis he knew no more than me.

'I must say it's very unlike Ashe to take a holiday, particularly an extended one. When he does go away there's usually some business reason or other. Felicia takes off to Biarritz and Paris from time to time, with friends. He prefers London, and his various interests here.' He gave me the charming, confiding smile I'd seen rather less frequently of late. 'He likes to watch the money coming in.'

I had never been sure how much the Jarvises knew about Ashe's 'interests', and I was always discreet, for personal as well as professional reasons: any information of which I was the exclusive holder was valuable, both morally and materially.

So it was not through my agency that one piece of information had leaked out. Since returning from New York Jarvis had been disinclined to work and this morning he was apparently in the mood to talk. He swung his feet on to the desk, and lit a cigarette.

'Suzannah's recovered, apparently.'

'Has she?' I shuffled papers into a neat pile. 'That's good news. I was sorry to hear from Mrs Jarvis that she's not been well.'

'No idea what it was, but Georgina said she wasn't at Rintoul's place any more and had gone away for a while.'

'To the sunshine, perhaps.'

'Who knows? She's a perverse creature. Looks like the least puff of wind would blow her over, but paints those big, impressive canvases, and lives out of a suitcase, never stays anywhere more than a couple of months. Enough to wear down the strongest constitution.'

'Perhaps she likes to feel free.'

'But it isn't freedom,' protested Jarvis. 'Not from where I'm standing, anyway.'

'We all have our own ideas about that,' I said primly.

'Indeed.' He chuckled. 'And what's yours, Pamela?'

'Financial independence.'

The answer had come out a little too quickly, but he laughed again, out loud. 'Ask a silly question!'

'I didn't mean to sound rude,' I said, but as a matter of fact I was pleased to have cheered him up, albeit unintentionally.

'You didn't,' he said. 'You were your usual practical, straightforward, likeable self, but it poses a dilemma for me.' He paused. I said nothing, but he must have taken my silence as a prompt, for he went on: 'I was thinking of giving you a rise in pay, but now I see that as well as rewarding your splendid service I may very well be hastening your departure.'

He cocked an eyebrow. It was clear that some sort of response was required. I weighed my words carefully.

'What I said was true,' I admitted. 'But I'm very happy here, and there's a long way to go before I realise my ambition.'

'Thank heavens for that!'

His morale was so much improved that I decided to press my advantage.

'Mr Jarvis . . .'

'Mm?'

'Excuse me, but just now – you mentioned a rise?'

'I did. And it's yours, starting this week.' He gazed at me almost fondly. 'Amanda and I know when we're well off. Suzannah, and even, God help us, Dorothy, weaken from time to time, but you – never!'

I had no alternative but to take this as a compliment. Besides, I was delighted about the money. The little acorns in my savings account might not be great oaks for a while yet, but they were growing steadily, and notwithstanding what

I'd said to Christopher Jarvis, I intended to move out of my present room into a bigger flat of my own in the spring. Soon after that, I very much hoped to be able to take in and support at least one lodger by the end of the year.

Full financial independence might be a long way off, but before too long I would have the power to provide safety for someone else and that, to me, was of inestimable value.

Georgina had got engaged in the new year, and had pretty well lost interest in everything and everyone but herself, her fiancé, and their wedding plans. It was a source of fascination to me. I suppose her youth, and youth's natural self-centredness, ensured that she managed so easily to divorce herself from the painful complications of life. And love – yes, it must have been true love, because her intended, Giles Parker, was neither rich nor handsome nor even especially charming, but simply the nicest, most downright, most unaffected man imaginable. I wasn't that much older than her, and had been in love once – perhaps twice, but I could not recall ever having been so wrapped up in myself as a result. Quite often over the ensuing months, between engagement and wedding, I found myself thinking of Georgina and Giles, and touching the ring Alan had given me – twin touchstones of normality, stability and hope.

Dorothy noticed the ring first.

'That's pretty, Mrs G,' she said, taking my hand and examining it. 'Give us a proper look.'

I took it off and handed it to her. She studied it closely, turning it from side to side in the light like an expert, and then asked, without looking up:

'Who gave it to you then, the doctor?'

'Yes, actually.'

Now she gave me one of her cheeky sidelong glances. 'So are you going to marry him – actually?'

'No.'

'But he wanted you to.'

I could only nod. At once, she was mortified.

'I'm ever so sorry, I am a stupid cow. Here.' She handed the ring back. 'It's lovely. Lucky you, I say. Bet I'll never have one like that.'

Like a true friend, she had given me time to recover from my moment's discomposure, and I appreciated it. In the short silence that followed, I had one of those ideas which formed only a split second ahead of my putting it into words.

'Dorothy – quite soon I want to move to a bigger place, a place of my own. Would you like to live with me?'

For only the second time since I'd known her, I could tell she was thrown off balance. Her face was an absolute study as a whole series of emotions raced across it, jostling for position: astonishment, disbelief, amusement, and finally a wary curiosity.

'Pardon?' She leaned one ear towards me. 'I'm not sure I caught that . . .'

'I asked if you'd like to live with me. When I get a new place of my own.'

'I thought that's what you said.' She gazed at me, her brow knitted, as though trying to read my mind. 'Why?'

I paused. I had moved too fast for both of us, and needed a moment to express myself simply and clearly.

'Because I'd like your company, you'd have a place to call your own—'

'No I wouldn't,' she interrupted tartly. 'It'd be yours, you just said so.'

'I'd buy it, but we could run it as a partnership.'

'Run what?'

I wasn't quite ready to outline my whole plan, so said lamely: 'Run our home. Together. I'd continue to go out to work for the time being, and you could manage the domestic side of things.'

'So I'd be your housekeeper, would I?'

'Sort of.'

'Blimey.' She dropped her head into her hands and then looked up, still baffled, her hair on end. 'I can't really see it, can you?'

'Yes, I can. Or I wouldn't have suggested it.'

'Tell me something,' she said. 'Why would I want to be your housekeeper when I've got a perfectly good job here?'

It was a fair question, and I could no longer avoid answering it. 'Because you'd be my partner, Dorothy – my business partner. I've got plans.'

'Haven't you just?' She gave a sceptical little laugh.

'There isn't time to go into them all now, but I want to help people – women like you and me. And you and I could work well together.'

'What's all this, "women like you and me"? You and me aren't alike, we're chalk and cheese.'

'That's what I mean, all sorts of women. And as for you and me, opposites can get along well.'

'That's true . . .' She sat back in her chair with her arms folded. I knew what she was going to say.

'I don't say it's not kind of you, and I appreciate it, I really do. But I've got a home already. And I've got my job here. Mr and Mrs Jarvis have been good to me, so I don't want to rock the boat, or leave them in the lurch.'

I felt as if a plug had been pulled out somewhere inside me and all the warm hopes and good intentions of a minute ago had drained away, leaving me empty.

'It's all right, Dorothy,' I said dully. 'I understand. Forget I mentioned it, please.'

She didn't forget, of course, and neither did I. It was one of those conversations which, though in no way fatal to our friendship, I would have erased from the record if I could. It rattled around at the back of my brain for days, mocking me with its (wholly unintentional) patronising tone, its condescension and presumptuousness. I believed then, and know now, that Dorothy herself did not notice any such horrors herself; she was simply baffled and taken aback. But that didn't prevent me from feeling like a pompous idiot. The exchange had created an unprecedented awkwardness between us. For a while, I returned to my original, somewhat unbending self, but there was none of her old, importunate teasing.

There were house guests, of course. Edward Rintoul came and went (with no news of Suzannah); Georgina, too, with quantities of shopping, selecting and ordering to do for the wedding, was a frequent visitor – once with her jolly, loud-voiced mother who was the very opposite of the martinet conveyed by her daughter. Her twin cries were 'On we go!', and 'No peace for the wicked', but under a jovially over-bearing manner she was the best-natured woman you could hope to meet. There was a sort of amiable wrangling going on, outside Georgina's hearing, about 'the fiancé'. The Jarvises claimed, not altogether seriously, that while Giles was pleasant he wasn't nearly good enough for Georgina, a shortcoming he shared with almost every man on the planet. Molly Fullerton propounded the view – also humorously – that anyone with his own teeth, hair and a steady income, and who was safe in taxis, was quite good enough, and to be welcomed with open arms.

To my great embarrassment, even I was dragged into this light-hearted debate. Mrs Fullerton came into the drawing room one morning when I was going through the diary with Amanda. Georgina was still in bed, having apparently not managed breakfast due to a headache.

'It must be bad to affect her appetite,' said her mother,

sitting down on the sofa. 'The girl eats like a horse and always has done.'

'Let's hope Mr Parker can afford to feed her . . .' murmured Amanda without looking up. They all loved this game, but it made me feel slightly uncomfortable.

Mrs Fullerton snapped open *The Times*. 'Now then, Hatches, Matches and Despatches . . . What do you think of my daughter's fiancé, Mrs Griffe?'

Amanda looked at me with a wide-eyed smile. 'There's a poser for you, Pamela. Molly, what a perfectly horrid thing to do.'

'No it's not,' said Mrs Fullerton. 'It's a straight question and I shan't think any the worse of her whatever she says.' She peered over the paper at me, eyebrows raised. 'Come along, Mrs Griffe, you can be the arbiter – a good catch or not good enough?'

'Well, Georgina certainly thinks he's a good one,' I said, sounding, as I always did when on the back foot, rather too sharp. 'And she's the only one who matters. If she's happy, it's not up to anyone else to throw him back in.'

'Well said, Pamela . . .' Amanda patted my hand. But Mrs Fullerton wasn't about to let me off so easily. Putting the paper down with a little heave of the shoulders, she addressed herself to me challengingly:

'A very diplomatic answer, my dear, and nothing wrong in that. But I'm going to be beastly and put you on the spot. What do *you* think of him? Personally, I mean. And you may speak freely.'

She was wrong to think me diplomatic. I had spoken freely the first time, and needed no invitation to do so again.

'I don't know him. But,' I added, before she could prompt me, 'he strikes me as kind, honourable, and generous.'

'Hmm . . .' Mrs Fullerton bridled mischievously. 'Are you saying my future son-in-law is a tiny bit dull?'

'Yes,' whispered Amanda in her direction. 'She is!'

Suddenly I'd had enough of these two older women playing their silly game. I got up and excused myself.

Five minutes later Amanda Jarvis came into the office and seeing that her husband wasn't at his desk, said: 'I'm sorry, my dear . . . Just now – that was inexcusable. But it was only a bit of silly nonsense. None of our business, and none of yours so Molly shouldn't have dragged you in.'

'It doesn't matter,' I said, a touch frostily.

'Well, no, but . . .' Amanda all but wrung her hands in mortification. 'He's a dear young man, and we're all so pleased.'

'I know.'

'Georgina's *so* happy.'

'Yes, she is.'

I wished she would go. I had work to do and the episode had meant less than nothing to me anyway. I began to type, but Amanda was hellbent on setting the record straight.

'What you said about Giles was absolutely true. He's a gem. Christopher and I like to tease Molly, but Georgina's very dear to us and believe me if we didn't like some man she'd taken up with, or really believed he wasn't good for her, we should say so *immediately*.'

Such was her sense of urgency and the importance of what she had to say that all of this came out in a continuous, fluent stream without the usual hesitations and flutterings. I had to reply with whatever was in my power to restore her peace of mind.

'Of course you would, Mrs Jarvis. I know that. And you're right, it's none of my business. It was nothing, let's forget it. In fact I already have.'

I smiled at her, was rewarded by a smile in return, and then she went, closing the door very discreetly, as though she had been dismissed.

When she'd gone I sat there wondering at how far I'd travelled in the past few months, and what I'd turned into. From
the reserved, unsure amanuensis of last spring, I'd become a
woman who spoke her mind, dictated terms, and interfered
in the lives of others. In other words I no longer knew my
place. This realisation was both shocking and invigorating.
The phrase 'self-determination', if it had even been coined,
was not then in common currency, but with hindsight it was
most certainly what I was engaged in. However, I reminded
myself sternly, common civility and respect for my employers
remained not only desirable but essential if I was to achieve
my goals.

One morning towards the end of February there was a
message waiting on my desk in Jarvis's racy, slipshod handwriting:

> *John Ashe telephoned. Returned last night, but would like
> you to go to his home address this afternoon. Hopes that
> won't be inconvenient.*

Just seeing his name on the sheet of paper put a cool cat's-
paw of apprehension on the back of my neck, so that I
suppressed a shiver. Jarvis came into the room and said
breezily:

'Morning, Mrs Griffe! Ah – you're reading that . . . He
called early this morning at some perfectly ungodly hour, I
swear he never sleeps. Anyway, do cut along early if you feel
you need to.'

I said I was sure that wouldn't be necessary. My plans
depended on the continuation of my work for Ashe, but I
wasn't looking forward to it. I had very readily slipped back
into the gentler and more random rhythms of life at
Crompton Terrace where, for the moment at least, the most

exciting event in the offing was Georgina's wedding.

And the spring exhibition, of course, the subject of today's work.

'As you know, I like to present new, young artists in the spring,' said Jarvis, shuffling absent-mindedly through the papers on his desk. 'It seems like the seasonal thing to do, creative vigour rising with the sap, so to speak . . . I do very well out of established artists, but the greatest satisfaction for a parasitic fellow like me is to launch the career of someone new.'

'Like Suzannah Murchie,' I said.

'Very much like Suzannah,' he agreed. 'She has a wonderful talent, and I flatter myself I was the first to spot it. But her output is so erratic. Scarcity value is one thing, but one has to be a little more firmly embedded in the minds of art buyers before that registers.'

'Do you know if she's working at the moment?'

'No idea. Don't know where she is, what she's doing, or with whom. What can I do? She comes and goes and disappears – she's not susceptible to any kind of management.'

There flashed into my mind that awful photograph: the attenuated, childlike limbs; the swollen, savagely scribbled belly; the bowed head with its shock of unkempt hair. A once-free spirit not just in captivity, but in servitude – humiliated.

'I think she needs someone to take care of her,' I said. 'She'd be more free if she was safe.'

Jarvis drew his brows together and looked keenly at me as though I'd voiced some remarkable insight instead of stating what, to me, was obvious.

'Do you know, my wife says that. But the thing of it is, Suzannah resists care. Even when she's here she leads her own life, and we take our tone from her. Like a cat!' he exclaimed, warming to his theme. 'A dog needs care and gives unstinting affection and loyalty in return. A cat graces you with its presence from time to time without a word of thanks, and then the moment something bad happens that you're powerless to prevent, it goes off in a huff and dies alone.'

This begged a question which I could not bring myself to ask, but which we both felt was hanging in the air.

'Not that we have either,' he said. We dropped the subject and got down to work.

When, later that afternoon, I presented myself at the house in Piedmont Gardens, the same butler answered the door and showed me not into the grand drawing room where I'd met Felicia, but into what he told me was Mr Ashe's study on the opposite side of the hall. It was more like a library than a study, solid and opulent with the feel of what I imagined to be a gentleman's club. Three walls were lined with books, from polished floorboards to the ceiling twelve feet away. I had got so used to seeing John Ashe in the sterile, flatly lit whiteness of Soho Square that he seemed quite out of place here. I reminded myself that this was his home, presumably designed to his taste and for his comfort, but it still felt strange.

Also, he was not alone. He sat in a leather armchair by the fireplace, and another man was standing in front of him, with his back to the door. It made one of those tableaux in which the seated figure held all the power. The visitor's attitude was that of a boy reporting to the headmaster. He didn't so much as look round when the butler announced me, but Ashe got up at once.

'Mrs Griffe – thank you for coming over. Mr Allinson was just leaving.'

Dismissed, the visitor turned to go. It was the usually genial vicar from St Xavier's, looking serious and preoccupied. I said, 'Good afternoon,' and he responded in kind but appeared not to recognise me. There was no reason why he should; in the church he was a distinctive, authoritative figure, while I, on the few occasions he'd seen me, had been one face among many.

'Excuse me for one moment,' said Ashe, and accompanied his visitor out into the hall. Through the open door I saw the butler bring the vicar's coat, hat and scarf and then withdraw. Ashe remained, and the two men spoke quietly – or at least Ashe spoke, and the vicar listened attentively with his hand to his brow. When Ashe suddenly looked over his shoulder I felt a sharp dart of shock. I turned away and stepped back into the room, but not before I saw him walk with long, swift strides towards the door. I heard it click shut. I had not meant to spy, nor to eavesdrop – I could not hear what was being said – but Ashe had, as always, drawn my fascinated attention and I had been caught out. Furious with myself, I walked to the far end of the room. It was L-shaped, with the arm of the 'L' extending to the left beyond the fireplace, away from the windows that overlooked the road. On the wall at the end hung the portrait of John Ashe.

It was disconcerting, having escaped his accusing stare once, to be immediately confronted with it again. But thrilling, too, because I knew the painting was Suzannah's. Even before I read the initials in the bottom right-hand corner I detected her distinctive trademarks: the huge scale, the muted, almost monochrome shades, the powerful and disturbing narrative quality that drew you into speculation and imagination – all were there. I could hardly breathe for excitement as I drew closer to the picture. For the moment, her achievement eclipsed her humiliation. No matter what had happened, nor what she had suffered or submitted to, her work would rise above it, and live on.

The likeness she had created was perfect; I might have been standing in the room with the man himself. He was depicted as if emerging from, or retreating into, deep shadow, with only the unmarked right half of his face showing. This device added greatly to the portrait's intensity, as if all Ashe's cold energy and power were gathered into the small part of himself that he chose, on this occasion, to reveal.

He was dressed in the plain dark suit and crisp white shirt he often wore; I could almost smell the dry freshness of that always-spotless shirt. A full three-quarters of the canvas area was cast not just in shadow but a deep, opaque darkness in which his pale face floated like a chilly half-moon on a stormy night. I realised with a shiver of pure delight that Suzannah, in creating this memorial to John Ashe, had taken control as only a true artist can. No matter what her sitter's instructions, something here was entirely hers – her vision, her genius, her message to everyone who looked at the picture. It took me back, yet again, to those days at Osborne's, when I had marvelled at the alchemy which brought strange and wonderful stories from the most unlikely people.

While I stood before the painting I was oblivious to everything. The windows could have blown in and I would scarcely have noticed, or so I thought – until the soft click of the door told me Ashe was back in the room.

I tried not to appear self-conscious as I rejoined him. But he rarely played on a feeling beyond the moment, and was his usual pleasant self.

'I apologise for keeping you waiting, Mrs Griffe. And for dragging you across town on this cold afternoon.'

'It doesn't matter at all. Did you have a good trip?'

'We did, thank you. I wasn't sure how long I'd be with my other appointments, and it seemed to me that what I have to discuss could as easily be dealt with here.'

I waited. He invited me to sit, and did the same himself. I chose a hard chair in which I could sit upright and alert; I was never wholly relaxed in his company and I hoped that always appearing businesslike helped to conceal this.

But having got me, so to speak, in place, he seemed in no hurry to get down to business. He remarked conversationally:

'You were looking at the portrait, I dare say.'

'I was admiring it, yes.'

'Of course it's hard to assess objectively a picture of oneself, but I think the artist has done a good job, would you agree?'

'Certainly.'

'I believe you like her work, as I do.'

'Very much – what I've seen of it.'

A short pause followed during which I felt him looking at me, and I studied my hands, trying not to fidget. Then he said:

'And what about my work – what you've seen of it?'

It was the second time he'd probed me on the subject, and I was determined not to be drawn. Any power I had lay in keeping my counsel.

'That's not in the public domain. It's not for me to judge.'

'No, indeed.' He sounded almost amused, but I knew better than to pick up on his mood. My defences, these days, were solid.

'That's what I like about you, Pamela – may I call you that?'

'I should prefer Mrs Griffe.'

He nodded. 'What I like, and have always liked, about you is your ability to keep impersonal those things which should be so. It's a rare quality, particularly among women.'

'Business is business,' I said. It was a clichéd response, and I dare say I looked the epitome of the discreet secretary perched there on the edge of my chair. Ashe couldn't possibly have guessed how deeply, fiercely personal business had become to me, nor how wildly I was exulting in my concealment.

'Precisely. Which is why I intend to ask you for something

for which I've never asked anyone else. Woman or man.'

I waited. It took all my concentration to keep my hands loose in my lap.

'I ask for your loyalty.'

'You already have it.'

'Now, yes – I refer to the years to come.'

'In other words, unconditionally.'

'That is the word, yes.' I didn't answer, so he went on: 'You see, Mrs Griffe, you are already in an extremely privileged position. There is no one in whom I can confide, except you.'

'I wasn't aware that you had ever confided in me,' I said.

'No? But you're closer to me than my wife.'

It was an exact echo of a remark of Louise's, which had made me laugh at the time. Still, I knew he never said anything without having previously calculated its effect. I could only hope he didn't see how taken aback I was. In my anxiety to seem unperturbed, I answered almost too quickly:

'I'm sorry if that's the case.'

'There's no need to apologise,' he said, his voice softer and silkier with offence. 'It's not something over which you had any control, believe me. But as far as I'm concerned it's an entirely satisfactory situation, and one I would like, with your agreement, to perpetuate.'

'You want me to be your confidante?'

'No. I would like things to remain as they are. Whether or not there is much work for you to do. I want you to remain – in place.'

How odd, I thought, that only days ago I was congratulating myself on being someone who no longer knew her place and now, it appeared, I had one, and was being invited to remain in it indefinitely.

'I don't know,' I said carefully. 'What you're asking is a big undertaking. I shall need time to think about it.'

'Naturally. Take a week.'

The whole conversation was so out-of-the-ordinary that I saw no harm in asking one more question.

'May I ask – you'll appreciate I have to know before reaching a decision – will I continue to be paid at or above the present rate? However much, or little, work I am doing?'

'You mean – let's see.' He tilted his head quizzically. 'Unconditionally?'

I opened my mouth to answer, but he cut across me: 'The answer is yes.'

'And there is one more thing.'

'The floor is yours.'

'As you know, I have plans for a project of my own that I want to launch in due course. When I do, my position with you would have to take account of that. I should need the time and the freedom to do my own work, as well as yours.'

'I shan't be asking for any more of your time than you give me at present, though it might occasionally need to be more flexible. As for freedom, I wouldn't dream of depriving you of it.'

This was a lie, and he must have known that I recognised it as such. I had seen the red room, the photographs, Parkes, Louise – and Suzannah – more than anything, Suzannah . . . But we were engaged in a game of bluff in which, I sensed, I was very slightly ahead. I would say nothing. I, too, could be secretive.

'So,' he said, 'you'll let me know this time next week?' I nodded and he got to his feet. I did the same, and would have left there and then, but he went on: 'I believe you told me this project of yours was some kind of charitable venture.'

'It is, yes.'

'Don't worry, I haven't the least desire to know more about it. But it occurred to me that you might be interested to know something about the good works of Ashe Enterprises.'

'I didn't—' I began, but he cut in at once.

'Know there were any? No, you wouldn't. In fact I was misleading you slightly; they have nothing to do with the company, more a case of doing good by stealth.' He smiled affably. 'A miserable sinner's bid for redemption.'

I remembered seeing Ashe – 'our Mr Jameson' – in the darkened crypt, and again in the church quite recently. I waited.

'Please,' he said, 'sit down for a few more minutes. I'd like to show you something.'

I obeyed. He went into the other section of the room, where the portrait hung. Beyond me, the rest of the house was very still. I wondered where his wife was, and whether she had any idea I was here, or what had taken place between us.

Ashe returned, carrying a framed photograph about eighteen inches by nine, and handed it to me.

' "C" Company,' he said, sitting down. 'The men of my regiment with whom I served during the war.'

I looked at the rows of faces, mostly young, the sharply peaked caps lending gravitas to their solemn expressions. The officers, many of them no older, sat in the front row. A company of Matthews, ready for anything except what lay in store.

'Which one is you?' I asked.

'I can understand your difficulty. It was a long time ago. I'm third row, sixth from the right.'

I followed his directions with my finger, but when I got there I wouldn't have known that it was him. Just another young soldier, straight-backed and clear-faced.

'You weren't an officer?'

He didn't answer; his eyes were still on the picture. 'Can you see Lieutenant Christopher Jarvis?'

I scanned the faces, and pointed. 'There?'

'Right first time. He hasn't changed as much as me.'

'You were friends?' I ventured.

'Comrades,' he said, correcting rather than agreeing with me. 'Brothers in arms. And fortunate – the majority of those men are dead.'

'It was a terrible time,' I said quietly. 'A terrible waste. My own husband was killed in the war.'

The minute I'd said this I regretted it, and was afraid that I had given away too much, but to my relief Ashe either didn't hear or chose to ignore my remark.

'The conduct of private soldiers in war is extraordinary,' he said reflectively. 'Their faith in their leaders, and each other; their courage, their capacity for humour and comradeship. The nobility of ordinary men and boys was endlessly fascinating to me. Inexplicable.'

'You were one of them,' I pointed out.

'No.' He shook his head. 'Never. I served and fought alongside them, but I was always an outsider in the ranks. Not well liked – but that didn't bother me.'

I handed him the photograph and he placed it carefully, face down, on the table next to him. 'Since the war I've done what I can to help the less fortunate survivors. The ones who left part of themselves out there and hadn't the strength to cope when they got back.'

'I've seen you in the square,' I said. 'And in St Xavier's.'

'They do good work, and I give them money to help them continue. Money's easy to give if you have it. Rather less often, I give time.' He was staring at me fixedly. I wished I still had the photograph in my hands, for something to look at. 'You know, Mrs Griffe,' he said, 'there is very little that disgusts or shocks me. It's an advantage that I begin each day by looking in the mirror.'

I said nothing. He went on: 'Consequently I make it my business to acquaint myself with men by whom other people are repelled – poor, deranged, drunken, crippled, filthy men, men that our society treats shabbily – on the grounds that some of them might have been in that photograph. Or another like it.'

For the first, and probably the only, time I believed that he was seeking my approval. But I had no intention of giving it.

'You must find that satisfying,' I said.

He laughed. 'Right. I mustn't detain you any longer, you're a busy young woman.'

He didn't, as he had with the vicar, show me out himself, but rang for the butler. When he arrived, Ashe said: 'I'll see you in the office next Tuesday. Business as usual.'

The study door was closed. The butler walked just ahead of me across the hall. The huge space was cold. There seemed to be no other lights on downstairs.

The butler brought my coat and helped me on with it. He opened the door on to the street and stood holding it for me. A wave of icy air enveloped me as I put on my hat and tied my scarf. From some far-off room in the upper reaches of the house I heard, tiny but distinct, the sound of a baby crying.

Chapter Twenty-One

I could hear a baby crying now, as I stood here in the scrubby, ill-kempt back garden of Woodlands; the desultory crying of an ordinary, healthy baby asking to be fed, or fretful because it had fed too quickly. The sound didn't make my flesh creep, or fill my mind with terrible imaginings. On the contrary, it was a comfort, a sign that all was right with the world – the cry of a baby safe in its mother's imperfect, loving care.

Notwithstanding the trials and tribulations of the last few hours, I had achieved everything that I set out to achieve. What did it matter if the locals saw me as that daft woman who ran the hostel up the road? Their ignorance gave me a perverse satisfaction. They could never in a million years have guessed how my eccentric philanthropy was financed – and if they could, how astonished they would have been!

I worked for John Ashe for another sixteen years, until his death just after the war. We became as close as two people could be who were not disposed to share the least intimacy. By the end, there was almost nothing I didn't know about his business, or the people he dealt with. I knew the names of all the women he'd photographed, and of those who were his agents, running other women, and of the managers of his clubs up and down the country. I travelled, sometimes with him and sometimes on his behalf, and the people I dealt with saw me as his familiar. Several times I went to Paris, to the elegant *appartement* of M. Cabouchet who ran the Libellule 'international escort agency' – he was Ashe's Gallic equivalent, as smooth as silk and not to be trifled with. Most of the others, even Dimarco, recognised my position and my influence, and I'm afraid I can't pretend I didn't play, in my own small way, on the resentful respect in their eyes. I learned to enjoy my little bit of borrowed power.

No wonder Ashe had made a fortune. As I had observed, and he had as good as told me, the strength of his empire lay in its most intangible resource, human nature; particularly the pride, vanity and weakness of women. In all the years I worked for him I never saw him show the slightest respect for a woman. Oh, he could affect good manners towards women for form's sake, but they were all grist to his mill – creatures, for him to use for pleasure, or profit, usually both. He didn't like women, and I was sure he could never love one. No wonder he married an object – 'the most beautiful woman in London' – as brittle and cold as a diamond. She needed only what his money could buy. And for him that was a modest price to pay for the pseudo-respectability which marriage afforded. Louise was quite wrong to suppose that he was deprived of marital love. He neither sought nor wanted it. In that respect, theirs was the perfect marriage.

You'll notice I say 'they' when referring to the women in his life because in all modesty I make an exception in the case of myself. I've thought about it often over the years. He may originally have employed me out of curiosity. Perhaps I represented some sort of amusing challenge – a sensible, businesslike girl for him to explore and manipulate. There was no doubt that his powerful, pervasive influence had caused me to turn away from Alan. But after that I had somehow (and I can scarcely take credit for something I don't quite understand) managed to defend my privacy and preserve my independence. My dream of a place of safety for women and children, and my dream of revenge, were one and the same.

And because of them I not only survived, but in every sense prospered in his employment.

Don't misunderstand me, we were never friends. In fact, as I understood him more, I liked him less. His attachment to the city's derelicts – by no means all of them war veterans – I found sentimental and self-regarding, more to do with himself than with them. Whatever he'd said about doing good by stealth I was convinced it was an exercise in vanity, which may seem an odd word to use of a man like him, but in his way he was the vainest man I ever knew. It would not be an exaggeration to say that I saw his other work as a kind of perversion. He associated with these men out of curiosity: to him they were specimens, who held a certain fascination for him but inspired no real pity. Besides, the money with which he endowed St Xavier's and similar ventures was blood money – I'd seen the record of that suffering with my own eyes.

In the late nineteen thirties he went to the States and came back two months later with a much-improved face. When I told Dorothy she said now that's what she *called* charity work, it was about time he thought of the rest of us.

I believed him when he said he had never been popular with his army comrades. There was no warmth in John Ashe – no pleasure in the small weave of life, no capacity for ordinary human happiness. Something had gone bad in him a long time ago and it coloured whatever he did. I suspected that as well as the pornography, prostitution and blackmail that made up his stock in trade he engaged in much worse things. When people left Ashe's employment, they suddenly disappeared. It was eerie. But I never enquired about anyone because of a distinct sense that to do so was to endanger them further: my discretion worked both ways.

In the spring of 1930, exactly a year after coming to work at Crompton Row, I made a down payment on a modest little terraced house in Queen's Park, off the Kilburn High Road. Upstairs were two bedrooms and a boxroom; downstairs, a kitchen, and a parlour. Apart from the kitchen sink the only water came from a tap in the outside lean-to which also housed the usual offices. At the back was a small yard, in the front a postage stamp of 'garden' separated from its neighbour by a snaggle-toothed fence and from the road by a privet hedge. I made two growing-boxes out of old drawers, filled them with wallflowers and petunias and put one front and back. The flowers flourished at the front of the house, but grew straggly and sad at the back, where they didn't get enough sun. The next summer I put them both in the front and had a wonderful show.

I loved that house with a passion, and a devotion, that most women reserve for their husbands and children. It was mine – courtesy of the mortgage company, but still mine. I spent every free moment and spare penny on it. I cleaned and made curtains, and kept it neat as a new pin. My mother should have been proud of me, but if so she wasn't letting on. When I finally persuaded her to come and visit one Sunday she was restless and unappreciative, as if she were there under duress and couldn't wait to be gone. At lunch she pushed my unexceptionable meat and veg around the plate suspiciously, and as she sat in the front room her eyes were constantly darting around, making calculations and assessments, and her hands fingered things for quality and cleanliness.

'So Mum, what do you think?' I asked her. In spite of everything, her approval mattered to me. But it was as if the sophistication and understanding she had displayed about my separation from Alan had been at the expense of tolerance in other areas.

'It's a bit big for one,' she said. 'I'm surprised you'd want all this to be rattling around in.'

Her 'all this' made it sound as if I were living in the equivalent of the Brighton Pavilion, but I was determined not to rise.

I said, as pleasantly and casually as possible: 'I'm thinking of taking lodgers.'

'What on earth would you want to do that for?'

'I've had it in mind for some time.'

'You never said.'

I refrained from pointing out the obvious, that I knew what her reaction would be. 'No – well, I didn't know how soon I'd be able to get a house.'

'But you don't want to be doing for other people!'

She kept on talking about what I did or didn't want, as if she knew what that was better than I did myself. But to tell her now the kind of people I intended 'doing for' would be like a red rag to a bull.

'Don't worry,' I said, 'I'll be very careful who I take. And I like the idea of being my own boss – not being answerable to anyone.'

She gave a shrug that was like a sniff. 'Strangers in your own home, Pam . . . They'll be round your neck like a mill-stone.'

I took deep breaths. 'Anyway, I'm going to give it a try. But it's quite a way off at the moment.'

'Good,' she said. 'You never know, you might—' She paused, and I knew exactly what she had been going to say. She'd been about to mention marriage, but in a somewhat tardy fit of tact she changed it to: 'You might change your mind.'

It was a relief when she'd gone, but I didn't hold any of this against her. The contradiction, as she saw it, of my single domesticity discomforted her. She was still disappointed to see me on my own, and my contented self-sufficiency made her feel usurped. A married daughter with a well-run home was one thing. An unmarried daughter, out to business, most of whose life remained resolutely mysterious, but who still managed relatively dust-free skirting boards, was quite another.

I had taken the first step towards realising my ambition, but it was a short one, and many more remained. In fact I was by no means sure what the next step was. All my time during the week was taken up with my work for the Jarvises and, increasingly, John Ashe. In order to help anyone, I – or someone – had to be there.

When I'd been living in Queen's Park for just about a year, Dorothy left the Jarvises to take up a job in a shoe shop. It was no better paid, but nearer to where she lived and one up, she told me, from domestic service. To begin with the whole household, including me, suffered shock, but things had never been quite the same since her 'illness' and pretty soon Amanda broke with tradition and took on a live-in couple, Mr and Mrs Speight. He looked after the heavy jobs, the garden, and the car, and she was housekeeper. They spent their time off at the old-time dancing club in Archway, and they didn't mind the mural.

They were a nice couple, but I missed Dorothy, and their arrival meant I had less to do at Crompton Terrace and spent more of my working days at the Sumpter. Since over the corresponding period I was doing more for John Ashe, that fitted in quite well.

I've always been what you might call an open-minded atheist but every so often something happens to make me suspect the existence of a benign deity of some sort. One summer evening I heard a knock on the door and I opened it to find Dorothy standing there. She'd been promising to come and visit me for such a long time that I somehow doubted she ever would. And now here she was in the low evening sunshine, a smiling rebuke to my faithlessness.

'Guess who?' she said. 'Well, I never . . . Aren't you snug!'

I showed her round my shoebox of a domain with considerable pride. I sensed her surprise that I was actually managing: she probably thought me as impractical as the Jarvises when it came down to it, that I was playing the dilettante when I helped out with chores. But unlike my mother, Dorothy was openly admiring and generous in her praise.

'Tell you what, Mrs G,' she said when we were sitting in the kitchen with tea and biscuits. 'You'll make some lucky man a lovely wife.'

Knowing her as I did, I was pretty sure she was sounding me out.

'Not if I can help it,' I said cheerfully. 'I keep house for myself.'

'Want some help around the place?' she asked.

'Why?' I asked. 'Do you know anyone?'

'Might do.'

'It doesn't pay much.'

'It doesn't have to.'

'And it's living-in, of course.'

'Well, it would have to be, wouldn't it?'

'There's something else,' I said. By now I was certain we understood one another, and that her own involvement was under discussion. 'I'd want to have another lodger pretty soon, so there'd be more work.'

'A bit of work never hurt anyone.'

I smiled. 'When can you start?'

She smiled back. 'End of the month?'

'I'll look forward to it.'

So Dorothy, bless her, hitched her sturdy wagon to my distinctly uncertain star. The relationship between us never changed, at least not outwardly. She never quite let go the manner of a slightly importunate, and impertinent, housemaid, and I kept something of the prim, businesslike secretary. This was because it suited us to do so. We were firm friends, but the maintenance of these superficial differences helped in the forming of a working partnership that was to last for what at this moment counts as for ever.

Suzannah's fate didn't bear thinking about. Not long after she'd had the baby she died, alone, in rented rooms in Bermondsey. She had initially gone to her friends down in Brighton, but left after a few days, they didn't know where to – like everyone, they were accustomed to her moving on when it suited her and without explanation. The Jarvises only found out some time afterwards; it had been a lonely death, the few, pathetic facts of which became blurred and confused by posterity. Apparently the post-mortem showed she had died of peritonitis (though Alan had said that in single girls that was often a euphemism for post-natal complications of some sort). Whatever the case, she must have been in terrible pain at the end, and still, somehow, turned her face to the wall.

I assumed Ashe would want to know of her death since she was, after all, the mother of his and Felicia's child. But when I told him, all he said was: 'Really? I'm sorry to hear that.'

As far as he was concerned, Suzannah was erased from the record. But I noticed that not long afterwards he acquired another of her paintings – he must have known the value would go up. The bleak, desolate nature of her death, and his icy disregard, made me all the more determined to succeed in my enterprise. It might be too late for Suzannah, but I had only just begun.

Louise, on the other hand, flourished. In her case my early fears and gloomy prognostications proved unfounded. She was what is now known as 'a survivor'. For years she lived as the pampered mistress of a series of infatuated and indulgent men, having in each case the good sense to move on to fresh fields before it became necessary to do so. She had a true courtesan's mentality, and managed to bring a spirited independence to what was – materially anyway – a situation of complete dependence.

Needless to say she was delighted with my plans, especially when she heard they were largely funded by John Ashe. She came to visit in a Bentley with a driver, her mink wrap, potty hat and vertiginous heels making her as rare as a cheetah in our road.

'Oh, but it's too delicious!' she cried. 'Does he have any idea what you're doing?'

I shook my head. 'None. It's not his business.'

'It certainly is not! Here, I want to give you some money, too.'

She opened her crocodile-skin bag, took out her wallet and handed me a sheaf of notes. I pushed them away.

'Louise! Put it away, I can't possibly take all that.'

'Yes you can. You must! I want you to have an enormous mansion full of fallen women.'

'They're not fallen women,' I said, but I was laughing, and she took advantage of this to press the money into my hand.

'Please, Pamela – indulge me. And I'm going to give you more whenever I feel like it, too, so there. Bobby is absolutely rolling and completely besotted. Provided I buy the odd diamond bracelet to satisfy his ego, he doesn't mind what I do with his money.'

I did indulge her, of course. It was impossible to resist, when she took such pleasure from it all. Her occasional visits were like being called upon by a particularly exotic species of royalty – flighty, glamorous and amusing – and I justified my acceptance of her donations on the grounds that it would have been simply too po-faced to refuse. Besides, I was well aware that my philanthropy, to be in the least effective, had to take advantage of whatever was on offer.

Dorothy was dazzled by Louise, and perhaps the tiniest
bit jealous. She had no need to be. Neither friendship was
conventional and I made no comparison between them. When
I told her the story of the young man smuggled out of the
house wearing Louise's clothes she shrieked with delight.

'She never!'

'I promise it's true.'

'She's always been a bit of a girl, then.'

'She has. Like you, Dorothy.'

'Me? I'm not that sort!'

Those few words taught me a lesson I was to forget at my
peril in the years to come. Bad luck was one thing, loose
behaviour another, and it could never be assumed that the
one was the offshoot of the other. Dorothy's admiration for
Louise was genuine, but it went only so far. In Dorothy's
eyes Louise, no matter how good a show she put on, was
'that sort'.

The distinction, I realised, was love. Dorothy, who I was
certain my mother would have described as 'no better than
she ought to be', had loved her faithless, pale-eyed Irish boy,
in the same way Alan loved me. She had accepted him as he
was, and accepted too her own powerlessness. She had not
wavered. Whatever latitude she had permitted previous
admirers, she had only given herself to him, and had borne
the consequences philosophically. Louise, scot-free and heart-
whole, was another kettle of fish altogether. In all the years
we were to work together, this difference remained constant
between Dorothy and me: in my eyes the girls were victims,
in hers they had slipped up. In this she was very like my
mother.

Our first girl, Leslie, seven and a half months pregnant,
arrived when we were in the chaotic process of having a bathroom put on at the back. Leslie's son, Martin, was delivered
at home two days later, 'not quite cooked' as the midwife put

it but still weighing in at a healthy seven pounds. The builder's men must have thought us all quite mad, but Dorothy kept them sweet. Maybe word got round through them, because almost at once another young woman arrived on the doorstep, this time clutching the infant she'd refused to give up for adoption. Dorothy moved into my bedroom to make space for her. Six months on, she and I were sleeping on camp beds in what had been the front room and the little house was bulging at the seams.

They say God protects drunks and little children. I had no right to expect divine protection of any sort, and Dorothy and I were abstemious, so the babies must have been the reason we got through those early years. I had not wanted to turn people away, but neither had I ever intended so swiftly to become the Old Woman Who Lived in a Shoe, when I was still working for the Jarvises and Ashe. In 1937 I handed in my notice with the Jarvises, to their dismay and our mutual sadness. They were understanding, and even gave me a donation for the house. I still saw them from time to time and they always made me welcome and sent me invitations to whatever was on at the Sumpter.

During the war the seamier side of Ashe's business declined somewhat. Perhaps people had more important things on their minds. The clubs flourished, though; to these he added the organisation of entertainment for troops. He put on shows in big halls around the suburbs of London; mostly they featured scantily clad showgirls with the odd smutty comedian thrown in to give the appearance of 'variety'. I dare say he thought of these shows as part of his 'charity work', but they didn't impress me.

Dorothy and I, with our shifting population of dependants, resisted evacuation and got used to nights in the tiny coal cellar and under the kitchen table and, as the war drew on, in the Anderson Shelter. I vowed that when the war eventually ended I would go all out to purchase a bigger place.

In the snowbound winter of 1946, John Ashe crashed his car in terrible conditions on a lonely stretch of road around the Devil's Punchbowl. He'd been on his way back from Brighton and, unusually, had been driving himself. His funeral at a crematorium in North London was sparsely attended. Mourners – if that was what you could call us – comprised Felicia, as thin and sharply elegant as Wallis Simpson in tailored black, their adopted daughter Beatrice, the Jarvises, a handful of domestic and business employees, myself – and Louise, unashamedly splendid in mink and pearls. There was no encomium of any kind, nor any hymns. Just the prescribed words, expressionlessly delivered, and the coffin disposed of. A formal wreath of white lilies 'from Felicia' lay on the coffin. Louise walked to the front of the chapel and placed a single buttermilk-coloured rose next to it. So like her, I thought, to revel in this moment when she gave less than a damn about Ashe; and just as well, too, that Felicia's face was heavily veiled.

The girl, Beatrice, who must have been about seventeen, was taller than her stepmother, but had yet to acquire her poise. She was slim and gangling in a too-dressy hat and tailored coat which made her look even more awkward. Something simpler would have suited her, and the occasion, better. When she and Felicia walked down the aisle at the end of the service I studied her face, trying to catch something of Suzannah there, but she seemed all her father's – sallow and dark, with a brooding quality about her. She struck me as unhappy, and not only because of the occasion. I thought with a pang that Suzannah would have known how to dress this changeling child, and how wonderful she would have looked in the flowing, bohemian clothes her mother had favoured. To me, she seemed still that distant, crying baby that I'd heard years ago in the Ashes' mansion; but she probably didn't know the real reason for her cries, and they would never be heard now.

I missed Ashe only in the sense that he had been a part of my life for more than sixteen years. It was huge relief to be free of the habit of secrecy that he had imposed, and no longer obliged to treat with the cruel, dark underside of the business which had made him rich.

But it turned out I wasn't to be free of it. In his will, John Ashe left me, without comment or condition, twenty thousand pounds: a fortune in those days and more than enough to buy the large property I needed, with some left over for myself, my mother, anything I wanted. It was stupendous! Still, even as I crowed and exulted, and Dorothy and I literally danced like dervishes in the kitchen, disturbing the babies, I knew that our pact still held: Ashe had purchased my future – and my silence.

Alan had married early on in the war. I was pleased, both because it relieved my own conscience and because no one deserved happiness more than him. His wife, Heather, was a nurse when he met her, and the picture he sent me showed the two of them outside the kirk in Morningside, flanked by her beaming parents. One look at their faces showed what she was able to give, which had been beyond me. Like me, she was small and dark, but there the resemblance ended. Heather was pretty – 'bonny' was the word that sprang to mind – and over the next couple of years they had two children, Donal and William. Then I heard nothing for some time. He was always a better letter-writer than me and I was almost buried beneath the demands of the life that I'd made for myself. It had become accepted between us that two or three times a year he would write, and I would respond a good deal less fully, when time and energy allowed, usually around Christmas.

I heard from him again in the strange, euphoric period following Ashe's bequest. Heather had died. Alan, now a widower with two small boys to raise, was taking a new job at a private psychiatric clinic near Lancaster. He had found a housekeeper – 'a motherly woman who will spoil the boys and be strict with me' – and of his loss said only that 'I can never replace her, just as I could never replace you'. If there was any sort of invitation, no matter how discreet, implicit in the letter I chose to ignore it, and after that our communications became even less frequent. In 1954 he got married again, to the housekeeper, Irene. He was lonely and the boys needed a mother: it was a marriage of solid, cheerful companionship, and the last I heard (in the Christmas card which is now our only connection) they were still contentedly together.

I saw Beatrice Ashe only once again, a year after her father's funeral. It was the purest chance. I was walking down Bowne Street, having visited the latest exhibition at the gallery, when I spotted her on the other side of the road, talking to a young man. The impression I got was of warm enthusiasm on his side, and chilling indifference on hers. Oddly, it was her I felt for. She looked so utterly out of place in the situation. The young man, hardly more than a youth, was confident, garrulous, full of smiles and swank. She had become something of a beauty but an unorthodox one, taller than her admirer, ill at ease with his attentions. She was an heiress, and must have had to put up with a lot of this kind of thing, but she seemed to have acquired none of the simple social skills for dealing with it. She scuffed her shoe on the pavement, folded her arms, unfolded them and thrust her hands into her pockets. At one point she glanced absent-mindedly over the road in my direction. She could not possibly have remembered me from the funeral, but I still froze and pretended to search for something in my handbag. When I next looked her arm was raised, hailing a taxi, and when it pulled up she climbed in with almost indecent haste, nearly trapping the young man's fingers in the door as she slammed it shut. To avoid his entreaties, she turned her face to the window on my side as the cab pulled away, and for the first time, in her wary expression that was both fey and fierce, I caught something of her mother. It was like seeing a captive animal released – I was swept by a tremendous sense of relief, and pride, that after all Suzannah had been through she had not been completely subsumed by Ashe, but lived on in her daughter.

That summer I bought a larger house and Dorothy and I and our whole establishment moved to a property not far from Woodlands, where we finally ended up. My policy of never turning really desperate women away, nor turning them out, had proved to be self-regulating. In most cases, once they had recovered themselves and learned to look after their babies (by no means the natural process I'd always imagined), they moved on after six months or so. But we were so busy, I wondered what on earth I had done with my time till now. I had somewhat recklessly taken on responsibility for people's lives, and that meant I was never off duty.

'You're barmy,' was how Dorothy summed it up.

To which my reply was: 'So that makes two of us.'

As time went by, my visits to the Jarvises became more and more those of a friend than a former employee. They didn't change – Christopher was still as debonair as ever, and Amanda as apparently frail and distraite. But as they moved towards old age the constitutions of both were a tribute to the leisurely existence they'd always led. A testament, if you like, to the health-giving properties of happiness, and living well. I had been replaced by a smart, pretty girl who had been a secretary in the Ministry of Agriculture during the war, and Chef had gone, so the Speights looked after all their domestic needs. They worked hard, probably reckoning they had expectations. To keep Mrs Speight happy, the kitchen acquired an electric cooker, and a refrigerator – Dorothy was astounded when I told her! The house guests came and went as usual, some getting older and crankier (Rintoul had knee trouble), the new ones young and 'bohemian', but no more averse to the Jarvises' kindly patronage. Bob Sullivan had married a canned-food heiress, and they went to the States for the wedding, but Christopher Jarvis had enjoyed a couple of romantic passions since then, and the two of them had a wonderful time mixing with the American millionaire set. By then I'd formed the firm opinion that far from being silly or put-upon, Amanda was a natural sophisticate, who loved her erring husband and knew that if he was happy, so was she. If theirs was a lavender marriage, it was a sweetly scented one. When Georgina, belatedly after a series of miscarriages, gave birth to her daughter Daphne, they were the most doting honorary grandparents imaginable.

One evening in the late June of 1954, in response to an invitation from Amanda, I left Dorothy in charge and drove up to Highgate in my shiny Austin A40 (an indulgence courtesy of Ashe) to have supper with them. It was to be my last visit for over ten years.

Afterwards we sat outside. Mr Speight had done his stuff, but the bottom of the garden was as overgrown as ever, the little path wriggling away invitingly into the mysterious green darkness. Amanda may have guessed what I was thinking, for she said:

'I have to restrain Mr Speight, Pamela, or he'd make the whole place look like a municipal park. I like to keep a little bit of wilderness, even though it gets on the poor man's nerves . . .'

I said I absolutely agreed with her. Christopher Jarvis wasn't so sure.

'It's not as though we ever use that end,' he said. 'We could have a pleasing prospect instead of a wall of vegetation.'

'It's not big enough for a prospect,' protested his wife. 'Isn't that right, Pamela?'

'That's right.'

'You're ganging up on me,' he said. 'I give in.'

The evening sank into night, but a big, mottled, golden moon rose, and upstairs lights shone from several of the neighbouring houses, so it wasn't completely dark. Half an hour later Amanda got to her feet.

'If you'll excuse me, Pamela, I'm going to bed.'

'Heavens, is that the time?' I rose immediately, conscious of having stayed too long. 'I'm sorry, I had no idea. I must be off.'

'No, no, you stay – you look tired, and it's so lovely out here.'

To my surprise, Christopher added: 'Yes, stay for a little while, why don't you? Have a snifter.'

Amanda patted my shoulder as if giving her permission. 'A very good idea.'

I declined the snifter, but he poured himself one and then returned, and we sat for a while in easy silence, breathing in the scent of the garden.

'How's the good work going?' he asked in the gently teasing tone he used on this subject. 'Is business brisk?'

'As much as we can handle,' I replied.

'Dorothy OK?'

'I don't know what I'd do without her.'

'Hmm . . .' I could almost hear him smiling. 'We used to say that, about both of you.'

'Yes,' I said, 'and look how well things turned out.'

'The Speights are fine but they're not interesting.'

To change the subject, I asked: 'Do you see anything of the Ashes these days?'

'Good grief, no.' He put his glass down and I heard the sounds of him lighting a cigarette, then saw the small red spark flare and subside as he took the first drag. 'Not since he died. I never cared for Felicia, and I'm afraid all that business with Suzannah stuck in my craw.'

'What business?'

'Getting her in the family way and then adopting the child as though he were doing her a favour, when he didn't give a damn for either of them. Anyway, they're not interested in us.'

I sensed a sore point, but it was out of curiosity, not a desire to hurt, that I asked: 'You were in the army with him, weren't you?'

'I was.'

'He showed me a photograph, years ago.'

'Did he.' It wasn't a question.

'Yes . . . "C" Company, I think he said. I was very clever, I picked you out.'

'Did you pick him out too?'

'No, but then he looked very different.'

Quite a long silence followed, during which I sensed that Christopher Jarvis was conducting an internal debate. He must have reached a conclusion, because he broke the silence by saying: 'Let me tell you something I learned in the army.' He glanced at me. 'Would that be all right?'

I wondered why he needed my permission. 'Of course.'

'It's this. In war, you develop a sort of sixth sense about who you can trust. It has nothing to do with a man's other qualities. In civilian life he could be a philanthropist or a thumping crook – it's simply a question of whether you can rely on him under fire.' He drew on his cigarette. 'I trusted John Ashe. He was an odd chap – not well liked even then, without the damage. He gave nothing away about himself, but he made it his business to know about other people.'

'He didn't change, then.'

'I forget – you knew him, too. So you'll understand something of this. Anyway, whatever else, in my view Ashe was a man I trusted with my life. He was my batman, did you know that?'

I was astonished. 'No. He didn't say.'

'Why would he? And anyway, after the war our positions became if not actually reversed then at least tilted in his favour. He made millions out of his dubious goings-on.'

'I know.'

'Left next to nothing, apart from the house. God knows where it all went.' Jarvis glanced at me. 'He liked you, Pamela.'

'Perhaps.'

'Well, as much as he liked anyone, especially any woman. He always preferred his own company first and foremost, with men second and women a poor third.'

'I guessed that.'

'Anyway, I was fond of him. It wouldn't be too much to say we grew quite attached to one another. And as I told you I'd have trusted him with my life.'

I listened intently, almost holding my breath. Above us, the light went off in Amanda's bedroom. The sense of secrecy was intense and overpowering. I didn't want to break the spell, but I couldn't help myself. I asked:

'And were you right?'

'I was,' he said, so quietly that I could only just hear him. 'I was. But there was a price to pay, for both of us. And there has been ever since.'

I knew there could be no more questions, that he considered he had said too much already. Perhaps, from his point of view, he had. Christopher Jarvis was an old man, trying to make sense of the distant past. I had half my life ahead of me, and much to do.

I heard his breathing grow deep and slow, as if he were asleep. As I rose to go, another sound stopped me in my tracks. Liquid, sweet and plaintive – the song of a nightingale rippling softly from her secret, hidden place.

The baby upstairs has stopped crying. The only sound I can hear is the soft, surging roar of the traffic on the busy road beyond the house. But the house itself – my house – is still, and safe, its occupants slipping into rest in their different ways.

One by one, the lights go out. In the kitchen, the light is still on, and I can see Dorothy filling the kettle at the sink beneath the window. Peter Archard is with her; she must have let him in. They're laughing together. He likes her but he doesn't stand a chance. Neither of them can see me, out here in the dark.

But I'm watching – and all will be well.